Death Takes
a Ride

Death Takes a Ride

A Novel

Lorena McCourtney

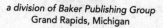
Revell

a division of Baker Publishing Group
Grand Rapids, Michigan

© 2014 by Lorena McCourtney

Published by Revell
a division of Baker Publishing Group
P.O. Box 6287, Grand Rapids, MI 49516-6287
www.revellbooks.com

Printed in the United States of America

Library of Congress Cataloging-in-Publication Data is on file at the Library of Congress, Washington, DC.

ISBN 978-0-8007-2160-2 (pbk.)

This book is a work of fiction. Names, characters, and incidents are the product of the author's imagination or are used fictitiously. Any resemblance to actual events or persons, living or dead, is coincidental.

14 15 16 17 18 19 20   7 6 5 4 3 2 1

To a wonderful stepdaughter,
full of fun and adventure,
whose life ended much too soon.
Jane

1

A light shone dimly in the front office attached to a larger metal building looming behind it. A sign identified the building as H&B Vintage Auto Restorations, and a neon Closed sign glowed in the window. Two vehicles stood out front, one a drab SUV, the other a vintage Corvette convertible, sleek and low and flame red.

"Never mind," Cate consoled her old Honda. Even standing still, the Corvette looked as if it might be breaking the speed limit. She patted the Honda's well-worn dashboard. "You have an inner beauty."

She spotted shadowy movement inside the front door, but Aunt Rebecca had said to go to a side door. Cate nosed the Honda around the far corner of the warehouse and stopped by a door with an Employees Only sign illuminated by a bare bulb overhead. She hesitated before turning off the engine.

Maybe that sign should read Muggings-R-Us. She couldn't even see the front parking lot from around here. Bare metal showed through the old paint on this hidden side of the building. Weeds grew in a crack between the metal and the asphalt, and a pile of discarded tires out back looked as if it might harbor anything from murderous thugs to mutant rats. A bicycle leaned against the tires. Was that something moving beside it?

Nah. Cool it, Cate. You're not working a PI case tonight. Nothing's moving. Just a trick of shadows in the moonlight. Cate dropped the keys in her pocket beside her cell phone, grabbed her purse, and punched the button to lock the door behind her. She shouldn't be inside more than a few minutes, but who knew how fast mutant rats could get inside an unlocked car?

The night air, even as far inland as Eugene was from the Oregon coast, held a tang of sea that reminded her of sunny beaches and booming surf. Hey, she and Mitch should run over to the coast for the day sometime soon.

She pressed a button by the warehouse door, and the harsh response from inside buzzed her ears. The dead bolt lock snicked and the door opened, silhouetting a husky female figure against a maze of shelves.

"Rebecca sent me," Cate said. In spite of her uneasiness with the gritty surroundings, she couldn't help a laugh because the statement sounded so cloak-and-daggerish.

The woman didn't miss a beat. "You got the password?" she growled back.

"How about, um, carburetor? Or spark plug?" Which was about the extent of Cate's knowledge of auto parts. "Or maybe shock absorbers?" She'd just had those replaced on the Honda.

The woman opened the door wider. "That'll work." She smiled and stepped aside to let Cate enter. "C'mon in. I'm Shirley Brackinbush."

Shirley loomed over her, broad shouldered and solid bodied in khaki coveralls, sheepskin-lined vest, and heavy boots. She looked fully capable of toting or tossing the heavy car parts lining the wide shelves behind her. Maybe wrestling mountain lions in her spare time. Fiercely curled black hair framed a face weathered and ruddy, but her smile beamed a friendly warmth. Cate put her at mid or late fifties, with considerable time in sun and wind.

An oversized creature bounded up and skidded to a halt beside Shirley. Cate took a step backward. The creature's broad head stood higher than Cate's waist, its eyes a surprising pale blue, ears floppy, body covered with a shaggy mottle of bluish-grayish-blackish hair. The tail, long and skinny, looked as if it had been added as a we-need-a-tail-here afterthought. It wore a wide leather collar studded with pointy brass triangles. Dog? Maybe. If you were willing to give the term a broad definition.

"What," she asked warily, "is that?"

The creature didn't growl at Cate, but it looked ready to ask for more than a password. Maybe a bribe? Something like half a beef?

"This is Clancy." Shirley gave the animal an affectionate stroke on his big head. "He can be a little intimidating, but that's just because he doesn't know you yet. Clancy, this is—I guess I don't know who you are either. What happened to Rebecca?"

"I'm Cate Kinkaid. Rebecca is my aunt." Cate kept a wary eye on the oversized animal. "She had to go over to the church early to help with refreshments, so she called and asked me to pick you up for the Fit and Fabulous meeting."

"Right. My old pickup conked out. The trailer park where I live isn't far, so I've just been walking to work. I can't leave until the meeting is over," Shirley added as she motioned toward an office sign sticking out over a door about halfway across the warehouse.

"A company conference?"

"Just Matt Halliday and Kane Blakely. They're the H and B of H&B. Mr. Halliday runs things here, and Mr. Blakely manages the Salem branch. Clancy belongs to Mr. Blakely, but Mr. Halliday didn't want a dog in his office."

At mention of his name, the dog waved his skinny tail like an animated whip. He stretched his nose toward Cate and sniffed up and down her leg. Did he smell Octavia's cat scent on her? Did he turn into Psycho Dog when he smelled cat?

"So, what you need is to be properly introduced," Shirley said. "Clancy, this is Cate Kinkaid. She's a friend. Cate, this is Clancy."

Cate had never been formally introduced to a dog before. She stuck out her hand, intending to give the dog a careful pat on the head, but he filled the hand with an oversized paw.

"Nice to meet you," Cate murmured.

Clancy replaced his paw with a friendly slosh of tongue. Cate started to wipe her hand on her jeans but decided that might be some breach of doggie etiquette and put the hand behind her for a more surreptitious swipe.

"I'm sorry this will make us late for the meeting," Shirley said.

"I don't think they'll lock the doors at the church if we don't get there on time."

"Yeah, but I need every minute of it." Shirley inspected her stubby fingernails and weathered hands. "Though I think that woman has her job cut out for her, making anything 'fabulous' out of me."

The special presentation at the church on this Tuesday evening featured a well-known inspirational author speaking on "Fifty and Beyond: Fit, Fabulous, and Faith-filled."

Weekly classes, based on the speaker's workbook, would follow. Shirley had never been in the church before, but the series had been mentioned in the Eugene newspaper, and Shirley had called about it.

"Look around, if you'd like," Shirley invited. "We've got some interesting stuff."

Cate moved to a shelf and fingered an unidentifiable car part with a maze of coils and wires. The metal roof disappeared in shadows high overhead, and the air smelled faintly chemical, maybe vehicle fluids or some special paint for metal. Splatters of soaked-in oil made peculiar figures on the floor. Rorschach inkblot tests for the mechanically minded?

Cate jumped when a male voice spoke out of an intercom speaker mounted on the wall above a computer on a nearby countertop.

"Shirley, could you bring those inventory sheets to the office now, please?"

"I'll be right there." Shirley grabbed a pile of papers next to the combination printer and fax. "Help yourself to some coffee," she said to Cate.

She waved toward a coffeemaker on the counter and took off in long strides toward the office, boots clunking on the concrete floor. Clancy raced after her, but she closed the door to keep him out of the office. He came back to join Cate.

"We have been formally introduced," Cate reminded him, just in case he'd forgotten.

She got a Styrofoam cup from a nearby stack and filled it half full from the coffeepot. Hey, good coffee. She strolled along the shelves labeled with names of various car brands to identify the items in that area. Corvette. Impala. Oldsmobile. They didn't seem to be in any particular order. Movable ladders that rolled on tracks anchored on the top shelf gave access to the upper shelves. A forklift stood between the shelves, apparently to lift larger items to the upper shelves.

Cate shivered in her light windbreaker. No wonder Shirley wore that heavy vest. The warehouse was cold. Morgue cold. Now where had *that* morbid thought come from? She'd never even been in a morgue. Probably, as Mitch would no doubt say grumpily, PI thinking.

Cate leaned over to study something large and spiky on a bottom shelf. A car part? Or maybe a misplaced medieval weapon? A yell from the office area interrupted her contemplation.

Then a muffled *bang*. Gunshot? Nah. This place restored vintage vehicles. Backfire bangs were probably commonplace. Although a backfire after hours in the office didn't seem likely—

Another *boom*. Cate slammed her Styrofoam cup on a shelf and ran for the office door. Clancy bounded past her when she opened the door, but she stopped short. The door opened into the dimly lit area she'd seen from out front, but it was a sales area more than office. No *bangs* here. Not even any people.

Then she realized that the actual office was sectioned off from this room, with the opening up front. Clancy's toenails screeched as he skidded around the corner.

She followed him. The door to the sectioned-off room stood open.

And something sprawled on the floor just inside it.

2

A body, male, big, and brawny in dark pants and hoodie. Face covered with a garish blue-and-red ski mask, gun on the floor near his hand. Bloody wound in his chest.

Cate stared in disbelief. The disbelief deepened when her gaze lifted to the far end of the metal desk in the office.

Another body slumped in a chair, blood trickling from a wound in his head, blood-spattered papers littering the desk in front of him. A wide-brimmed cowboy hat lay on the floor.

Two shots. Two bodies. Two scents. The raw smell of blood and the sharp tang of a just-fired gun. Or guns?

Shirley and a man in similar khaki coveralls stood behind the desk. Shirley still had an inventory sheet clutched in one hand, eyes wide with shock. The man held a gun. A frozen tableau, without sound or movement. Cate was a part of it, she realized, as if time had momentarily stopped for all of them.

Clancy was not frozen, however. He jumped over the body on the floor and thrust his nose into the hand dangling from the body in the chair at the end of the desk.

Then the man with the gun behind the desk moved too. He looked down at the gun in his hand as if he didn't know how it had gotten there.

"I-I *shot* him," he croaked. He looked between the two bodies, then at the gun again, his expression as disbelieving as Cate's own.

"He shot Kane first!" Shirley pointed an accusing finger at the body on the floor. "He was going to shoot all of *us*!"

Cate had seen dead bodies before. Even though Uncle Joe insisted Belmont Investigations didn't do murders, sometimes it seemed they gravitated to Cate like mud to her clothes when she was a little girl. But never two at the same time before, and never before had the sound of the death weapon actually echoed in her ears.

Cate grabbed the cell phone in her jacket pocket. "I'll call 911."

The paper in Shirley's hand fluttered to the floor. She darted to the body slumped in the chair. "Mr. Blakely!" she cried.

911 answered immediately. Cate gave the operator a terse explanation of the situation. Her name and the address. Two gunshot bodies. The woman on the line wanted more, but Shirley suddenly waved at her frantically.

"Tell them to send an ambulance. Kane isn't dead!"

Cate knew they'd probably send an ambulance without being asked, but she passed the information along, answered a few more questions, and dropped the cell phone back in her pocket.

"I need something to put against the wound to stop the bleeding!" Shirley yelled. Right now she was holding his bleeding head against her chest, blood staining the khaki coveralls. Clancy had his big front paws on the chair and was frantically licking the man's face.

Cate dug in her pockets again, but all she came up with was the cell phone, keys, and a crumpled Snickers wrapper. Not exactly life-saving equipment.

But with the cell phone in hand, Cate's PI instincts kicked in and she quickly snapped several photos: the ski-masked man on the floor, Shirley and Clancy huddled over Mr. Blakely, the dazed-looking man holding the gun. Halliday? Apparently.

Shirley was already improvising by grabbing Blakely's jacket from the back of the chair and holding it hard against the wound, her arms again cradling his head against her ample chest. Cate discarded the irrelevant thought that under different circumstances, he'd probably have enjoyed that. Even with a bullet wound in his head, Kane Blakely had a certain silver-fox charisma, as if he might at any moment open one eye and give her a conspiratorial wink.

Halliday suddenly came to life. He rushed over to Shirley and leaned across her to touch his partner on the shoulder.

"Kane, are you okay?"

"No, he's not okay," Shirley snapped. There was an unspoken "you idiot!" in there somewhere. "He's shot in the head! But he's alive."

"Hang on, buddy," Halliday said. He patted Blakely's arm. "You're going to make it. Just hang on."

Cate, avoiding the pool of blood, squatted beside the body at her feet. Now she saw his right hand. Tattoos. Four of them across the man's hand in front of his knuckles. Four *skulls*. She forced herself to ignore them, felt his wrist and then his throat for a pulse. She was no expert, but she was reasonably certain this man was all-the-way dead. She wanted to go to Shirley too, see if she could help somehow, but she found herself squeamish about simply stepping over the dead body as if it were no more than a heap of old clothes. Even if poor aim was all that was keeping him from being a killer.

Halliday apparently realized the gun still dangled from his hand. He set it on the desk, his movements slow and careful, as if he were afraid the weapon might explode in his hand. He flexed his fingers and stared at the hand as if it were an unfamiliar appendage. This hand that had *shot* someone.

"Mr. Halliday, are you all right?" Cate asked.

His numbness turned to a sudden blast of fury. "Who is this guy? What's he doing here? He shot Kane! Just ran in and *shot* him." He sprinted around the desk and, before Cate realized what he was going to do, yanked at the ski mask.

"Hey, I don't think we should touch—"

Too late. The ski mask came off in Halliday's hand, leaving the dead gunman's face exposed. He was probably in his forties, with thinning brown hair pulled back into a skimpy ponytail, a beefy face, coarse skin, and thick neck. His eyes stared sightlessly upward.

"Do you know who he is?" Cate asked.

Halliday shook his head. "I have no idea. But he must have known . . . how could he have known?" He glanced toward his partner as if looking to him for an answer to the question. Cate wasn't sure what the question was.

Halliday looked as if he might slump to the floor at any moment. Cate hastily grabbed a plastic chair from the corner and eased him into it.

"I-I'm okay," he said. "I think." He ran a shaky hand across his chest as if uncertain whether he, too, had been shot.

"What happened?" Cate asked.

"I-I'm not sure. We needed the inventory sheets from the Salem warehouse, and Kane went out to his car to get them—"

"The Corvette?"

"Yeah. Kane likes to drive our flashiest restorations for a while." Halliday looked over at the unconscious man and half-smiled, as if this trait of his fallen partner's were a flaw, but an endearing one.

It must have been Blakely she'd seen at the door when she first drove up, Cate realized. She took another look at the head cradled in Shirley's arms. Kane Blakely was about Shirley's age. Distinguished looking, in a rakish kind of way. Even the gunshot wound in the head didn't hide the fact that he was a good-looking guy, his thick hair elegantly silver, with matching mustache and stylishly trimmed beard. His dark slacks and pale blue dress shirt, although blood-streaked now, contrasted with Halliday's workaday khaki coveralls and scuffed shoes. On the street, Blakely and that vintage Corvette no doubt drew admiring glances.

"He must not have locked the front door behind him when he came back in," Halliday went on. "This guy in the ski mask busted in and just started shooting. I don't even remember doing it, but I must have grabbed the gun out of my desk and shot back."

"Did he say anything?"

"No . . . Yes, he did! He yelled 'I want the money.'"

"You keep large amounts of money here?"

"No, not usually. Practically never, in fact. But tonight . . ." Halliday straightened in the chair, lines ridging his forehead.

Cate's gaze followed his, and she saw what she hadn't noticed before. Money spilling out of the pocket of the jacket Shirley had wrapped around Blakely's head. Hundred-dollar bills. The pocket bulged as if it contained many more of them.

"How could this guy know we had money here tonight?" Halliday demanded again. He put his fists to his eyes as if he wanted to shut out the scene or wipe away what had happened.

Cate gave him a more thorough inspection. Pleasant looking, in an inconspicuous sort of way, the kind of looks that went with the drab SUV out front. About the same age as his partner, mid to late fifties, but his receding hair was a drab mix of gray and brown. A grease streak on the sleeve of his coveralls suggested he worked on the old cars here himself. He looked like the kind of guy more apt to own a Clancy-type dog than Blakely did.

She took a quick glance around the room. A drawer on the nondescript desk hung open. A computer sat on a stand against the back wall, its screen dark. A photocopy machine stood in the corner. Several color photos of gleaming vintage cars hung on the walls.

"Do you always keep a gun in your desk?" Cate asked.

"Yes, ever since a service station up near Beltway was robbed. Though I never expected to have to use it. Nobody knew about the money except Kane and me."

Apparently not true, if this guy on the floor blasted in with a gun-enforced demand for the money. Unobtrusively, she snapped another cell phone photo that showed his face. Although it was possible, she supposed, that he was simply on the prowl, found a business door unlocked, and figured there'd be money inside.

Cate went to the main front door and peered out at the parking area. Nothing there but the Corvette and the SUV she'd seen earlier. How had the gunman gotten here? Was an accomplice hiding somewhere with a car? Sirens wailed in the distance. She went back to where Halliday was still slumped in the chair where she'd placed him.

"Is there someone we should call about Mr. Blakely?" Cate asked. "Someone who'd want to be with him?"

"His ex-wife Candy lives up in Salem. I doubt she'd be in any hurry to get down here and comfort him no matter how bad off he is." Halliday sounded bitter about his partner's ex-wife. "His son and daughter live back east or down south somewhere. I suppose I'll have to call Candy to get phone numbers for them."

The police car arrived, the reflection of the light bar on top shooting garish flickers of red and blue into the office. Two officers charged through the unlocked front door, neither of whom Cate recognized from past encounters with the Eugene police.

The older officer's experienced gaze took in the scene without shock or emotion. "Check the premises," he told the younger officer.

"There's no one here but us," Halliday said. He jerked a hand at the body on the floor. "And *he's* dead."

Although the thought had apparently occurred to the officer, as it had to Cate, that there could be an accomplice lurking somewhere with a getaway car. The younger officer headed toward the warehouse door. The older officer knelt by the body on the floor. His competent-looking touch apparently confirmed what Cate already knew. Dead.

The officer, with none of Cate's squeamishness, stepped over the body to get to Blakely. He felt at Blakely's throat but didn't touch the cascade of hundred-dollar bills. "Ambulance is on its way." He patted Shirley's shoulder. "Good work."

Clancy eyed the officer, and a warning rumbled deep in his throat. He was ready to defend his owner, but the officer didn't give him reason to have to do it. The officer stepped back and spoke into the mic attached to his shoulder to tell someone what the situation was here.

Halliday started to stand up but plopped weakly back into the chair. He held the ski mask out to the officer. "The guy on the floor was wearing this. He shot Kane and then I-I shot him." Again the brief stutter, as if what he'd done had affected even his ability to speak.

"The guy was going to shoot both of us!" Shirley said. Clancy tried to paw his owner, obviously upset with the lack of response from Blakely.

"All of you were here in this room?" the officer asked.

"I wasn't," Cate said. "I was out in the warehouse. I ran in when I heard the gunshots. I didn't see it happen."

"I was right here. I saw it all. The guy just ran in, yelled something about money, and then shot Mr. Blakely. He didn't even have a chance to give him the money!"

The ambulance siren died in the parking lot, followed a moment later by two EMTs rushing into the office. Cate stepped back to give them more room. One went to Blakely while the other checked the body on the floor. Then they both concentrated on Blakely. One man carefully removed the jacket Shirley had pressed against his head, more hundred-dollar bills fluttering, but Cate couldn't see what the wound looked like. She noticed now a mark on the wall behind Blakely. Did that mean the bullet had grazed or passed through his head? Was that good or bad? A third man rushed in with a stretcher.

"Where will you take him?" Shirley asked.

"Sacred Heart, RiverBend. Are you his wife?"

"No, but I'm coming along."

"Sorry, but you can't ride in the ambulance, ma'am."

Cate offered a quick prayer for Blakely as they carried him out on the stretcher. Shirley had to grab Clancy to keep him from running after them, but she looked ready to run and jump in the ambulance herself, no matter what the EMT said. Was there some relationship between them that Shirley hadn't mentioned? She turned to Cate.

"Can I use your car?"

"Well, uh, sure, I guess so." Cate dug in her pocket and fished out her keys.

"Hey, you can't leave," the younger officer objected. "We need to get your statement—"

Shirley snatched the keys out of Cate's hand. She gave the officer a defiant try-and-stop-me glare and barreled past him to get to Cate's car through the warehouse. He turned to look at Cate as if this were somehow her fault.

"And you are . . . ?"

"Cate Kinkaid. I'm just an, um, acquaintance." Abandoned now, Clancy came over and thrust his nose into the hand of the only person remaining that he knew, Cate.

"We'll get to you later," the older officer interrupted. "Don't leave before we get your statement." He turned to the body on the floor again.

Two more officers arrived. They herded Halliday, Cate, and Clancy into the outer office and repeated the don't-leave instructions. She had a chance to give the sales and reception area a more thorough inspection. A counter and cash register, shelves, and several spin-type display racks with fuses and miscellaneous small parts, a computer on a desk behind the counter. More posters of vintage cars. A long shelf held gleaming trophies. She caught a glimpse of her own car as it zipped by with Shirley at the wheel.

She turned back to the action in the other room. She couldn't see all that was going on around the body on the floor, but she knew the general procedure. Photos, measurements, bagging of both guns, bloody jacket, money, and anything else that might be relevant. No moving the body until someone from the medical examiner's office arrived.

There were a couple of plastic chairs in a corner of the outer room, apparently for waiting customers. Cate nudged a still-dazed Halliday toward one. More lights were on now, and the fluorescent bulbs overhead emphasized hard angles and shiny surfaces. And lines in a face.

"Can I get you something?" she asked Halliday. Shooting and killing someone had obviously hit him hard, even if he'd done it in self-defense. "There's coffee out in the warehouse."

"I don't want anything." Halliday's throat moved in a convulsive swallow. "I shot a man. I *killed* a man."

"You didn't have much choice." Cate's cell phone tinkled in her pocket. Mitch, no doubt wondering where she was for their pizza date. She let the call go to voice mail. "Not everyone could have reacted as quickly as you did in such a scary situation. Or had the courage to do it."

"Matt Halliday, hero?" His voice went croaky again. He shook his head. "Maybe, instead of shooting him, I could have . . ."

Halliday apparently couldn't think of anything else he could have done, and neither could Cate, but guilt obviously swamped him anyway.

"I wonder how the guy got here?" Cate said. "I don't see a car or any other transportation out there."

Halliday gave a powerless lift of shoulder, as if rational explanations in this situation didn't exist. "I can't believe it. That someone just . . . waltzed in here and started *shooting*." He stood up. "I'm going to the hospital too."

He started toward the door, but an officer intercepted him. After a brief but heated discussion, the officer led him back to the chair and pulled out a notebook. He waved Cate to the far side of the room.

She couldn't hear the officer's questions, but she caught some of Halliday's agitated answers about the money, how the gunman had gotten in, why they were here after hours, and the identity of the woman who had left.

Cate's interview was considerably shorter. The officer didn't recognize Cate or her name, but he did recognize the name of Belmont Investigations. Cate explained that her presence here tonight had nothing to do with her position as an assistant private investigator. His last questions were about Shirley, but Cate had no information to give about her. The officer gave her the usual line about contacting them if she thought of anything else and then told her she could leave now.

Sure she could. How? Saddle up ol' Clancy and ride off into the night? Shirley had her car.

With a certain feeling of déjà vu, she fished out her cell phone and hit the top number on her contact list.

3

Mitch answered on the first ring. "I have a bad feeling about this call," he muttered without preliminaries.

Sometimes Mitch had way too much intuition for a six-foot male with enough computer skills to hack his way into secrets of the universe. Although that hacking thing was long in the past, he'd assured her. High-school stuff. He was strictly legitimate now.

"I'm sorry I'm so late calling," Cate said. "I couldn't answer when you called earlier. Things were a little hectic here."

"Hectic," he repeated in a tone that suggested he suspected the word was a euphemism for something more dire. "Where are you?"

"At a place that restores old cars out on Maxwell."

"Are you okay?"

"Nobody tried to kill or kidnap me, if that's what you mean."

"Given your past record, I'm glad to hear that. Although I think I hear a *but*, don't I?"

"But I need one of your famous knight-on-a-white-horse rescue missions. Can you come get me?"

Dependable Mitch might occasionally be a little snarky

about her propensity for getting into difficult situations, but he didn't demand explanations or even sigh before he now said, "I'm a little short on white horses, but I'm always available to aid a beautiful damsel in distress. Should I bring a weapon? Fire-fighting equipment? Maybe a safety net?"

"Do you own any of those?"

"No, but it's a situation I should probably correct. I could acquire a gun. Or maybe I should have something with more firepower? A grenade launcher, perhaps?"

"Your snarkiness is showing." Although Cate had to admit all the items on his list could have come in handy on past occasions.

"Yeah, it is, isn't it? Sorry." He sounded at least semi-contrite. "But I know you, Cate. And I worry. I wouldn't say you go looking for trouble, but it does seem to find you. An occupational hazard, I suppose."

"This didn't have anything to do with my being a PI," Cate protested. "I just came to pick up a woman to take to the Fit and Fabulous meeting at church. But then there were some gunshots and the police and an ambulance came and then Shirley needed to use my car—"

"In other words, just an average day in the life of Cate Kinkaid, spunky assistant private investigator."

"Soon to be Cate Kinkaid, fully licensed private investigator," she reminded him tartly. Hopefully.

The state required a test of investigator competency from the Department of Public Safety Standards and Training, plus a certain amount of time working for a licensed private investigator. Cate had now successfully completed both, and the application for her own license had been submitted. Along with fingerprints, a surety bond, recommendations, photos, and a hefty fee.

Mitch didn't comment on her coming change of status. He just asked again, "Where are you?"

Cate gave him the address on Maxwell. "It's out past the residential area, a place called H&B Vintage Auto Restorations. You'll know it when you see the police vehicles out front."

"Police vehicles, plural. Why doesn't that surprise me? How *many* police vehicles?"

Cate peered through the window. "Five, I think. Oh, wait, there's another one turning into the driveway now."

"Six! Impressive."

"I just happened to be here. This isn't a case."

"Keep reminding yourself of that," he grumbled, but he also added, "See you in a few minutes."

Cate felt the weight of 120 or so pounds of dog leaning against her hip as she slipped the phone back in her pocket. She dropped a hand to Clancy's big head. He looked up at her with those amazing blue eyes, now obviously confused and anxious with his master gone. What about Clancy for tonight?

"You can probably sleep out in the warehouse," Cate comforted him.

She went back out to the warehouse to retrieve her purse, Clancy following like a shaggy shadow. Then she waited by the front door for Mitch, Clancy at her feet. Halliday came over and stood beside her, hands jammed in the pockets of his coveralls. Another vehicle arrived, unmarked this time.

"I'm sorry, I know we talked earlier, but I'm a little vague on who you are," Halliday said.

Cate gave him her name and explained about being there to give Shirley a ride. She didn't mention being a private investigator. Halliday's skin was so gray and washed out that she said, "You look as if you need to get out of here. Do you have to stay?"

"I don't think so. Apparently they're through questioning me. At least for now. But I think I should be here to make sure everything is locked up when they're through."

"I'd guess they'll be here most of the night."

Halliday groaned. "I don't understand what they're doing." He glanced back at the office now crowded with officers and crime scene people. "They don't have some big crime to solve here. The dead guy shot Kane, and I shot him to keep from getting shot myself. And Shirley too. No big mystery about any of it."

"I think the police have to investigate any not-natural death, even in circumstances such as this, and it takes a while."

"I'll go over to the hospital, then. As soon as I think I can drive without running off the road." Halliday held out a hand that was noticeably unsteady, then touched his stomach as if it too were in an uncertain condition. "I've never shot at anything but a target on a shooting range before. Hitting a man is different. Even someone who just shot your best friend. And some of the police questions were . . . disturbing."

"Disturbing?"

"They almost sounded like accusations."

"Accusations about what?"

"So many questions about the money. It feels like they think I shot the guy to protect the *money* more than in self-defense. I didn't even *think* about the money. I just saw the gun turning toward me. And Shirley." He hesitated a moment. "They had a lot of questions about Shirley too. How long she's worked here, what her relationship with Kane is, all kinds of stuff."

Cate remembered that the officer had asked her about Shirley too. Of course they were interested in Shirley. She was a prime witness. And yet, looking at it from a police view-point, Cate saw a different possibility. Were they considering a conspiracy here, that Shirley could have told the gunman about the money, with a deal to split it? But Halliday's quick action had thwarted that.

"It looked as if Mr. Blakely had way more hundred-dollar bills than people usually carry around in a pocket."

"He did. Thirty-thousand-dollars' worth. We got together tonight mainly to talk about closing down the Salem branch, but a few days ago he said he needed money, cash money, so I got it for him."

Halliday spoke as if there was nothing unusual in this. You had a friend and partner, he needed money, you didn't ask questions, you just supplied it for him.

"Company money?" she asked.

"No, it was a loan from my personal funds."

They both moved farther away from the door as two more people in plainclothes arrived. One a detective, Cate guessed. The other probably someone from the medical examiner's office. The media would no doubt show up soon to add their bells and whistles to the scene.

"Did he say what he needed it for?"

Another question that was definitely none of her business, although Halliday didn't seem to notice. He shook his head.

"I didn't ask. I figured it must be important, or he wouldn't have needed it." His gray face twisted in a grimace. "Though it probably has something to do with Candy. She's a real leech."

"And you have no idea how this guy in the ski mask could have known about the money?"

"All I can think is maybe Kane told whoever he owed money to that he was getting it here tonight. And then that person blabbed it to someone else. Still sounds like Candy to me. She's a big mouth, and no telling what kind of scumbag friends she has."

No lost love between Halliday and Blakely's ex-wife, obviously.

As if he'd heard Cate's unspoken thoughts, he made a rueful lift of shoulder. "Sorry. I get a little hot under the collar about Candy. She did everything she could to alienate Kane's kids and break up his relationship with them. And grabbed every asset she could get hold of in the divorce. She works for some politician there in Salem. Though she's probably trying to snag him as a husband. But he'd better watch out. Candy may look like a trophy wife, but she's more like a poison pill in spike heels."

"Have you and Mr. Blakely been partners for a long time?" Cate asked.

"About five years. We're not much alike, but we've been friends since way back in high school, when we were both running our old cars in the local drag races."

Cate saw the gleam of the Corvette under the outside lights that had now been turned on, the workaday SUV a dull hulk beside it. "He's a little more on the flashy side?" she guessed.

Halliday smiled at the way she phrased it. "Yeah, I guess you could say that. But it makes for a good balance in our business. Me on the stodgy side. Kane flashy. He's great at the promotion part of the business, meeting people and getting publicity. Last month he led a parade over on the coast in a '57 Thunderbird we restored, and he's won a lot of prizes with our restorations at car shows." He waved a hand toward the shelf of trophies. "Me, I'd rather hide under the hood and work on an old engine than get out in public."

A motorcycle turned from the street into the parking area. Cate recognized it immediately. She was momentarily surprised. She'd assumed Mitch would bring his SUV. She should have asked him to. But she knew she shouldn't be surprised that he was on the Purple Rocket. He loved roaring around on that big two-wheeled machine. Sometimes it was hard to know where Mitch fit on a stodgy-to-flashy scale.

"It looks as if my ride's here," Cate said.

Then she hesitated. Her murder cases had slipped under Uncle Joe's radar a couple of times, but he was still adamant that Belmont Investigations did not do murders. Yet this wasn't murder, she rationalized. Blakely wasn't dead, and Halliday had acted in self-defense when he shot the gunman.

"If I could be of any help . . ." She fished a business card out of her purse and handed it to him.

"You're a private investigator?" Halliday said the words in that same astonished tone most people used when they discovered 30-year-old, 5'4", redheaded Cate was a PI.

"Assistant private investigator," Cate corrected, as honesty always made her do. The thought occurred to her that once she was fully licensed, she could carry a gun. Did she want to? Sometimes carrying a weapon sounded like a good idea, but right now she suspected she'd be even more of a basket case than Halliday if she actually had to shoot someone.

"So if I can be of any assistance, give me a call," Cate said. She saw Mitch dismounting the motorcycle and opening the trunk behind the seats to get her helmet. "I'll put Clancy out in the warehouse for the night."

"No! I don't want him out there getting into everything and leaving smelly dog piles all over the place." Halliday spoke with a vehemence that suggested he put Clancy in the same undesirable category as Blakely's ex-wife Candy. "I don't know why Kane hauls that animal everywhere with him. Put him out in the Corvette."

"Well, uh, okay."

Clancy looked up at her—although he didn't have to look all that far up—as if he knew he was about to be further abandoned. But what else could she do with him?

She grabbed his studded collar and opened the door.

And immediately wished she hadn't gotten such a good grip.

◆ 4 ◆

She belly-skidded across the concrete walkway fronting the building, hitting a couple of stray rocks as she went, but she finally managed to let go of Clancy's collar before he dragged her into the gravel. She looked up to see the dog barreling across the parking lot, although not to the Corvette. Instead he aimed straight for the Purple Rocket. A flying leap landed him on the seat. Mitch, Cate's helmet in hand, stared in astonishment for a moment before dropping the helmet and running to Cate.

"Are you okay?"

"Do I look okay?" she grumbled as Mitch helped her to her feet. She felt as if the surface of the concrete were imprinted on her body. She brushed her knees and the front of her clothes. "But yeah, I'm okay."

"What's with the dog and my bike?" he asked.

"I have no idea." Clancy waved his skinny tail lazily as they approached the bike. "His name is Clancy. They took his owner to the hospital. I was going to put him in the Corvette. I don't know what *he* has in mind."

Cate grabbed Clancy's collar again to pull him off the motorcycle. Clancy resisted. Cate felt like a mouse trying to pull an elephant. A somewhat worse-for-wear mouse.

"You think maybe you could help here?" Cate suggested to Mitch.

"Like how? Call in a bulldozer?" But Mitch went around to the far side of the motorcycle and pushed, first with his hands and then his shoulder. Clancy dug his toes in, as if he had about seventeen of them on each foot, but he finally landed on the ground. Cate dragged him to the Corvette.

Locked.

"I'll go see if I can get a key." She transferred her grip on Clancy's collar to Mitch. Inside, a different officer was now talking to Halliday. Cate hesitated to interrupt, but she had to do something. She hoped neither Halliday nor the officer had seen the Two-Stooges-and-a-dog scene outside. Halliday shook his head when Cate asked about a key to the Corvette.

"Kane probably had it on him. Or it was in that jacket they bagged up."

"I'll have to put him in the warehouse, then."

Cate assumed Halliday wouldn't object now that there was no choice, but he was already shaking his head when the officer backed him up.

"I'm sorry, but the dog can't remain here unattended while we're working the crime scene." The officer peered out the window. Sounding more like a baffled bystander than a law officer, he added, "Why is he sitting on that motorcycle?"

Clancy had apparently gotten away from Mitch and again planted himself on the motorcycle seat. The brass studs on his collar gleamed under the yard light.

"Kane has a big bike," Halliday said. "He lets the dog ride in a special box he had made for it. Or sometimes the dog sits in front of him on the seat. He has goggles for it to wear. He says the dog loves it."

Great. A monster-sized mutt with a motorcycle fixation.

Cate went back outside and reported the no-key situation and what both Halliday and the officer had said about the dog not staying on the premises.

"Now I don't know what to do. I can't just dump him out here in the parking lot."

"What Clancy obviously has in mind is a bike ride," Mitch said. He draped an arm over the dog. Although they had not been formally introduced, Clancy squeezed up against Mitch. Maybe motorcycle possession was sufficient recommendation for a new friend.

"I guess I'll have to take him home for the night," Cate said reluctantly. "Halliday says Clancy likes riding on a motorcycle, and I don't know what else to do with him."

"What's Octavia going to think of a doggy visitor in her Kastle?" Mitch asked.

"I guess we'll see."

Mitch eyed dog and motorcycle. "How do you have in mind doing this?"

"Mr. Halliday said Clancy's owner had a box on his motorcycle for Clancy to ride in."

"Unless you have an instant Honey-I-Shrunk-the-Dog kit in your pocket, he's never going to fit in the Purple Rocket's trunk."

"Then I guess he'll just have to ride between us."

Mitch slid a foot over the bike. Clancy generously made room for him. Cate put on her helmet and clambered on behind the dog. He didn't seem to mind being pancaked between them.

"Remember, if anything goes wrong, this was your idea," she warned the dog.

A skinny tail whapped her leg.

"Okay, here we go," Mitch said.

He cautiously eased across the parking lot and onto the main road. Clancy shifted on the seat to get a better view over Mitch's shoulder. One big rear paw dug into Cate's thigh. Mitch speeded up. Clancy turned his head, and a long wet tongue and a flapping metal license tag slapped the faceplate of her helmet. Then, despite the faceplate, she got a mouthful of dog hair.

Oh, this was going to be a fun trip.

At the corner, where Maxwell turned onto River Road, experienced bike-rider Clancy shifted his weight into the turn.

"You okay back there?" Mitch asked.

A flapping dog ear blocked Cate's view. Another hind foot scraped her other thigh. Dog hair clogged her teeth. A tail whapped her ribs. "Yeah, we're fine," she muttered. Clancy added a wiggle and bark.

Mitch drove slowly and cautiously. A sedan pulled around to pass. Cate saw pointing fingers and laughing faces. A pickup passed them. A guy rolled down the window to yell, "Who's the good-looking one in the middle?"

By the time they roared up the steep driveway to her house, Cate felt as if she, Clancy, and Mitch had been melded into some inseparable lump.

"How do we get off?" she asked.

Clancy solved that problem by squirming out from between them and jumping to the ground. Cate stumbled off the bike and removed her helmet. She spit out dog hair, wiped what she suspected was dog slobber off her neck, and brushed ineffectually at enough dog hair on her jacket to knit into a mutt suit of her own. Mitch's back, she noted, was neat and tidy. His smooth jacket shed hair as if the leather had a Teflon coating.

"I'll come in and help you get him settled," Mitch said.

Cate's house key was on the key ring she'd let Shirley have, so she had to go around back to retrieve the spare she kept hidden under a brick. Clancy loped along with her. In the backyard, she spotted movement along the far fence.

Cate stopped short, imagination in overdrive after what had happened out at H&B. Burglar? Killer? Beside her, Clancy's muscles bunched as he readied for attack.

She grabbed his collar just in time as she saw what was moving by the fence. Not a killer. A skunk!

Clancy was perfectly willing to give her another belly-skid across the yard to go after the skunk, but this time she managed to grab a patio post before he got in full gear. She yelled, and Mitch came running. He still had a tight hold on the dog when they went around front and Cate unlocked the door.

Octavia met them in the foyer. Her white fur instantly bristled into porcupine spikes. She skidded into a turn, then apparently remembered this was *her* house, built especially for her, actually. She took a stiff-legged stance that practically shouted "C'mon, dog. Make my day!"

Clancy, for all his size, plopped his hind end on the floor and looked up at Cate uncertainly.

Octavia advanced a step and let out some warning yowls. She couldn't hear herself because she was deaf, but that had never inhibited the volume of her yowls. Clancy stood up as if he might take Octavia up on her challenge after all. Octavia, apparently deciding she'd made her point and discretion was the better part of valor, made a dignified turn and then scooted up the padded pole that led to her private walkway near the ceiling.

"I think you can let him go now," Cate said.

Mitch released the dog's collar, but Clancy just sat there until Cate patted her thigh in invitation.

"C'mon. We'll see if we can find you something to eat."

In the kitchen, broad-minded Clancy gulped dry cat food. Then he explored the house at race-dog speed, around the coffee table, down the hall, through the laundry room and bathroom, before finally jumping on Octavia's prized, pillowed window seat. He sniffed it thoroughly, turned around a couple of times, and curled into a shaggy ball. Octavia, from her walkway, hissed disapproval. Clancy rumbled matching disapproval.

"I don't think this is going to work," Cate said.

"It isn't fair to expect Octavia to stay up there all night," Mitch agreed.

"I suppose I could lock Clancy out in Octavia's play area. It's screened in."

Mitch straightened the shade on a lamp Clancy had knocked askew. "It's going to get cold out there tonight." His glance flicked between Octavia, now prowling her walkway, and Clancy, still claiming the window seat. "I guess I could take him home with me for the night," he finally said with all the enthusiasm of volunteering to walk the nearest plank into some bottomless sea.

"They allow pets in the condo?"

"I see other people with them. Mostly snuggly little lap-dog types."

"I imagine Clancy would be glad to snuggle in your lap, if that's required."

"That's what I'm afraid of. The headline may read 'Condo Resident Smothered by Hairy Animal of Unknown Origin.' But I'll have to go get the SUV to take him home in. I can't carry him on the bike without you along to hold him on. Do you still feel like pizza?"

Cate hadn't had anything to eat since lunch. Earlier, out

there at H&B, she'd have said no way to food of any kind at any given point in the near future. Right now, she felt as if she *shouldn't* be hungry, after what had happened. But she was. Mitch was surely hungry too. He often got so busy on a Computer Solutions Dudes project that he didn't even bother with lunch.

"Canadian bacon and sausage? With olives and sliced tomatoes?" she asked.

"You got it. I'll pick up some dog food too."

As soon as the Purple Rocket rolled down the driveway, Cate tossed the hairy jacket in the laundry room and used her cell phone to call Rebecca. She gave her aunt a minimal explanation about why she and Shirley had missed the Fit and Fabulous meeting at the church. Rebecca suggested that Cate talk to Uncle Joe about the shootings at H&B, but the landline phone in Cate's office rang, and she excused herself to answer it.

Actually, she was grateful for the interruption. She hadn't placed the events at H&B into the category of a *case*, but she didn't want to give Uncle Joe the opportunity to tell her to stay out of this. Halliday's question kept jogging around in her head. How had that gunman known about the money?

She picked up the phone. "Belmont Investigations. Assistant Investigator Cate Kinkaid speaking."

"Cate, this is Shirley. You're a *what*?"

"Assistant private investigator. But it's my home phone too."

"Oh." Shirley paused as if she had questions but apparently decided she hadn't time for them. "I'm glad I found your number in a phone book here at the hospital. It finally hit me that I'd left you out there at H&B without any transportation."

"A friend came and got me. How's Mr. Blakely doing?"

"They won't tell me much. You know how they are about privacy regulations. But I do know he hasn't regained consciousness. I don't think that's good."

No, not good at all. "Mr. Halliday intended to come to the hospital, I think. Did he get there?"

"Yeah. He's really shook up about all this. He's worried about Kane, but he also feels guilty about shooting that guy. I guess I'm not that bighearted. I'm just glad he did it. He and I would probably both be dead if he hadn't."

"I think so."

"A couple of policemen were here too, and asked me all kinds of questions."

"They can get really nosy."

"Yeah, *really* nosy. But—" She broke off, as if not certain she wanted to go on, but finally she added, "But I got the funny feeling they think I might know something about the gunman. Maybe even had something to do with the shootings. And I don't know anything about *anything*!"

Everybody, it seemed, put their own nervous spin on being questioned by the police. Cate kept silent about the fact that a similar thought about Shirley had slithered into her own head.

"But what I called for, I can drive the car to your place and then call a cab to come back here to the hospital."

"You're not going home?" Cate asked.

"I want to be here with Kane. I don't really know him very well, but . . . I feel as if someone should be here."

And maybe, if Blakely recovered, he'd be very grateful for Shirley's caring concern. The situation strongly suggested that Shirley had feelings for him.

"I don't need the car tonight. You keep it there and bring it here in the morning. Then I'll take you home from here. Do you usually use a bicycle to get to and from work?"

"A bicycle? No, since my pickup broke down, I walk. A guy there at H&B is working on it. But if Jerry can't fix it, maybe I will be riding a bicycle pretty soon."

Which meant the bicycle Cate had seen out there by the piles of tires near the warehouse didn't belong to Shirley after all. Biking and hiking were popular around Eugene, and maybe crooks needed their exercise too. But surely a gunman intent on snatching $30,000 would have a higher-tech getaway plan than pedaling off into the night, wouldn't he?

"Does someone else who works there have a bicycle?"

"Not that I know of. Why are you asking?"

"Because I saw a bicycle leaning against that pile of tires when I parked back there by the employees' door."

"I've never noticed one there. Somebody probably just dumped it to get rid of it. People are always dumping stuff there. I suggested to Mr. Halliday that the area ought to be fenced off, but he hasn't done it." Shirley asked for Cate's address and said she'd be at the house in the morning. "Oh, I'm so jittery I forgot to ask about Clancy. Did you leave him in the warehouse?"

"No. Mr. Halliday said he couldn't stay there."

"That figures. He isn't much of a dog person."

"I brought him home with me, but he and my cat aren't getting along, so a friend is taking him for the night. We can take him out to your place in the morning."

Silence on the other end of the line until Shirley said, "We'll have to, uh, figure that out tomorrow."

Cate started to ask what Shirley meant by that disquieting statement, but she'd already hung up.

♦ 5 ♦

Cate planted herself between the hostile animals to await Mitch's return.

"Some cats and dogs live in perfect harmony," Cate chided them. "Don't you two realize you both have blue eyes, and that's unusual in both cats and dogs? Think of it as a special bond between you."

A whap on the wall with Clancy's tail. A hiss from Octavia.

Well, that went over great. Like she'd suggested they both go on vegetarian diets. Octavia and Clancy were obviously not planning to pose for warm-fuzzy calendar shots of two-species togetherness.

While Cate waited, she scratched. Somehow dog hair had migrated under her shirt. Under her waistband. Shouldn't Clancy be missing some hair, considering all that had transferred to her? But no, his bluish-blackish-grayish coat looked as thick and shaggy as ever. She desperately needed a shower, but she didn't dare leave these two alone.

Mitch finally arrived, a fragrant pizza box in hand. Clancy sat up and sniffed as if he were familiar with the smells and eager to join in a pizza fest.

"Stay," Mitch said sternly to the dog. Clancy obediently

plopped back down on the window seat. Mitch looked surprised but pleased with his unexpected dog management skill. "Hey, I should have tried that earlier."

Cate gave him a congratulatory thumbs-up gesture. She doubted he'd do as well ordering Octavia around. Fortunately, her cat didn't care for pizza anyway.

While they ate, Cate gave Mitch a rundown on the evening's events, including the oddity of the gunman apparently knowing about the money. She showed him the cell phone photos she'd taken.

"No one there recognized the gunman?"

"Not Halliday. I haven't showed the photos to Shirley yet, but she didn't say anything about recognizing him when Halliday yanked off the ski mask. Blakely is in no shape to talk, of course."

She didn't mention her own semi-suspicion of Shirley, but, with no hints from her, Mitch came up with a similar thought about the possibility of an insider conspiracy, since the gunman apparently knew about the money.

"Shirley may be a little rough around the edges, but she seems nice. And very shaken up about Blakely. I don't think she could have been involved." Although Cate had to wonder, even as she said that, if it was herself more than Mitch that she was trying to convince.

Mitch separated another slice of pizza. He ate a string of cheese from the dangling end up to the crust. "Maybe she didn't count on the guy shooting Blakely. Maybe he was supposed to grab the money and run, and then they'd split it later."

Uneasily, Cate realized she didn't know enough about Shirley to argue with that scenario. But still she protested mildly. "Shirley struck me as a basically good person. Nice," she repeated.

"What is it your Uncle Joe says? 'In the PI business, you have to be suspicious of everyone.' *Nice* doesn't necessarily cut it."

"Now you're thinking like a PI."

"Yeah. Sometimes I do that," Mitch muttered. He sounded as if that was more like discovering a bad case of toenail fungus than a welcome surprise. In an abrupt change of subject, he added, "Something unexpected happened today. We got an offer on Computer Solutions Dudes."

Cate almost dropped her Pepsi. "I didn't know you were even thinking about selling the company."

"We haven't been. This Portland outfit wants to expand into the Eugene area, and apparently they think buying us out would be better than starting cold here. Or competing with us."

Mitch and his partner, Lance McPherson, had been in business together since before Cate and Mitch had met. Computer Solutions Dudes specialized in complete computer setups, including writing software, for small businesses.

"You're not thinking about taking the offer, are you?"

"It's a very good offer."

Cate took a big gulp of Pepsi, but the fizzy liquid didn't fill the sudden hollowness that billowed inside her. "But what would you both do if you sold?"

"Lance has contacts with people in a big computer company in Dallas. I think they'd jump at a chance to hire him. I'm not sure about me."

Mitch wouldn't leave the Eugene area . . . would he?

"I don't think I want to go to Texas. I'd be more inclined to try Seattle or the Bay area."

So he *was* thinking about leaving the Eugene area. "Oh."

Cate wondered if she sounded as dismayed as she felt. She

and Mitch didn't have any solid commitment between them, true, but somewhere in the back of her mind she'd kicked around the idea that their relationship might grow into something permanent. If Mitch could ever get past his hang-up with her being a PI. But maybe it was an even bigger stumbling block for him than she'd realized. With his computer experience and expertise, some Seattle or Bay area company would no doubt welcome him with open cyberspace arms.

"Or, if Lance wants to sell and I don't, our initial partnership agreement gives either of us the right to buy out the other partner's share of the company."

Relief whooshed through Cate. She picked up another piece of pizza. "That sounds like a great idea, don't you think?"

"I'd have to borrow a lot of money to do it."

Where Cate couldn't be of any help. Until Uncle Joe hired her, she hadn't been able to find a steady job for over a year. She had no helpful investment fund socked away. Unless you counted the jar of found pennies on the kitchen counter. That might finance a couple of Snickers bars, but not half of Computer Solutions Dudes.

"How does Robyn feel about this?"

Lance and Robyn had been married less than a year. Both Cate and Mitch had been in their wedding. Fashionista Robyn had turned out to be not nearly as shallow and status/money conscious as Cate had first thought, and she was very supportive of her husband. But right now Cate found herself hoping Robyn would stomp a Ferregamo-clad foot and reject Dallas as if it were some hick cowtown.

"I haven't heard what her reaction is yet, but I'm guessing she'll be fine with Texas. Dallas is a lot larger than Eugene."

Cate almost yelled, "Don't do it! Don't go running off to Seattle or somewhere! I want you to stay here!" But he hadn't specifically asked her opinion, and without a commitment between them, she didn't feel she had the right to say anything. So all she did was loop a strand of melted cheese around her pizza and try to sound thoughtful when she said, "I'm sure you and Lance will make the right decision together."

"What I need to do is talk it over with the Lord, of course," Mitch said, and Cate gave herself a mental whack. Of course. That's what she should have said too instead of thinking mostly about how selling the company would affect *her.*

"You're going to have some decisions to make too, you know, when you get your PI license," Mitch said.

Right. Uncle Joe was talking about fully retiring and turning Belmont Investigations over to her once she was licensed. He and Rebecca wanted to buy a motor home so they could, as Joe put it, just drive off into the sunset. See all the places they'd never seen. Cate thought it was a great idea for them.

But was she a good enough PI to go it alone? Or would she flounder and wind up working as a Christmas elf at the mall again? Investigating nothing more than the identity of the sticky purple stuff some child left on Santa's suit.

And maybe all without Mitch.

There were a few crumbs and half a piece of pizza left when they finished eating. Mitch put the box on the floor and called Clancy over. The dog scarfed down the leftovers. Mitch grabbed his studded collar in preparation for taking him out to the SUV.

"You're sure taking him to the condo is going to work out okay?" Cate asked.

"No, but that's the kind of thing we noble knights on Purple Rockets do to aid damsels in distress."

"I appreciate it, Noble Knight." Cate dipped her head in a little bow. "And I appreciate your coming to get me too.

Along with your admirable humility." She leaned over the dog and kissed Mitch on the cheek.

Mitch didn't comment on her snarky observation about his humility. "I think this double rescue rates more than that." His kiss was more directly targeted, lasted longer, and made Cate breathless enough to forget even a belly button full of itchy dog hair.

Finally she came right out and said it, breathless still. "I hope you don't leave Eugene."

"We'll see. I'm considering various possibilities."

Which wasn't exactly the full assurance she was looking for.

◆ 6 ◆

Cate wouldn't, however, let herself go all teary and emotional about the situation. She stepped back. "Clancy could use a good brushing when you get him home. He seems to have a lot of excess hair."

Mitch scratched his neck as if he'd acquired a few dog-hair itches of his own. "This is just for tonight, right?"

"I'll take him out to Shirley's trailer tomorrow as soon as she brings my car back. I'll call you."

"Okay. Talk to you then."

After Mitch and Clancy left, Octavia cautiously climbed down from her walkway. She was sniffing like a bloodhound following an escaped prisoner when Cate headed for the shower.

◆◆◆

Cate had coffee started and a plump scoop of tuna in Octavia's cat dish by 7:00 the next morning. Shirley arrived a few minutes later.

Her black curls looked as if they were still in high-voltage mode, but her eyelids drooped and she was still in yesterday's bloodstained coveralls. She held out the key ring.

"I filled the gas tank," she said.

"Oh, you didn't need to do that. But it's really thoughtful of you. Thank you! How's Mr. Blakely?"

"Nobody's telling me anything, but they did let me in to see him. For about twenty-nine seconds." Shirley sounded grumpy about the time limitation, but the fact that they'd let Shirley see Blakely at all surprised Cate. Probably a tribute to her persistence and determination. "He's never regained consciousness, and he looks . . . terrible."

"I think the crime scene people were digging a bullet out of the wall, so hopefully that means they won't have to do surgery to get it out of his head."

"He has tubes everywhere. And machines with beeps and green lines keeping track of everything. He looks terrible," she repeated.

Shirley didn't look so great herself, and impulsively Cate said, "How about breakfast before I take you home?"

"I wouldn't want you to go to all that bother—"

"No bother."

"That'd be great! Mr. Halliday said not to come to work today. Some outfit is coming in to clean up."

Cate stepped back to let Shirley inside. "There was a lot of blood." An understatement about the scene that Cate was trying to keep out of her mind.

"I'll go home and get some sleep before I go back to the hospital. Hopefully Jerry will have my pickup fixed by today."

"You can freshen up if you like. Bathroom's down there."

Shirley started in the direction Cate pointed, but then she spotted one of the unique features of the house. She was too polite to comment on the oddity of painted planks circling the living room about a foot below the ceiling, but she eyed them doubtfully.

"That's Octavia's special walkway," Cate explained. "And that's Octavia," she added, as her white cat padded over to inspect the newcomer.

"I guess I'm more of a dog person myself," Shirley said warily as Octavia, tail swishing, looked as if she might be considering climbing up Shirley's leg. Cate scooped her up. "You made a special walkway for the cat?" Shirley asked.

Cate explained the basics of how she'd acquired both cat and house. "I was living with my uncle and aunt when I took Octavia to keep her from going to the pound, and then it turned out her former owner had in her will that whoever got the cat also got the house. But then the house that was here burned down, so the lawyer who was executor of the will had this new one built."

Cate left out the fact that a killer had started the fire in an effort to kill Cate and another woman in the burning house. It was one of the incidents that reinforced Mitch's negative attitude about her work as a PI.

"Cats like to walk around up high?"

"Oh yes. Octavia spends a lot of time up there. The window seat"—Cate pointed at the padded seat below a picture window—"is so she can be warm and comfortable and still watch birds and squirrels outside. She has an outdoor, screened-in playroom too." Octavia also had a trust fund, although Cate didn't mention that.

"Wow," Shirley said, which was apparently all she could think to say about a house that Mitch called the Kitty Kastle. She hesitated and then looked toward the bathroom as if wondering if it had any peculiar cat features.

"It's a normal bathroom," Cate assured her. "Octavia uses a litter box like any ordinary cat."

Although Octavia's litter box had her name written in gold

script over the arched doorway, and she was extraordinary in other ways as well. In spite of her deafness, she had some uncanny knowledge about when the landline phone was about to ring. Cate sometimes reminded her she shouldn't feel all superior about that; she didn't seem to have any special ability concerning cell phone calls. Octavia also gave Cate occasional advice on PI situations. Cate always assured herself the helpfulness of that advice was surely only coincidental.

"She does like to nap in the bathroom sink occasionally," Cate added.

"Well, uh, okay," Shirley said.

Cate heard the bathroom door close firmly. Apparently Shirley didn't want sink company.

◆◆◆

By the time Shirley came out to the kitchen, Cate had coffee perked, orange juice poured, and scrambled eggs, hash browns, and toast ready to dish up. Shirley had folded the coveralls so the blood was concealed on the inside, and she was now in the gray sweatpants and T-shirt she'd been wearing under them. Cate found a plastic bag for the coveralls, and they sat down to eat together.

There were various things Cate wanted to know, but Shirley seemed more inclined to eat than talk. Cate suspected she came from a hard-working family where mealtimes were solely for consuming food, not for bonding experiences.

Finally, however, Shirley had cleaned her plate and leaned back to enjoy a second cup of coffee. They talked a little about what a great hospital RiverBend was, and the beautiful wooded grounds between the hospital and river.

"I don't see any man stuff around, so I guess you're not married?" Shirley asked.

The unexpected question momentarily jolted Cate. No subtle small talk before getting right into the nosy stuff for Shirley.

"No, not married."

"Boyfriend?"

Answering that question was a little more complicated. Cate and Mitch had a steady relationship, but he was still uncomfortable with her being a private investigator and kept offering her a job at his Computer Solutions Dudes company. Although he'd given her a special pen that was really a video camera, great for the possibility of undercover work, plus a voice-activated wrist cell phone, and he'd several times helped with her PI cases. He was closer to boyfriend than *non*boyfriend. "Um, yeah, I guess I have a boyfriend."

"Of course you do." Shirley's hazel eyes appraised Cate. "You're nowhere near fifty, and you're definitely fit and fabulous."

"I don't know about that . . . though I thank you for the compliment. You know, you can still go to the Fit and Fabulous sessions even if you missed that first one," Cate said. "There's more to it than just the fitness stuff."

"I've never been much on churchgoing. Will this woman, uh, preach at us?" Shirley's eyebrows scrunched, as if this might be a deal breaker.

"I don't think there will be any actual sermons, but the speaker is supposed to have some good insights on connecting faith with being fit and fabulous." Now, given Shirley's blunt questions and comments, Cate shot back a few of her own. "How about you? Married?"

"I was. Thirty-six years. But Hatch got killed three years ago."

"I'm sorry to hear that." Impulsively Cate added, "I'll bet he thought you were fabulous."

Shirley looked surprised, then smiled and nodded. "I think he did. Though that word would never have occurred to him."

"You lived over on the coast?"

"Hatch and I had a commercial fishing boat for years, and he always bragged that I could clean a fish as fast as he could, and a crab even faster." Shirley's smile turned rueful. "But, yeah, I need the fabulous stuff. You don't see anyone bragging about fish- and crab-cleaning talents on those internet dating sites."

Cate hadn't visited any of them, but she figured Shirley's statement was probably accurate. "Boyfriend?"

"Before Mr. Blakely came down from Salem, he asked me to go to dinner with him after his meeting with Mr. Halliday last night. He told me to call him Kane too. We have a larger inventory of parts here than in the Salem branch, so Kane and I often talk on the phone or email back and forth."

"More than business talk?"

Shirley's ruddy cheeks reddened further. "Sometimes."

"I'm assuming you said you'd go to dinner with him?"

"No, I told him I couldn't go, because I'd already promised Rebecca I'd be at the meeting. She sounded so friendly and nice. I think she was concerned that not many women had signed up, and I told her I'd be there for sure."

So, if Shirley made a commitment, she kept it. Even if it meant missing dinner with an attractive man who interested her. Admirable.

"But then I got up my nerve and suggested, since he was spending the night in Eugene, maybe we could go out for breakfast. And he said great."

"Good for you! He probably thinks you're fabulous already."

Shirley shook her head. "When he got here, he said he

wouldn't be able to make breakfast after all because he had to meet with a client." Shirley brushed a finger over her right eyebrow, which, in some misguided attempt at taming, she'd plucked to the skinny line of a road to nowhere on a map. "Maybe that was true. But I think, after he met me in person, he just changed his mind." Her throat moved in a hard swallow.

"So he gave you his dog to babysit for the evening." Cate couldn't keep the indignation out of her voice.

"Yeah. But I don't blame him for backing off. I mean . . ." Shirley pulled a black curl out from her head and let it go. It boomeranged right back to her scalp.

Honest, forthright, tell-it-like-it-is Shirley. No oversized ego here. Okay, Shirley's dye job was a little too crow-black, and her wiry curls looked as if they had popped out of her head with an electric *s-p-r-o-i-n-g!* Her boots would do fine for military combat. But the warmth and frankness about her were surely more important than hairdo and eyebrows, and Blakely should have seen that. A fish-cleaning ability wasn't to be downgraded, either. Mitch would likely approve a fish-cleaning talent more than he approved of Cate being a private investigator.

Blakely didn't deserve shooting for hurting Shirley's feelings, Cate granted. But a few heavy car parts thrown at him in the warehouse when he backed out of the breakfast date might have been appropriate.

Now Shirley leaned forward, elbows on the table. "But I'm thinking, if I could learn enough at these Fit and Fabulous sessions, Kane might feel differently."

Make yourself over for a man? That grated on Cate's nerves, but she made herself keep quiet. For the moment, anyway. She switched to a different subject.

"Has anyone besides you been at the hospital?"

"Just Mr. Halliday. He showed up again as I was leaving to come here. I talked to him for a minute, and he said he'd gotten hold of Kane's son and daughter. He didn't know if they're coming. Kane isn't very close to them."

"Did you know about the money before the gunman tried to steal it last night?"

"No. Mr. Halliday must have given it to Kane before he called me into the office. I was shocked when I saw all those hundred-dollar bills falling out of Kane's jacket when I was trying to stop the bleeding with it."

"So you don't know what Mr. Blakely wanted the money for?" Cate asked. Shirley shook her head and grabbed a leftover piece of toast on the plate. "Mr. Halliday seemed to think he needed it for something to do with the ex-wife," Cate added.

"When Kane and I talked on the phone, it was mostly about old cars or car parts, or sometimes fishing and crabbing, but he mentioned his ex-wife a few times. Candy got the house and most everything else. I don't know why she'd be entitled to any more money from him." In spite of what Cate thought was definitely rudeness from Kane Blakely about their date, Shirley sounded protective of him.

"Is Candy the mother of his children?"

"No. His first wife was killed in a car accident a long time ago. His son lives in Georgia and his daughter in Florida. Candy wouldn't go visit them, so Kane hasn't seen them much since he married her. He feels bad about that."

The ex-wife separated Kane from his kids? Not a particularly admirable stepmotherly trait. Not a particularly admirable fatherly trait either, however, letting a new wife do that.

"Did Mr. Blakely go out to his Corvette to get the inventory sheets before or after you went to the office?"

"Before, I guess. He didn't leave while I was there. Actually, I wasn't even supposed to be there last night. Radine, she's the office manager, was supposed to stay for the meeting. But her daughter got sick about noon, and she had to leave, so Mr. Halliday asked me to stay in case they needed details about the inventory or something."

"How did you happen to get a job there?"

"After I moved over here from the coast, I got into a special program for disadvantaged older workers at Lane Community College. And then Mr. Halliday was generous enough to hire me, even without experience."

So if Shirley didn't know about the money being there that night, she couldn't have been in on any conspiracy with the gunman. If she was telling the truth, of course. Cross-my-heart-and-hope-to-die probably wasn't written into the criminal creed of behavior. But it was getting ever harder to think of Shirley as a criminal. Was filling the gas tank of a borrowed car the kind of thing someone involved in a robbery conspiracy would do?

"I was really surprised when you said you're a private investigator," Shirley said.

"Assistant private investigator," Cate corrected automatically. "My Uncle Joe, who owns Belmont Investigations, is Rebecca's husband."

"You investigate murders and bank robberies and arson?" Shirley, like many other people, had an exaggerated idea of the glamour and excitement in a private investigator's life.

"We do mostly background checks and insurance investigations, sometimes surveillance work or locating witnesses for a lawyer, things like that."

"Did you always want to be a private investigator?"

"It wasn't my plan in life, that's for sure. But sometimes God has different plans for us than we do for ourselves."

"I don't think God is interested in me or my plans."

"You might be surprised."

"I'm going to try to make Kane part of my future plans," Shirley declared with the kind of determination that said minor events such as a shooting weren't going to stand in her way.

Kane Blakely should be grateful that Shirley was interested in *him*, Cate decided. Granted, even with a bullet wound in his head, he'd looked like an attractive older guy. But even so, with big, hairy Clancy part of the package, some women wouldn't be interested.

Shirley got out her cell phone and called the mechanic who was working on her pickup at H&B. She reported that he said her pickup wouldn't be ready for several days, but he'd loan her another pickup of his own.

Cate gathered dishes and carried them to the dishwasher. "We'll go by Mitch's condo and pick up Clancy on the way to your place."

Shirley looked in her empty coffee cup. She cleared her throat. "Well, there's a, uh, problem."

7

"The manager of the trailer park just sent around a notice that tenants can keep any pets they already have," Shirley said. "But no new pets are allowed."

"Surely that doesn't mean you can't keep Clancy for a few days, just until Mr. Blakely can take him back?"

"I'll ask, but Mrs. Noonan is a real fussbudget."

"But Mitch didn't plan on having Clancy more than one night!"

"Maybe I can find a kennel that will take him."

Of course. A kennel. Easy solution. Cate relaxed. She called Mitch to explain that she'd come for Clancy as soon as they found a place in a kennel for him. "How'd he do last night?"

"I left him in the living room when I went to bed, but it sounded like a pack of wolves howling in some old Western movie out there. So I fixed a blanket on the floor so he could sleep in the bedroom."

"Problem solved?"

"He quit barking, but then he whined like a lost puppy."

"So?"

"So I let him sleep on the foot of the bed." Mitch sounded grumpy but also defensive, as if he didn't like admitting he'd caved in to the dog's mournful whines.

"So everybody lived happily ever after."

"Well, more or less. Except for the snoring."

"Yours or his?"

Mitch answered that question with an unappreciative snort. "I'm going to take him to the office with me. Who knows what he might do here alone?"

Cate suspected Mitch was taking Clancy along because his soft heart didn't want the dog to be lonely, but some macho pride wouldn't let him admit that.

"You're a good man, Mitch Berenski," Cate said. *And I hope you don't pick up and leave Eugene.*

◆◆◆

Cate took Shirley to the trailer park, which was on a side street a few blocks from H&B. She came out of the office with a quick answer about Clancy. Mrs. Noonan was adamant. A rule was a rule, and bending it for one renter apparently would lead to some sort of trailer-park anarchy.

Shirley's mobile home, which she said she'd had moved over from the coast, was an older single-wide, modest but well maintained. Cate didn't want to leave until Shirley had found a kennel for Clancy, and she could relieve Mitch of his foot-of-the-bed guest, so she went inside with Shirley. The interior of the trailer was roomier than Cate expected, clean and faintly pine scented but totally lacking in feminine touches. The only decorations were a couple of calendars with fishing scenes hung on the walls. A basic computer setup filled a small wooden table, printer on the floor.

Shirley started calling kennels. One apparently asked what kind of dog Clancy was. Good question.

"Well, he's kind of black and gray, with some bluish hair too. So maybe Australian shepherd? But he's bigger than that, so maybe some Saint Bernard. And he has a long, skinny tail that might be Great Dane." After a pause, apparently in response to a question about weight, Shirley said, "Well, uh, over a hundred pounds, I guess."

"Where did Kane get him?" Cate asked, after that kennel declined to take Clancy.

"He found him on the beach when he was over at the coast a few months ago. All wet and cold and hungry."

If Clancy had come up out of the ocean, maybe he had a few sea-monster genes in there too. But you had to give points to a man who was willing to take in a wet, hairy, hungry dog.

It took Shirley two more calls, but she finally found a kennel for Clancy. Cate got the address and said she'd take Clancy out to the kennel. It was a rather awkward question, but she had to ask it. "Is paying for the kennel going to be a problem?"

"I'm sure Kane will be happy to pay the bill when he gets out of the hospital."

And what happened if Kane didn't get out of the hospital? Cate reluctantly decided that was a worry for another day.

"I'm so sorry to bother you with all this," Shirley added. "Would you like some coffee before you go?"

"Thanks, but I'd better be on my way." No telling what kind of damage Clancy might be wreaking in Mitch's computer world.

"I wish I could afford to hire you," Shirley said suddenly.

Cate turned at the door. "To do what?"

Shirley's narrow eyebrows scrunched as if she wasn't sure of the answer herself. "It's just that all this seems so . . . peculiar. Maybe it needs investigating."

"Crime often is peculiar. But you know who shot Kane, and you saw Mr. Halliday shoot the gunman. Not much to investigate, and I'm sure the police will do whatever is necessary."

"I know. But who was that guy? How did he know about the money? Why didn't he just grab the money and run?" Shirley blinked and swallowed. "He didn't have to shoot Kane."

"He might have panicked and shot without really intending to." Or maybe the guy just felt like shooting someone. It was a disturbing fact that there were people like that.

"I guess." Shirley's agreement sounded more frustrated than convinced. "I still wish I could hire you."

"I took some photos last night," Cate said. "They're kind of gross. But if you'd like to see them . . . ?"

"I would."

Cate pulled out her cell phone and brought up the pictures. Shirley's throat moved in a harsh swallow at the picture of a bloody and unconscious Kane Blakely, but she didn't back off. She went on to study the picture of the dead man on the floor. Cate asked if she'd ever seen him before.

She shook her head. "Out there in the warehouse, I hardly ever see customers. But what is it criminals do? 'Case the joint'? Maybe he's been in, and Radine would recognize him."

"Have you seen the morning newspaper?"

"No. I can't afford a subscription, but I sometimes look at local news on the website."

"It's possible the police have identified the gunman by now. They may already have all the important facts available for the public."

"I'll bring up the website. Learning to use a computer was really tough for me, but now I can surf the internet without even getting seasick." Shirley sounded proud of that accomplishment. She pulled up a stool in front of the desk. The computer was slow booting up and connecting to the internet. "But I'm still on dial-up," she added, a hint of apology in her voice now.

Cate knew she could probably find information faster with her cell phone, but she didn't want it to look as if she were trying to one-up Shirley with technology, so she waited. Shirley found the site, and Cate leaned over her shoulder to read. The information was minimal. The dead man's identity was either not yet known to the police or they were not yet releasing it. No mention of the money or Kane Blakely's condition.

"I guess I can't help wondering if Kane's ex-wife is involved," Shirley said. "Can't you find out more from the police than what gets in the news?"

"Because I'm a private investigator?" Cate asked, and Shirley nodded.

Oh, if only that were true. But Cate had trouble getting information even on cases in which she was actively involved, let alone ones in which she didn't even have a client. Private investigators on TV shows and in books always seemed to have a friend in the police department to supply insider information, but Cate didn't have any more "in" with the police force than she had with the Pentagon.

But all she said was, "I'm afraid not. I'll call and let you know about Clancy after I get him to the kennel."

Shirley supplied her cell phone number, and Cate headed for Mitch's office with various speculations rambling around in her head. Halliday and Shirley both suspected ex-wife Candy could be involved, maybe because Kane owed money to her. But if that weren't true, did she know about the money anyway? And hire a gunman to go after it? How did one go about hiring a hit man? Cate had never seen a "hit man" section in the yellow pages.

Or maybe some other woman was involved. It was probably unfair to classify Kane Blakely as a Don Juan type on the basis of his silver-fox good looks, but maybe some messy triangle that included an unhappy boyfriend or husband was complicating his life. Or maybe it wasn't a woman complication, and the gunman was an unhappy customer taking a do-it-yourself route to a refund. But Halliday would surely recognize an unhappy customer. Although not if that customer was from the Salem business . . .

Not your case. Mind your own business. Which at the moment was relieving Mitch of one big, hairy dog.

◆◆◆

Computer Solutions Dudes didn't have a parking lot, but Cate squeezed the Honda into a space on the street. Inside, fortyish receptionist/secretary Maggie Bones, in jeans and Oregon Ducks sweatshirt, gave Cate a shoulder wiggle in place of a wave. Her hands and ears were busy multitasking on a landline phone, a cell phone, and a computer. Maybe Mitch was always offering Cate a job because they really could use some extra help here, not just because he wanted to get her out of the PI business?

When Maggie was semi-free, Cate asked, "Is Mitch around?"

"No, he went out on a job first thing this morning."

Cate peered around. There didn't seem to be any oversized creature lurking in the office. "Alone?"

"He took Clancy with him."

"Did Clancy cause any, um, problems here?"

"He knocked a vase of flowers off my desk with his tail."

"Oh, I'm sorry—"

Maggie dismissed the flower accident with another shoulder wiggle. "Actually, I think it was a comment on the guy who sent them. The more I think about it, the more I realize what a jerk he is. Dogs are good judges of character, you know."

Cate wasn't convinced of that line of thinking, but, if Octavia could do PI work, maybe Clancy could do long-distance boyfriend evaluations. "Okay. Tell Mitch I'll call him later."

Cate was just going out the door when she met Mitch and Clancy coming in. The dog gave her hand a slurp of familiarity. His bluish-blackish-grayish coat looked almost silky. Definitely brushed.

"I came to get Clancy. Shirley found a kennel for him." Cate held out her hand for the leash.

"Oh. Good." Mitch's tone was neutral, but he kept a tight hold on the leash. "Have you checked out the place?"

"Checked it out how?"

"You can't leave an animal just anywhere." He sounded indignant. "What's the staff like? How clean is the place? Do they exercise the animals or just leave them sitting in a cage all day?"

Cate granted that knowing all that would no doubt be an excellent idea, but she was a little surprised by Mitch's vehemence.

"Actually," Mitch added, looking down at the dog, "I don't think he's going to be happy locked up in any kennel."

"I don't see any alternative." She explained why Shirley couldn't keep him.

Mitch seemed to weigh that on some invisible scale. It tipped in an unexpected direction. "I suppose I could keep him for a few more days, until his owner gets out of the hospital."

"Sleeping on the foot of your bed?" Cate asked doubtfully.

"That was a temporary arrangement. He'll sleep on the floor tonight."

Cate looked at Clancy now sprawled at . . . well, *on* . . . Mitch's feet. Dogs couldn't smile or wink, but Clancy had a smirky expression that strongly suggested if anyone slept on the floor tonight, it wasn't going to be him.

8

Cate tried to call Shirley to let her know Clancy was taken care of, but she had to leave a voice mail message. She spent the day on the continuation of a job locating a wife who'd taken off with papers important to a Belmont Investigations client. She followed several leads until one took her out to Junction City and she located the woman at a cousin's home. Routine stuff, the kind that paid a PI's bills.

Cate and Mitch had tentatively planned to watch a DVD at his condo that evening, but he called to say he had to do an emergency virus removal job for a client.

"What about Clancy?" Cate asked.

"I'll take him along. He's okay with waiting in the SUV. Actually, he's kind of useful. I don't think anyone's going to break into it when he stands up in the seat and looks them in the eye."

Shirley called from the hospital to check on Clancy too. She'd gotten there by cab, but she said she'd have transportation by the following day. Her mechanic friend Jerry was loaning her a pickup he'd acquired as a basket case and put back in running order.

"How about if I take you home tonight, then?" Cate suggested.

"I don't want to bother you—"

"No bother. What time?"

"Oh, 8:30 or so would be great. By that time, there's no possibility I'll get in to see Kane."

"You didn't see him today?"

"No. But neither did his ex-wife." Was that a hint of satisfaction in Shirley's voice?

"She's there?"

"Oh yes. High heels. Blonde hair. Earrings down to her elbows. Fur jacket. She's running around crying and carrying on, but she isn't letting it mess up her mascara, of course." Shirley gave a muffled gasp. "Oh my, that was really catty, wasn't it?"

Oh yes. Catty, with claws and sharp teeth, Cate agreed, although Shirley sounded so appalled with herself that Cate felt no comment was needed. "Did you talk to her?"

"Me? Oh no. She and Mr. Halliday were arguing about something. He's usually so calm and even tempered, but he looked ready to rip that fur jacket off her and stuff it down her throat."

"I wonder if she's staying here in town."

"She yelled something at Mr. Halliday about him not getting rid of her by being a bigger jerk than ever."

Cate picked Shirley up at the hospital just after 8:30. Shirley hadn't personally been able to find out anything more about Kane, but she said Halliday had managed to get some information. The bullet hadn't stuck in Kane's brain, but it had hit a critical place or gone deep enough that his condition was considered a coma now.

Back at Shirley's trailer, an older gray Toyota pickup was parked in the driveway.

"Oh, Jerry brought the pickup over early!"

"He must be a really nice guy."

"He is. Mr. Halliday says he isn't much good on the fancy details with restorations, but he can fix anything. Sometimes parts for old cars just aren't available, and Jerry can make them."

Jerry hadn't gone in for cosmetic details here. The small pickup had a dinged-up rear fender and dents in the tailgate, and splotches of darker gray paint looked like stray continents migrating across the doors and hood. But the tires were crisp and new.

Shirley opened the car door. "Thanks so much for everything."

"Keep in touch. Even though you missed that first Fit and Fabulous meeting, I'm sure you can still get in on the coming weekly sessions," Cate reminded her.

"I really can't afford to go buy a lot of fancy makeup and hair and fingernail stuff, so maybe there isn't much point in it anyway."

"You could come to see what the faith part is about."

"Well, I'll, uh, think about it."

◆◆◆

Cate didn't expect to hear from Shirley again until Kane was well enough to get his dog back, so she was surprised when Shirley called the very next morning.

"I'm here at the hospital again. I intended to stop in just for a minute before going to work, but there was a fire here last night, right there on the floor where Kane is—"

"Is he okay?"

"They caught it before it got beyond the restroom."

"Maybe someone was smoking in there, even though they're not supposed to, of course. Accidents—"

"This was no accident. The door had paper towels stuffed under it to brace it open so smoke and fire would get out in the hallway. But I don't think anyone was actually trying to burn the hospital down."

"But you think someone deliberately set it?"

"I think it was a, what do you call it? Diversionary tactic. Someone wanted to distract people and keep them busy so he—or she—could sneak into where Kane is without being noticed in the confusion."

"For what reason?"

"It wouldn't take an expert to finish Kane off. Just yank out some wires and tubes and stuff, and he'd be gone."

"Shirley, you're talking about murder!"

"That guy at H&B tried to kill him. Maybe someone wanted to finish the job."

"You're suggesting it wasn't just a robbery at H&B? That the gunman was actually out to kill Kane?"

Shirley gave a combination sigh/groan. "Sounds pretty wild, doesn't it? I guess I'm not sure what I'm thinking. I'm just so worried and scared!"

"Do you have someone in mind who might do this?"

"The fire was in the women's restroom," Shirley added in a way that said the location was meaningful.

"In Kane's condition, he must be in an area that's under constant observation."

"Yes, but he isn't under *guard*. And maybe that's what he needs. A guard. Protection."

Under the current circumstances, Cate doubted the police would expend their limited financial resources on a guard for Kane. Especially when this might well be some paranoid imagining of Shirley's. "Did anyone see someone trying to get into where Kane is?" she asked.

"I heard a couple of nurses talking about one of the patients being upset because he thought he'd seen someone in his room last night. Maybe she just blundered in there while trying to find Kane."

Shirley didn't have to spell it out. *She*. Ex-wife Candy.

"Are the police there?"

"Oh yeah."

"Have you talked to them?"

"Not yet, but—"

"Shirley, I don't think you should be throwing around unsubstantiated accusations. I mean, maybe Candy isn't exactly Miss Congeniality, but why would she want Kane dead? As you said, she already managed to get almost everything in the divorce. And according to Mr. Halliday, she has her eye on a new husband candidate."

"You think I'm silly, don't you? Getting all worked up about a man I barely know. Lonely older woman desperate to latch on to any available male, alive or half dead, right?"

"Oh, Shirley, I didn't mean it like that—"

"Yeah. Okay, I'm going to work now. I'm sure they're tired of seeing me around here anyway."

Cate repeated what she'd said before. "Keep in touch."

◆◆◆

Back home, Cate checked the newspaper's website for more information about the shootings at H&B and found that the gunman at H&B had been identified with the name Mace Jackson. Identification on the body showed an address in Salem, and fingerprints from previous offenses confirmed the identification. The gun used in the shooting had been stolen in a Salem burglary a few weeks ago. The victim in the shooting was listed as being in a coma from the gunshot wound. No mention of a fire at the hospital.

As far as Cate could tell, Shirley might be the only person connecting the fire with Kane's presence in the hospital. Which didn't mean she was wrong about a connection.

But the new information sent several thoughts skittering around in Cate's mind. Did guys with robbery and/or murder in mind usually carry identification to the scene of the crime? Was that meaningful? Jackson was from Salem, where both Kane and his ex-wife lived. Had he come to Eugene with information about, and a deliberate plan to go after, the $30,000 at H&B? The stolen weapon and previous offenses pointed out that this wasn't a first-time foray into crime for Mace Jackson.

Cate didn't have a dog-hair itch now, but she definitely had an *itch*. Maybe this was the real occupational hazard of being a PI. The itch of curiosity.

9

Uncle Joe called to tell her he and Rebecca were heading up to Corvallis to look at a motor home. The third one this week.

Cate spent some time on the internet doing a background check on a potential employee for an accountant's office. Octavia's catwalk didn't extend to Cate's office, but the cat took her usual place in a wire basket atop a file cabinet to oversee Cate's work. Once she came down to sit beside the computer and after a while inserted a paw that clicked on a site Cate had decided to pass over. Which turned out to have some incriminating and helpful information on a company the potential employee had formerly worked for.

"Coincidence," Cate scoffed at the white cat. "You're always batting at something, and you just lucked out this time."

Octavia gave a condescending "whatever" flick of tail.

Cate realized she was almost out of paper for the printer and decided to run out to Staples and get a box. Which was when she discovered an envelope on the floorboard on the passenger's side of the Honda, apparently fallen out of Shirley's purse. Nothing mysterious, just a power company bill, but, after picking up a ream of paper at Staples, she decided to go on out to H&B and return the bill to Shirley.

There were several cars in the parking area this day. Kane Blakely's Corvette, Shirley's borrowed Toyota pickup, Halliday's SUV, and a sleek burgundy Lexus. Knowing it was a Lexus was not a leap in Cate's vehicle recognition skills. She read the name on the rear of the car when she parked behind it.

This time Cate went through the front door at H&B. A dark-haired, thirtyish woman sat at the computer behind the counter, cup of coffee beside the keyboard. This must be office manager Radine. The door to Halliday's office was closed.

The woman started to stand up, but Cate waved her to go on with her work. "Is Shirley out in the warehouse? I need to give her something she left in my car." She held up the envelope.

The woman pointed to the door that led out to the warehouse. "Sure. Just go through that—"

The door to Halliday's office burst open, and a blonde tornado in black denim, high-heeled boots, and gray fur stormed out. She headed for the front door but spun and aimed for the counter instead. Cate knew who she must be. The infamous ex-wife. Definitely trophy-wife material. Cate had to admire the spin. In those heels, she'd have gone down like a sack of potatoes.

"I want to see your insurance file," the woman snapped at Radine. She didn't appear to notice Cate's presence or to consider that Cate might be a customer who'd been there first. "Everything that you have on insurance. *Now.*"

Radine stood up, her back stiff. "I'm sorry, but I don't have—"

"I know there's insurance. A *lot* of it." Candy tossed her head, long earrings flashing like *Star Wars* weapons. "I remember very well Kane telling me when we got married that the business was set up for a half-million-dollar payoff if anything happened to him, and I want—"

Radine picked up her cup of coffee and regarded Candy with ice in her eyes. "As I'm trying to tell you, Mrs. Blakely, I don't have an insurance file." A lift of her chin suggested that even if she had it, Candy was more likely to get that cup of coffee thrown in her face than the file.

Insurance. Interesting. So maybe ex-wife Candy did have a motive for murder? Although you'd think she'd be a little more discreet about displaying her interest. Had she also been sneaking around the restroom and hallways at the hospital with accelerant and match in hand? At the moment, she looked fully capable of pulling a gun out of that pink Coach handbag—a gun fully color coordinated with handbag and fur—and blasting away.

Cate almost injected a comment. *You're divorced. Kane wouldn't have kept you as his beneficiary*. But she managed to clamp her jaw shut. Not her case. It was also possible Kane had neglected to change the beneficiary, and Candy actually had grounds for demanding information.

Halliday stepped around the corner of his office. "Aren't you getting a little ahead of yourself, Candy? Kane's not dead. No matter how much you might wish he were."

"What's *that* supposed to mean?"

Halliday smiled, not pleasantly. "Exactly what you think it means."

"I don't want him dead! I just want . . . whatever I have coming."

"That's what I think you should get too. Exactly what you have coming."

The snarky implication was clear. Whatever Halliday thought Candy had coming, it wasn't a big insurance payoff.

"I'll have my lawyer—"

Halliday lifted a hand and motioned toward Cate. "Candy, meet my private investigator, Cate Kinkaid. Cate, this is my business partner's ex-wife, Candy Blakely." Halliday's smile was a home-run winner now. "Cate will be looking into the details of the shooting. And the fire at the hospital last night."

I will? Cate blinked. Now, for the first time, Candy noticed Cate's existence.

She was not, Cate could see, instantly intimidated. She looked Halliday's investigator up and down as if Cate were a scruffy mannequin in a secondhand thrift store. Cate owned a pair of high-heeled boots. She wished now that she'd worn them instead of her jeans and old Reeboks. She yanked out a business card and handed it to the woman to affirm that she was indeed a private investigator.

Unfortunately, Candy instantly picked out the incriminating word on the business card. "*Assistant* private investigator? What does that mean? You're the bargain-rate substitute because Matt was too cheap to hire the real thing?"

Cate had been willing to give Candy the benefit of the doubt, but apparently she *was* fully as obnoxious as Halliday and Shirley had said.

"I have full confidence in Ms. Kinkaid," Halliday said.

"And I have full confidence in my lawyer," Candy snapped. Another spin—how did she *do* that in those heels?—and she clacked to the door on the hard-surfaced floor.

The three of them watched her slide into the Lexus. Radine rolled her eyes and turned back to her computer. Halliday looked at Cate. He smiled ruefully.

"I'm sorry to put you on the spot like that. But that woman always makes my blood pressure go up like a rocket blasting off." He shook his head. "So, how about it? Do you want to be my private investigator?"

"I'm not sure there's anything to investigate," Cate said. Yes, she was curious about several aspects of the situation, but still, it was basically a cut-and-dried case. No mystery about who killed whom to solve.

"My feelings exactly," Halliday agreed. "What's to investigate? But Candy apparently intends to keep everything as stirred up as possible. There's no telling what she may try to pull or what trouble she may cause."

Radine leaned against the inside of the counter. "Maybe what should be investigated is *her*."

"As you can probably guess, we're not exactly charter members of the Candy Blakely fan club here," Halliday said. "In any case, I'd appreciate knowing I have you on my side if something does come up."

"I can send over a rate sheet on how Belmont Investigations charges for services."

"Yes, do that. I'm uneasy about this fire at the hospital last night. It never occurred to me until Shirley brought it up earlier that the fire might have something to do with Kane. First the attack right here, now a fire. Maybe somebody *is* out to get him."

◆◆◆

Before going out to the warehouse, Cate showed Radine the photo of the dead man on her cell phone. "Any chance you've seen him around? It's possible he came in to check things out sometime before charging in with a gun."

Radine studied the photo. "The police showed me a photo too. I didn't recognize him. But someone lying there dead maybe looks different than a live person." She shivered and looked up from the cell phone. "Are you going to work for Matt and investigate this?"

"I'll have to discuss it with Uncle—with Mr. Belmont."

Cate took the power company bill out to Shirley but didn't stay to chat. A tall string-bean of a guy in the standard H&B coveralls leaned on the counter while Shirley packaged a car part for shipping to a customer. Shirley introduced the guy as the mechanic Jerry, the one who'd loaned her the pickup. A guy who was interested in more than car parts, Cate suspected, from the way his eyes followed Shirley's every move.

Cate was surprised when she went out to her Honda to see that the Lexus hadn't actually left the parking lot. Candy had pulled around behind Halliday's SUV. She tapped on the horn to get Cate's attention, then slid out of the Lexus and purposefully high-heeled it toward Cate's car. Those dangling earrings flashed like sharpened knives.

Cate warily touched the button to roll down the window. Candy was smiling, but those elongated silver earrings winked warning signals.

"I want to apologize for what happened in there." Candy shook her head, creating a charming flurry of tousled blonde hair. "I've just been so upset about Kane, and then Matt always can push my buttons. It's a good thing there weren't any sharp car parts lying around, or I'd probably have thrown some at him." Another smile, this one winningly rueful. "You really are working for him?"

Cate didn't smile back. "Our client information is confidential."

"I stuck my foot in my mouth in there, didn't I?" Candy put a hand on the window frame, as if suspecting Cate might raise the glass barrier between them. "I'm sorry. Actually, before you handed me the card, I thought maybe you were

Matt's girlfriend, and he was trying to scare me by making me think he had a private investigator poking around."

"Girlfriend!"

Candy grimaced. "Okay, ghastly thought, right? I'd be horrified too, if someone thought I was Matt's girlfriend. But I realized right away, of course, that you're much too bright and attractive to be a girlfriend of his."

Bright and attractive. Now Candy was trying to butter her up?

"It's just so hard to get my head around this whole situation." A brightness in Candy's blue eyes suggested imminent tears, although Cate had to wonder if they were real or if she had an instant supply of them at her disposal. "Matt dislikes me so much that he isn't about to give me a clue about what's really going on. I wouldn't put it past him to threaten me with a private investigator even if you were a termite inspector or spark-plug salesman."

Hmmm. Why would Candy think a private investigator was a threat if she hadn't done anything?

"You threatened him with a lawyer," Cate pointed out.

In a mercurial switch of emotions, Candy laughed as if she were delighted with herself. "I did, didn't I?"

Cate didn't laugh with her. Bluntly she said, "Maybe what really upsets you is that you figured Kane would be forking over that thirty thousand by now, and he isn't. Why was Kane getting the money for you?"

"He wasn't! I didn't know anything about—" Candy broke off and thrust her head forward as if she might go into earring-attack mode. Instead, she straightened and offered another smile. "I have questions. You have questions. Maybe we can help each other out here."

Cate hesitated. There *were* questions she'd like to ask the ex—Mrs. Blakely. But Candy's suggestion smacked of underhanded collusion between them. "I don't think so."

"Matt and Radine told you a lot of unflattering stuff about me, didn't they?"

"They didn't tell me all that much, but I don't think you can count on a helpful reference for a résumé from either of them."

Candy's second big sigh struck Cate as melodramatic. "Maybe we could just back up and start over?" Her nicely shaped eyebrows lifted hopefully. "I know I've come off as the Wicked Witch of the West here, but I do have some redeeming qualities."

Maybe a snake had redeeming qualities too, but Cate wasn't inclined to get close enough to the forked tongue to figure out what they were.

Candy smiled again, and now the smile was rich and warm as a fresh cappuccino. "I brush my teeth and see my dentist regularly. I make great lasagna. I dote on babies and kittens and puppies. I even like that big, hairy mutt of Kane's. In fact, the dog must have been down here with Kane, and I'm worried about what's happened to him. I don't suppose you'd know?"

Candy's concern about the dog made a small dent in Cate's antagonism toward the woman. "A friend of mine is taking care of the dog temporarily. I'd have done it, but my cat and Clancy didn't get along."

"Really? He and my Persian do fine together."

Several surprises in that offhand statement. One, that Candy had a cat. Two, that the cat and Clancy got along. Three, that this must mean Candy and Kane had some relationship close enough to involve her cat and his dog.

Was it possible Candy Blakely wasn't quite the obnoxious,

money-hungry witch that Halliday, Radine, and Shirley had made her out to be? Although, if she wasn't, she'd certainly done a credible impersonation of one back there in the office.

Maybe it wouldn't hurt to see what information she could glean from Candy.

10

"I could use a cappuccino," Cate said tentatively. "How about you? The Valley River Center mall isn't far from here. Are you familiar with it?"

"Does a duck know where the closest water is? Of course I know where the mall is! One of my favorite places when I lived here. I'll meet you at the food court in fifteen minutes."

◆◆◆

At the food court, Cate spotted Candy already in line at the espresso stand. Cate got in behind her. They both ordered caramel cappuccinos. With their drinks in hand, Candy wound through the maze of tables to a far corner. She draped her fur jacket over the back of a chair. Cate decided she'd let Candy take the lead in this unexpected discussion and see where she ran with it.

"So, are you a Eugene native?" Candy asked. She spooned a fluff of whipped cream off the cappuccino.

The ask-you-about-yourself approach, no doubt to be followed by a good-listener response.

"I came up from California a couple years ago, but I was raised down in southern Oregon. Gold Hill, to be exact."

"Gold Hill! Oh, I've been there. Kane and I went to some funny celebration down there once. They had outhouse races!"

Right. Perhaps not one of the small town's finer moments. "How about you?" Cate asked.

"I grew up in Beaverton, started college at Oregon State, got married and never graduated. Got unmarried, had a few jobs, started modeling in Portland, and came down to Eugene to do a fashion show here at the mall. Met Kane and got married six weeks later. Where we became Candy and Kane. Say that fast and you get visions of sugarplums dancing in your head." Candy wrinkled her nose as if the combination was not one of the more appealing aspects of the matrimonial merger.

Cate tried to make her "um" sound thoughtful.

"We lived here for a while and then moved up to Salem when Kane and Matt decided to expand H&B to a second city."

"Did something happen to precipitate the animosity between you and Mr. Halliday?"

Cate expected Candy to downgrade the open hostility, or perhaps even reveal some pre-Kane relationship with Halliday that went down in flames, but Candy just frowned.

"I didn't even meet Matt until after Kane and I flew down to Vegas to get married, but he seemed to dislike me from day one. I guess I have to admit the feeling is mutual. The man is boring as an old car-repair manual. Picky as a disinfectant salesman with a germ fetish."

Cate didn't encourage this line of criticism, but Candy didn't need encouragement.

"Finding a transmission for a Model A is his idea of big excitement. He'd rather spend his time putting a carburetor in an old Mustang than do anything fun. Kane and I went out to dinner with Matt and Marilee a few times, and he was so nitpicky it was embarrassing. He'd practically get out a magnifying glass to inspect the silverware, and then he'd dip a napkin in a water glass and start scrubbing. Then he always found something to argue about on the bill."

"Kane isn't boring or nitpicky, I take it?"

"He at least reads a book occasionally, and can talk about it, and he likes to play tennis and golf and go to a movie or dancing. He's fun, always joking and teasing. We learned scuba diving together. Kane had his flaws as a husband, but being boring wasn't one of them." Brief hesitation before she added, "I loved him."

"There was some friction between you and Kane's son and daughter?" Cate asked.

Candy tilted her head. "Let's see—you're pointing out that I don't get along with Matt. That there were problems with Kane's son and daughter. You make it sound like I'm as prickly as a porcupine with a personality disorder!"

"Sorry."

Candy leaned forward, arms on the small table. "Yes, there was 'friction.' Having your new stepdaughter call you a tramp who seduced her dad into marriage can do that. Having a stepson make a pass at you behind his father's back, and then, when you won't play, threaten to tell his father *you* made the pass, that'll generate some friction too. Especially when he *did* make that pass."

All of which would tend to produce some family discord, Cate had to agree. Although the be-suspicious-of-everyone trait that had rubbed off on her from Uncle Joe made her add to herself, *If she's telling it the way it really happened.* "You must not be much older than the son and daughter."

"Marrying an older man isn't a crime!"

True. Kane had led Shirley to believe the family split with his son and daughter was Candy's fault, but maybe his children's attitude was a big part of the problem. Although six weeks from meeting to wedding might make some people think someone was railroading a rush to the altar. But, if you didn't make a prejudgment, maybe that someone was Kane.

Two sides to everything.

"So what broke up the marriage?" Cate asked.

Candy shrugged. "We started getting on each other's nerves. We had money problems. Kane didn't like my interest in politics. I got tired of his obsession with watching every one of those CSI shows on TV."

"He got boring?" Cate suggested.

"Or maybe I did. I don't know. Even though we were short on money, he started spending most weekends over on the coast. Without me."

"Another woman?"

"I figured there might be, but I never really knew. I probably should have hired someone like you to investigate or follow him." Candy frowned as her appraising inspection took in Cate's red hair and old green sweater, as if she wasn't convinced Cate could find pickles in a pickle jar, let alone a straying husband. "Do you do that?"

"Occasionally."

"But I didn't do it. So I still don't know." In a sharp change of subjects, Candy added, "The hair color's real, isn't it?"

"Would I dye it this color?" Cate asked.

Candy laughed. "You could touch it up, you know, just so it wouldn't be so tomato-on-fire looking."

Apparently the buttering up was over.

Candy fumbled in her purse and dragged out a pack of

cigarettes. Then, apparently remembering the Oregon law about smoking in restaurants, she shoved the pack back in the Coach bag. "I've been trying to quit, but I'm so upset about Kane I can't do it now." She put a mint in her mouth instead.

"I understand that you pretty much took him to the cleaners in the divorce."

"You don't pull any punches, do you?" Candy said. It was not a compliment. "Okay, I admit it, I grabbed everything I could get my hands on. Kane didn't want me modeling after we got married, so I dropped that, and it isn't something you can step right back into. I had something coming to make up for giving up my career for him, didn't I?"

Cate pressed the mental voice button that turned on her all-purpose "um."

"Although there wasn't all that much to get. Kane was a big spender. He liked to impress people with something like sending a hundred-dollar bottle of champagne over to their table at a restaurant. Treating everybody in a bar to drinks. Making a big event out of donating money to some charity. But, as you may or may not know, the Salem branch of H&B has been floundering financially. They'll probably close it. That's what Kane and Matt were having their big powwow about."

"You knew about the meeting ahead of time?"

"Kane told me he was coming down here to meet with Matt."

"But he didn't tell you about the money?" Cate didn't try to keep a hint of skepticism out of the statement.

"No, I didn't know about the money." Candy gave an exasperated roll of eyes.

"The car you drive isn't exactly a low-budget model."

"No, but it's a hybrid. Good for the environment." Then

as if she were annoyed with herself for responding to Cate's comment about her vehicle, she snapped, "And what does my car have to do with anything anyway? I'm paying for it, not Kane. I'm working for Mark Gillerman. He's in the state legislature now, and he'll probably be our next senator in Washington DC. I can't rattle around in an old junker."

Cate murmured the all-purpose "um."

"I got the house. Big deal." Candy threw up her hands. "The mortgage payment is a killer." She stopped short, as if thinking that wasn't the most sensitive way to put it, under the circumstances. Then she shrugged. "I love the place, but I'd unload it if I could. But the real estate market is in the pits. I may wind up losing it to foreclosure."

So Candy needed money. Big money. Car payments. House payments. Pink Coach handbags. Maybe she'd eyed that $30,000 too? If it wasn't intended for her, had she been ruthless enough to go after it with a hired gunman?

"How did Matt get ahold of you anyway?" Candy demanded. "Just look in the yellow pages under private investigators? Or maybe you tack flyers on doors or advertise on TV?"

"Belmont Investigations is in the yellow pages, but no, that isn't how—" Cate broke off as she realized what this question meant. "You didn't know I was there at H&B when Kane was shot?"

Candy's blue eyes widened. "No, I didn't know that! The newspaper didn't mention you. And Matt didn't tell me. You mean you *saw* Kane get shot?"

Cate explained about being out in the warehouse, although not on PI business, and running in when she heard the gunshots.

"So now you're working with the police investigating this?"

Well, no. The police and Cate were not exactly on BFF status.

"The police have their investigation. I have mine," she said with a lofty inflection, as if the separation were her choice. She sat back and purposely dropped an out-of-the-blue subject into the conversation. "So, how do you know Mace Jackson?"

Candy sloshed cappuccino on the table, apparently startled by the abrupt question. She busied herself wiping up the puddle with a napkin, but she didn't pretend not to recognize the name. "The gunman Matt shot and killed after the guy shot Kane? All I know is what I read in the newspaper. Why would you think I know him?"

Maybe because you hired him? "He's from Salem."

"You're from Eugene. Do you know every scumbag who lives here?" Candy challenged.

Good point. Although, since becoming a PI, Cate had gotten to know more of the local scumbag population than she'd ever expected. Candy saying she didn't know Jackson didn't necessarily mean she *didn't* know him. Cate jumped subjects again.

"I haven't met Matt's wife. Marilee, that's her name?"

"She isn't his wife now. Didn't I mention that? Matt was pretty broken up when she picked up and left. Which surprised me. I didn't think he had that much emotion in him. Maybe he didn't realize what he had until she was gone."

"What was she like?"

Candy leaned back and sipped her cappuccino thought-fully. "I didn't really know her very well. They didn't have kids, but she was, you know, housewifey. And I'm not. She was into arts and crafts, painting, that kind of thing. She hardly ever said anything. Of course, if she did say anything, Matt just put her down, like her thoughts or opinions were worthless."

"Did she resent that?"

"She never seemed to. But sometimes I thought, maybe she was one of those meek, quiet women you hear about who finally has had enough and just up and poisons or shoots her husband. And everyone is so astonished, because she was such a sweet little wife."

"Did she get a big settlement in the divorce?"

"As far as I know, she walked away with nothing."

A vengeful ex-wife hires a gunman to storm in and get rid of the ex-husband who wronged her, and pick up a $30,000 bonus? Except that wasn't what happened. Mace Jackson shot Kane Blakely, not Matt Halliday. Unless he made a mistake and got the wrong guy?

"Where is she now?"

"I have no idea. I don't think Matt does either. Hopefully, she's living it up with someone more exciting than Matt."

"That's your standard of excellence in a husband, then, how exciting he is?"

Candy let the unflattering question go unanswered. Her mouth pinched. "Oh, I know. I'm probably being unfair to Matt. In his own boring, pompous, nitpicky way, he's steady, dependable as an old Volkswagen Bug."

"Being boring, pompous, and nitpicky aren't exactly in the top-ten sins."

"I suppose not. And Matt has no bad habits, no vices. He's loyal, responsible, and trustworthy. Punctual too. You could set your clock or calendar by Matt. He must have a bundle socked away for retirement. He sure never spends anything now."

Cate remembered how Halliday had described himself. *Stodgy.* "But when Kane needed money, Mr. Halliday was quick and generous enough to provide it for him."

Candy didn't bother with applause. She leaned forward, and Cate saw a distinctly predatory gleam in her eyes.

"So, what about the money?" Candy asked. "Thirty thousand, isn't it? Who gets it?"

"I presume it's in police custody now. But I should think Kane would get it back eventually."

"If he lives."

Cate nodded, at the same time thinking that Candy didn't sound all that concerned about her ex's well-being now.

"But if he doesn't live, who gets it?" Candy prodded. "His kids, as part of his estate? Or does it go back to Matt?"

"That may be a question for lawyers to squabble about. Mr. Halliday seemed to think Kane needed the money for some obligation to you." Cate tossed out a possibility. "So maybe you're entitled to it."

Candy nodded, but Cate couldn't tell if the nod was agreement that the money should be hers, or wild hope.

"What does Mr. Halliday have against you?" Cate asked.

"At this point, I think he figures I had something to do with Marilee leaving him. That I encouraged her, maybe even helped her do it."

"Did you?"

"I would have helped her, if she'd asked me. But she just up and left, all on her own. But even before that, I think Matt figures I led Kane astray. That I lured him into doing something besides taking care of H&B business 24/7. We spent ten days in Vegas on our honeymoon." She rolled her eyes and slapped her hands to her cheeks, as if in imitation of Halliday's horrified reaction to the time away from H&B.

"Mr. Halliday didn't approve?"

"You'd think we'd taken a six months' vacation on company money while he labored back here in the salt mines.

We didn't start out intending to stay that long, but we were having such a run of luck and such a great time that we almost *couldn't* leave."

"A run of luck at gambling, you mean?"

"Kane played blackjack and poker, and he must have come out at least $5,000 ahead. Card games aren't my thing, but I just kept hitting the jackpot on slots. I came away with $1,742. It was like we couldn't lose." Candy's face lit up at the memory.

What Cate also noted was that Candy knew right down to the dollar how much she'd won. A woman who kept track of money. A woman who'd had her eyes on $30,000 and now insurance money? Except Kane wasn't dead. Yet.

"Kane is Mr. Halliday's friend. He feels protective about him. He may have been concerned Kane was going to get hurt in a relationship with you," Cate suggested.

Halliday was also protective enough to whip out a gun when Kane was attacked.

"Protective," Candy reflected. "Yeah, I suppose so. Another of Matt's admirable traits. I told Kane once that I wouldn't trust his good buddy Matt any farther than I could throw him. But that was no doubt unfair. Sometimes I wonder, how can the guy have all these admirable qualities and still be such a jerk?"

Maybe jerk-ness, like beauty, was in the eye of the beholder.

Cate changed the subject. "You asked Radine about insurance."

"And you saw how far I got with that. She closed up like a bank when you need a loan."

"I would think, given that you and Mr. Blakely are divorced, that he's probably changed the beneficiary by now."

"Maybe he has. But maybe he *hasn't*. I want to know. I have a right to know."

"That may be something for your lawyer to investigate."

Candy leaned back in her chair. Her eyebrows, which Shirley probably envied for their graceful shape, twitched in a frown, and she gave an unladylike snort. "I don't have a lawyer. The one I had for the divorce got kicked out for appropriating money from some client trustee accounts. I just threw out the lawyer thing to Matt because . . . oh, you know. He's such an overbearing, know-it-all jerk."

Cate made no comment on that.

"Okay, now I have a question for you," Candy said. "Matt said something about a fire at the hospital. What was that about?"

Candy didn't know about the fire? Or was this question a diversionary tactic designed to make herself look innocently ignorant of the fire?

"All I know is that there was a small fire on the same floor that Kane is on at the hospital. I don't think it affected him or any of the other patients."

"Knowing Matt, he probably thinks I set it," Candy said with a sour smile.

"I presume you're staying at a local motel?"

Candy gave Cate an odd glance at the apparently unrelated question. She named a chain motel over close to I-5 and the hospital.

"Were you in your room all night?"

"What kind of question is that? Where else would I be?" Candy looked puzzled, but then realization kicked in. "Oh, I get it. That's a PI question. Make all the suspects account for their whereabouts during the time of the crime. Which means you suspect *I* set the fire. And my point in doing that would be . . . ?"

"It appears Kane may be worth more dead than alive to you."

"Okay, maybe I wasn't in my room all night. My nerves were jittery, and I went over to a little bar for a drink. But I never went near the hospital."

"You and Kane are still seeing each other in Salem?"

"Why would you think that?"

"You mentioned your cat and Kane's dog get along."

Candy shrugged. "We see each other occasionally, but we aren't *seeing* each other. You know what I mean. Sometimes Kane comes over to the house to look for something he forgot when he moved out. Sometimes I let him keep one of the restored cars in the garage if they run out of room at the shop. He always has Clancy with him. We're on good enough terms that I don't meet them with a shotgun or a blast of pepper spray, and I keep some doggie treats around for Clancy."

"You're seeing someone else now?"

"Maybe you should just give me a questionnaire to fill out!"

"Actually, I just happen to have one with me . . ." Cate reached for her purse, and Candy swung her booted feet around as if ready to run.

Then she laughed, a laugh that for the first time sounded earthy and genuine. "You're kidding, right? But I made a mistake. I thought I could pull information out of you, and instead I'm answering your questions. I guess I should have known better than to try to match wits with a private investigator." She clapped her hands lightly. "Bravo, Ms. Kinkaid. Job well done."

In spite of an occasional slip, Candy was also doing a good job of buttering her up, Cate decided. In fact, if the butter got any deeper, Cate might whoosh right out of the chair. A sweet-talking tactic Candy had borrowed from her politician employer/husband candidate?

"Okay, another question," Cate said. "Why are you here in Eugene now?"

"I'm not wholly indifferent to what happens to Kane."

"Or maybe it's because of the insurance. So if Kane does die, you'll be right here to stake your claim."

Candy lifted those groomed eyebrows. Cate wondered if she knew about Shirley. Although there wasn't actually much to know. Shirley's relationship with Kane hadn't gone beyond long-distance chats and something of a crush on Shirley's side.

"Apparently, Tact and Sensitivity 101 isn't required for assistant private investigator status," Candy said. "You just dig right in."

"Yeah, I got an A in Digging In 101."

Candy abruptly stood up. "This has been a lovely conversation, but I think we're done now. Nice meeting you." She did the spin on her heel thing—*Doggone it, I should have asked her to show me how she does that!*—and headed for the exit.

Cate grabbed their empty cups and napkins and dumped them in a trash can. As she also headed for the exit, her thoughts about Candy jumped back and forth, like Octavia chasing after a moth. Cate saw a possibility that Kane hadn't turned out to be as financially well-off as Candy had first thought, and her trophy-wife status had developed a layer of tarnish. She'd decided to do a *delete* on the marriage and then make a grab for whatever assets Kane had. Maybe she'd also hired a gunman to go after that $30,000. Shooting Kane may not have been part of her plan. Or maybe it was. With Kane dead, she could go for the big prize, his insurance. Maybe she'd lucked out with Halliday shooting the gunman, because now the dead guy would never be able to incriminate her with the revelation that she'd hired him.

Or was she an innocent woman wrongly labeled and maligned as a gold-digging trophy wife? Candy's profession of love for Kane had sounded sincere, and her concern for Clancy was a check in the plus column too.

Maybe a ten-page questionnaire would have been helpful.

Outside the mall, Cate momentarily lost track of Candy. Then she spotted the slim figure in fur jacket just off to the side of the main doors. She had a cigarette in her mouth now. She put a flame to it, and a thought occurred to Cate.

A cigarette lighter. A handy accessory for someone engaged in midnight fire-setting in a hospital restroom.

❖ 11 ❖

Cate finished up the day at home still working on the background check of the potential employee for the accounting office. He looked a little doubtful to her after she found he'd worked for a company that got in trouble for not turning over to the IRS some payroll tax deductions they'd made. But Belmont Investigations just offered facts, not recommendations.

Just out of curiosity, she looked up another name. Marilee Halliday. She found a couple of references, but they were from back when she was still married to Matt Halliday. Nothing current. Which meant what? That she was using her maiden name? Remarried? Moved out of the country?

She called Uncle Joe and gave him a report on the status of the incidents at H&B, including that Matt Halliday might be interested in hiring the services of Belmont Investigations.

"You know how I feel about jobs that involve murder," Uncle Joe said.

Cate started to argue that this case wasn't really about murder. The victim wasn't dead, and the man who was dead had been killed in self-defense. Before she could say anything, Uncle Joe continued.

"Of course, you've managed to circumvent my stand on murder cases a couple of times already," he grumbled.

"It wasn't on purpose," Cate protested. "Those cases just kind of . . . dragged me in."

Although that might be like claiming those fantastic boots at Macy's just dragged you into the store to buy them.

"Anyway, you'll be running Belmont Investigations, or whatever you decide to call it, before long. We're really interested in this motor home we looked at in Corvallis. We may be waving good-bye from our home on wheels very soon. So I think it's time you start deciding on your own what cases you want to accept or decline."

"Even murder?" Cate asked.

"I have to admit, I'd rather not see an ad in the yellow pages with a picture of a skull and crossbones and the motto 'We specialize in dead guys,'" Uncle Joe said.

Fair enough. "You think I can handle a PI business on my own?" Cate asked.

"I'm counting on it."

Cate took a deep breath. "Thanks, Uncle Joe."

"We'll get the legalities taken care of when your PI license gets here."

Cate looked up H&B's website and found an email address to send the Belmont Investigations' information sheet to Matt Halliday. A website that could definitely use some jazzing up. It was mostly hard-to-read text about car parts, the occasional photo so tiny that it was difficult to tell if the item was a wiring system or a dish of spaghetti. Dull. Boring. She could almost hear Candy saying, "Well, what would you expect from someone like Matt?"

Mitch came over for dinner that evening. Cate fixed shrimp tacos. He left Clancy in the SUV, although Octavia prowled around as if she suspected the dog was lurking somewhere nearby. After dinner, Cate suggested Mitch bring Clancy in for a few minutes with the hope the animals might have a change of attitude.

The meeting was semi-successful in that it didn't involve any steeplechases over furniture, but there were still hisses as Octavia proclaimed her territorial rights. With responding barks from Clancy to show he was not intimidated. They did not appear to be heading toward a pastoral era in which the lion lay down with the lamb.

After dinner, they took Clancy out for a run under the yard light in the backyard. This house was not as large as the big old Gothic monster that had once stood here, so the oversized yard was great dog-running territory.

Mitch tossed an old tennis ball for Clancy to chase, and the dog seemed inexhaustible in his enthusiasm for retrieving it. Between throws, Cate pointed out the corner area where she'd like to put in a garden.

"I can borrow a rototiller from Hank Bowman at church. I've used it before on a Helping Hands project," Mitch said.

"That'd be great!"

"Will you plant carrots? I love those little baby carrots."

"Sure." And peas and lettuce too, like her mother always planted in an early garden. With tomatoes and green peppers and cucumbers for later. "Of course, Clancy couldn't run back here if there was a garden."

"We could fence it in. But it doesn't matter anyway," Mitch said. "He'll be going back to his owner before long."

Cate kept waiting for Mitch to mention the offer on Computer Dudes again. When he didn't, she finally asked about it. They were standing by the corner of Octavia's screened-in playroom, the sky above clear but rain clouds looming off to the west. Octavia watched Clancy's antics as if she were a newscaster giving a play-by-play description of tennis action.

"We're still talking about the offer," Mitch said in answer to her question. He threw the ball for Clancy again. The dog caught it in midair.

"What does Robyn think?"

"She's all in favor of Dallas. But Lance thinks we should counter with a higher offer."

"What do *you* think?"

"I wouldn't object to getting more money out of the deal."

"A higher counteroffer might make them back off entirely."

"I wouldn't object to that either."

Cate fist-tapped his shoulder. "Sometimes you can be as dense as Octavia."

"Maybe that's because I'm not sure myself what I want. God isn't offering any definitive instructions."

Yes, that was the way God sometimes worked. And God had his own timetable.

Clancy brought the ball back and dropped it at Mitch's feet. An abundance of dog drool on it didn't deter Mitch from picking it up and throwing it once more. He just wiped his hands on the grass at his feet between throws. This time a bounce dropped the ball next to the screen around Octavia's playroom.

Clancy ran up to retrieve the ball. Cate expected Octavia to hiss and retreat, but she stood her ground. The two animals touched noses with the screen separating them before Clancy bounded off with the ball. Octavia stood at the screen as if she'd like to follow and get in on the fun. Then, flicking her tail with haughty indifference at being excluded, she headed for the kitty door to the interior of the house.

If Octavia were a person, Cate decided, she could definitely execute that spin-on-a-heel thing that Candy did so well.

◆◆◆

Next morning, Cate had just started to make French toast for breakfast when Octavia looked at the phone expectantly. "You do not know when the phone is going to ring," Cate said firmly.

Oh yeah?

Cate picked up the phone when it rang. "Belmont Investigations." She made a face at her cat. "Cate Kinkaid, Assistant Private Investigator, speaking."

"Cate, this is Matt Halliday at H&B Vintage Auto Restorations. You may remember me."

Was that a hint of dark humor from Halliday? Yes, one did tend to remember a person holding a gun over a dead body on the floor.

"Yes, I remember you, Mr. Halliday."

"Call me Matt." The suggestion was businesslike, definitely nothing flirty about it.

"Thank you." He'd already called her Cate, so she didn't have to mention that.

"Why I'm calling, I'm not sure you do this kind of work—I don't have any experience with private investigators—but I thought I'd ask. It doesn't have anything to do with Kane or his wife or the man who shot Kane."

"Okay."

"What I'm hoping is that you can find someone for me."

"That comes within our scope of operations." *Scope of operations.* Cate was pleased with that professional-sounding phrasing. She drew a line in the air, giving herself a point. "You received that Belmont Investigations information I emailed you?" she asked. It had more than rates, of course. There were also various details of their business operations and specifics about their not engaging in illegal activities of any kind in the course of an investigation. Uncle Joe said he'd had potential clients ask him to do everything from break into an office to tell them how to conceal an embezzlement.

"Yes, I received it. Everything looks fine." He sounded impatient to get on with it.

"So, what can we do for you?"

Cate expected him to tell her he wanted to locate the long-gone wife Marilee, but he surprised her with a totally different business-type request. No doubt proof, as Candy had indicated, that Halliday was business 24/7.

"What I need," he said, "is to find a guy who came in a while back and wanted to sell me an old Indian motorcycle—"

"An *Indian* motorcycle?" Cate repeated doubtfully. Her knowledge of Indian culture was minimal, but none of the Native Americans she'd seen on TV westerns had been roaring around on bikes.

"It's a brand name of motorcycle. Oldest motorcycle outfit in the country, I think, though it's owned by some other company now. This kid had a '48 Chief model. It needed restoration, of course, but it was in pretty good shape considering its age. He rode it in here. The '48 Chief is a real classic, and you don't often run across one."

"I didn't realize H&B did motorcycle as well as car restorations."

"We don't often do bikes, but they're kind of fun."

Halliday's idea of fun, as Candy would no doubt point out. Working 24/7.

"But you didn't buy it?"

"No. They're worth a bundle, but this kid had about a

three-bundle price on it. He was also scruffy and looked like he had issues with getting too cozy with a bottle of shampoo. The kind of person you figure you'd better not get too close to or you'll find your wallet missing. And probably into drugs. Buying, selling, using, whatever. At the time, I suspected the bike might be stolen, and I didn't want to get involved with that."

Commendable. "But now?"

"I checked with the police a few days ago, and they have no record of any stolen bike of that description. It just happens that a customer called the other day looking for that particular brand and year of bike. He's a collector with money to burn. If I can find the kid and get him down on his price, H&B can make some good money on a restoration and sale to this collector."

Business went on, even as his partner lay in a coma in the hospital. Cate scratched that critical thought. Yes, business did go on. As it would with Belmont Investigations, even with Uncle Joe leaving. At least she hoped she could keep it going. For a mini-moment, *Kinkaid Investigations* blazed across her mind.

She doused the blaze. "What can you tell me about him?"

"His name is Andy Timmons. He's probably twenty-five or twenty-six."

Not exactly a kid, then, from Cate's thirty-year-old perspective. But older people often seemed to have a different view on "kid."

"He's scrawny, wiry build, about five foot five, maybe 135 or 140 pounds. Dark hair, long and straggly. A mustache, like something out of a costume store."

"You mean it looked phony?"

"No. Just too much mustache." Halliday's impatience was

showing again. "Sharp features, kind of weasel looking. Nervous eyes. Like I said, probably a druggie."

"Do you have an address for him?"

"At the time, he gave me an address over on Jefferson Avenue. A rooming house, I found out when I went there myself a couple days ago. But he'd moved and didn't leave any forwarding address, and I have no idea where to go from there. I'm hoping you can do better."

Cate jotted down the address he gave her. "Hiring a private investigator may be an expensive way of finding him," she warned.

"No problem."

"I have a couple of other small cases I'm working on, but I can get on this right away."

"Good. And when you locate Timmons, you don't need to talk to him or approach him in any way. In fact, I'd rather you didn't. I just need to know where to find him."

"Are you saying he could be dangerous?"

"Oh, I don't think so. I wouldn't be sending you after him if I thought he was dangerous. It's more that I don't want him knowing how eager I am to buy the bike or he'll jack up the price even more. Just find out where I can get in touch with him, and I'll approach him about the bike myself."

"Okay."

"In fact, I want this kept confidential all around," Matt added. "I don't want our customer to find this bike before I do and buy it himself. It can be a good moneymaker for us."

"Our work is always confidential."

Cate spent the morning serving a subpoena on an uncooperative recipient and worked on another case on the computer that afternoon.

She was trying to locate a husband who had skipped out on paying his child support, and, as so often happened, she wound up wishing she had Mitch's computer expertise. Taking a break from that case, she tried digging up something on Andy Timmons and/or his motorcycle.

She found some Andy Timmons information, but the name wasn't all that unique, and most of what she found wasn't connected to the man Halliday wanted to locate. One thing she did determine was that the old Indian motorcycle was registered to him. She made a note of the address, which was not the Jefferson Street address Matt Halliday had tried.

Purely out of curiosity, she also tried Mace Jackson's name on a search engine and then on a couple of Uncle Joe's PI databases. The Jackson name wasn't uncommon, of course, and she didn't know if Mace was real or a nickname, so she didn't find much that she could identify as specifically him, not even a vehicle registration or driver's license. Which must mean there had been something else on the body that the police used to identify him the night he was killed.

What she did find in a small newspaper article from a Salem newspaper was that someone by the name of Mace Jackson had placed second in a fifty-mile bicycle road race there. It seemed an unlikely activity for a gunman, but there was that bicycle she'd seen out back at H&B. Crime and an interest in bicycling were not necessarily exclusive, she supposed. Maybe she could check—

She interrupted herself. No. No checking. Because, as she sternly reminded herself again, that wasn't her case. Finding Andy Timmons and an old Indian motorcycle was her case.

To get her brain out of cyberspace, she went for a run at about 4:00. Later, Mitch brought Clancy over for another playtime in Cate's backyard. He thought the big, active dog needed more exercise than just a walk on the sidewalks around the condo.

"Now don't get your tail all in a twist about this," Cate advised Octavia when she left the cat inside and went out to join Mitch and Clancy in the backyard.

Mitch had a new ball for Clancy. Cate saw Octavia watching from the window seat first, then from the outdoor playroom. When Clancy ran for a ball near it, she took a flying leap and buried her claws in the screen, apparently Octavia's interpretation of a ferocious flying tiger. Clancy jumped back, but then he edged over to sniff at her furry white form clinging to the screen. Octavia, perhaps huffy that her leap hadn't been more intimidating, untangled her claws from the screen and jumped to her jungle-gym apparatus. She watched from there until Mitch took Clancy back to the SUV and brought the sub sandwiches he'd picked up earlier into the house.

Cate noted Mitch's sandwich had one end missing, and he admitted he'd broken off a chunk to give to Clancy out in the SUV. Cate, conscious of Octavia's reproachful eyes on her, evened the situation by offering a bite of ham from her sandwich. She and Mitch talked about his day setting up a new computer system for a bakery, and hers chasing down various people.

Mitch crumpled the wrapping paper when he finished the sandwich. "Any news yet about Clancy's owner and when he'll take his dog back?"

Cate stood up. "I'll call Shirley and ask." She'd been thinking about talking to Shirley anyway.

Mitch lifted a hand. "Hey, no hurry. You don't have to do it right now." He sounded almost alarmed, as if he hadn't expected such express action from her.

Cate called Shirley's cell phone anyway, but the call went to voice mail. She was stuffing the wrapping from their sub sandwiches in the trash when her cell phone jingled.

"I'm sorry I couldn't answer when you just called." Shirley sounded breathless. "I was on my way in to see Kane. I think they gave me a whole minute this time."

"How is he?"

"His eyelids twitched. I think he was trying to open them!"

Cate suspected that could be a normal movement even in a coma, but she wasn't sure. "Will you be at the hospital again tomorrow?"

"Saturday is just another work day at H&B, and I'm cooking dinner for Jerry tomorrow night. But I'll come out to the hospital between when I get off work and when I start dinner."

"What are you cooking for him?"

"Jerry is a meat and potatoes kind of guy, so I'm making fried chicken, mashed potatoes, green beans, and apple pie."

"He'll love that. You know the old saying, the way to a man's heart is through his stomach."

"I'm not trying to get to Jerry's heart." Shirley sounded

appalled, as if Cate had just suggested she was setting a bear trap for an innocent bystander. "He's at least ten years younger than I am. He won't take any money for letting me use his pickup, and I just wanted to do something to repay him."

"Okay, keep in touch. But remember that a relationship with a younger man is not a crime."

"It doesn't have to be a crime to be *ridiculous*."

Cate didn't, of course, tell Shirley she was also working for Matt Halliday now. Confidential. But she passed Shirley's information about Kane's eye twitch along to Mitch.

His opinion was the same as her own, that an eye twitch wasn't necessarily meaningful. "So, looks like I'm stuck with Clancy for a while yet," he added.

"Where's he sleeping now?"

"At the foot of my bed."

"On the floor at the foot of the bed?"

Mitch paused before he made a more specific admission. "Well, uh, no, he's on the bed. His staying with me is just a temporary arrangement, of course, so I figured that letting him sleep there was more practical than trying to retrain him."

Oh yes. Very practical.

◆◆◆

At midmorning on Saturday, Cate located the rooming house on Jefferson easily enough. She'd decided this address Halliday had given her was probably more recent than the one on the motorcycle registration.

It was an older, big blue house, not shabby, but it hadn't had any recent contact with a paintbrush. A small sign said Rooms for Rent. A porch covered the front, with dormer windows above. There was a single doorbell beside a windowed door with a saggy lace curtain, which suggested the renters didn't have separate entrances. A tiny older woman in tight purple leggings, kneesocks, and Birkenstock sandals opened the door.

"I'm full up," she said.

"Thanks, but I'm not looking for a room. I'm trying to find a man named Andy Timmons. I understand he lived here?"

"You a social worker?"

"Did Mr. Timmons have a social worker?"

"He was always tellin' me, when his rent was late, that he was about to get disability payments, or a grant to go to school, or some other wild scheme he'd cooked up. I finally told him to take his old motorcycle and find some other living room to park it in."

"He kept his motorcycle in the living room?"

"He was renting my studio apartment." She jerked a thumb toward a detached building that looked like a garage remodeled into living quarters. Cate suspected "studio apartment" upgraded its status. "And yeah, I found out he was keeping his old motorcycle in there. On my carpet! Renters. You can't believe the things they come up with."

Cate had to admit that if she were a landlady, she might also object to a motorcycle in the living room, but all she said was, "The motorcycle may be a fairly valuable antique model."

"Yeah, well, I don't care if it belonged to Elvis himself. Nobody brings a motorcycle in and parks it on my carpet. No way I'm ever going to get the oil stains out of that shag."

"I'm wondering if you have any idea where Mr. Timmons went after he left here?"

"How come him and his old motorcycle are so popular all of a sudden?" She peered at Cate as if looking for concealed weapons. "Some guy was here looking for him a couple-three days ago too."

Mr. Halliday, no doubt. Unless the potential collector-buyer of old motorcycles had his sights on Timmons too.

"But you don't know where Mr. Timmons might be now?" Cate asked.

"No, I'm just glad he isn't here. Rent always late. Always feeling I'd better count the silverware after he did come pay it."

"He used the motorcycle to move out?"

"I don't know how he moved out. He was just gone. He drove an old Ford pickup sometimes. But maybe the pickup belonged to that girl. Andy was only paying rent for one person, but I know she stayed overnight sometimes."

The landlady's face puckered in disapproval, although Cate couldn't tell if she disapproved of the girl staying overnight or if the rent differential between one and two people was what concerned her.

The face of an older man considerably taller than the tiny landlady appeared over her head. "Ladies, excuse me," he said. "If I can just slip out the door without disturbing you . . . ?"

He had an air of faded elegance with his bolo tie and dark jacket, silvery hair combed back in a style of yesteryear, but his blue eyes were bright and a bit mischievous.

"Hey, Duane, you were on friendly terms with that guy with the old motorcycle when he was living here, weren't you?"

"Andy? Yes, of course. A young man with potential, but wasting his life, I'm afraid." The man smiled, teeth so white and perfect Cate knew they couldn't be his originals. "And, sadly, not open to counsel from someone who's been there, done that, and now knows better."

"Would you happen to know where he went when he left here?" Cate asked.

"I believe he had a young lady friend who was going to

let him stay with her for a while. At a trailer park, I think it was, out on Cushingham."

"Do you know her name?"

"I'm afraid not. I never actually met her, but I saw her a few times. A lovely young woman. Beautiful dark eyes. Very pale blonde hair."

"Okay, thanks. I appreciate the information." Cate had the feeling the man could use some money and wondered if she could pay him for the information. She also realized this man would surely be insulted if she tried to do so. So all she did was repeat the words as he strode jauntily down the steps. "Thanks again. You've been very helpful."

"'Lovely young woman. Pale blonde hair,'" the landlady mimicked. She snorted. "She had hair bleached so hard it could stand up by itself. And enough mascara and eyeliner to start a clown store."

Cate used her all-purpose noncommittal "um."

"Duane is a lovely man himself. He always sees the best in everyone." The landlady sighed and shook her head as if that attitude were a naïve fault. With a dark huddle of eyebrows, she added, "He wouldn't think everyone was so wonderful if he was a landlord for a while."

Or, Cate had to agree, if he were a private investigator.

Back in her car, Cate used her cell phone to locate two trailer parks on Cushingham. The road ran south out of town, a hilly, wooded area not far from I-5. The first trailer park she came to was for recreational-type vehicles, not the big single- and double-wides that were situated in the park where Shirley lived, although many of the RVs had small yards and fences and looked at least semi-permanent. Cate stopped at a fifth-wheel trailer with an office sign out front.

A beefy guy in black work pants and a cap with the trailer

park name on it opened the door. Hoping Andy Timmons may have done a legal registration with the park management before moving into the woman's RV, Cate asked about him by name.

The man didn't need to check registration records or wasn't inclined to bother. "No one here named that."

Cate offered the description of Timmons that Matt Halliday had given her, skipping his derogatory details of Timmons looking like a druggie and/or weasel. "He may be staying with a blonde woman who drives an older Ford pickup. And he has an old Indian motorcycle. A '48 Chief."

"Don't ring no bells. And I'd of noticed an old Indian bike, that's for sure. Had one when I was a kid."

"Okay, well, thanks. Is it okay if I just drive around and see if maybe I can spot them?"

"Help yourself."

The RVs were parked on both sides of the long driveway that ended in a turnaround at a board fence highlighted with red reflectors. She stopped and asked a gray-haired woman working in her yard if she knew anyone named Andy Timmons. The friendly woman tried to be helpful, but she shook her head when Cate added the description of man, woman, and motorcycle.

Cate went on to the next RV park farther down the road. A palm tree stood out front, its straggly condition testament to the fact that Eugene was not palm-tree friendly. The spaces here were smaller, the RVs crammed into them close enough for a window-to-window handshake. No one answered her ring at the office, so she drove on by. A sign said "5 mph speed limit. Strictly enforced."

Perhaps enforced by the bathtub-sized potholes dotting the street, Cate decided as she cautiously eased past the parked

RVs. One man walking his dog shook his head when she inquired about an Andy Timmons, but she got a potential hit with the second person she talked to.

This was a middle-aged woman, gray hair held back by an embroidered headband, down on her knees pulling weeds around the trailer hitch of her RV. She stood up, put a hand to her lower back, and came to the low picket fence.

"That sounds like Lily Admond and her boyfriend. She lived right down there." The woman pointed a gloved hand toward an empty spot about four spaces down the street. "She had a trailer, about a twenty-five-footer. I never knew her boyfriend's name, but I did see his old motorcycle a couple times. Usually he kept it all covered with a tarp. My husband thought it was something real special, but it was just a dinged-up old motorcycle, far as I could see."

"She moved out?"

"She mentioned going down to Arizona. Said it was hard finding a job here. But I don't know if that's where they went."

Cate could sympathize with the difficulties of finding a job. It was the reason she'd turned into an assistant PI. That and the fact that she finally figured out that God may have plans for her life that hadn't been on her own agenda.

"Young couple in the fifth wheel down there next to them might know more," the woman added. "I think they were friends."

"Okay. Thanks."

Cate nosed the Honda on down to the fifth-wheel trailer next to the empty space. At one time, "fifth wheel" would have been meaningless to her, but now, courtesy of Uncle Joe, who'd considered various forms of living quarters on the road, she knew what it was. Fifth wheel meant a trailer that, rather than hooking to a hitch at the back end of a vehicle, fastened to a big wheel-like thing in a pickup bed, similar to the hookups on big commercial eighteen-wheeler truck and trailer rigs.

The couple from the fifth wheel, with a baby in the woman's arms, were getting into a pickup when Cate pulled up behind them. She tapped the horn to get their attention, and the woman opened the pickup window when Cate approached.

"Hi. I'm trying to find Lily Admond and her friend Andy Timmons. I think they were parked there." Cate motioned to the empty space. "I'm hoping you might know where they went?"

The woman glanced over at her husband, as if uncertain about responding. The husband leaned around the woman to look at Cate.

"You a friend of theirs?"

Cate suspected he was really wondering if she was a bill collector or some similar unwanted company.

"Actually, I haven't met them. Does he still have his old bike?"

"Oh yeah. He was thinking about selling it when his unemployment checks ran out. I wouldn't of minded buying it off him, but Shauna here"—he gave the woman an affectionate glance—"she had this stuffy idea we should buy groceries and diapers and stuff like that instead."

Cate smiled and gave the woman a thumbs-up gesture. "So, do you know where they are now?"

"Lily told me she was going to dump him," the woman offered.

"Yeah?" The husband looked surprised. "He told me they might go down to Nevada and get casino jobs."

If Timmons had picked up and gone to Nevada or Arizona, Matt Halliday probably wouldn't be interested in tracking him all the way there to find the motorcycle. She'd have to talk to Matt again.

"I appreciate the information," Cate said. "I'll stop by the office again and see if they left a forwarding address. If you happen to hear anything more about him, would you give me a call?"

She started to fish a Belmont Investigations card out of her pocket, then thought better of it. Private investigator might scare them off. She scribbled her name and cell phone number on a page from her small notebook instead.

Cate stopped at the office again, but the woman who answered the doorbell this time said Lily Admond hadn't left a forwarding address with her. "I didn't even know she was leaving until one morning she was gone."

"Is that unusual?"

"Oh no. That's what RV life is about, you know? Freedom. Sometimes I think that's what I should be doing, instead of just sitting here watching them come and go."

Although what she really seemed to be saying, as her doleful gaze followed a motor home rolling past the office, was, "Instead of sitting here watching life pass me by."

Okay, she'd try Andy Timmons's address from the motorcycle registration next, Cate decided. A long shot, but maybe someone there would know something helpful.

❖ 13 ❖

That idea resulted in a display of the changing face of the city. What may have been a modest residential area where Andy lived earlier was now a new and bustling strip mall. A tantalizing scent drifted from a small restaurant with a banner proclaiming "Best Barbecue in Town!" The hair-and-nails salon next to a dry cleaners reminded Cate her nails were beginning to look as if she shared Octavia's love of the scratching pole. And the tattoo parlor brought back memories of the time she and college friend Tangela decided to fill one dateless Saturday night by getting tattoos. But God had wisely confused their way and given them a flat tire to boot. If not for those impediments, she might right now have a fire-breathing dragon circling her ankle. *Thank you, Lord!*

But she felt a twang of disappointment that wherever Andy Timmons had once lived was obviously gone. Another dead end. However, disappointment did not plunge her appetite into depression, and the pulled-pork sandwich she had in the barbecue restaurant was great, meaty and juicy. Hey, she'd have to tell Mitch about this place.

It wasn't until she got home that the thought occurred to her that concentrating her search on Lily Admond might be the best way to find Andy. She got on the computer and, using a database Uncle Joe subscribed to for Belmont Investigations, found a rural address for a pickup in Lily's name. Cate knew it was probably an old address, but hopefully worth checking out. She thought about going out there yet today, but a call from Uncle Joe made her decide to put it off until later.

She called Mitch to see if he wanted to run over to Uncle Joe's with her, and he came by a few minutes later. Clancy was riding shotgun in the front seat when Cate opened the SUV door. He offered her a sloppy face kiss, which Cate managed to detour to her elbow. Mitch shooed him into the backseat, where he curled up in a red-plaid, padded doggie bed.

"You bought Clancy a bed?"

"I leave him here in the SUV a lot. I didn't want him to be uncomfortable. He can take it with him when he goes back to his owner." Mitch changed the subject. "So they really did it."

"That's what Uncle Joe said."

The truth of that was verified when Mitch parked in front of Uncle Joe and Rebecca's house. A motor home filled the driveway, big and bulky as a tyrannosaurus rex on wheels. A mural of a desert scene, complete with cactus and howling wolf, decorated the back wall. Uncle Joe stepped out of the door, can of Pledge in hand. He beamed the same way Mitch had when he'd just bought his Purple Rocket motorcycle. Men did like their motorized toys.

"You're going to drive that down the highway?" Cate said. "It's enormous!"

"Not all that big," Uncle Joe scoffed modestly. "It's only a thirty-footer, and they make them a lot bigger than that. C'mon in and take a look around."

"Where's Rebecca?"

"In the house getting sheets and blankets to make up the bed."

"Is she going to drive it too?" Cate asked.

"She says not, no way. But I'm thinking she'll change her mind after a while. Drives like a dream."

Cate eyed the metal hulk again. Dream, nightmare, whatever.

Uncle Joe held the door open, and Cate and Mitch stepped inside. Clancy was still in the SUV.

Cate strolled the interior length of the motor home. Two big seats up front for driver and passenger were on a higher level than the living area, wide console between them, TV above. A sofa and small upholstered chair, kitchen counter with double sinks, propane kitchen stove, microwave. A dinette with upholstered bench seats overlooked a window across from the kitchen, a refrigerator/freezer beyond. Bathroom on one side of the aisle, small tub and shower on the other. Queen-size bed in back. Storage cabinets tucked in everywhere. Not an inch of wasted space. And, Cate had to admit, all quite cozy and comfortable looking.

"So, how soon are you taking off in it?" Mitch asked.

"Well, not within the next fifteen minutes." Uncle Joe grumped, as if fifteen minutes was the time frame he'd prefer. "We're still waiting for Cate's PI license. And I have to get a tow bar put on the car so we can pull it behind the motor home. We'll probably take a couple of short trips to see how everything goes, but I'm thinking we'll be seeing the northern states this summer and hitting the Florida beaches by fall."

◆◆◆

Cate and Mitch went to church together on Sunday, as usual. It was a gorgeous spring day, blue skies with a decorative sprinkle of fluffy clouds, the kind of day that made Cate think maybe God was showing off just a bit. Oak trees with a haze of new growth, red tulips along the walkway to the church, scent of freshly mowed grass. Clancy waited in his red-plaid dog bed in the SUV. After church, Cate asked Mitch if he'd like to take a drive out in the country.

"A see-the-countryside drive or a working-type drive?" he asked.

Hmm. Mitch knew her all too well.

"I could check on an address that might be connected with a case I'm working on," Cate admitted. To sweeten the prospect, she added, "But we can find a place for Clancy to run out there too."

"Okay. Sounds good."

They went by Mitch's condo and then Cate's house to change out of the clothes they'd worn to church. Octavia sniffed at Cate's shoes as if she suspected Cate had been fraternizing with a hairy dog.

"Yes, we're taking Clancy along," Cate admitted to the cat. "But you don't even like to ride in a car, so you shouldn't be complaining."

Deaf Octavia couldn't hear her, of course, but it always seemed as if the cat got the gist of their conversations. Sometimes Cate suspected her of some super-cat ability to read lips. She considered that possibility now as Octavia gave her an accusing, blue-eyed stare.

Nah. That was *Twilight Zone* stuff. Cats could not read lips. But in case this one could, Cate added, "But you know you're my favorite furry creature in the whole world."

Following Cate's directions, Mitch headed west on the road to the coast, then, a few miles out of town, turned off to the south. More turns brought them to Mad Crow Road.

Trees, a few nondescript cattle, and a couple of big-eyed deer, not people, populated the area. Cate didn't spot any crows, mad or otherwise. A hand-scrawled sign at a gravel driveway identified the address she was looking for, a Wood For Sale sign tacked to the post below it. A double-wide mobile home sat beside several outbuildings well back from the road. Of more interest to Cate was the travel trailer under a nearby madrone. She felt a flutter of excitement. Had she hit the jackpot and found Lily and Andy already?

"Yeah, I know Lily," the guy who came out from behind a mountain of firewood said in answer to Cate's question. The statement wasn't rude, but his up-and-down assessment of her held a hint of "what's it to ya?" challenge.

He was tall and lanky, with heavy boots and a black stocking cap that revealed a shock of hair as red as Cate's own. The tail of a blue-plaid flannel shirt hung over his faded jeans, and a chain saw dangled from one hand.

Cate tried not to think about those old chain-saw massacre movies. Which, of course, made her think of them in full gory detail. Plus more stray thoughts about chainsawed bodies, body parts tucked away in freezers and basements. Or maybe woodpiles.

"What do you want to know for? She in trouble?" he asked. The unfriendly attitude suggested their both having red hair did not establish an instant bond with Cate.

"No, nothing like that," Cate assured him. "Actually, it's a friend of hers I'm trying to find."

"That punk Timmons? I told her she was off her rocker having anything to do with that deadbeat. He's bad news all the way."

Cate revised her hope that Andy Timmons might be found with Lily in the nearby trailer. Chain Saw Man's attitude suggested that if Timmons showed up, he'd run him off the property. Maybe off the planet.

"You're Mr. Admond?" Mitch asked. Apparently he was thinking the same thought that had just occurred to Cate, that this might be an ex-, or even current, husband.

"Lily's my sister. She divorced that scumbag Admond, so Connie and I were letting her stay in our travel trailer. He come sniffin' around once, but I don't think he'll be coming again." He gave a shark-in-a-flannel-shirt smile of satisfaction. A chain saw was no doubt an effective ex-husband deterrent.

"Lily got tired of being stuck out here in the boonies, so I pulled the trailer into town for her. I wouldn't of, if I'd known she was going to take up with that Timmons jerk."

Either Lily was the world's worst at picking men, or her brother was unfairly prejudiced about her choices.

Cate glanced toward the small trailer out back. "But now she's come back alone?"

"Her and Timmons wanted to take the trailer down to Arizona or Nevada or somewhere, but I said no way. I went and got it. I tried to talk some sense into Lily and get her to move back out here, but she wouldn't do it. I should of drug her back out here anyway."

He could probably see, as Cate could without even knowing Lily, how far he'd have gotten with that.

"So they went on down to Arizona without the trailer?" Cate asked. She kept a wary eye on the chain saw.

The guy looked her up and down again. The inspection apparently did not upgrade her status. "I don't see any reason I should be blabbing to you about where she is."

The brother might not approve of his sister's choices in men, but he was still protective. Cate hesitated, wondering how close she had to stick to Halliday's "confidential" instructions. Before she could decide, the brother turned and clomped back to the far side of the woodpile. A moment later the roar of the chain saw put a final punctuation mark on their visit.

"I don't think we're going to get any more information here," Mitch observed. "Why *are* we looking for this woman and her friend?"

Cate started to tell him, but that matter of "confidentiality" shot up like a stop sign. She sometimes shared generalities about cases with Mitch, and he'd helped her several times and come to her rescue more than once. She couldn't imagine that his knowing details of this case could matter. But clients had a right to confidentiality, and Matt Halliday had been specific about it in this case.

"It doesn't have anything to do with murder or dead guys or anything like that," Cate assured him.

Mitch swiped a hand across his forehead and shook the pretended sweat toward the ground. "Whew. That's a relief. For a minute there I figured now we'd be looking for a place to dig up a dead body."

"Don't be ridiculous. If that were the case, I'd have brought a shovel and a body bag," Cate said primly.

For a moment he looked as if he believed that, then he grinned. "True. You're quite efficient. Okay, then, what now?"

"Now we find a place for Clancy to run."

Which they did. A clearing along a creek, where Clancy roamed with his nose to the ground and his tail waving like a skinny whip above the tall grass. He dug a hole, dirt flying behind him. He chased something unseen in the tall grass. He splashed in the creek and came back to happily shake cold water all over them. Mitch found an old towel in the SUV with which to dry him off, but Clancy had other ideas.

He grabbed the towel in his teeth and ran away with it. Mitch took after him and enveloped him in a flying tackle. They rolled around in the grass and dirt, Clancy's tail wagging all the time. Uh-oh, Clancy was getting away again—

Cate dove into the mêlée. And then all three of them were rolling around in the dirt and grass. Dog hair. A flying foot—Mitch's, not Clancy's. A floppy ear in Cate's mouth. A dog footprint on Mitch's forehead. Whap of dog tail across her leg. Cate clamped an arm across Clancy's neck. Sloppy dog kiss. Smells of grass and earth and wet dog.

Clancy wiggled away, but then he jumped back on top both of them and everything scrambled together like some new brand of wrestling match. The People vs. Clancy!

The People are winning! Cate has the towel. Mitch has a dog tail. Clancy is down.

No, Clancy is up! Clancy has the towel. Cate has a handful of nothing. Mitch is flat on his back. The People are down.

The People are giggling. Clancy is plopped down, panting. If dogs can grin, that's what Clancy is doing.

Cate flopped onto her back in the tall grass. *Hey, I'm happy!* She was here with Mitch and Clancy and the sun was shining and the grass smelled like spring and sunshine. *Thank you, Lord!* She spread her arms and legs and made an angel figure in the grass. Mitch spit out dog hair or dirt. Maybe both. He grinned at her. Clancy offered her the towel.

Mitch staggered to his feet. He offered Cate a hand to help her up. She gave him a foot instead. Clancy jumped up and stuck his nose in her ear. Cate giggled some more. Grass tickled her nose. Mitch scooped her up in his arms. Clancy jumped and danced and barked.

Mitch looked into Cate's eyes.

Then he dipped his head and kissed her, long and thoroughly. She couldn't hear Clancy barking now. Cate wrapped her arms around Mitch's neck and kissed him back.

"I think we lost the battle," Mitch murmured. "Clancy still isn't dry, and he has the towel again."

"Who cares?" Cate stretched up for another kiss.

When Mitch finally set her down, he said, "I believe we'll have to dry the dog off more often."

◆◆◆

When they got back to town, Cate showed Mitch the restaurant she'd discovered, and they shared a big platter of barbecued ribs. Cate thought he'd take some bones out to Clancy, but Mitch said cooked bones weren't good for dogs.

"Neither are chocolate, coffee, or macadamia nuts," he added.

"All of a sudden you're the big dog expert?"

"You can find anything on the internet."

Where Mitch had apparently spent a fair amount of time surfing in the dog world. If it weren't for the fact that he kept asking when Blakely would take his dog back, she might think he was getting attached to the big hairy mutt.

She knew she was.

◆◆◆

By that evening, Cate reluctantly decided she'd have to call Matt Halliday first thing Monday morning and tell him she'd reached a dead end on Andy Timmons. Failure rankled her, but she didn't have any more leads. A call from someone else on Monday morning changed her mind. Maybe she did have a lead.

Cate never answered her cell phone with the Belmont Investigations name, so all she said was, "Hello?"

"I'm looking for Cate Kinkaid?"

"This is Cate."

"Hi. You talked to us about Lily and her boyfriend? At the RV park?"

"Yes, I did."

"I happened to run into her later. Well, not exactly *run into* her. I saw her working at the counter in the convenience store behind the station where I gassed up. The baby was asleep, and I didn't want to leave her alone in the pickup, so I didn't go inside. Sometimes awful things happen, you know?"

"Right. You shouldn't leave a baby alone in a car." Cate asked for the address of the convenience store and jotted it on a scrap of paper. "I really appreciate your calling."

"I'd rather you didn't mention to Lily that it was me who told you about her, okay?"

"Okay."

"My husband wouldn't want me calling you. He says we should keep our noses out of other people's business."

Cate was curious why the woman did call. She didn't ask, but the woman seemed to feel obliged to offer an explanation.

"I probably wouldn't of called, but I didn't like that Andy. Lily acts kind of tough, but she's okay. Just kind of . . . mixed up."

Using information acquired from the brother, Cate said, "She went through a divorce a while back."

"Yeah, and she's scared of that guy. He knocked her around a few times. I don't think Andy hits her or anything like that, but it sure looked to me like he was mooching off her. She works so hard, and all he ever seemed to do was watch TV or tinker with that old motorcycle. Although I never did see it even running. I just thought if you found her . . ." Her voice trailed off as if she wasn't certain what she'd thought, but she'd like to see something better for Lily. "Well, maybe she's dumped him by now. I hope so."

"Thanks again for calling me."

Cate grabbed a jacket and headed for the convenience store.

◆ 14 ◆

No one matching Lily's description was working behind the counter. Cate took a quick tour through the aisles, but all she saw was a young guy stocking a shelf with Froot Loops. The store was busy, and she bought a cappuccino from a machine to sip while waiting for a lull.

When the lull came, she stepped up to the counter. "Hi. I'm looking for Lily Admond. I think she works here?"

"Yeah, but she's just part-time, on weekends, so she isn't here today." The middle-aged woman in jeans and blue sweatshirt busily rearranged a candy display as she spoke. "During the week she works for some house-cleaning outfit."

"Do you know where she's living?" Actually, Cate doubted the question would get her anywhere. It wasn't information an employer was likely to hand out to some stranger. To make the request sound more personal, she added, "She moved out of the RV park where she's been living, and I'm worried about her."

Worried was stretching it, Cate thought guiltily. But that woman from the trailer park had sounded worried. So maybe there was something to worry about.

"She's had this guy hanging around," Cate added in a meaningful way.

"Yeah, he's been in here a couple times. Not someone I'd want hanging around *my* daughter."

Apparently, if all these non-fans got together, Andy Timmons might qualify as the Guy Most Likely to Be Voted Off the Planet.

A customer stepped up with a six-pack of beer and a sack of taco chips. His impatient look told Cate to buy something or get out of the way. She got out of the way but stepped up again when he was gone.

"I'd really like to find her before Andy talks her into leaving the area or something," Cate said.

"Lily hasn't worked here long, but . . ." The woman touched an I'm-thinking finger to her chin. "She must of filled out one of those forms for tax records and stuff when Everett hired her. It might still be here, if Everett hasn't given it to the bookkeeper yet." She opened a drawer and shuffled through a clutter of papers. "Hey, yeah, here it is."

She pulled out a printed form with information scribbled in the blanks and gave Cate an address on Van Buren. Cate hastily wrote the information in her notebook, thanked the woman, and scurried out before she could start asking questions about Cate's relationship with Lily.

◆◆◆

The address wasn't a house, as Cate had assumed from the address number. Four apartments were strung out in a row leading away from the street. Big rhododendron bushes overhung the driveway, and a lake-sized puddle stretched between them. The apartment building wouldn't qualify as slum-sleazy, but moss greened the roof and plywood patched a hole in a window. But when she slid out of the car, a wonderful sweet-fresh scent of cedar from the big trees looming over the parking area greeted her. She could close her eyes and feel she was miles out in the woods. The scent improved the ambiance of the area considerably.

The apartments were numbered, but since Cate didn't know what number she was looking for, that was no help. Lily either hadn't put the apartment number on the form, or the woman at the convenience store hadn't noticed it when giving Cate the address. A couple of cars stood along the walkway out front of the building, but no Ford pickup or old bike.

Cate hesitated, that old warning to kids, "Don't talk to strangers," jumping up like a pop-up computer ad in her head. But talking to strangers was exactly what a PI had to do. Cate pumped up her confidence, took a deep breath of the reassuring scent of cedar, and approached the first door.

A woman a little younger than Cate, in cutoff shorts over dark leggings and a gold hoop in her nose, answered the doorbell. "You come about the TV we're selling?" she asked hopefully.

"No. Sorry." Cate offered names and descriptions of Andy and Lily, but the woman shook her head. She also said she hadn't seen a motorcycle.

"It's a really great TV," she added, following Cate a few steps onto the walkway. "And we're only asking a hundred bucks for it."

She sounded so wistful that Cate almost wished she needed a TV. But she already had two. Lawyer Ledbetter had been generous in furnishing the house. He'd even inquired if Octavia might want a TV of her own. "If I hear of anyone needing a TV, I'll send them here," Cate said.

The buzz of the bell at the second door brought a middle-aged older woman in a pink robe. A plastic cap covered her head, foamy stuff inside, and a brownish streak dribbled down her cheek. She said some new "kids" had moved into the end apartment, but she didn't know them. Also hadn't noticed if they had a motorcycle. A timer dinged behind her, apparently marking some crucial point in the hair-coloring process, and with an apology, she scurried off.

Yes, time was of the essence. Cate remembered an occasion back in college when some miscalculation had turned her red hair as green as the mossy roof.

An older man at the third door held a beer can in one hand. His belly sagged like a T-shirted avalanche over his jeans, suggesting beer might be the foundation of his food pyramid. He scowled and told her she shouldn't go around knocking on strange doors, something bad might happen to her. She asked about the new renters in the apartment next door. He said he didn't know them.

"Do they have a motorcycle?" Cate asked. "An old one?"

"Maybe. Seems like I seen one when they first moved in, but I ain't seen it since. They got an old Ford pickup."

A Ford pickup! "Okay. I'll contact them later."

"You pay attention now, young lady," he warned with a severe shake of beer can at her. He said "young lady" as if she were a ten-year-old. At some point in life looking younger than she was might be an advantage, but not now. "You shouldn't go around knocking on strange doors."

Actually, she hadn't knocked on any doors. She'd rung doorbells. But, same difference, as Mitch would no doubt point out.

"I'm sure that's good advice," she said brightly.

◆◆◆

Cate intended to ask Mitch to go with her back to the apartment house where Lily and Andy might be living, but he and Lance were meeting to go over some figures to present to the company interested in buying Computer Solutions Dudes that evening, so she didn't mention it to him.

She hesitated about going alone. Maybe not the smartest idea. But if she was going to run Belmont Investigations on her own, she couldn't scurry to Mitch every time she had misgivings.

◆◆◆

The apartment area looked different after dark. Not an improved difference. With those big bushes on either side, she almost missed the driveway when she drove by. She didn't miss the big puddle between the bushes when she turned in, however. Water surged around her car like a parking lot tsunami. The lights above two of the apartment doors had been turned off or burned out, and the yellowish bulbs that shone dimly above the other two doors failed to illuminate the narrow driving area behind the vehicles filling the parking spaces. A scent of cooking onions from one of the apartments overpowered any scent of cedar now, and dark caves lurked in the shadows beneath the looming trees. An older, light-colored pickup stood in front of the apartment at the far end. A curtain twitched in the window when she stopped behind the pickup.

Good. Someone was home. She'd just give Halliday the information that Timmons was at this address—

Reluctant logic interrupted that thought.

Timmons *might* be here. Or he might not. Cate had no personal sighting or positive confirmation from other tenants that he was here. Halliday had specifically told her not to contact Timmons, but she needed more concrete information than what she had at this point.

There was no place to park, but she waited for several minutes behind the pickup, engine running, hoping someone might enter or exit. Nope. Everything was Christmas-story quiet, not a creature was stirring, not even a mouse.

Okay, she'd park out on the street and walk in. If Timmons answered the door, she should recognize him from Halliday's description. She'd pretend she'd bumbled into a wrong address, back off, and provide Halliday with the address information. If Lily answered, she'd inquire about Andy. If he came out from another room and confronted her, she'd simply have to tell him Matt Halliday wanted to talk to him about the bike.

A good plan, she assured herself.

Right. So why did some old saying about plans suddenly pop into her head? Something about the best laid plans of mice and men . . .

Well, she was neither mice nor male, so she should be fine.

She returned to the street and parked in front of an old SUV. The street at this point was not much better lit than the apartment area, and Cate's car turned to a dark blob in the shadows of an overhanging tree the moment she walked away from it.

One foot plunged into the forgotten puddle as soon as she crossed the dark entryway into the apartment area. She stopped short. But by now her foot was already covered, water oozing around her toes, so she grimly decided she may as well keep going. She started to slosh on across the puddle, but something rustled in the oversized bushes.

She paused, listening, both feet in the puddle now. Was that something . . . someone . . . breathing there in the shadows?

Maybe she should back off and ask Mitch to come with her tomorrow evening. Or she could call him, and after he and Lance were through with their business discussion tonight—

No! She straightened her shoulders. She could do this. Alone. Okay, so it was darkish and kind of creepy here, and her feet felt as if some unknown puddle monster might be nibbling at them in the water. But it was only a few steps to the concrete walkway in front of the apartments. The chatter of a TV came through an open apartment window. A car honked on the street only a block over.

With the parking spaces in front of the apartments filled with cars now, everyone must be home. If she screamed, any number of people would come running.

Another rustle. A moving shadow caught in the corner of her eye. Something touched her back. Her nerves froze. Muscles turned to jelly.

Okay, maybe it was time to scream now—

Except it was really hard to scream with a hand clamped over her mouth.

15

Cate frantically tried to twist her head out of the trap, but the hand tightened and fingers dug deeper around her mouth. Her teeth cut into her stretched lips. Another arm wrapped around her neck, cutting off her air. Panic whipped through her.

She couldn't talk, couldn't even gasp for a breath, and only a frantic *glug* gurgled deep in her throat. She squirmed and tried to kick, but all she managed to do was make tidal waves in the puddle. He wrestled her over to the side of the driveway and shoved her into the bushes. Leaves still wet from this morning's rain smashed into her face and hair. Water spidered down her neck. Panic perspiration ran down her ribs. Glug, glug.

"Who are you?" he demanded. His mouth was so close to her ear she could feel his hot breath. A scent of garlic blasted around to engulf her face. "What do you want? Why are you running all over town asking questions about us?"

She gurgled and glugged some more, and he finally loosened both grips to where she could snatch a breath and gasp something. "Let—me—go!"

She couldn't see him, but she could tell from the closeness of his mouth to her ear that he must be no taller than she was. But pit-bull strong. She grabbed at the hand over her mouth. She couldn't pull it away, but she dug her only two decent-length fingernails deep into the skin. *Gotta grow longer fingernails.* But even if she had only two fingernails to work with, he yelped with surprise, and the hand let go.

"You do that again and you're gonna be face down in that puddle," he threatened.

"Got—to—breathe," she managed to gasp before the hand closed over her mouth again. *Lord, what do I do now?*

He shifted the other arm down to clamp around her waist. "Okay, breathe. But you make one sound, and you're a dead woman."

"Andy?" she guessed. "Timmons?"

The question didn't jolt him with surprise. He obviously already suspected she'd been looking for him and/or Lily. Had he talked to the guy at the trailer park? Or maybe Lily had stopped in at the convenience store? Maybe Beer Can Man had mentioned something.

All Timmons said was a surly, "So?"

"I just need to talk to you for a minute—"

"Who are you? Dirk sent you snooping around to find Lily?"

"Who's Dirk?"

"You know who Dirk is!"

"No. I was coming to your apartment, but there wasn't any place to park. So I went back out to the street—"

"I saw you sitting in your car outside our apartment. What've you got? Some kind of fancy listening equipment so you could hear everything we said inside the apartment? You just tell Dirk—"

"Fancy listening equipment" might be a great idea, but

Cate didn't have any. She didn't even have any *unfancy* listening equipment. Maybe she should discuss that with tech-expert Mitch. Although by now she had a good idea that Dirk must be the ex-husband Lily was afraid of, the "scumbag Admond," as her brother had referred to him. Okay, give Andy points for being protective of his girlfriend. Take a whole bunch of points away for lousy problem-solving technique.

"I keep telling you, I don't know Dirk. It's *you*, not Lily, I'm looking for," she said.

"Why?"

"It's about your motorcycle."

"You from the outfit that manages the apartments? Just because we didn't mention the bike on that application form—"

"No. It's about *buying* your motorcycle."

"You don't look like no bike buyer."

Was that an insult? If so, it was the least of Cate's worries at the moment. "Not me, someone else."

He considered that. Thinking seemed to intensify the garlic breath. It wafted around her like a toxic storm.

"Okay, we're gonna walk over to the apartment. Nice and easy. And you're not going to try to run away or make a ruckus. Because of this."

A gun barrel rammed the middle of her back.

"You can't shoot me right here!"

"Try me."

"People will hear. They'll come running! They'll call the police."

"First one comes running, cop or anyone else, gets a bullet in the belly. Just walk toward the apartments. You're not gonna get hurt, and neither is anyone else, if everything's like you say and this is just about buying the bike."

Cate did not comment that this was not a great sales technique. She felt the harder pressure of the gun barrel against her back and started walking. Her feet squished in her wet shoes. Water from the wet bushes trickled from her hair into her eyelashes and dribbled over her lips. She blinked, trying to clear vision that seemed to double everything around her. Double the apartment building. Double the vehicles. Double the dim lights. His wet shoes squished behind her. She wanted to scream like a girl in a horror movie when the bug monster is about to get her.

Instead she yelled inwardly at herself. *No. No screams. Don't get some innocent bystander killed.*

Past the first apartment door, the second, the third. At the last door, he told her to knock.

She remembered Beer Can Man's advice: don't go around knocking on strange doors. At this point, she didn't seem to have much choice. But she still procrastinated. "There's a doorbell."

He jabbed her twice in the back with the gun. "Knock."

Cate knocked.

A female voice answered warily, "Andy?"

Andy kept the gun in the middle of Cate's back, but he leaned toward the door. "Everything's okay, sweetie. Do like I told you. If it's a knock, not the doorbell, it's me. Open up."

The door opened, and a petite blonde stared at her. Duane at the rooming house had been grandfatherly sweet in his assessment of her, the landlady more realistic. Her bleached hair did look stiff enough to withstand anything from a demolition derby to a tornado. But, without makeup, she also looked young and scared and vulnerable.

"What'd you bring her here for?" she demanded. She didn't *sound* vulnerable. She was holding a big spoon covered with spaghetti sauce across her chest like a shield, paper towel underneath it to catch the drips. The apartment smelled like Andy's breath. Maybe someone should tell Lily she should cut back on the garlic in her cooking. "Who is she?"

That was when Cate spotted the motorcycle. Actually, she couldn't miss it, since it stood in the middle of the living room floor. This was the bike Halliday was so hot to acquire? It looked old and beat up enough to qualify as junkyard sculpture, but the name Indian was written on it in metallic script. This no doubt explained Andy's worry that she was from the apartment management company. Keeping a bike in the living room was probably universally frowned on by landlords.

Although newspapers were spread on the carpet under it. The feminine touch, perhaps?

Andy shoved Cate inside, locked the door behind her, and stood in front of it to further impede any escape. She turned to look at him. Halliday's description had been accurate. About 5'5", 135 pounds, wiry build, but she knew he was much stronger than his size and build suggested. Sharp features, scraggly dark hair. Halliday had been right about the mustache too, oversized and droopy, like the stereotype of a Western movie bandit. All he needed was a belt lined with brass bullets slung low across his skinny hips. Hey, wait a minute—

"You aren't carrying a gun!"

He cocked his hand and fingers into the shape of a gun. He blew across his forefinger, as if it had just blasted hot lead, sly triumph in his smile.

Some PI you are, Cate Kinkaid. You can't even tell a finger jabbed in your back from a real gun.

Andy folded his fingers back and rubbed the hand where her fingernails had cut crescent imprints in his skin.

Lily stabbed Cate with a gaze. "You can just tell Dirk—"

"Dirk didn't send her. She said she's here about the bike."

Lily threw the spoon at him. It bounced off his wiry chest and splattered an abstract spaghetti-sauce portrait of Andy's mustache across the carpet. "How do you know Dirk didn't send her to spy on me? Andy, you're so gullible. You believe anything anyone tells you."

Maybe Lily was wishing she'd dumped Andy, as she'd told the woman at the RV park she was going to do?

"And you're both dripping muddy water all over the carpet." Lily grabbed sheets of newspaper from the sofa and stuffed them under Andy's feet. Cate obligingly lifted one foot at a time so Lily could do the same with her.

"I vacuumed in here just yesterday," Lily fretted.

"Sorry," Cate said. She didn't point out that Lily had herself sabotaged the vacuuming job with her addition of spaghetti sauce to the carpet.

"Maybe she's an undercover cop," Andy suggested. He took a protective stance in front of the bike.

An undercover cop. Cate felt mildly flattered.

Lily turned to him again. "Why would she be an undercover cop? Are the cops after you for something I don't know about? You been dealing pot or meth again?" she added darkly.

"No! I told you, I'm not into that stuff anymore." Andy moved away from the bike, expression wary, as if he feared she might produce more throwing artillery and he didn't want the bike in her line of fire. With a cagey look at Cate, he added, "Not that I ever was."

"I really am here about your selling the bike," Cate interrupted. "A, um, business associate is interested in buying it. He wanted me to locate you so he could contact you. That's the only reason I'm here."

Lily planted her hands on her hips. "Oh yeah? Who is this 'business associate'?"

The time for confidentiality was past. Lily might indeed have additional and more lethal artillery. Or Timmons might come up with a real gun. Halliday would just have to live with the fact that Andy knew he was interested enough in the bike to send someone looking.

"His name is Matt Halliday, from H&B Vintage Auto Restorations out on Maxwell. Actually, you offered to sell the bike to him awhile back." Cate lifted wet eyebrows at Andy. "Remember? He wasn't interested then, but he is now."

"Who are you?"

Cate sometimes wished she had a better imagination, but the only name that came to mind was her own. "Cate Kinkaid."

"You work for H&B?" Andy asked.

"No. I'm in a business that, um, sometimes finds people for other people." Cate started to pull out a Belmont Investigations card, but she felt a sudden reluctance to provide him with any further way to connect with her.

"He *paid* you to find me?" Andy said.

"That's my job." She shoved the card deeper in her pocket.

Halliday had said Andy had nervous eyes, and Cate saw them in 3-D action now. Eyes that flicked from door to her to bike to Lily, with a long stop at the end to squint into space while he thought about something. Probably not quantum physics.

"How much?" he demanded.

"How much will he pay for the bike? I don't—"

"How much did he pay you to find me?"

"I haven't calculated the bill yet."

"You sure you don't owe this guy money or something, and that's why he sent her looking for you?" Lily demanded with a hands-on-hips glare at Andy.

Cate didn't wait for Andy to try to soothe Lily with assurances about his credit rating. "So I'll just be running along now," she said brightly, as if this had been a pleasant social visit. "I'll tell him you're living here, and he can contact you."

"Well, I dunno," Andy said. Cate could almost see dollar signs playing tag in his head, and he sounded cagey, as if he figured that now he could afford to play hard to get with the bike. "If it's the stuffed shirt I talked to at H&B, he wasn't all that nice to me."

"Nice, nasty, who cares?" Lily threw up her hands in exasperation. "Sell the bike. I'm tired of it sitting in our living room like a big ugly pet we have to pamper." To Cate she added, "He acts like I should bow down every time I pass by it."

"Why *do* you keep it in the living room?" Cate asked Andy.

Andy frowned, as if this were an irrelevant question. "It's a valuable old bike, a real classic." Andy moved a few steps to rub a smudge on a fender. Which seemed like an exercise in futility given all the dents and rusty spots elsewhere on the bike. "Very hard to find a '48 Indian these days. I'm not leaving it out where someone can steal or vandalize it."

Lily crossed her arms over her chest. "I think your opinion of its value is highly overrated."

Cate thought that might be true too, although she didn't comment. Apparently Andy considered the old bike a prime investment, his personal IRA.

"Oh, I think Halliday is going to be willing to pay plenty." Andy's smile and nod were smug, as if he knew something neither Lily or Cate knew about bike values. "How're things going out there at H&B now? I heard on the news they had kind of a messy shootout there."

"Yes, there was," Cate agreed.

"One man dead, another one almost dead," Andy observed. "But business is still chugging along?"

"All I know is that Mr. Halliday is interested in buying your bike."

Andy unlocked the door, all the polite, considerate host now. "You don't need to tell Mr. Halliday anything. I'll get in touch with him myself. I might be at work or something if he called or came here."

"Work?" Lily said, as if *work* and *Andy* were an unlikely combination.

Andy opened the door and motioned Cate toward it, apparently eager to be rid of her now. "I'll call him and set up an appointment. You don't have to do anything. In fact, I'd rather you didn't."

Halliday didn't want her to talk to Andy; Andy didn't want her to talk to Halliday. It sounded to Cate like a strange way to do business. But then, choreographing their negotiations was not in her job description anyway.

Cate wiped her feet on the newspapers so she wouldn't track more muddy water across the carpet. At the door, she looked back at Lily.

"If you're worried about your ex-husband, it might help to get a restraining order against him."

Cate knew something about restraining orders. She and Uncle Joe had worked on a stalking case in which the stalker had turned out to be the guy's ex-wife.

"I don't know how to do that."

"You can go to the police and fill out a form. Or there's a free legal aid service where you can get help. They're in the phone book. I think you can get a temporary order right away, and then you go before a judge to have it made permanent.

Just be sure you know specific dates when he harassed or threatened you, and what he said or did."

"You don't need any restraining order," Andy scoffed. "I can take care of you. Or maybe we'll just take off and go someplace better."

"We don't have any money."

"We will have. Plenty of money. Soon."

"The bike can't bring that much." Lily gave it a glance that would wither whole cornfields. "It isn't even running. We had to haul it over here in the pickup."

"You just wait and see."

"Mr. Halliday seemed to think you were kind of high on your price before," Cate warned. "If you really want to sell, it might be best to put a realistic price on the bike."

"I know how to deal with Halliday."

Lily came to the door and elbowed Andy out of the way. "Thanks," she said to Cate. "I really appreciate the information about a restraining order."

Andy got in the last word to Cate, however. "Remember, you don't say anything to Halliday about me. I'll take care of it."

❖ 16 ❖

Cate drove home with the scent of garlic still thick in her nose. Which was because, she realized when she walked into the house and the smell was still with her, it had also saturated her clothes. A new hazard connected with the PI business that she'd never anticipated. Was wardrobe contamination an acceptable business deduction on your income tax return? Although Octavia seemed more interested in than repelled by the scent.

Octavia followed Cate into the bathroom and curled up on the garlic-scented clothes Cate tossed on the floor. Now she'd have a garlic-scented cat? After showering and washing her hair, Cate went to the computer in her office to write up a report for Matt Halliday. Andy had said she didn't need to give Halliday any information, that he'd rather contact the man himself.

She wouldn't go along with what Andy wanted. Halliday was her client, not Andy. Using information from the .notebook she kept in her purse, she listed dates, times, who she'd contacted, and what she'd done on the case, hours and minutes it had taken her, miles she'd traveled.

The report told Halliday what she'd learned about the location of the motorcycle and Andy. But when she was correcting punctuation and grammar, she noticed a time didn't seem right. She turned away to retrieve the notebook to check for accuracy, and when she returned to the computer, she found Octavia strolling across the keyboard.

Cate looked on the screen at what the cat tracks had written: 'pl/ijmbgyesx. Octavia plopped down on her rump beside the computer and looked up expectantly.

"And that is . . . what?" Cate asked. "Advice? Compliment on a job well done? Dinner order?"

Octavia flicked her tail and batted a pen off the edge of the desk, which Cate interpreted as exasperation with Cate's denseness. Cate studied the letters on the computer screen again.

"This doesn't make any sense at all," she finally declared. "So don't expect me to believe you're giving me some important message in code."

Although an unexpected wave of apprehension shivered up her spine. Was Octavia's peculiar sixth sense perceiving something and trying to warn her? That perhaps the situation wasn't exactly as it seemed, and unknown dangers lurked?

"No way," she said firmly. "It's just cat gibberish."

A quick *delete* took care of the strange line of letters.

Case closed!

She printed out two copies of the report, one for Halliday and one for the files. Uncle Joe didn't trust having records on the computer only; he wanted paper copies too.

◆◆◆

Next morning, reading the newspaper, she saw a big feature article interviewing both Halliday and Shirley about the shootings at H&B, with photos. There were letters to the editor too, several readers praising Halliday for his quick reaction. Somehow she doubted Halliday would be pleased, even though everything lauded him as a hero. He didn't seem to like the limelight.

Cate called and discussed the amount of the bill for Halliday with Uncle Joe. He'd seen the article and letters too. Afterward, instead of mailing or faxing both report and bill, Cate decided to run them out to H&B. She wanted to remind Shirley that this evening was the second Fit and Fabulous session.

Cate was surprised to see a police car pulling out of the H&B lot when she arrived. Did that mean they were still investigating the events that had happened here? The Corvette was no longer in the lot.

Inside, Halliday's office door was open. Cate gave Radine a little wave and went directly to the open door.

"I have a report for you," Cate said from the doorway. She held up the envelope. "About Andy Timmons and his motorcycle."

Halliday shoved some papers aside. He was in the khaki coveralls all the H&B people except Radine wore, smear of grease on the sleeve, and he smelled like her dad when he came in from working on his old tractor.

Halliday's creased forehead and compressed mouth looked serious and worried, but then that was how he usually looked. As if he lived under a dark cloud from which bad news could rain down at any moment. "Already? Good work. Come on in."

Cate stepped inside and handed the envelope to him. He opened it, skimmed what she'd written, and glanced at the bill. No explosion there. Good. It was in the report how Timmons had ambushed her in the puddle, but she now offered an expanded explanation about why she'd had to tell him Halliday was interested in the bike. "I hope this doesn't complicate your negotiations with Mr. Timmons."

He waved a hand, dismissing her concerns. "I'm just sorry you had to go through that. I suspected Timmons was sneaky and unreliable, but maybe he's also more dangerous than I realized."

"All in the day of a private investigator," Cate assured him. "As it says in the report, Timmons plans to contact you himself, so you'll probably hear from him soon."

"Actually, the situation has changed, and I don't think I'm interested in buying the bike after all. I talked to the client just this morning, and he said he'd bought an old Indian bike over in Idaho." Halliday frowned, but he added a little shrug that suggested that was just an everyday business annoyance.

He opened the desk drawer and pulled out a checkbook. He wrote out the check for Belmont Investigations himself rather than having Radine do it. He held it out to her. "I appreciate your good work."

"Thanks. We appreciate the prompt payment." She tucked the check in her purse. "Good interview in the newspaper this morning."

"I felt like an idiot when I read it." Halliday grimaced. "When you see something you've said in print, it comes out different than what you intended to say."

"People writing to the editor really approved what you did."

"Those I appreciated."

"Well, um, if you ever need anything else, Belmont Investigations is available."

"You never know."

"I see the police were here again," Cate said tentatively. "I thought their investigation was concluded by now."

"There was that fire at the hospital. The police now seem to think it could be connected with what happened to Kane. It really worries me."

"Connected how?"

"They didn't spell it out for me. You know police. But they asked questions about clients Kane may have had problems with. Also relationship problems, personal enemies, financial problems. They didn't get to people who didn't like his dog, but they covered everything else. But I think what they have in mind is that someone may have been trying to get to Kane right there at the hospital. To finish him off."

"You mean that his original shooting here could have been something more than a robbery? That Kane was an intentional target? And someone is still out to get him?"

"That's what it looks to me like they're considering."

Halliday stood up. He arched his back and rubbed his neck as if both were tight with tension. "What I'm thinking is, if it involves some kind of grudge against H&B . . ."

Maybe they'd come after him too.

Unexpectedly, he offered both a smile and another grimace. "Listen to me. Kane is in the hospital with his life on the line, and I'm worried about some weirdo coming after me."

"Have they ever connected the gunman to any dealings with H&B?"

"Not that I know of."

"So they're thinking someone may have hired him to kill Mr. Blakely?"

Halliday smiled ruefully. "The police don't include me in their loop."

Yeah. Cate too.

"So maybe he was a hired assassin, or maybe it was some

conspiracy of buddies out to get him," Halliday added. "I don't know."

"Is there any specific customer you think could have been unhappy enough to do this?"

"Not really. Although even in the best of businesses, there are always a few unhappy customers. Recently, one guy was all bent out of shape because the charge on restoring his old LaSalle came in considerably higher than we'd estimated. Or Kane may have had problems up at the Salem branch that he didn't tell me about." He paused. "And then there's Candy, of course."

"Is this something you want Belmont Investigations to check into?"

Halliday frowned as if considering that, then shook his head. "Not at this time, no. Maybe I'm reading something into the police thinking that isn't there. This whole situation has been—and *is*—very disturbing."

"I see Mr. Blakely's Corvette is no longer in the parking lot. Did the police take it?"

"No. I had one of our employees tow it around to the shop and put it inside to keep it safe. Kane would be really upset if anything happened to it."

"Good idea. Is it okay if I step out in the warehouse and talk to Shirley for a minute?"

"Yes. Of course."

◆◆◆

Cate found Shirley in the middle of the warehouse, head tilted toward an upper shelf. Jerry, the string-bean guy who'd loaned her a pickup, was moving a ladder on its rails to a different position on a shelf, his coveralls streaked with the trademark grease of anyone who worked here. Shirley put a foot on the ladder, but he kept a hand on it.

"I can do this for you."

"Jerry, it's *my* job."

Shirley briskly started up the ladder and climbed to the top shelf. Jerry's worried gaze followed her every movement. She came down carrying one of those unidentifiable car parts. She handed it to Jerry and spotted Cate. "Hey, Cate, hi!"

"I had to come out and see Mr. Halliday, so I thought I'd stop in for a minute."

"I'd better get back out to the shop. Thanks for locating the generator for the Olds." Jerry headed for the open door on the far side of the warehouse. Cate suspected he was disappointed that her appearance had shortened his brief time with Shirley.

Shirley went back to a big box on the floor beside her computer.

"We've had some stuff coming down from Salem. I'm cataloguing these hood ornaments right now."

"Because Mr. Halliday is closing the Salem branch?"

"I guess." Shirley's frown suggested she wasn't particularly pleased about that, no doubt because of Kane.

"I saw you got interviewed by the newspaper."

"Yeah. And some magazine in Portland called too. But I didn't do anything with them. It all makes me feel kind of . . . slimy. Like I'm capitalizing on Kane getting shot."

Cate had been right. Neither Halliday nor Shirley were publicity hounds. She peered into the box. The mixture of silvery, gold-toned, and bronze ornaments weren't individually wrapped, just jumbled together. A dolphin. A football player. Silvery steer horns, a foot and a half wide. She picked up an upright metal bear, surprisingly heavy when she hefted it in one hand.

"I don't think I've ever seen any of these on cars."

"Some brands of vehicles use specific ornaments, like the ram figure for Dodges, but these are random ones some company made. Mr. Halliday said Kane must have picked them up on a company closeout. Sometimes a customer wants something, you know, different. Jerry said they mounted real steer horns on a pickup once. Though I don't know who'd want *this*."

Shirley picked up an oddly diabolical-looking goldy figure with big feet and a peaked hat. Clown? Witch? It was hard to tell.

"I'll just catalogue them and stick the whole box up on a shelf somewhere. We may never use them. How's Clancy doing with Mitch?" Shirley added.

"Great. We took him out for a run in the country on Sunday afternoon. Anything new with Kane?"

"I don't think he's getting any better," Shirley said gloomily. Then she determinedly brightened. "But I don't know that he's any worse either. His son is here now."

"What's he like?"

Shirley lifted a shoulder. "Oh, okay, I guess. I introduced myself, but we didn't actually talk much."

Not much enthusiasm from Shirley for the son, and Cate figured the guy had just blown her off. He wasn't making any pass at Shirley, as Candy had said he'd done with her.

"What about the ex-wife?"

"I think she went back to Salem when Kane's son got here."

"How'd your dinner with Jerry go?"

"Just fine." Her sturdy face brightened. "He really liked the fried chicken and apple pie, and we played chess afterward. Hatch and I used to play chess a lot out on the boat. Jerry got my pickup fixed, so I gave him back the one he loaned me."

Cate wanted to put in a plug for Jerry, what a great guy

he seemed to be, but she doubted it would do any good right now. Shirley had a fixation on Kane.

"I was wondering if you're going to make it to the Fit and Fabulous session tonight."

"I don't know. I guess I'd forgotten."

"You can still go, even if you missed that first session," Cate reminded her.

"I don't know . . . I mean, with Kane still in a coma . . ." Shirley's shoulders slumped and her voice trailed off, but a sudden spark of determination straightened her back. "Yes, I will go! Maybe, by the time Kane comes out of the coma, I can surprise him. I'll be a whole new woman for him!"

"You're a great woman already. Kane should appreciate that."

"You're saying I don't need to go?" Shirley stretched one of those black curls out from her head. It looked as if she let go too suddenly, it might boomerang full force into her scalp. "With hair that looks like wire that fell into a bucket of black paint? Eyebrows like they were plucked by a post-hole digger? Clothes that look like they came out of an ad in *Fisherman's Digest*?"

"You're being much too hard on yourself."

"I have a mirror, Cate. I can see the problems. I just don't know how to fix anything. I want to learn."

Shirley could use some basic assistance on makeup and hair and clothes. It might help her self-esteem and self-confidence considerably. But Cate didn't want to see Shirley get her hopes up about a makeover jump-starting a relationship with Kane and then wind up being hurt by him. Because Cate just didn't think Kane was the kind of guy who'd go for even a madeover Shirley for long. And that $30,000 he'd borrowed from Halliday still puzzled and troubled her. Why did a man desperately need that much cash?

But all she said was, "It starts at 7:00. Maybe I'll come too."

"You're already fabulous."

"Tell that to my cat. She thinks I'm just part of the staff she's rightfully entitled to."

Cate went out the way she'd come, through the main front entrance. She was just scooting into the Honda when Matt Halliday opened the door and yelled something. Cate couldn't hear what he said, but there was no mistaking the urgency of his upraised arm motioning her back.

17

"Something wrong?" Cate asked when she reached the door Halliday held open for her.

"The mail just came. I want you to see something."

Inside, Radine stood by the door to Halliday's office with a brass letter opener in one hand. Mail scattered the counter, some opened, some unopened, as if she'd abandoned the job in mid-slash. She looked as horrified as Cate had felt the time she'd opened a plain envelope and discovered she'd somehow gotten on a porno mailing list.

"Everything's okay, Ray," Halliday soothed her. "It's probably just someone's weird idea of a joke."

Cate followed Halliday into the office, Radine trailing behind until the phone at her desk rang and she went back to answer it.

Halliday picked up a sheet of paper with fold lines and held it out to Cate. She started to take it but then got a glimpse of what was on the paper.

"I don't think you should be touching that," Cate said.

He dropped the paper as if it had turned to a letter bomb in his hand. "You're right. What was I thinking? There could be fingerprints."

Cate cautiously used a couple of envelopes from Halliday's desk to spread and flatten the page without actually touching it. The sender hadn't used any great imagination in creating the message. It was done in words cut out of a newspaper and taped to the page, practically the gold standard for anonymous messages. Most of the words were from regular newspaper print, a couple in capitals from headlines.

We got Blakely your NEXT con MAN

The sender had a little problem with both punctuation and word usage, but the meaning was plain enough. *You're next, con man.* Or to be fair, maybe he couldn't find "you're" in the newspaper.

"Where's the envelope?" Cate asked.

Without touching it, Halliday pointed to a face-down envelope on the desk. Cate used a pen to flip it over.

Halliday's name and the H&B name and address were on yellow paper, apparently cut from a phone book. It was a Eugene postmark, yesterday's date. Legal-size envelope, standard issue, no identifying marks.

"I guess threat makers aren't into return addresses," Halliday said.

"What does 'con man' mean?"

"I'm assuming the person is saying we 'conned' him in some business deal with H&B, and he's getting even. First with Kane, and I'm next."

"You should call the police immediately. This is a definite threat."

"I will. Of course. Right away." Halliday paused, the lines that seemed permanently etched into his forehead cutting even deeper. "Although . . ."

"Although?"

"I don't mean to criticize our local law enforcement, but

they don't exactly work at warp speed. I'm not sure I want to wait for them to figure out who's behind that guy who shot Kane. Because whoever it is may get to me before the police figure out who it is."

A worrisome possibility, Cate agreed.

Halliday glanced around nervously, as if he thought another gunman might burst through the door at any moment. "You said earlier that if we needed anything more, Belmont Investigations was available. I want to take you up on that."

"There's a possibility, of course, that the sender is one of those crank types. People do this kind of thing. Everything from giving the police imaginary leads to confessing to a crime they didn't commit."

"Really?" Halliday seemed taken aback by this information.

"It can be a big problem for law enforcement. They have to follow up on leads, even ones that sound weird."

"I don't think I can take the chance that it's just some weirdo crank."

"Neither do I. I can start looking into it right away. But you still need to bring in the police." She tapped the envelope with the dull end of the pen. "I'll need a list of names and addresses of anyone H&B has had any problems with in the last year. Or even before that, if you remember someone who was exceptionally angry. From both here and in Salem."

"It doesn't sound like Candy, does it?" Halliday sounded regretful, as if he'd like to nail Kane's ex-wife for making threats.

No, it didn't sound like Candy. But Cate wasn't jumping to conclusions. Candy wasn't dumb. She might try to make a personal vendetta look like a business grudge. Although, if she was really out to get Halliday, why bother giving him advance notice? Why, in fact, would anyone give advance warning with an anonymous threat? Why not just whack him? A solid threat just got his guard up.

"The police will probably want to take this letter to check for fingerprints. Can you make a copy for me now?"

Conscientious about not adding more fingerprints, Halliday used another piece of paper to scoop up the anonymous letter and carried it to the photocopy machine.

Cate picked up the clear copy that rolled out. "Do you mind if I use this when I'm asking questions, or is it something you'd rather keep confidential?"

"It isn't exactly a flattering recommendation for H&B, is it? Implying we conned someone. But yes, use it however you need to. I'll have a list of possible unhappy clients ready for you in an hour or two. In general, we have very good relationships with our customers."

"Email the list to me as soon as you can."

"I will. Though I think the problem must be something up at the Salem branch, not here."

"In addition to unhappy customers, how about former employees? Any problems there?"

Halliday shook his head. "The only employee who's left recently was the stock clerk, the job Shirley has now. But he left because of health problems. I'm not sure about Kane's employees in Salem."

"Okay. Thanks."

◆◆◆

A problem in Salem, with either a customer or former employee, sounded plausible. Mace Jackson was from Salem, and the "*We* got Blakely" indicated this person making a new threat was associated with the gunman in some way. Candy lived in Salem too . . .

153

At home, Cate grabbed her file with her notes about Mace Jackson and photos she'd printed from her cell phone. She stuffed everything in a seldom-used briefcase. She'd pick up Halliday's email message with her phone later.

As a last-minute thought, she packed a bag and put out enough food to last Octavia overnight. Salem wasn't all that far, no more than commuting distance for some people, but she might decide to stay overnight. Octavia, suspecting something was going on that she wouldn't like, stalked around like some queen of the jungle unhappy about the loss of a good slave.

"If you don't like being left home alone, you should learn to like riding in a car," Cate informed her. To which Octavia cat-stomped out to her screened-in playroom. Lipreading again?

◆◆◆

Salem wasn't more than an hour and a half away, mostly green farmland with bluish mountains in the distance on either side of I-5, but Cate wasn't really familiar with this capital of the state. She used her phone to locate the H&B address in a busy, semi-industrial area. She passed a wholesale import business, a company that manufactured windows, and another that built horse trailers. She couldn't pick out specific sounds, but the area had an indefinable hum of activity.

The H&B building was considerably smaller than the Eugene warehouse and shop, but classier, with brick and decorative rock on the front. A white-and-red restored '56 Chevy Bel Air, an identifying placard and a silvery trophy beside it, stood in an oversized display window. Low shrubs and green grass surrounded a freestanding H&B sign. Nicely paved parking area, but no vehicles in it.

Certainly not ostentatious, but it suggested a considerably more stylish and upscale business than the workaday setup in Eugene. It also looked prosperous, although that look apparently wasn't reflected in bottom-line profits. Nothing indicated the business was now closed, but the door wouldn't move when Cate tried it. A big, furniture warehouse truck rumbled by, and, from somewhere, the ding-ding-ding of a piece of equipment backing up. Now what?

That was when she heard banging around back. She circled the building and found a separate metal shop with an open roll-up door. A motorcycle stood outside, a small one without the Purple Rocket's muscle and speed. The banging came from around front of an oversized vehicle in process of restoration.

"Anyone here?"

No one appeared, but a voice yelled, "Yo!"

"I'd like to talk to someone, if you have time," Cate called back.

"Sure. Gimme a minute."

A husky guy a couple years younger than Cate finally appeared in the doorway. Linebacker shoulders filled green coveralls, but he had baby-blue eyes in a freckled, boyish face. Rowdy blond curls stuck out from under a green cap with the company name embroidered in gold. He was wiping his hands on a greasy rag. His interest perked up when he saw Cate, but he said, "We're kind of closed," as he tossed the rag aside.

"I just need a little information." She handed him a business card.

"Seth Erickson." He stuck out a hand, and Cate shook it.

He didn't seem as startled or intimidated by the information on the card as some recipients were. Instead his gaze inspected her from red hair to daisy-painted toenails she'd experimented with a few days ago. She thought he was about to make some flirty remark, but then he asked a question.

"You carry a gun?"

Oh, *that's* what he was looking for. Gun lumps. The whole world apparently thought every PI carried a Glock in one pocket and a Sig Sauer in the other. Well, maybe she *wouldn't* carry a gun, even after she got her license and *could* load up on Glocks and Sig Sauers and fifty-bullet clips. Just to show that you could be a PI without one.

"No, no gun," she snapped.

"You shouldn't tell people that," he reproved. "I could be a really bad guy."

Yeah, maybe she was too honest. She didn't admit that, however. She just stared him in the eyes even as she thought, *Baby-blue-eyed guys can be killers too*. She had a momentary impulse to turn and run, but she shoved it aside.

"Okay, bad guy, do you have time for a few questions?"

He grinned. "You aren't with the police?"

"No. This is a private investigation. Have the police been here?"

"After Kane got shot, I figured they would be, but I've never seen anyone. I guess you're here about the shooting?"

She nodded. "But you're *kind of* closed?"

"We are closed, I guess, although I'm not sure what's going on. If you're an investigator, you probably know more than I do."

Not necessarily.

"Have you worked here long?" Cate asked.

"About a year. I'm here alone now. We didn't get any paychecks last week, so Angie, she runs the office, took off to look for another job. My buddy Carter started job hunting too. But I hated to give up on this old gal." He jerked a thumb toward the unfinished hulk with huge fins. "So I thought I'd hang around for a while. How's Kane doing?"

"Neither the hospital or police are releasing much information. Right now, I'm looking for more information about Mace Jackson, the man who shot him. He was from here in Salem."

"I read the name in the newspaper. I'd never heard it before that."

Cate pulled out a copy of the photo she'd enlarged with her computer. Erickson's head jerked back at the sight of the obviously dead man sprawled on the floor, gaping wound in his chest.

"Sorry," Cate said. "It's the only photo I have available. Have you ever seen him?"

"Nope. Stranger to me." Erickson handed the photo back. "Interesting job you have." He smiled. "Most women just take pictures of flowers and dogs and kids."

Cate returned the photo to her briefcase. "Do you know of any problems with customers? Someone who might have a grudge against H&B?"

Another nope before Erickson added, "Well, there was a guy a couple months ago whose wife was all perturbed about the paint job on their Lincoln. She said it was too pinkish. I ask you, how can a blue be pinkish?"

"How about former employees? Any hard feelings there?"

Erickson shook his head. "Guys come and go. This isn't a big bucks kind of place to work. But I don't remember anyone getting fired. Angie wasn't mad. Neither was Carter. Though I guess we're all shook up about the place closing. Puzzled too. It's always seemed like business was good."

"Did you find out about the closing before or after Mr. Blakely was shot?"

"Kane warned us a couple weeks ago it might happen. To give us a chance to look for other jobs, I guess. He isn't the kind of guy who'd dump something like that on employees at the last minute. Mr. Halliday has started moving inventory down to Eugene this past week."

"So you'll definitely be out of a job."

"Yeah. Though, like I said, we don't seem to be getting paid anyway. It doesn't affect me much, because I'm going back to school next quarter anyway. But I'm sure Kane was unhappy about it. He really loves tooling around in something hot looking."

"Wearing his big cowboy hat?"

Seth smiled. "Yeah. He loves that ol' hat too. And his dog."

"Clancy."

"Yeah, Clancy."

"A friend of mine is taking care of him," Cate said.

"I'm glad to hear that. We all liked Clancy. He always made rounds to say hello to everyone." Now Seth sounded reminiscent, as if, whether he consciously realized it or not, he figured Kane and Clancy wouldn't be back.

"So you don't think Mr. Blakely wanted to close?"

"I think it was the other guy, Halliday, the partner down in Eugene, who said they had to do it. I've never met him." The statement, either unconsciously or with deliberate subtlety, lined Seth's own feelings up on Kane's side of any conflicts between the two partners.

"You like Kane?"

"Sure, Kane's a great guy. He works here in the shop right along with us. He's better at the promoting stuff, though, a great glad-hander. But I don't mean that in a bad way," Seth added hastily. "Lots of times he has pizza or sub sandwiches delivered to the guys working in the shop."

"Can you think of any reason someone would want him dead?"

"*Want* him dead?" Erickson repeated, a touch of alarm in his voice. "I understood that guy just busted in and tried to rob the place."

"There may be more to it than a robbery attempt." Cate pulled out one of the copies she'd made of Halliday's anonymous letter.

"Wow! Sounds like someone has a killer grudge about something, doesn't it? Has Halliday gone into hiding?"

"No. He just put me on the case to find out who's behind this and what they have against H&B. Hopefully I can come up with an answer before they get to him."

"It doesn't necessarily have to be a customer or employee, does it?"

"Do you have something in mind?"

"Hey, no." Erickson's feet shuffled and he lifted his hands, palms out. "Not me! I don't know Kane outside of working for him here."

Cate gave that hasty denial and the alarmed look in Erickson's clear blue eyes a quick evaluation. "But you know something."

He took a step backward. "Well, uh . . . Look, I don't want to say anything that will make Kane look bad or make waves for him or anything."

"We need to know everything we can to protect Mr. Halliday from whoever is behind this."

"This doesn't have anything to do with H&B or Halliday, but I was over on the coast for a weekend a while back. I'm no gambler, but a friend and I wanted to see an Elvis impersonator at a casino. He was supposed to be really good. Anyway, I just happened to spot Kane at a poker table, and he was betting. Betting *big*."

"Winning or losing?"

"I didn't watch that long, but I know my nerves would have sizzled like a bug on a burner if I were betting that kind of money. One other time he came in on a Monday morning and handed everyone a fifty-dollar bill. Someone asked how come, and he said he'd had a great weekend and wanted to share his good fortune."

Maybe Kane had found a stray sack of fifty-dollar bills or gotten a big income tax refund, but this sounded to Cate like a successful gambling weekend. Seth apparently interpreted it that way too.

"Do the casinos allow unlimited bets?" Cate asked.

"There are table limits, I think. But if Kane is really into gambling, he might be doing it outside the legal casinos. I hear those gambling syndicate guys can be pretty hard-nosed if someone runs up a gambling debt and doesn't pay off. The kind of guys who'll take you for a one-way boat ride down the river."

"But why would they be after the other partner too?" Cate asked.

"I don't think they care who they collect from. Just so they get their money. But look, like I said, I don't want this to be anything against Kane. He's a great guy."

Cate nodded, a little stunned by this new information. This lined up with what Candy had said about Kane spending weekends over on the coast without her. She'd suspected another woman—but maybe gambling, not other women, was Kane's weakness.

Kane's involvement in some big-time, illegal gambling would explain his rush need for that $30,000 he was borrowing from Halliday. And apparently he'd specified he needed it in cash.

Did Halliday know about his partner's gambling and where this loan was headed? Boring, solid citizen Halliday would surely disapprove of his money going to pay off a gambling debt. But, out of loyalty to his partner and perhaps fear of the consequences for Kane if he didn't pay up, Halliday would probably provide the money even if he knew and disapproved. So why was Kane shot if he was planning to pay up? Could the debt have been much larger than $30,000, and that amount was just a down payment? Which didn't impress a hard-nosed gambling syndicate? Killing Kane in a robbery would have netted them $30,000 and sent a powerful message to other "customers" about what happened to gamblers who didn't pay up.

"I appreciate knowing this," Cate said. "You have my card. If you think of anything else, would you give me a call?"

"You'll be here in Salem?"

"I may stay overnight." After a moment's hesitation, she added, "I'll put my cell phone number on the card, in case you think of something I should investigate while I'm here."

He handed her the card back, and she scribbled the number on it. She didn't usually give out her cell phone number.

"Thanks." He looked at the card and then tucked it in a pocket of his coveralls. "I sure hope Kane comes out of this okay. Mr. Halliday too, of course."

"A couple more things. Do you know Kane's ex-wife, Candy?"

"I don't know her personally, but she's been around a few times. She and Kane got into some screaming battles right there in the office." Seth put his hands over his ears, as if the memory were a noisy one. "We could hear her clear out here in the shop."

"Arguing about money?"

He grinned. "How'd you know? You must be a great private investigator."

"Lucky guess. It's what exes usually argue about."

"I don't have one, so I'll take your word for it."

"Do you know where I can reach the woman who worked in the office?"

"Angie said she was going up to Seattle to stay with a cousin and see if she could find a job there. I don't know how you'd get in touch with her."

One of those all-too-familiar dead ends. "Okay, thanks."

"I'll call if I think of anything."

◆ 18 ◆

Cate used her cell phone for directions to Candy's address and was headed that way when the phone jingled its guitar riff. She peeked at the caller identification and pulled into a McDonald's parking lot to answer.

"Hey, Mitch. You got my message?"

"That you were heading up to Salem? Yes." He didn't voice disapproval, but his tone equated this with an announcement that she was poised for a leap into a vat of boiling oil. "You're in Salem now?"

Cate briefly explained about Halliday's anonymous message and how she was here to try to find out more about who may have been in with, or behind, Mace Jackson on the shooting. And also what she'd unexpectedly learned from Seth Erickson about Kane's possible involvement with a gambling debt.

"You plan to just drop in on some illegal gambling operation and start asking questions?" Mitch's question was dry but not without snarkiness.

"My plans were a little more mundane. Your idea sounds much more exciting. Could I get into their inner circle by placing a bet? I could probably come up with $1.98. Maybe even $2.98."

"Cate—"

"Although I'm not sure how to locate a gambling syndicate. Is there an 'illegal gambling' section in the yellow pages? Or do I find a sleazy bar and whisper, 'Hey, buddy, you know where I can find some action on the races?'"

A small noise sounded like teeth grinding. Cate expected at least a mini-lecture from Mitch, both for her being here and for not treating the situation more seriously, but instead he said, "I think you're kidding . . . aren't you?"

Cate considered that for a moment. "Probably. Anyway, at the moment, I'm on my way to see Kane's ex-wife."

"I wish I were there to help."

The first words that came to Cate's mind were a snappish, *I don't need a caretaker or a babysitter*. Then she surprised herself by thinking about Mitch a moment more and agreeing with him. If he were here, he *would* help. "I wish you were here too."

Moment of silence while they both digested that exchange.

"Are you thinking the ex-wife knows more about the guy who shot her ex-husband than she's letting on?" Mitch asked.

"That, and I also want to talk to her about Kane's gambling."

"This isn't any connection with the ex-wife or gambling, but didn't you say earlier that you'd seen something in a newspaper article about Mace Jackson winning something in a bicycle race?" Mitch asked.

"I didn't find much on the internet about him, but I did find that."

"How about checking with bicycle shops, some places where they might be familiar with bicycle events and who participates?"

"That hadn't occurred to me," Cate admitted. She also had to admit, "It's a good idea. I'll check it out. Thanks."

"Your message said you might stay overnight?"

"Yeah, and now that you've suggested the bicycle shops thing, I'm sure I will."

"Me and my bright ideas," Mitch muttered.

"You think of things I don't. I appreciate that."

"If you're not going to be around, I'll take Clancy over to Alton Baker Park after work for a run. So talk to me again later, okay? And be careful. Watch your back. Call me if you need anything."

"Like you could zoom in and do a white-knight rescue from seventy or eighty miles away?" she teased.

"A trifling obstacle for a knight on a Purple Rocket," he assured her. "We specialize in zooming."

◆◆◆

Yeah, killer mortgage payments, Cate decided when she saw Candy's house. Not a mogul mansion, but definitely not a cookie-cutter tract house. One of those bulky places with complicated roof lines, enough square footage for a Brady Bunch family, and garage space for anything up to and including an eighteen-wheeler. Maybe your average UFO as well. All on a professionally landscaped, oversized lot. No seven-foot walls with electronically controlled gate to keep unwanted visitors out, however.

Cate parked at the curb and walked up to the main entrance. With volatile Candy, Cate braced herself for anything from earring attack to stomping by high-heeled boot.

A Herculean-sized brass knocker was centered on the door, but it didn't look as if it were actually meant to be used. She punched the doorbell off to the side of the door. No answer. A couple more punches with the same result. Had Candy gone back down to Eugene? Maybe. Cate checked her watch.

But she could be here in town, just not yet home from her job with the husband/senator candidate.

Now she felt let down. She'd primed herself to be sweet and friendly or confrontational, whatever the situation called for, and all she had to work with was a closed door.

Okay, no big deal. She'd hit some bicycle shops now and come back later.

◆◆◆

It was almost 6:00 when Cate parked in front of Candy Blakely's house again. Visiting three bicycle shops had been a big bust. No one knew anything about Mace Jackson.

This might be a big bust too, she decided wearily. No Lexus stood in the driveway. Although, hopefully, that might only mean Candy had put the car in the oversized cave of a garage. Cate started to get out of the car, then decided to check email with her phone first.

Halliday had sent the list of unhappy clients. It did not look particularly helpful. A man who thought H&B did an unsatisfactory job with his upholstery. A couple who split up during the restoration of their 1961 Cadillac and dragged H&B into the battle over who got the car. Another mention about the man who objected to the charge for restoring his LaSalle. Nothing on any problems with customers here in Salem.

Cate tucked the phone in her purse, but she hesitated a moment before opening the car door. She really did wish Mitch were here. But he wasn't, and if the Computer Dudes sale went through, he might be off to who knew where, out of her life forever.

Okay, Ms. Almost-fully-licensed-PI, just get on with it. Candy couldn't do any more than slam the door in her face. Hopefully.

She gave the doorbell a brisk punch, and it jerked open a moment later.

The ex-wife gave her an unfriendly appraisal. "Well, if it isn't the hotshot assistant private investigator, all bright and perky. Did Matt send you all the way up here to harass me?"

Candy was still wearing what Cate assumed she'd worn to work that day, a navy blue suit with a nipped waist that emphasized her curvy figure. Her gold-spiral earrings ended in a point sharp enough to drill through concrete. Was there a jewelry shop that specialized in lethal earrings, and Candy was their best customer? But her feet were bare, the toenails a delicate pink, not some flamboyant color Cate would have expected. Candy saw Cate eying them.

"So I have a bunion problem," she said with a hint of what's-it-to-you challenge.

Cate started to say "My grandma had bunions" but snapped off the words before they escaped. Candy would probably not appreciate being equated with Cate's grandma.

"What do you want?" Candy demanded. "Why are you here? You are working for Matt, aren't you?"

Working for Matt obviously being on a level with door-to-door salesman of sleazy magazines.

Cate pulled out a copy of the threatening letter Halliday had received and handed it to her. "It appears the person who shot Kane wasn't working alone. And that person is after Mr. Halliday now. Is it you?"

She didn't expect a sudden confession, but she thought the blunt question might startle Candy into some giveaway reaction. No such luck.

"I wouldn't mind swatting Matt with a two-by-four," Candy said. "But if I were going to do it, I wouldn't send him a warning notice."

Candy's grumpy statement echoed Cate's own earlier thoughts. Candy was shifting back and forth on her feet now. Nervous? Or maybe that bunion really hurt.

Candy handed the letter back. "And if I did send a threatening letter, I'd certainly do a better job with the spelling and punctuation than this person did."

"You sound as if you're even more unhappy with Mr. Halliday than usual," Cate suggested cautiously.

"Yes, I am. Well, no, not really," Candy corrected. Her shoulders lifted and drooped. "I guess it's not Matt's fault. What I mean is, well, I feel kind of, oh, guilty, I guess, saying anything nasty about Kane, the condition he's in and all. I'd rather be mad at Matt. But Kane lied to me!"

Cate wanted to ask "About what?" but she murmured a less intrusive, "That's too bad," instead.

"Oh, you might as well come in," Candy muttered. "I could use some company, even yours. It's my own fault, I suppose, for not checking a long time ago."

Candy headed back into the foyer. She left the door open but didn't look back to see if Cate followed.

It wasn't exactly a warm welcome, but Cate had already decided that, for a PI, anything other than a door slam in the face worked as an invitation.

19

Candy bypassed a formal living room and turned into a more lived-in looking family room. The seating arrangement of suede sofa, love seat, and upholstered chairs centered on an oversized flat-screen TV, but a lineup of well-tended plants flourished under a big picture window. A chandelier in wagon-wheel shape hung over a pool table behind the seating arrangement. A bar filled half the rear wall, and a piano and drums stood next to the bar.

Candy dropped into the suede sofa. Cate was apparently free to sit wherever she liked. She chose the suede love seat, vaguely wondering how many cattle had given up their hides for all the suede in this room. Candy frowned at the coffee table, another wagon wheel topped with glass, and didn't speak.

Cate finally made a conversational thrust. She wiggled her fingers toward the piano and drums. "You play?"

"No. I decided once that I wanted to learn piano, so Kane bought that for me, but I never got around to taking lessons. A long time ago, back in high school, Kane played drums in the school band, but he never had a set of his own. So he bought those. You know, middle-aged man fulfilling youthful fantasies." She interrupted this rather dour account of the couple's musical history to repeat, "He lied to me!"

Cate let her lame attempt at small talk fizzle and waited for Candy to fill the empty space. After a few moments, she did.

"Kane told me he had this big insurance policy, a half-million-dollar policy, through H&B."

"I believe we had an earlier discussion about insurance."

"I didn't marry him *because* of the insurance." Candy glanced up as if checking to see if Cate believed that. "I mean, you don't marry someone for something that probably isn't going to happen until way off in the future."

No, you marry him for his current assets and income. Cate added an addendum to that. *Unless you have in mind a fatal catastrophe hurrying the event from future into the present.* But all she said aloud was her frequently used, non-committal "um."

Actually, although she hadn't discarded suspicions entirely, she was more or less beyond thinking Candy had anything to do with Kane's shooting.

"But he's a lot older and I could expect, statistically, you know, to outlive him. A woman has to think about these things and look out for herself."

"But there isn't any insurance?"

"Oh, there's insurance, all right. I just don't get any of it."

"Kane isn't dead anyway," Cate pointed out. Hey, hadn't they also had this not-dead conversation before? Had Candy shrugged then? She did now, as if the non-death were an irrelevant road bump. "He changed his beneficiary so the insurance goes to his children?"

"Not them either. It is, and always has been, a business thing with the partnership. It was set up when Kane and Matt started H&B. Both partners are insured, and if something happens to either of them, the insurance payoff goes into the business. I guess it's a common type of arrangement. It's intended to make sure the business doesn't collapse if something happens to one of the partners." She sounded momentarily reasonable, even understanding about that setup, but then she hit her mantra of outrage again. "Kane lied to me!"

"It's possible Kane didn't know or understand the, oh, fine points about the insurance," Cate suggested.

Candy scowled but finally nodded. "Kane has never been much good with financial details. He'd rather spend money than keep track of it. Although I still wouldn't put it past him to lie to me."

"How did you find out about this aspect of the insurance?"

"Radine called. Sweet Radine. You could hear the glee in her voice when she told me I wasn't entitled to anything and why. Sometimes I think she has the hots for Matt."

"Matt asked her to call you?"

"I suppose. He'd rather talk to an IRS agent or a two-headed alien than have a conversation with me."

Was it possible Halliday also hadn't earlier realized the consequences of how the insurance was set up? Cate doubted that. If she were a betting woman, she'd bet Halliday knew every word, clause, comma, and semicolon in the insurance policy.

Bottom line was that if Kane Blakely died, Halliday lost a friend and partner but he—because he *was* H&B if Kane died—gained a half million dollars.

Did the police know that? Probably. As Matt had said, they didn't work at warp speed, but Cate's experience was that they usually covered all the bases.

Another bottom line, however—what difference did it make? A few seconds more and the gunman would have finished Halliday off, and, if Kane lived, he'd be the survivor in line for the insurance bucks. He still could be, if the person sending that threatening note to Matt managed to make good on the threat.

Candy stood up. "I need a drink. You want something?"

"No thanks."

She followed Candy to the bar anyway and watched her clunk cubes from an ice maker into a stubby glass. Without any diluting additions, Candy covered the ice with an amber liquid from a shelf under a mirror on the back wall. She stood behind the bar, elbows on the counter, glass cupped in both hands, frown turning her mouth into a downward curve.

The bar was done in a rugged, Western saloon style. Suede-covered stools, scarred counter, two "bullet holes" in the mirror. A colorful poster showed a barroom girl with upswept hair and revealing bodice swooped into a dip by a lanky cowboy. After a moment, Cate realized the poster was actually an enlargement of a photo from one of those fun photography places, and those were Candy's and Kane's faces. They looked happy. Which was not how Candy looked now.

"Don't you have a cat?" Cate asked. "I remember you mentioning a Persian."

"She's probably asleep on my bed upstairs. When she realizes we have company, she'll come around to check you out." She took a sip of her drink. "So, about this letter Matt received. Was it sent from here in Salem? Is that why you're investigating here?"

"The envelope had a Eugene postmark, but, according to the police, the man who shot Kane was from here in Salem. The threatening letter sounds as if Mace Jackson was the hired hit man or part of a conspiracy that intended to kill Kane but didn't get the job done."

"Yet."

"Yet," Cate agreed.

"And now they're after Matt." Candy took a sip of her drink. "Look, I'd like to help. I really would. I'm not such a bad person that I want to see Matt murdered. But, as I already told you, I never saw Mace Jackson before and I don't know anything about him. Or anyone else who'd try to kill Kane or Matt."

"Some other information turned up today, possibly related. Kane may have been into some very high-stakes gambling. If he lost big, gambling creditors may have payback rules they enforce with guns."

Candy clunked the glass down hard on the counter as if she were about to argue. But then a light went on in her eyes. "That's what he was doing all those weekends he was gone, isn't it? Gambling in some casino over on the coast!"

"Could be." Cate suspected Candy was relieved to hear this and know it wasn't another woman who'd captured Kane's time and interest.

Candy tapped glossy fingernails on the counter. "I know he's been hurting for money."

"My understanding is that H&B here in Salem hasn't been profitable lately. That's why they were closing it. So he may have been short of money for that reason, in addition to gambling losses."

"Maybe a shortage of profits at H&B was *why* he was gambling. Because he needed money. As I told you, he did great with gambling on our honeymoon."

"Gambling isn't exactly a sure-thing investment. You can lose everything you have in casino gambling, I suppose. But the casinos are well regulated and controlled. I don't think they're going to let you gamble with an IOU. You have to have the money up front."

"You're saying Kane borrowed money from some loan shark? Or he was gambling somewhere outside the casinos and going in debt to do it? Something illegal? A bookie or someone like that?"

"I don't know much about illegal gambling or how you do it," Cate admitted. Bookies were well outside her experience. All she had was a mental picture, no doubt from some old movie, of a heavyset guy wearing suspenders, smoking a cigar, and talking out the side of his mouth. Candy's suggestion about a loan shark was something new. She hadn't considered that before. Loan sharks were also noted for a nasty attitude about nonpayers.

"But why kill him?" Candy demanded. "He was getting the money to pay them off."

Candy might be unhappy that Kane had sneaked around to gamble, but now she also sounded resentful that his gambling or loan creditors hadn't been more patient. Cate expected Candy to demand to know where she'd acquired information about Kane's gambling, but she was apparently so instantly convinced of his involvement that she didn't need details.

"Can you remember anything, maybe suspicious phone calls he made or received, anything that could have been contacts with a loan shark or some illegal gambling setup?"

"I don't remember anything from before we separated. And I wouldn't know about phone calls to the apartment where he lives now." Candy gave Cate a sideways glance. "But I have a key."

"To the apartment?"

"Kane took Clancy with him almost everywhere, but once he flew down to a big antique car auction, Phoenix or somewhere, and he gave me a key so I could go in and feed Clancy. Actually, when I got there, poor Clancy was so lonely

I brought him here. Kane never asked for the key back, so I still have it."

"So you're saying . . . ?"

Candy's eyes flashed a blue glitter of excitement. "We could go over and see if we can find something helpful about this gambling stuff!"

"Belmont Investigations doesn't do anything illegal, even if it might aid an investigation."

Candy rolled her eyes. "Don't be such a wimp. There wouldn't be anything illegal about this anyway. It isn't as if we'd be breaking in. Kane *gave* me a key. I've used it a couple of times."

Cate was curious about why Candy had used the key and what she'd been doing in her ex-husband's apartment.

As if Candy recognized a pending question, she added flatly, "And no, I'm not telling you why I was there. C'mon. We'll take the Lexus."

When Cate still sat there undecided, Candy dumped the remainder of her drink down the sink. "I'm going upstairs to change clothes. You think about it. If you want to find out who's threatening Matt, this is the place to start looking."

But going into someone's apartment . . . Cate was still mulling the idea after Candy went upstairs and the cell phone in her purse gave its guitar riff. She looked at the screen. Mitch? No, an unfamiliar number.

"Hello."

"Cate, hi. This is Seth Erickson. You talked to me earlier, out in the shop at H&B?"

"You thought of something more about Mr. Blakely or H&B?"

"I tried. I really, really tried. But to be honest, I'm as blank as that blue screen of death on a computer."

"So you're calling me because . . . ?"

"I'm thinking, if you're staying in Salem overnight, you have to eat dinner, right? So I'm also thinking we could have dinner together. Maybe a movie afterwards, to relax you from a hard day of private investigating."

Seth Erickson was asking her for a *date*? She considered the invitation briefly. No, she didn't consider actually accepting it. She and Mitch had their differences about her being a PI, but they had something strong going between them. Neither of them dated anyone else.

"That's really thoughtful of you, Seth. I appreciate the invitation. But no, I don't think so. I'm . . . involved."

"Oh. I should have guessed that, shouldn't I? Beautiful private investigators no doubt have their pick of law officers, detectives, FBI men, etc."

"You don't object to a woman being a private investigator?"

"Object?" Seth sounded surprised. "Why would I?"

"Sometimes dangerous situations are involved. Dangerous people. On my first case, two different people tried to kill me on the same day."

"Hey, awesome! I'd like to hear all about it."

Cate had to smile at the boyish eagerness that matched Seth's boyish-looking face. "Again I appreciate the invitation. But no. It's an important involvement."

"If you change your mind, just give me a call."

"Okay. Thanks, Seth. It was nice meeting you."

Cate was smiling when she slipped the phone back in her purse. No, she hadn't been tempted to go out with Seth Erickson. But at the same time, it gave her something to think about. Not all guys were as opposed to the investigative business for a woman as Mitch was.

She suddenly wanted to talk to Mitch again. *Needed* to talk to him. Right now. She clicked on his number.

As often seemed to happen, technology did not cooperate. It sent her to voice mail. She dropped the phone back in her purse as Candy returned to the family room and twirled in front of Cate.

"How do I look? Proper outfit for a PI . . . what's the word? Caper! Am I properly dressed for a PI caper?"

Skinny black jeans. Black turtleneck. Black scarf tied biker style to conceal her blonde hair. Stiletto-heeled black boots. Yeah, she looked ready for a PI caper. Or maybe a cat burglar jewel heist. Although those heels might be a liability. Then Cate remembered Candy's ability to do that impressive 180 in heels. The woman could probably scale walls or do Tarzan swings in high-heeled boots.

"Perfect," Cate finally said. Good thing they weren't headed out to investigate a strip club, or no telling what suitable attire Candy might have chosen.

20

Candy had been there before and did not have to wander around to find Kane's apartment. She drove straight to it and pulled around back to a cramped parking area. She pointed to a gray lump in a shadowy corner space.

"That's Kane's SUV."

The vehicle surprised Cate. No flash here. The old SUV looked as if it should have cat tracks on the hood and a "My son was Student of the Month" sticker on the bumper.

"But he'd rather drive one of the H&B restorations or his bike," Candy added. "He really liked that Corvette he drove down to Eugene. His bike must be out at H&B."

The apartment was in an older house divided into separate units. Kane's apartment, on the third floor, had an outside entrance reached by stairs that looked weather-beaten but solid. Even so, Cate stopped with one hand on the railing.

"You're not backing out now, are you?" Candy looked down from four steps above her.

No, Cate wasn't backing out now. Halliday's life was on the line, and she needed to find out who was after him. Which still didn't totally cancel the squeamishness she felt about prowling in someone's private residence. At the landing at the top of the stairs, Cate half-expected "do not cross" police tape blocking the door, but there was only a spiderweb.

Light spilled on the landing when Candy opened the door and reached inside to flick a switch. She stepped inside without hesitation, and Cate followed cautiously. The apartment smelled faintly musty, even though Kane hadn't been away from it all that long. The scent was almost like a foreshadowing of emptiness and disuse to come, as if the apartment didn't expect him back.

Dump it, Ms. PI, Cate scolded herself. *Get on with it. You're an investigator; stop smelling and start investigating.*

Burgundy drapes covered a skimpy window. A cream leather sofa faced a flat-screen TV, much smaller than the one at Candy's house. An L-shaped desk in a corner held a laptop. A two-drawer wooden file cabinet stood beside the desk. Pages of a local newspaper littered the floor, and papers and photos, some loose, some in wire baskets, covered the desk space around the laptop and the top of the file cabinet as well.

Only a counter separated the living room and kitchen, and a short hallway led to what was probably a bedroom and bath area. The kitchen sink and counter displayed dirty dishes. A TV dinner container stuck out of the top of a trash container. Cate sniffed. Maybe that was what she smelled. Aging trash. Two cabinet doors stood open. Not totally a rat-magnet kitchen, but it wouldn't win any housekeeping awards.

Candy planted her hands on her hips. "Kane needs a *wife*," she declared. "Where should we start?"

"With finding him a wife or finding something here?"

Candy rolled her eyes at the facetious question.

"Okay, what are we looking for?" Cate asked.

"You tell me. You're the private investigator," Candy snapped, as if this had all been Cate's idea. "I'll see if I can find anything back in the bedroom while you dig through stuff out here."

Cate approached the desk and started looking through the jumbled mess. She was tempted to organize and neaten the papers as she plowed through them, but she restrained herself from doing so. She didn't want to leave evidence they'd been here even though the entry was surely legal enough with Candy's key coming direct from Kane.

After a few minutes, she realized there was nothing personal among the scattered papers and photos. Everything had to do with projects for H&B. Vehicles available for restoration, past restorations, specifications for work in progress. Nothing about gambling or loan sharking.

Cate tried the file cabinet, but Kane didn't have any helpful folders labeled "Gambling" or "Loan Shark." A file labeled "Personal" held a disorganized collection of papers about the divorce from Candy, death certificate for Kane's first wife, a rental agreement on the apartment, and some medical information. She closed the file quickly. She really didn't want to know the details of Kane's hemorrhoids or an itchy skin condition.

He must have had considerable trouble with the SUV because there was a separate file labeled "Repair Shop," with some yellow receipts. Why didn't he just fix the vehicle himself, or have someone like Seth at H&B work on it? Lumps at the bottom of the file turned out to be a collection of crumbs, apparently fallen into the manila folder while Kane perused his car troubles.

Yes, Kane definitely needed a wife. Or at least a housekeeper. She closed the file cabinet and eyed the laptop. If Kane kept any gambling records, that must be where they were.

She turned the laptop on and at the same time heard clunks

and clatters from the rear of the apartment. She found Candy going through the medicine chest in the bathroom, tossing everything on the counter as she went. Band-Aids, Pepto-Bismol, various over-the-counter sleeping pills, allergy medication. She was now frowning at a half-empty bottle of generic aspirin.

"Kane never used aspirin. It upset his stomach. He always used acetaminophen or ibuprofen."

"So?" Cate asked, impatient with this triviality. "I doubt it has anything to do with his gambling or debts."

"It might mean someone else has been here with him."

Someone here in the apartment wolfing down aspirin and running a gambling operation? Unlikely. Then the truth dawned on her. Candy was thinking some other woman had been here in the apartment with Kane. Which was why she'd used the key to get in the apartment before. Then and now, she was snooping for signs of Kane and another woman. A definite ambivalence in her feelings about her ex-husband.

"If someone was here, and she was guzzling aspirin, it doesn't sound like the kind of relationship flaming romance novels are written about," Cate said.

"I'm not worried about Kane's love life! I'm just—" Candy broke off. Her small smile held embarrassment, but it also hinted at relief. "But I guess a half-empty bottle of aspirin doesn't suggest romantic interludes, does it?"

"I'm not sure how long we should be in here. Maybe you could concentrate on looking for something to do with gambling or debts, something like that?"

"Okay. Sure." Candy's tone went grumpy. "I was just looking in the medicine cabinet because, well, you never know where a man may hide something."

Candy flounced out and started thunking drawers in the

bedroom. Cate went back to the laptop. And found, of course, exactly what she feared. Kane had the laptop set up to require a password. Why did the man need a password? He was the only one here to use the laptop.

Unless, of course, there *was* some aspirin-gulping woman friend here. Or maybe he needed the laptop to work a complicated gambling system? And he wasn't about to have some unauthorized user steal his system? She tried various password possibilities. Kane. Blakely. Kane and Blakely together. H&B. Candy. Clancy.

"What's Kane's birth date?" she called to Candy.

"Why?"

"I'm trying to figure out a password on the laptop."

Candy came out of the bedroom and looked over Cate's shoulder at the screen. She gave a September date, and Cate typed it in. The laptop was unimpressed.

"Any other ideas?" Cate asked. "Maybe a password he used for something else? Some people stick with the same one for everything."

Candy shook her head. "It must be here somewhere. Kane didn't have that good a memory. Maybe the file cabinet?"

Cate had already been in the file. No passwords. What she needed was Mitch. Mitch and his computer expertise. He'd figure some way to do this.

Cate tried a few more guess words and numbers she'd heard were common passwords, but she finally gave up. She turned the laptop off. There was a drawer below the computer that she hadn't looked in yet. She opened it and poked around. Receipts, paper clips, stamps—hey, an address book.

Cate skimmed through it. Friends? Clients? It was a long-used book apparently, because addresses and numbers had been crossed out and new ones written in. Cate would like to make a copy of the pages, but Blakely hadn't conveniently outfitted his home office with a copier.

Candy came out of the bedroom, shaking dust off her hands and grumbling that all she'd found were boxes of old-car magazines under Kane's bed and a full dirty-clothes hamper.

"He must not have done laundry in a month," Candy fussed. Cate couldn't tell if she was disgusted or worried. Then she spotted the address book in Cate's hands. "Let me see that!"

Candy grabbed the address book and scrutinized it.

"Hey, I know her." She stabbed a name in the book. "Diane Reed. Has Kane been seeing *her*?"

Cate reached to take the address book back, but Candy held it out of reach. "I'm taking this," she declared.

"Candy, you cannot take Kane's personal, private address book out of his apartment. Even if you have a key."

"I can make a copy and bring it right back."

Cate had to admit to being momentarily tempted by that idea. She'd like to have a list of Blakely's contacts. But she firmly nixed it. "No. Morally, ethically, legally *wrong*. We just came here to look, not to take anything." She wrestled the book out of Candy's hand and jammed it back in the drawer. "C'mon. Let's go."

Cate thought Candy might argue, but she did her heel-spin and went to the door. They turned off the lights, locked the door, and tromped down to the Lexus. Cate remembered something she hadn't seen in the apartment. A dog bed. Which no doubt meant Clancy sacked out on the sofa or the foot of Kane's bed. The lump of vehicle in the shadows caught Cate's eye again. An unexpected thought jumped out at her.

"Is the SUV running?"

"As far as I know. It's kind of an old beater, and a little low profile for Kane's taste, so he only uses it when he's hauling something around. Why?"

"There was a folder in his file cabinet for a repair shop. I thought it was about repairs for the SUV."

"I can't imagine Kane taking a car to some repair shop. He'd do it himself or have someone at H&B do it."

"Let's go back up to the apartment."

"Why?" Candy glanced over at her with interest. "PI intuition?"

"Maybe."

What Cate thought of as her "inner PI" did sometimes toss out something useful. Was this one of those times? Maybe!

Back in the apartment, it wasn't the laptop Cate headed for. Instead she opened the bottom drawer on the file cabinet and yanked out the "Repair Shop" file. Too hurried to be cautious now, she dumped the contents on the desk clutter.

There were the receipts she'd seen earlier, all from some place called Pete's Econo-Rite Parts and Repairs, with the motto "Always right at Econo-Rite, right parts, right price!" At least they were made up to look like ordinary receipts. But were they?

Because there were also scribbled letters and figures on the back of a yellow receipt. WSU—UW 2,000. PS 3. With a line slashed through it.

And many more similar notations of letters and numbers. An exclamation point rather than a slashed line followed a few notations.

Meaningless, unless you put a certain interpretation on them.

"What's it about?" Candy asked.

"I think it's college football games. With how much Kane bet on each one. This first one is Washington State University versus University of Washington." Cate studied the figures a little more. "I think the slash means his two-thousand-dollar bet was bad. He lost. An exclamation point shows he won."

The record-keeping was cryptic, definitely not something meant for the IRS. Slashes heavily outnumbered exclamation points, perhaps an indication of how Kane got $30,000, or more, in debt.

"But I have no idea what the PS and a number means," Cate added.

"Point spread," Candy informed her. "Most of the time, betting isn't just on who wins or loses, but on how much difference there is between the scores."

Cate looked up at her.

Candy shrugged. "My boss and his friends have an occasional betting pool. It usually involves point spreads. Or sometimes they have really dumb bets, like whether some new secretary's boobs are real or who's going to catch the biggest fish on some fishing trip."

Cate didn't see anything like the "dumb" bets Candy mentioned, but not all the betting was on college games. Some of the initials suggested professional teams. And he'd bet $1,000 on something called Dingbat. With a slash through it. The name of a horse in a race? A slow horse with an appropriate name, apparently.

Candy had been looking over Cate's shoulder, and finally she said, "You're thinking Kane was placing bets at this Pete's place?"

Cate didn't answer with an instant yes. It was possible the receipts for vehicle repairs and the betting weren't connected. Kane's messy filing system might put actual repair receipts in with his peculiar form of record keeping on his bets, and they were separate matters entirely.

"Although I guess a car repair place would be a good front for an illegal gambling setup, wouldn't it?" Candy said thoughtfully.

"One way to find out," Cate said.

Candy turned a yellow receipt over so they could both see the address. She pushed up the sleeve of her black turtleneck to look at her watch. "It's close to nine o'clock. A repair shop wouldn't be open this time of evening."

But if it *wasn't* just a repair shop . . .

Cate repeated what she'd just said. "Only one way to find out."

21

Cate used her cell phone to find the exact location of the street. Candy drove that direction as if her gas-pedal foot had suddenly developed a debilitating affliction.

"You think this is a good idea, just the two of us going out to this place alone?" Candy asked as they turned a corner at tricycle speed.

"What did you have in mind? Asking your next-senator friend to go along?"

"Don't be ridiculous."

Agreed. Which didn't keep Cate from again wishing Mitch were here to go along.

Pete's Econo-Rite Parts and Repairs, the name painted in red on a wooden sign across the front of a nondescript concrete block building, was in a commercial area of similar businesses. A tire shop stood on one side, and a tavern blinked a purple sign in the shape of a bubbling cocktail on the other. Parking areas separated the buildings, no sidewalks.

Two roll-up doors on Pete's Econo-Rite building were large enough for truck-sized vehicles. Cartoonish vehicles painted on the front windows blocked out all but a few chinks of light. Nothing indicated the business was open for customers, but several vehicles occupied the parking spots along the side of the building. Candy pulled into a smaller parking area up front.

"Well, here we are." Candy's hands tightened on the steering wheel, a protective clutch that suggested she feared some wrench-wielding mechanic might rush out and start removing parts from her Lexus. In spite of her snazzy spy outfit, her enthusiasm for investigation appeared to have fizzled. "Be careful."

"You don't want to go in with me?"

"I don't know anything about this kind of thing. I might say something that would mess things up." Candy's fingers flexed on the wheel as she smoothly rationalized what she didn't want to do. "I'll keep the engine running in case you need to make a quick getaway."

Cate suspected that if a quick getaway were needed, she'd find herself smelling burned rubber while Candy spun out on her own.

Cate slid out of the car and approached the door. The knob turned in her hand. She hesitated. What was her game plan here? She couldn't just start throwing out incriminating questions about gambling. Okay, this was, supposedly anyway, a car-parts store. She needed a part for her car.

Inside, her quick glance took in a counter, cash register, shelves of air filters, oil filters, various brands of oil, spark plugs, and windshield wipers. All normal looking for a car-parts store. A fiftyish man in jeans, plaid shirt, and heavy boots clomped through an open door to a back room. Cate heard voices and laughter, but she couldn't tell if they came from actual people or a TV.

"Can I help you?"

"I'm lucky to find you open! Most car parts places are closed by now."

"We try to accommodate our customers. And you need . . . ?"

Nerves suddenly jumbled Cate's thinking. Maybe this was exactly what it looked like. A not-too-prosperous parts store and repair shop, and her suspicions were foolish. But then, maybe it was all a staged setting, phony as a cavalry-and-Indians chase in a Hollywood Western. And outsiders who got too nosy might find themselves migrating to the top of a hit list?

She eyed the shelves again. "A spark plug," she said brightly. "I need a spark plug."

"*One* spark plug?"

"No, I need, um, spark *plugs*. However many it takes for a car."

"What kind of car?"

A semi-panicky blankness emptied her head. She should have asked for something more generic. Windshield washer stuff. Car polish. Too late. She was already into spark plugs. "Honda, four-door sedan." She named a year.

"Four or six cylinder?"

She surprised herself by actually knowing the answer to that. A smidgen of confidence returned. "Four."

The man reached up high in the spark plug area. He returned with four spark plugs and rang up the sale. She paid and received change. The man put the spark plugs in a plastic bag with the store name and motto on it. She'd probably need spark plugs someday, she decided philosophically, so it wasn't wasted money.

"Anything else?" he inquired.

Cate stood by the counter, trying to think where to go with this, when he surprised her with a tentative-sounding question.

"Did someone . . . recommend us?"

Her interior antennae pricked to attention. Was he asking if someone had recommended them for car parts and repair work—or for something else?

"Yes, a terrific recommendation!" Cate put all the watts she could gather into a smile. "He said you had great repairs and parts. And sometimes offered, you know, games? Entertainment? For while a customer was waiting?"

"I'm not sure what you mean. We used to have some video game machines, but I took them out a while back."

"I was thinking maybe something . . . more profitable?"

His eyes squinted, as if he were assessing *profitable*. "Sometimes we get a poker game going. A few of the guys got a game going right now." He jerked a thumb toward the open door, then gave her a conspiratorial grin. "But don't tell my wife. She thinks we play pinochle."

"You're Pete?" When he nodded, Cate took a little gamble herself. "You could make bets on pinochle too, couldn't you?"

"Yeah, but pinochle's a women's afternoon game. You know, bunch of old ladies get together and have tea and crumpets and gossip. Men like poker. Of course, we don't bet much. Five-dollar limit."

"Women like to gamble too," Cate said, "On poker. Or . . . you know . . . sports events? Races? Something with a little more excitement?" She felt as if they were in a verbal ping-pong match, cautiously batting words back and forth to feel each other out. Feeling as if she were tossing out bait, maybe dangerous bait, she added, "But I'd like to bet more than five dollars."

"Yeah?" He looked her up and down now as if assessing the extent of her assets. And probably doubting, correctly, that she had any. "What kind of poker you like?"

There were different kinds of poker? Uh-oh. In over her head. She'd never played any kind of poker. The further she got into the PI business, the more subjects seemed to turn up that she knew nothing about. "Oh, all kinds," she faked airily.

"You don't look like a poker player."

Cate could see him now assessing her red hair and the sprinkle of freckles across her nose. She should have added some makeup, something that said "this is a real poker playing, gambling woman."

He laughed. "But with our luck, you'd turn up a royal flush and we'd all lose our socks."

Royal flush. Somehow she doubted he was talking about a blushing queen of England. She decided she'd better try to back out of this gracefully before he knew she was bluffing about gambling and was actually snooping for information.

"Who is this person who recommended us?" Pete asked with a sudden edge to his friendly banter.

Probably she should make up a name, something totally fictitious. But this was what she'd come to find out. Cautiously she said, "I think his name was Mace something. A big guy, ponytail, tattoos of skulls on his knuckles." She made a fingertip movement across the front of her own hand.

"I have no idea who Mace Something is, but he doesn't sound like anyone I'd want to get into a friendly poker game with."

Pete could be lying, of course, faking a relaxed answer, even if he knew exactly who Mace Jackson was. But Cate's sometimes-working inner PI told her Mace Jackson really wasn't in Pete's memory bank and the name *had* relaxed him.

"Enjoy your spark plugs," he added cheerfully.

Quick, hoping his guard was down, she threw out another name.

"If it wasn't Mace, then it must have been someone else. Maybe Kane Blakely?"

If she hadn't been looking directly at him, she wouldn't have seen the reaction. Because it wasn't much. Just a momentary flicker in his eyes, a minuscule tightening of mouth.

He shook his head, which told her that even if he recognized the name, and she was certain he did, the name had closed, not opened, doors.

"Hey, would you look at the time?" He glanced at a plain round clock on a side wall. A red second hand moved in quick jerks. "I should have closed up a long time ago."

He didn't touch her, but he definitely herded her toward the door. It burst open before they reached it.

"Hey, Pete, am I too late to put fifty on—"

"Wes, don't tell me that old Chevy is giving you trouble again?"

The guy stopped short, his expression puzzled, but then he glanced at Cate and some light apparently went on in his head. He smiled at Pete.

"Yeah, the ol' clunker sounds like a load of ball bearings going through a washin' machine. I keep you in business buying parts for it, don't I?"

"My favorite customer," Pete agreed. To Cate he said politely, "Have a nice day." Then, "A little piece of advice?"

"Uh . . . okay."

The smile was gone now. "I know kids your age go looking for fun and excitement. Maybe your friends heard something and elected you to come in and check us out here. But looking for some big betting action is a bad idea. A really lousy idea. You could get in real trouble. Hanging around with some guy with skulls tattooed on his knuckles is bad news too. And find yourself a guy your own age, not someone like—"

Cate was almost certain he'd started to say "like Kane Blakely," but he changed it to, "Not someone way older than you."

In a rough kind of way, the advice sounded almost fatherly. Like Beer Can Man at Andy Timmons's apartment, Pete thought she was younger than she was. Younger and foolishly looking for excitement and fun. Which meant he had no idea she was a private investigator working on a case. Relief zapped through her. "Oh. Well, uh, thanks."

Cate went back out to the Lexus. She wasn't running. In fact, her movements felt as jerky as the second hand on that clock. But she'd no more than slid into the car than Candy shot out of the parking area like a bullet on wheels. Nothing wrong with her foot action now.

They were a mile away before Candy finally slowed and Cate could ask, "What was *that* for?"

"You had this funny look on your face. An I've-just-seen-a-ghost look."

"I didn't see any ghosts."

"So?"

Cate held up her plastic sack. "So I bought some spark plugs."

"That's it?" Now that they were safely away from the danger zone, Candy's attitude turned incredulous. And scornful. "That's all Matt's hotshot assistant private investigator can come up with, spark plugs? Oh, wow. Let's party."

Cate managed not to throw said spark plugs at Candy. Candy was, after all, driving. "I mentioned Kane's name. I'm pretty sure the guy recognized it. And that guy who came in as I was leaving? He was there to place a bet. They tried to make me think otherwise, but I'm sure of it."

"I wonder how these things operate. I mean, do they pay off

a big win with their own money? Or is this part of something bigger, like a gambling syndicate thing?"

"I don't know. Bigger, I think."

Bigger and meaner, and willing to use a gun to protect their territory from deadbeats who didn't pay their gambling debts.

They drove a few more blocks before Candy said, "What about Mace Jackson? Did you try his name?"

"I did, but I don't think his name or my description of him meant anything to the guy I talked to. Except he advised me I shouldn't be hanging out with that type of person."

"How sweet of him."

"He also told me I shouldn't be going around looking for fun in all the wrong places. And to find a guy my own age. I think he was referring to Kane."

"You must bring out some dormant protective-male instinct." The statement did not sound complimentary, although Candy finally added, "I suppose that could be useful as a PI."

Cate ignored the comments and considered the past few minutes. She was reasonably certain some kind of illegal gambling was happening at Pete's Econo-Rite Parts and Repairs, something more than backroom poker. But would a guy who seemed honestly concerned about a young woman's welfare also sic a killer on someone who owed a gambling debt?

"I don't think he hired Mace Jackson to kill Kane."

"So now what?"

Yeah, now what? Cate could go to the police and tell them she thought an illegal gambling operation was going on at Pete's Econo-Rite Parts and Repairs. She could picture the reaction.

Did you place bets there?

Well, no, but—

Do you know someone who placed bets there?

Not for sure, but I think—

So, young lady, what makes you think this is some sort of undercover gambling establishment?

Cate could give them reasons. She thought Pete recognized Kane's name, and Kane was a gambler. A guy rushed into the store, and she was almost certain he was there to place a last-minute bet on something.

Thank you for the information, Ms. Not-yet-fully-licensed-PI, but I think we'll need more than that before we get a search warrant and start battering down their door.

Okay, maybe she needed something more solid before she went to the police.

At the house, Candy turned the Lexus into the driveway and pushed the control clamped on the sun visor to raise the garage door. Cate reached for the door handle so she could get out and go to her own car parked at the curb.

Candy tapped the steering wheel. "Do you want something to eat before you go?"

Although Cate hadn't until then thought anything about food or missing dinner, her stomach rumbled a comment.

"I guess we could go somewhere for a burger or something," she said.

"I have ham and eggs and cheese in the fridge. We could make an omelet. Kane said that if he hadn't married me for other reasons, he'd have married me just for the omelets."

"An omelet sounds great."

The kitchen was oversized, of course. With cabinets of some exotic wood, six-burner stove, oversized refrigerator, and a lineup of every kitchen appliance known to man. Or woman. Cate eyed a contraption with a metal funnel-like thing on top and a clear, square box below.

"What's that?"

"It's a snow cone machine. That thing next to it is a combination pressure cooker, rice cooker, and slow cooker. The next thing is a soymilk maker."

Making soymilk had never occurred to Cate, let alone buying a machine to do it.

"You keep all this equipment out because you use these things regularly?"

"I had a brief-lived housewifey era and bought all this stuff. It's all sitting out now because I *don't* ever use any of it. I was always afraid the pressure cooker might explode, and the only time I tried to make tofu in that wooden mold, we were picking wood slivers out of our teeth. Anyway, I thought maybe I could get a few bucks selling everything. Or just give it all away, if I have to. You want something? Maybe that bread-making machine or that chocolate fountain?"

"No, I don't think so. But thanks."

Candy gave Cate the job of chopping green onions and grating cheddar cheese. She waved at a couple of appliances that would probably chop and grate anything up to and including granite blocks, but Cate chose to use the old-fashioned hand method.

The Persian, silvery-gray, with the trademark flat face of Persians, joined them. Candy said her name was Scheherazade. The cat caged a smidgen of ham out of Candy. Cate expected the cat to turn down her own offering of a bite of cheese, but Scheherazade accepted it with queenly grace.

Candy laughed. "She may look like royalty, but she's really a garbage-can alley cat at heart."

Candy thawed blueberry muffins from the freezer to accompany the omelet and made a pot of some fragrant tea, deep fuschia colored when she poured it into cups.

Before eating, Cate took time at the table for a moment of silent thanks. When she opened her eyes, Candy was looking at her curiously.

"A hotshot private eye is into blessings and prayers?" Candy commented.

"Believers come in all shapes, sizes, and occupations."

Candy didn't comment further, but her head-tilted expression looked thoughtful.

"Mmm, what is this?" Cate asked after sipping her cup of tea. She tasted hints of raspberry and blueberries, cherries and grapes, maybe something tropical too. "It's so good."

"It's a sangria rooibos and hibiscus blend. I buy it online, specially blended for me."

"Oh." Exotic tea. Another subject about which Cate was grossly ignorant. Mitch usually preferred coffee, but even he might like this.

"But this is the last of it, and I can't afford to buy any more once this is gone," Candy added gloomily.

"I appreciate your making some of it tonight."

The omelet was indeed the-way-to-his-heart delicious. Candy seemed to have temporarily put aside her hostility toward Cate for working for Matt Halliday, and their late-supper talk was about cats and tea and the potted plants by the living room window.

Finally Cate drained the last of her second cup of tea. She stood and picked up her plate. "I'll help clean up before I go."

"You're driving back to Eugene tonight?"

Cate made the quick decision that yes, she was driving home. Motels tended to make her uneasy, and it would probably take her as long to find and get settled in one she felt comfortable with as it would to drive home. She could make an early trip back up to Salem in the morning. Octavia would be glad to have her home too. She nodded to answer Candy's question. "So I'd better get going."

"But you still have work to do here, don't you?"

"I'll come back tomorrow and try to find out more about Mace Jackson."

After a moment's hesitation, as if she wasn't too sure she wanted to do this, Candy finally said, "You could stay here. There's plenty of room. No need to drive all that way."

The invitation surprised Cate. She doubted Candy cared enough about social politeness, at least where Cate was concerned, to make the invitation out of courtesy.

So her instant question was why? Did Candy have some ulterior motive? As if Candy guessed Cate wasn't about to jump on this with glee, she grabbed their plates and went to the sink with them. Her booted step had a hint of stomp in it.

"Look, I'm not inviting you to a BFF slumber party. And I'm not going to sneak in and smother you with a pillow in the night. It's just a place to stay. You'll have to make your own breakfast. I don't do breakfast."

Scheherazade took that moment to stroll over and wind herself around Cate's ankles.

"See? Even Zadie wants you to stay. If you leave your door open, she'll probably come sleep with you. She likes to make guests feel welcome."

Cate reached down and picked up the silky-haired cat. Who could resist an invitation to a room that included cat company? "Okay, thanks. That's very nice of you. Both of you," she added with a snuggle of cat to cheek.

Cate went out to move her car into the driveway and get her overnight case out of the trunk. Candy showed her to a second-floor bedroom with bath toward the rear of the house. Queen-sized bed with luxurious orchid comforter and enough pillows for her and any number of cats.

Before she went to bed, she called Mitch and gave him a quick rundown on the evening, ending with, "Tomorrow I'll talk to some more bicycle shops."

He gave her his usual "be careful" admonition, then told her about running with Clancy in the park and having dinner with Lance and Robyn. Yes, they'd heard from the company again after making the counteroffer. The company wanted further details.

"But it's looking good. I think they really want Computer Dudes," Mitch said. "So, I'll see you tomorrow?"

"I'm not sure what time I'll get back."

"I miss you." Moment of silence. "I'm thinking maybe we should . . ."

Cate waited, but whatever Mitch was thinking, he apparently decided he didn't want to continue with it now.

Cate continued it after she was snuggled in bed.

I'm thinking we should get engaged and start planning a big wedding?

I'm thinking we should elope and have a quick wedding without any fuss?

Or maybe it was something more prosaic.

I'm thinking we should take Clancy to the coast some weekend. I'm thinking we should try that new pizza Abby's is advertising. I'm thinking we should see Johnny Depp's new movie.

Or maybe it was, *I'm thinking we should recognize this is never going to work with you being a PI, and when the deal on Computer Dudes goes through, we'll just go our separate ways.*

❖ 22 ❖

Cate uneasily drifted off to sleep. Sometime in the night Scheherazade slipped through the door Cate had left cracked open and curled up behind her knees. She was still there in the morning, but she disappeared while Cate was showering. No doubt with a satisfied "my work here is done" swish of tail.

Candy stood by the counter finishing a cup of black coffee, no food visible, when Cate went down to the kitchen. Scheherazade was washing a hind leg.

"Coffee's made." Candy motioned to a coffeemaker that looked sleek and sophisticated enough to make secret weapons in its spare time. Today Candy wore a peach suit, short skirt, long jacket. No nonsense, but feminine and figure flattering.

"I have to get going," she said. "Mark likes to start early, and there's an important land use bill coming up today. Help yourself to anything in the fridge or pantry. Lock the door when you leave."

"Okay. Thanks for everything."

"If you decide to spend another night in Salem, you can stay here again."

"Thanks, but I'm definitely going home today."

"Look, if you hear anything about Kane's condition, would

you give me a call? The ex-wife apparently isn't entitled to know anything, and Matt sure isn't going to tell me what's going on. If Kane's released from the hospital, I could come down and get him." She paused and reflected for a moment. "If he needs care, he could stay here for a while."

Not if Shirley got to him first, Cate suspected. "Sure, I'll call."

Candy left for work carrying a different Coach bag than the pink one Cate had seen before. She found a granola-type mixture in the pantry, with a label from some health food store, and filled a bowl with the crunchy stuff for breakfast. Upstairs, she made sure the sink was clean. Scheherazade, her hostess duties fulfilled, had gone off to do whatever the schedule of the day was for a Persian princess.

Cate got a quick listing of more bicycle shops with her phone and headed for the closest one. No information about Mace Jackson there, but a bulletin board held flyers and a list of bicycle events from all around the state. The number and variety surprised Cate. Road races, track races, off-road races. Races for seniors, kids, and everyone in between. Sprints, long-distance races, races on mountain trails. A whole world of events Cate had never realized existed.

On to the next shop. There she approached one of the two clerks when he finished with a customer. He was young and lean, with a baseball cap turned backward on shaggy hair. There were racks of sleek biking clothes, but he wore baggy khaki shorts and a black T-shirt with a monster-sized bicycle ridden by a squirrel emblazoned on the front. Hmm. Secret symbolism or just odd taste? He shook his head at the Mace Jackson name and description Cate offered. But he gave her the location of a bigger shop that carried all kinds of bikes and gear and catered to racing enthusiasts, and Cate moved on.

This place, the Complete Biker, fit its name, Cate decided the moment she walked in.

More bicycles than she'd ever seen in one place before. She didn't know a mountain bike from a road race bike, but none of these remotely resembled the $20 secondhand bike she'd ridden as a kid. Some of the prices made her blink. She smiled when she saw the tandem bikes for two people. They looked like fun. Mitch? Maybe. Though he was really fond of his high-powered Purple Rocket. As she was too, she had to admit.

She wandered on to the clothing section. Socks, dozens of different kinds. Arm covers, pads for knees, shins, and elbows, giving a hint that bicycle riding might have some rough edges. Gloves, both whole hand and fingerless.

Cate hadn't identified herself as a PI in the other bicycle shops, but here she handed a business card to the young woman who came over with a usual, "May I help you?"

The woman looked at both sides of the card as if she thought the back side might have explanatory information. "You're not law enforcement?"

"No, I'm working on a private investigation. I'm trying to find someone who knows a guy named Mace Jackson."

"We have a customer database, but I don't think we can give out information from it."

"I don't know that he's a customer. I do know he placed second in a bicycle race here in Salem a couple months ago, a fifty miler. I was hoping someone might know local bicycle racers and remember him."

"That would probably have been the Winter Fun Run. I wasn't in that one." She smiled. "Actually, I was in the hospital having a baby."

"A baby two months ago?" The woman's midsection, a

sliver of skin visible between short top and slim jeans, looked racehorse hard and lean. No post-baby fat here.

"I'll be racing again by next month." Definitely a poster girl for the benefits of bicycle racing. "But, you know, I think Mark rode in that race." She spotted a guy over in the bicycle section and waved him over. "Hey, you rode in the Winter Fun Run, didn't you?"

"Yeah." Young guy. Also lean and hard. This was definitely a no-fat zone. "If you call coming in nineteenth being in it. I might as well have ridden my little brother's tricycle that day."

Cate again offered Mace Jackson's name, again got a negative shake of head. She added the description.

"Hey, yeah, I do remember that dude! Everyone else was wearing gloves that day. It was, like, arctic cold. But not him. Proving how tough he was, I guess. And I sure noticed those knuckles."

The woman clerk zeroed in on something else in how Cate had described the man. "He *was* about forty . . . ?"

"He's dead. He tried to rob a business and shot a man in Eugene not long ago, and he was then shot and killed by the business owner. Now there has been a threat against that businessman. I need to find out more about Mace Jackson."

The male clerk shook his head. "None of the guys I ride with knew him. He didn't have much of a bike, and I figured he was no competition. But he rode like he was on a two-wheeled tank and didn't care if he mowed you down with it. We were calling him Knuckles." He gave a wry smile. "Not to his face, of course. He looked like he wouldn't mind giving you a noseful of those knuckles."

Odd that the kind of guy Mace Jackson seemed to be had acquired an interest in bicycle racing. The well-rounded killer?

Maybe he was a secret ballet aficionado too. "You never saw him at any other races?"

"No, but he was in here not too long ago. I wouldn't have recognized or remembered him, except for those skulls. He was looking at racing bikes. He said he wanted the best on the market. I remember thinking he wasn't happy with wherever he placed in the Winter Run."

Cate nodded. "Did he buy a bicycle?" she asked, hopefully thinking she might be able to pry an address out of the database.

"No. He seemed really interested in our highest-priced racing bike and wrote down the brand and model. I figured he didn't have the money, but he said our prices were too high. Although he had one of our coupons from the newspaper and bought something. Socks, I think."

A bargain-shopping, coupon-clipping killer. While Cate was still digesting that, the clerk added a zinger.

"He said he could get a better deal on a racing bike down in Eugene."

"We can beat anyone's price." The woman sounded indignant.

Cate had assumed Mace Jackson had gone to Eugene specifically to rob and/or kill Kane Blakely. But if he'd instead gone there to buy a racing bicycle, how had he come to park his old bicycle at H&B and burst in with a gun? Even if he'd decided he needed a quick source of money to buy a bike, how did he know a significant amount of cash would be available at H&B that night?

"I haven't been able to find that he owned a vehicle," Cate said. "Would he ride whatever bike he owned all the way down there?"

"Sure. Why not? I've been in a couple of hundred-miler races."

This would explain how Mace Jackson was managing to get by without a driver's license. She still didn't know what ID he'd had on him that the police used to identify him, but she'd looked on the internet again and was reasonably certain he didn't have a driver's license. Had his driving privileges been revoked? But in that case, surely she'd have run across that information. Unless his legal name was something other than Mace. Or he'd lost the driver's license in another state. Maybe he was even wanted somewhere else? A good reason for keeping a low profile by using bicycle transportation? The police had surely taken his fingerprints. Had they turned up a different name for him? If so, they conveniently hadn't shared that information publicly.

"Did he have friends in that Winter Run race? Like a group riding together, or someone he seemed to be buddies with?"

"I think he was pretty much a loner. When he was in here, I didn't mention the race and that I remembered him from it."

"Was there a registration sign-up for the race?"

"Yeah, sure, there always is."

"Maybe someone I could contact who'd know more about him?"

The two clerks discussed it for several minutes and finally settled on a name: Danielle Stevens. Some other people had probably helped, but Danielle had been running things that day. She probably had a list of entrants somewhere, to be used for notification of new events.

Great! "Where do I find Danielle?"

Somewhere between Oregon and Florida. On a bicycle. Danielle and her new husband were on their honeymoon. With backpacks filled with lists of old entrants in Eugene bicycle races? Not likely.

Sometimes Cate wondered if this was how a rat stuck in

a maze felt. Running full speed, looking for openings and more often smacking into blank walls.

Cate spent a couple more hours in Salem, but all she accomplished was buying a couple of DVDs at a store having a sale next to another bicycle shop that had gone out of business.

◆◆◆

Cate got home by midafternoon, feeling as if she'd been away much longer than overnight. She found Octavia snoozing on a high perch out in her playroom. The cat looked down on Cate with one of her blue-eyed, "do I know you?" stares, cat punishment for abandonment. But when Cate coaxed, she finally deigned to come down and snuggle a bit.

Cate called Mitch to let him know she was home, and he picked her up at 6:00 to go out for the Wednesday night special on spaghetti and meatballs at an Italian restaurant they liked. In the SUV, Clancy's wagging tail and slobbery tongue gave her VIP welcome.

"Hey, he has a different collar."

"Yeah, I don't like that studded one. It has too much of a my-dog-can-whup-your-dog look."

"It was kind of macho," Cate agreed. This leather collar was big and masculine looking, definitely not lap-dog style, but gentlemanly masculine.

The spaghetti and meatballs were spicy delicious, and the garlic bread buttery soft. Cate told Mitch what she'd learned in Salem about Kane Blakely and gambling, and Mace Jackson and bicycles. She did not tell him about Seth Erickson's dinner and movie invitation. Since the Computer Dudes deal seemed to be rolling toward completion, she was ever more uncertain about her relationship with Mitch. But she would not go the cheap route of trying to make him jealous.

Back home, Cate asked if Mitch and Clancy would like to come in and watch one of the new DVDs she'd picked up in Salem. There was the usual confrontation between Octavia and Clancy before they could start watching the movie, although this seemed more like a formality than passion-felt hostility. Cate had just opened the DVD carton when a frantic banging on the door stopped her. She peeked through the peephole first and then yanked the door open.

"Shirley! What—"

"I just came from the hospital. Kane is *dead*."

"Oh, Shirley, I'm so sorry." Cate pulled the woman inside. Uneasily she had to ask, "A normal death? Or . . . ?"

"He never came out of the coma. No one did anything to him. He just *died*. His son was there."

"I'm so sorry," Cate repeated, feeling that helplessness that death so often brings. "Did you talk to the son?"

"I just happened to run into him out in the parking lot. I asked him how Kane was doing, and he said he'd been in there 'finalizing things.' So I asked what that meant, and he told me Kane died this morning."

There was no good way to break news of a death, of course, but it sounded as if Kane's son had been particularly unfeeling about this announcement to Shirley.

"I asked about services, but he's having the body shipped to California for burial. That's where Kane's first wife, the son's mother, is buried, and Kane will be buried beside her. No services here or there. All of which took Warren about three sentences to say, and then he walked off."

Blakely's son was under no obligation to tell Shirley anything about Kane, of course. He didn't know any relationship between them existed and might have been even more unfriendly if he had known.

Actually, Cate reflected, there *wasn't* any real relationship, only what Shirley had hoped for.

"It's almost like . . . he never was." Shirley dropped to the sofa and rubbed a hand across her eyes. It came away with a smidgen of wetness, but no big flood of tears. Clancy came over and laid his big head on her leg.

"His son didn't even seem particularly upset. More like having to come here was some big inconvenience. Somebody ought to care more than that!"

Cate patted Shirley's shoulder. "You did all you could."

"But somehow I feel more . . . let down than sad," Shirley admitted.

Cate heard a hint of guilt in the words, as if Shirley thought she ought to feel worse. She repeated what even to her own ears sounded like a banal platitude. "You did all you could."

Shirley's slumped shoulders straightened and she asked an unexpected question. "I wonder if his ex-wife knows? I don't think Kane's son would ever bother telling her. Maybe not Mr. Halliday either."

"I saw her while I was up in Salem. I just got back from there this afternoon. She asked me to let her know if there was any news about Kane. So I'll do that."

Mitch cleared his throat. So far he hadn't said anything, but now, with an uncomfortable glance at Cate, he asked Shirley, "What about Clancy?"

Shirley looked down as if only then realizing the dog's head was still on her leg, and her hand was absentmindedly stroking him. "I'd take him, but I can't because of the trailer park regulations. But Jerry might do it. I'll ask him."

"I could keep him," Mitch said. He strengthened the statement. "I'd *like* to keep him."

"You would?" Shirley looked surprised. Cate wasn't. She'd

seen Mitch's attachment to the big hairy animal growing day by day. "But I thought he was a real inconvenience for you."

"We've kind of gotten used to each other."

"Then I'd say, just keep him." Shirley nodded firmly. "Kane's son isn't going to care."

"I'd rather be sure. I wouldn't want something to come up later about him."

After thinking about it for a moment, Shirley said, "Mr. Halliday must know how to get in touch with Warren."

"I'm going out to H&B in the morning. I want to give Mr. Halliday a report on my trip to Salem. I can ask him then," Cate said quickly.

"Good. I'd appreciate that." Mitch ruffled the dog's shaggy hair. "Is there anything we can do to help you?" he added to Shirley.

"No, I'm okay. Jerry's coming over this evening. My kitchen sink faucet went bad, and he's going to fix it. Maybe I'll see you out at H&B tomorrow," she added to Cate.

Cate nodded, and another plan for tomorrow also plunked into her head.

23

After Shirley went home, Cate called Candy. Candy didn't burst into tears when she heard the news about her ex-husband, but neither was her reaction indifferent. Her voice went scratchy, and Cate suspected tears would come later. Cate passed along the third-hand information she had about Kane being buried next to his first wife but no services. Candy just muttered, "Typical Warren."

"If I hear anything more, I'll let you know," Cate said.

"Thanks. I guess I should tell you something."

"Oh?"

"I went back over to Kane's apartment today and got that address book. I wanted to know about his girlfriends." Candy's statement held a note of challenge, as if daring Cate to object to her taking the address book, but then her voice wilted. "Which seems . . . kind of sleazy now that he's dead, doesn't it?"

"I guess it doesn't matter now."

"What I thought I should tell you is that I found a name in there that really floored me. Marilee."

"As in Matt Halliday's ex-wife? That Marilee?"

"It doesn't have a last name with it, so it could be a different Marilee. But I don't think so."

"Why would Kane have her phone number?"

"That's what I can't figure out."

"You were looking for girlfriends," Cate pointed out.

"You mean, maybe there was something going on between Kane and *Marilee*?" Candy sounded flabbergasted and immediately answered her own question. "No way. Marilee was sweet, in her own mousy way. But Kane liked women the same way he liked cars. With a lot of flash and glitter. You know, *hot*."

"Are you going to call and tell her Kane is dead?" Cate asked.

"I figure if she wanted any contact with me, she'd have initiated it before now. No address, but it looks like a Portland area code. I thought you might like to have it. For PI purposes. But I'm not giving it to you if you're going to pass it on to Matt!"

Cate said no, telling Matt wouldn't be necessary. She wrote down the number Candy read off, and thanked her.

"You will call me if you hear anything?" Candy asked.

"About what?"

"Kane. Matt. The end of the world, whatever." Candy laughed, softening the snap in her words. "I don't know. I just feel as if everything is still . . . unfinished."

"If I hear anything, I'll let you know. You do the same, okay?"

Cate did a quick Google of the name Marilee Halliday but found nothing. With sudden inspiration, she did a reverse search on the phone number. That brought immediate information. The number was for an M. Hardee, with an address in Portland.

◆◆◆

Cate was at H&B shortly after 9:00 the following morning. Radine said Mr. Halliday was already working out in the shop. Cate found him with his head buried in the engine of a hood-less Oldsmobile that looked a long way from full restoration. Feet, probably Jerry's, stuck out from between the front wheels.

"I went up to Salem," Cate said to the back of Halliday's head. "I thought you might want to know what I found out there."

"Did you find out who has me next on their hit list?"

"No, not yet," Cate admitted.

"Then just put it in a written report. We're running behind here."

If Halliday was mourning his partner's death, he wasn't letting it interfere with work. Was it possible he didn't know?

Tentatively she said, "You know Mr. Blakely passed away yesterday, don't you?"

"Yes." Halliday lifted his head out of the engine compartment, wrench in one hand. "Terrible thing. Jerk just crashing in and killing a good man like Kane. Earlier I was all shook up about shooting the guy, but now I'm not sorry I exterminated him on the spot."

He swiped a hand across his forehead, leaving a streak of grease in one of those permanent frown lines. "Something happened the other night."

"Happened?"

"I'd stopped in at Walmart to pick up some groceries. I was crossing the parking lot to get to my car when a pickup came out of nowhere and practically ran me over. *Tried* to run me over. It didn't work as well as the driver probably hoped, but it knocked me down in the middle of a mess of smashed eggs and milk."

"You think it was someone trying to make good on the threat in the note?"

"They didn't stop to draw diagrams about their intentions, but that's what it felt like. But you're the investigator."

"Have you told the police?"

"Sure, I told them. But I didn't have a license number, and all I could say about the pickup was that it was an older model and light colored."

"So . . . ?"

"So I got a mini-lecture on how parking lots can be dangerous places and how everyone has to be careful, both drivers and pedestrians." Halliday tapped his palm with the wrench. "So maybe it was an accident, just another stupid driver."

Maybe.

"There's something else I wanted to talk to you about," Cate said hurriedly. She doubted Halliday was going to give her much time. "It appears Mr. Blakely may have had a gambling problem."

"A gambling *problem*? Oh, I don't think so. Kane enjoyed his poker, and he liked putting a few bucks on a horse race now and then. But gambling was never a *problem* for him. Unless Candy dragged him into it. Besides, what's that got to do with anything?"

"Gambling losses may have been why he needed the money you were loaning him."

"You know, I don't much appreciate your dumping on Kane when he can't defend himself."

"I wasn't—" Cate broke off. Halliday obviously wasn't going to think badly of his partner no matter what. She didn't want him to, of course. That wasn't her intention. But if Kane's gambling activity was what had gotten him killed . . .

Halliday leaned forward and fastened his wrench on something in the engine again, obviously not in a chatty mood, and Cate hurriedly asked her other question.

"I hate to bother you further, but a friend has been taking care of Mr. Blakely's dog. Now he needs to talk to the son about the dog. Could you tell me how he can get in touch?"

"I think Radine has a phone number. Warren's his name. Check with her."

"Okay. Thanks. I've also been wondering, did Andy Timmons ever get in touch with you about his Indian motorcycle?"

"No. I haven't talked to him. Like I told you, it doesn't matter now." Halliday sounded impatient, but he managed to add, "But I appreciate your good work in locating him. Look, if you'll excuse me . . . ?"

Cate left him to his engine restoration. Maybe work was how he was coping with the loss of his friend and partner. She intended to stop and see how Shirley was holding up, but Shirley was on the forklift, maneuvering cartons on a shelf, so they just exchanged waves. Out in the office, she asked about Kane's son. Radine wrote both a cell phone number and an address in Georgia on a page from an H&B pad.

"Do you know him?" Cate asked.

"Only time I ever met him was yesterday, when he came in asking if Kane had any life insurance through H&B."

Kane Blakely's insurance. Everybody was interested. Cate already knew the situation with the insurance, however, and she was curious how Warren took the news.

"Harder than he took the news of his father's death, I think," Radine answered.

As Candy would probably say, typical Warren.

The night before, Cate had made up a list of the bicycle shops in the Eugene area, and, back in the car, she studied the list. There were over twenty names and addresses, more than she'd expected. Bicycling was big in Eugene. She picked the closest address and headed for it.

The shop was small. Neither of the two clerks remembered anyone of Mace Jackson's name or description coming in to purchase a bike within the last couple of weeks. Similar results at the next half dozen places. It reminded Cate that while the crime itself might be remembered as a shocker, killing and getting killed in a shoot-out did not elevate your name to a memorable place in local history.

Cate took a break for lunch with salad at a Wendy's and called Mitch at the same time. She gave him Warren Blakely's phone number, and he said he'd contact him about Clancy. After the quick lunch, Cate started on the list again. Finally, at a larger shop with a creative décor—vine-y green plants trained to grow in bicycle shapes on the walls—one of the endless blank dead ends in her own PI maze cracked open.

"I don't remember the name. I probably wouldn't have gotten it unless he actually bought or ordered a bike," the middle-aged clerk said. "But I remember those knuckles. As I recall, he had a specific brand and model of bike in mind, but we didn't have it in stock. I offered to order it, but he said he was from out of town."

Yes! It all fit. "Did he say where he was from?"

"He either didn't say or I don't remember. But he wasn't alone. I think Monica knew the other guy. She was talking to him." He looked across the bicycles to a section of women's clothing, where a woman and another male clerk were in an animated discussion. "That's her over there."

Cate could hear the subject of the discussion as she approached. Twenty-six versus twenty-nine-inch wheels on mountain bikes. Fascinating. Right up there with a government info sheet on eradicating bugs in cauliflower fields.

The woman, another walking advertisement for the benefits of bike riding, broke off and smiled at Cate. "Sorry. Friend Aaron here is kind of a fanatic on certain subjects."

"*You* are a fanatic," Friend Aaron stated loftily, "whereas *I* am a learned authority on the subject." He grinned at both of them and headed off to the bicycle parts area.

Cate presented her business card to the woman and once more repeated Mace Jackson's name and description. "The other clerk"—she motioned back to the man now with another customer—"thinks the man I'm seeking information about may have been in here not long ago, and someone you knew was with him."

Monica, with an identifying name tag on her T-shirt, studied the card. "And you're looking for these guys because . . . ?"

Cate once more repeated the basic facts about that night at H&B.

"You're telling me that guy with Andy was the one who shot someone and then got shot himself?" the woman interrupted. "I remember seeing that on TV and thinking how *awful*, but I never realized—was *Andy* involved in that?"

"Andy?"

"This guy I hung out with a while back." Clerk Monica smiled. "My very short walk on the wild side. He was kind of fun, but I backed off when we went in a store and he shoplifted a can of bean dip to go with the tortilla chips I bought."

"This Andy," Cate said. She felt an odd little tightening

across her midsection. Maybe anticipation. Maybe dread. "Andy who?"

"Andy Timmons."

"Could you describe him?"

Monica described exactly the guy with the motorcycle whom Cate had tracked down for Halliday.

"Do you know anything about his relationship with Mace Jackson?"

"Not a thing. I'm sure I'd never met the Jackson guy before they came in here that day. Andy didn't even introduce us then. I know he had some friends who were pretty sleazy. Andy himself was on the sleazy side." She lifted both her hands and shoulders and smiled, as if her relationship with him was a puzzle to her too. "That was my rebellious stage, when I was practically *looking* for someone my folks would disapprove of."

"Where was Andy living then?"

"No idea. Just kind of hanging out here and there, I guess."

"Anything else you can tell me about him? Was he into gambling?"

"Gambling? You mean like buying lottery tickets or playing slots at a casino?"

"Maybe something less legal. Like betting with a bookie, something like that."

"Bookie? I thought the only place guys like that existed was in bad movies. There really *are* bookies right here in Eugene?"

"I don't know," Cate admitted.

"If Andy was into anything like that, I never knew it. He was definitely into buying and selling a little pot, but it's scary to think he had friends like this—what was his name again?"

"Mace Jackson."

"I'm just glad I dumped Andy when I did. It feels creepy even now, thinking I was standing right next to a *killer*."

Cate asked her to call if she thought of anything else, and the woman nodded. Cate went back to the car, undecided what to do next. Talk to Andy? That night at his and Lily's apartment, he'd made some comment about the shootings at H&B, but he hadn't indicated he knew the dead man. Why had he omitted that information? What would he do if Cate confronted him with it? Would Lily know anything? Even if she didn't know Mace Jackson by name, she might recognize the description. But Cate needed to talk to Lily without Andy present to monitor every word.

Cate glanced at her watch: 3:15. Lily would still be at the housecleaning job she worked on weekdays. But if Cate went to the apartment in the evening, Andy would probably be there.

New and disturbing thought. Had Andy Timmons sent that threatening letter? And Halliday had said the vehicle that ran him down in the parking lot was a light-colored pickup. Lily's pickup was light-colored, and Andy often drove it. Had Andy been good enough friends with Mace Jackson to be into payback for Halliday killing him?

Cate went home to find Octavia on her desk looking at the phone. About five seconds later, it rang. "So sometimes you're right," she grumbled. She glanced at the caller ID. "Hi, Uncle Joe."

"Hey, Becca and I were thinking maybe you and Mitch would like to come over for a celebration dinner tonight."

"You have something to celebrate?"

"Not me, you. Something came for you today."

"In the mail?"

"Yes indeed. First class, definitely not junk mail."

"From?"

"Well, let's see . . ."

Uncle Joe was enjoying stretching this out, Cate could tell. Her own heart did a little salsa dance. There was only one thing that could have come in the mail worthy of celebration.

"Department of Public Safety Standards, it looks like," he said.

"Did you open it?"

"Of course not. It's addressed to you. So you two be here for dinner at 6:30 and we'll see what's in it then. Becca says she's making your favorite carrot cake."

"We'll be there."

Cate's call to Mitch caught him helping the people at the bakery, where he'd set up a new computer system, so she just gave him a quick message about dinner. A half-second later, she gave herself a mental slap. She'd told Uncle Joe they'd come to dinner, but she should have checked with Mitch first. She and Mitch were together several evenings a week, but their relationship had subtly altered since the future of Computer Dudes was up in the air. Because that uncertain future meant the future of *their* relationship was drifting in the unknown too.

"I'm sorry. I should have asked first," she said hastily. "If you have something else planned—"

"Cate, I'm not about to miss your celebration dinner. It isn't every day you become a fully licensed private investigator. That is what this is about, isn't it?"

"That's obviously what Uncle Joe thinks. But who knows? Maybe the letter is a rejection notice. Maybe I'm disqualified because I capitalized something I shouldn't have on the application. Maybe they investigated my past and discovered that one time I copied answers off the test paper of the guy sitting next to me in US history class."

Not one of her more noble moments in education. Although she'd not escaped the strong hand of justice. The answers had been wrong and they'd both flunked the test. Lesson learned.

"Okay, then, if it's a rejection, I'm not going to miss commiserating with you about it." Something crashed in the background. "Look, I've got to go. I never thought someone could actually kill a computer, but I'm not so sure about this guy. I'll see you about 6:15."

24

Mitch brought Clancy inside with him when he arrived at the house. Octavia's fur electrified. Clancy's legs stiffened. Hiss . . . bark. Octavia surprised Cate by then tentatively touching noses with the dog, but she followed the touch with a "gotcha!" swipe of paw. Clancy's heavy shoulders stiffened, and he looked ready to retaliate with a snap of his big jaws, but he apparently decided a better payback was beating her to that window-seat spot they both favored.

"Have you called Kane's son yet?" Cate asked.

"I tried about an hour ago, but he didn't answer. I'll try again."

Cate thought he meant later, but he immediately grabbed the phone clipped to his belt. He lifted a finger to indicate to Cate that the phone was ringing this time.

Mitch identified himself and explained why he was calling. "I'm willing to pay—"

The response from Warren Blakely was brief. He broke in and ended the call before Mitch even had a chance to finish the sentence.

"He hardly listened to you! He wants Clancy himself?"

"He said he didn't even know his father had a dog. I was trying to tell him I'd pay for Clancy, but he didn't give me a chance. He just said, do whatever you want. He doesn't want a dog."

"Clancy could wind up in the dog pound, for all he knows!"

"Right."

"What a hard-hearted attitude."

"Yeah, isn't it?" Mitch's eyebrows momentarily scrunched, but then he grinned. "But who cares? I get to keep Clancy. Hey, Clance, c'mon over here."

Clancy deserted that favored spot on the window seat and ran to Mitch for a roughhousing on the carpet. Cate grabbed a lamp before it went down in the mêlée. Octavia climbed up to her walkway and stared down with cat horror on such immature behavior. Man and dog both got up looking considerably rumpled and rather embarrassed.

With somewhat more dignity, Mitch said, "Okay, you're my dog and I'm your person now. Want to shake on it?" He held out his hand.

Clancy offered him a big paw, and they shook.

"Now we have two things to celebrate," Mitch said to Cate. He offered her more than a handshake. He wrapped his arms around her and kissed her on the nose. He grinned again.

"You look awfully happy for a guy who started out making the big sacrifice of keeping a dog for a night and is now stuck with him permanently."

"Yeah, well, he's kind of worked his big, hairy, slobbery way into my heart."

"I'm glad. For both of you."

And she was. But where, she wondered when he looked

back at the dog with fond pride, did a certain redhead fit into his heart?

◆◆◆

Uncle Joe didn't make Cate wait when they reached the house. He handed her the envelope as soon as they walked in. She ripped it open and stared at the contents. Name spelled right? Yes. Address correct? Yes. Correct type of license, not one that gave her the right to spray for termites or sell insurance? Yes.

Cate Kinkaid was now a fully licensed private investigator in the State of Oregon! She also had an official identification card, with the reasonably flattering photo she'd sent them. She passed both around for everyone to see.

Uncle Joe and Rebecca both hugged her. Mitch kissed her cheek. Clancy stuck his nose into her armpit.

"Take a bow," Uncle Joe said. "You did it!"

Cate dipped into a little curtsy. She held up the newly minted license as if it were an Oscar award. Breathlessly she said, "I want to thank all of you for making this possible. I couldn't have done it without you! Thank you, Uncle Joe, for giving me this opportunity. Thank you, Rebecca, for putting up with me while I lived here. Thank you, Mitch, for your help when I needed you. Clancy, thank you for—whatever. And, of course, I want to thank my cat and my parents and my third grade teacher—"

"We get the picture," Mitch said.

Cate smiled at her own giddiness. "But I really do thank all of you."

Uncle Joe, as if he suspected this could get maudlin, headed for the dining room. "Okay, let's eat."

Cate stared at the license once more before following, and

this time she offered a special private thanks. *Hey, Lord, I didn't know I wanted to be a private investigator when you stuck me in this job. But you had plans, didn't you? Thank you. Help me to be what you want me to be and to do my very best for you.*

Dinner was Rebecca's special chicken and rice casserole, followed by the carrot cake. She'd decorated it especially for the occasion, with a detective figure bent over, peering through a magnifying glass, the red-icing hair unmistakably Cate's. Uncle Joe took photos of her, the cake, and Mitch in all possible combinations. Mitch grabbed the camera and got more combinations of people, dog, and cake. Then they ate the cake, with even Clancy getting his sliver to celebrate with them.

It wasn't until the meal was over and they were back in the living room that Uncle Joe got down to the more serious aspect of Cate's new status. First he told her the identification card should be carried with her at all times, and the PI license should be displayed on the wall of her office.

Cate said she'd do that but added, "Although I've never actually had a client in my office, so probably no one will ever see it anyway."

"But *you* are Belmont Investigations now, at least you will be as soon as we get the transfer made, so you may have an occasional client in your office. Actually, I think you should consider getting a professional office outside your home as soon as possible, because you never know what kind of clients may show up. You'll want to change the business name, of course."

"I'll be happy to leave it just as it is—"

"I don't need a memorial," Uncle Joe stated firmly. "Belmont Investigations is galloping off into the sunset. So you can pick something entirely your own. Let's see, what should it be? Hilltop Investigations, to suggest your location? Eugene Investigations? No, too generic. Cate and Cat Investigations?"

Cate laughed. Cate and Cat Investigations had a certain cachet. She was rather tempted by it. "I'm thinking along more traditional lines. Kinkaid Investigations."

Uncle Joe nodded approvingly. "I've already talked to our lawyer friend Ledbetter, and he'll draw up the papers transferring the business ownership to you. We'll move the files and my research library over to your place. We also need to transfer all the information off my computer onto yours, although I'm not sure how to do that."

"I can do it," Mitch offered.

"Good." Uncle Joe went on about getting a new business license in Cate's name, arranging for insurance and bond, joining the state association of private investigators, and various other details involved in running an investigative business. "So you come over tomorrow and we'll go through the files. Then, when we get back, we'll sign whatever papers need to be signed and—"

That made a dent in Cate's giddiness. "Back from where?"

"We're leaving day after tomorrow to spend the next week over on the coast. Or maybe we'll make it ten days—"

"Or two weeks," Rebecca put in. "Maybe three."

"Right," Uncle Joe agreed. "That's what retired people in a motor home do, you know. Free as birds with an open migration schedule."

Rebecca produced an oak frame suitable for the license, and then they all admired the framed license. Cate tried to look and sound happy. Hey, she was happy! For Joe and Rebecca. For herself. But some dismay apparently leaked through because Uncle Joe leaned over and picked up the license in its new frame.

He shook it at her. "That was the whole point of this, remember?" His voice gentled. "A business of your own for you, retirement for me."

Well, yeah, but . . . um . . . uh . . .

Uncle Joe reached over and squeezed her hand. "Don't worry. You'll do fine. You've already proved you can handle anything, up to and including killers."

Not on her current case, she hadn't. Somebody still had Halliday targeted, and she didn't know who.

Mitch had his news about Clancy to share too, and then everyone had to shake the dog's big paw in congratulations. It was close to 10:00 before the celebration broke up.

As Cate and Mitch headed to the door, Rebecca went to wrap up the cake leftovers to send home with Cate, and Uncle Joe said, "Oh, one more thing."

He went into his office, and Cate heard him unlocking the one desk drawer that was always locked. He came back carrying a black leather holster. With gun inside, big and dark and dangerous.

"This is yours now. Part of what goes with Belmont Investigations." He held the holster out to her, but she just eyed the gift warily.

"Uncle Joe, Dad let me shoot his .22 rifle a few times, but I don't know a thing about handguns."

"There are a couple of shooting ranges with instructors here in town. Take the gun there and learn."

"Do I really need a gun?"

"I haven't needed one often in my career as a PI. But when I did need it, it saved lives. Mine and several others."

Cate nodded slowly. She tentatively unwound her fingers

and stuck her hand out. He draped the belt of the holster over it. Heavy. Deadly. *Hers.*

Back in Mitch's SUV, she set the remainder of the cake on the console between them and laid the holster carefully across her lap. At the house, she just as carefully hung it on a hook on the far wall opposite her desk. It definitely gave the office a different ambiance.

An ambiance that said, "I'm a tough PI and don't you forget it."

It issued a blatant warning, "Don't mess with me. I've got a gun and I'm not afraid to use it."

Or maybe what it really said was, "This is just for show because this PI doesn't even know how to put bullets in a gun."

Octavia came and jumped on the file cabinet so she could inspect the gun. She backed off and hissed at it.

"Opinion duly noted," Cate told her. "Although you may change your mind if we're ever attacked by a herd of super-mice with an appetite for deaf cats and redheaded PIs."

Mitch had come inside with her. He didn't stay, but at the door he put his arms around her.

"I know I can be kind of a . . ." He paused, as if trying to think of a proper word, and Cate, even though some less-than-complimentary terms came to mind, didn't try to fill in for him. "I can be narrow-minded about your being a PI, but I really am proud of you. Getting your own license is a great accomplishment."

"Thank you."

"May I offer a congratulatory kiss?"

Cate smiled at his formality. "You may."

And he gave her that kiss. A kiss that was sweetly tender, a daisies and sunshine, violets and moonlight kind of kiss. But a kiss that deepened and went on until she felt it right down to her toes. A lightning and fireworks, flash-bang and sizzle kiss.

If she'd been wearing socks, it would definitely have scorched them off her feet. She felt breathless and giddy, as if she'd had one too many spins on some upside-down carnival ride, and she had to wiggle her toes to be sure her feet were still on the floor. She opened her eyes and looked up at him.

"I-I feel well congratulated."

He grinned. "That was my intention."

25

Cate spent most of the next day with Uncle Joe. He brought her up to date on a couple of minor but active cases she hadn't been involved in. They hauled files on old, long-closed cases up to the attic for storage.

He gave her contact information for experts he had consulted in the past, everyone from an authority on poisons to an expert on historic houses in the area. Then there was the beekeeping expert. Cate couldn't imagine ever needing that one, but Uncle Joe just smiled and reminded her that the PI business could be strange and unpredictable. They loaded as many of the books in his reference library as her car could handle. He gave her a couple of boxes of bullets to go with the gun.

She started setting up her own library when she got home. She put the boxes of bullets in a drawer near the gun, then stood back and considered both gun and bullets with a certain ambivalence. She'd thought often enough about the day she could actually carry a gun in her PI work. Now she had a PI license and a gun.

Be careful what you wish for; you may get it?

That evening, she and Mitch returned to Uncle Joe's, and

Mitch transferred all the relevant files from Uncle Joe's computer to hers. They loaded the metal file cabinet and the remainder of the reference library books into the SUV. Rebecca added some potted plants that wouldn't survive in the house without care. Her worried expression suggested she wasn't sure they would survive *with* Cate's care.

"I'm going to miss you guys. I suppose you're getting up at the crack of dawn to take off?"

Uncle Joe and Rebecca looked at each other. "No way," he said.

"We're throwing away clocks and calendars. God gave us this special time of life together, and we're going to enjoy it." In a whispered aside to Cate, but one which her husband surely couldn't miss, Rebecca added, "Sometimes I've been afraid Joe was going to wind up as the World's Oldest Working PI. I'm really glad the Lord sent you to keep that from happening."

Back home, Cate and Mitch unloaded everything, with Octavia inspecting each item. Clancy claimed the window seat while she was busy sniffing a book called *Diary of a Cat Burglar*, which was surely just another of those odd coincidences. Mitch seemed rather preoccupied this evening. Not really distant or withdrawn, but he definitely had something on his mind as they worked.

"Everything progressing okay with the sale?" she asked tentatively as they took a Pepsi break in the kitchen.

"Going good. Just a couple of minor details to work out yet. They've offered me a job, Coordinator of Special Projects."

"Hey, great!"

"It's in their Seattle office."

Cate concealed a ten-story plunge somewhere inside her. "Are you going to take it?"

"It might be the smart thing to do." Mitch paused, sloshing the Pepsi in the can reflectively. "The company Lance is going to work for down in Texas has contacted me too."

"Looks as if you have your choice then, of where you want to live and work." Cate tried to sound pleasantly supportive. She wanted to be glad for Mitch that he had good opportunities. She *would* be glad for him, even if it felt like trying to make cheesecake out of sawdust. "That's really great."

"But I think I'm ready for something new," Mitch said.

He didn't expand on that thought. Cate wondered if he was waiting for her to ask *what* something new, but her stubborn streak surfaced and she didn't do it. If he wanted to be male-mysterious, she wasn't going to beg for his thoughts. He'd be coming out of the sale of Computer Dudes with an impressive chunk of money. Maybe he had in mind loafing with Clancy in the Caribbean for a year, or making a man-and-dog world tour.

She gave herself a mental whack. Now she was sounding jealous of a dog.

"Hey, I was thinking. I need to talk to someone tomorrow morning, but maybe later we could take Clancy for a run somewhere?" Cate suggested.

"How about if while you're busy I come over and get the ground rototilled for that garden you were talking about? I've already talked to Hank Bowman at church about borrowing his rototiller this weekend."

Garden? Would Mitch be interested in planting a garden unless he expected to be around to benefit from it? Cate's spirits lifted with a trampoline bounce, then sank just as quickly. Yeah, Mitch would help plant a garden even if he'd be a thousand miles away when it started producing. Mitch was like that.

"I bought a bunch of seeds, so that sounds great," Cate said.

She could plan all kinds of menus with produce from the garden. Solitary Squash. Lonely Lettuce. Onions for One.

◆◆◆

Mitch arrived the next morning before Cate left for the convenience store to talk to Lily, rototiller and various other tools jumbled in the back of his SUV. By the time she left, Mitch and the machine were churning a trail through the dirt in a corner of the yard. Clancy sniffed every overturned clod, occasionally pausing to dig as if he sensed buried treasure. Although she had to wonder with some uneasiness exactly what Clancy might consider "treasure."

The visit to the convenience store was brief. Another clerk said Lily was working this weekend, but she wouldn't be in until 1:00. Cate drove to Lily and Andy's apartment and warily peered down the driveway from the street. Lily's pickup stood in front of the apartment, so she was home. Cate had no way of knowing if Andy Timmons was also there, and she couldn't think of any good excuse to offer for dropping in if he was home.

Maybe she should start a sideline of door-to-door sales so she'd always have an excuse for dropping in on anyone. And a backup career if the investigative business tanked. Kinkaid Investigations and Kitchen Gadgets? Kinkaid Investigations and Lingerie?

Cate wasn't sorry to hurry on home. It was a fantastic spring day, cloudless blue sky, warm sun, a day made for digging and planting. She changed into denim shorts and tank top and stepped out the back door.

Mitch's shirt was open, sleeves rolled up, shirttails flapping, dark hair falling over his forehead as he manhandled the rototiller. The ground hadn't been worked up in a long time, years probably, and occasionally the machine made a bucking-bronc leap, but he had the muscles to keep it under control. Cate couldn't say that muscular-male types had ever particularly impressed her, but now . . . Hmmm. She could see a certain appeal after all. Something attractively elemental about a man wrestling with machine and earth.

He made a turn at the corner, spotted Cate, and shut the rototiller off. He grabbed a piece of old towel out of his back pocket and wiped sweat off his face and neck as he walked toward her.

There was something unexpectedly appealing about honest male sweat too. And who'd have thought a streak of dirt across a cheek could be so attractive?

"Hey, how'd it go?" he asked.

"She hadn't come to work yet. I'll have to go back later."

"What do you think so far?" Mitch waved across the expanse of tilled earth.

He'd started by ripping an outline of the intended garden area and was working inward from there. The space was at least double the size Cate had intended. If she had any success growing things, she could supply a vegetarian army.

"It's, um, a little larger than I expected. But that's okay," she added quickly.

"I guess I kind of got carried away," Mitch admitted. "But you can learn canning and freezing and drying. All that good pioneer stuff."

Yeah, right. She might also learn to flap her ears and fly.

Perhaps realizing that, he added, "Or Helping Hands can always use donations of produce to give to needy families."

Donations she could do.

They worked until noon, Mitch rototilling, Cate raking, Clancy digging. All getting dirt-streaked and grubby. They stopped for a quick lunch, then went back to work. By 2:30, when Cate reluctantly stopped to shower, they had rows of carrots, radishes, and lettuce seeds in the ground. Perky little packets impaled on a stick at the end of each row identified what would soon be sprouting there.

Mitch plants, I water, God gives the increase. The biblical version of those words had a spiritual garden in mind, but maybe it applied to earthy gardens too. *You okay with that, Lord? Even if I'm not planting parsnips or rutabagas?* God had no doubt created them with good intentions, but she hated parsnips and rutabagas.

She was back at the convenience store by 3:10. She didn't spot Lily's pickup in the parking area, but inside the store she saw Lily in skimpy shorts and tank top working the cash register. No chance to talk to her, however. The little store was so busy that all Cate could do was ask Lily if she'd get a break soon.

Lily eyed her suspiciously. "Why?"

"I need to talk to you. It won't take more than a few minutes."

"Talk about what?" More suspicion.

"About someone you might know."

Lily's glossy pink lips compressed into a thin line, but she finally nodded. "Okay. I guess I owe you that. I tried to call you."

Cate couldn't think why Lily owed her anything, but she wasn't about to argue the point.

"I usually take a break about 4:00 if you want to wait until then," Lily said.

"I'll be out in my car."

"Sometimes Andy shows up about my break time too."

Was that a warning? Cate went to the car to wait and fidget about several things. Why had Lily tried to call her? How did she get the number? Cate purposely hadn't left a card at the apartment. Again, she thought Andy's keeping quiet about knowing the gunman at H&B was definitely odd. Maybe, that night she was at the apartment, he was afraid if he mentioned knowing Jackson, she'd tell the police and they'd pull him in for questioning? Details of Andy's lifestyle might not bear magnifying-glass inspection.

The car heated up on the warm spring day. She moved it into shade cast by a tree on a neighboring lot, angled so she could watch for Andy. No self-service gas in Oregon, and a steady stream of customers kept the attendants on the gas pumps busy. Many gas buyers also went into the store and came out with arms loaded. With nothing else to do, she started analyzing purchases: 60 percent of the customers bought soft drinks, 75 percent beer, and 90 percent some type of chips.

The fascinating life of the fully licensed PI. Kinkaid Investigations and Statistical Junk Food Analyst?

4:00 and 4:30 came and went.

Cate was about to expand her analysis into brand names of beer and soft drinks, or maybe just leave and try to catch Lily another time, when she spotted the woman coming out a rear door of the store. It was 4:35 by then. She had two soft drink cans in hand. Cate stepped out of the car and waved to her.

Lily didn't apologize for her lateness. "I brought Pepsi and 7UP." She held out both cans and Cate selected the green one. Lily went around to the passenger's door and slid inside.

"Thanks for taking time to talk to me," Cate said. "Andy didn't come to share your break today?"

"He has the pickup. He was going out to Junction City this afternoon. I guess he didn't get back yet."

"He's looking for a job out there?"

Lily gave her a what-planet-are-you-from look. "He went to look at a trailer for sale. It's supposed to be a nice one, and he says we'll have plenty of money as soon as he sells that old bike." She didn't sound convinced.

"You're still thinking about going down to Nevada or Arizona with him?"

Lily shifted in the car seat and ignored the question. "Look, I want to thank you for telling me about the restraining order and how to do it and everything. I think it got through to Dirk. That's what his sister said when I talked to her, anyway. So I really appreciate it. I tried to call and thank you."

"I'm glad I could help." But . . . "How did you get my phone number?"

"Andy got it somewhere. I don't know where."

Great. Now she was on a killer's friend's speed dial? Not that her number would be all that difficult to locate, but why had Andy bothered to do it?

"I guess I'm surprised you and Andy are still together," Cate said.

"He doesn't have any place else to go." Lily sounded mildly frustrated, as if Andy were a stray creature that had wandered in and she hadn't the heart to shoo him away. "But he keeps saying he'll have all this money coming in soon. I guess that stupid old motorcycle really is worth more than it looks like."

"He's talked to Mr. Halliday at H&B about buying it?"

"They're haggling over price or something. I keep telling Andy he should just do it, but he says the longer he holds out, the more the guy will pay."

Cate tapped the 7UP can against the steering wheel. None

236

of this corresponded to what Halliday had said, which was that he hadn't talked to Andy Timmons at all. Was Andy stringing Lily along by telling her some pie-in-the-sky story about a big chunk of money coming in soon?

Cate didn't reveal that Halliday had said he'd had no contact with Andy, but she asked, "Do you suppose it could be someone other than Mr. Halliday who's interested in the bike now?"

"I don't know. Maybe. Who knows? Andy likes to play games with his little secrets. Or maybe it's the truth he plays with. If he ever does get any money, I'm going to tell him, 'Great! Now take it and get your sorry butt out of here.'"

Cate blinked at the wording, but she figured the meaning was definitely a good idea.

"What I wanted to talk to you about is something to do with Andy. Actually, a friend of his," Cate said carefully. Lily, for all her snarky remarks about Andy, might reverse directions and get defensive if she thought he was threatened.

"You said before you're not police." Lily made a suspicious question out of the statement.

"I'm not. But in this situation I'm working on, I came across the fact that Andy knew Mace Jackson, the guy who shot the man at Mr. Halliday's place of business."

Lily straightened her slouch on the car seat. "Who says Andy knew him?"

Yes, definitely a hint of challenge or even hostility. Cate knew she had to maneuver carefully here.

"I talked with someone who saw Andy and Mace together at a bicycle shop here in town."

"Why would they be at a bicycle shop?" Lily scoffed. "Andy wouldn't ride a bicycle if you gave it to him."

"Mace Jackson was into bicycle racing," Cate said. "Apparently he also used a bicycle as his main transportation."

"Weird. I haven't ridden a bicycle since I was, oh, like twelve."

"I'm wondering if you knew him too?"

"You said his name was Mace something? Like in that stuff the police use in riots? Is that his real name?"

"It's what he was using."

"Why would anyone name a baby Mace?" Lily wrinkled her nose. "If I'm ever a mother, I'm going to name my baby something nice. Darcy if it's a girl. Shawn if it's a boy."

Cate gave a moment's thought to baby names. She rather liked Jacob. Or Mark. Maybe Eli. Definitely not Mace. Had Mitch ever thought about baby names?

Mental whack. How did they get off on this rabbit trail? Was Lily deliberately sidetracking her? Cate yanked the subject back to where she wanted it.

"Did you know Mace Jackson? Or hear Andy mention him?"

Lily shook her head negatively to both questions, but when Cate added the description, Lily's eyes widened within their framework of black eyeliner and sooty eye shadow.

"Hey, yeah, I remember *him*. I never heard his name, but I remember those awful skulls on his hand." Lily flexed her fingers. "He was at the trailer with Andy one time when I got home from work. We used to live in a trailer my brother owned. But I guess you knew that, didn't you?" She spoke as if knowing too much was a definite flaw in Cate's character makeup.

"What was Andy's connection with him?"

"They'd been smoking pot in the trailer. I could smell it. I was really mad. Andy had promised he wasn't into dealing or even using anymore. I kicked 'em all out of the trailer right then and there. But Andy had money the next day, and I was pretty sure he'd gotten it from selling pot to that Mace guy."

"Was Mace from around here? Or how did Andy know him?"

"The guy wasn't living here in Eugene when he was at the trailer. I remember because I asked. I wasn't about to have him hanging around all the time. I think he'd come down from Corvallis or somewhere up there."

"Salem?"

"Could be. Andy and him knew each other from some-where before. Maybe when Andy was growing up down in California. But I don't think they were really good friends. He even got Andy's name wrong and called him Artie once. And I don't know why he was here in town when he was at the trailer."

"Mace Jackson's name was in the news after he shot Mr. Blakely in the robbery attempt, and was then shot himself by Matt Halliday. Did Andy have any reaction to that?"

"I don't remember any."

So Andy wasn't shedding tears or stomping around in outrage about his friend's demise at Matt Halliday's hand. But maybe he was even then working on the old theory of "don't get mad, get even."

"It seems odd, when the shooting at H&B happened, that Andy didn't even mention he knew the guy or that you'd met him too," Cate said.

"Andy doesn't tell me things he figures I don't want to hear." Lily's eyes narrowed, but then, with her usual ambiva-lence about Andy, she added, "He says it's because he doesn't want to worry me unnecessarily."

Right. Andy the noble-hearted protector of the weaker sex.

"Why are you asking all these questions anyway?" Lily demanded. "What difference does it make if Andy knew this Mace guy?"

Cate pulled a copy of the threatening note out of her purse and handed it to Lily. "This is a copy, of course. The original, using words cut out of a newspaper, was sent to Mr. Halliday at H&B."

Lily studied the copy of the note as if it were a lengthy treatise, not just seven words. "And you think that just because Andy knew this guy, maybe *he* sent the note?"

"I don't necessarily think that. But I am investigating the situation." For the very first time, Cate pulled out her brand-new official identification card and held it up for Lily to see.

"You mean you *are* with the police?" Lily asked, her voice both shocked and accusing.

"No, we're a private investigative agency. No connection with the police."

Lily grabbed the identification card. "So I don't have to answer your questions if I don't want to." Lily flipped the official identification card back to her, apparently unimpressed, and Cate felt mildly deflated.

Lily picked up the copy of the note again. "What does it mean in here, 'con man'? Is this Halliday a crook or something?"

"Customers sometimes think they're getting ripped off even if a business is entirely honest and ethical."

"Yeah, I guess. Last weekend some woman was screaming about our charging way more for some cereal than they do at Safeway."

Cate nodded. "Exactly."

Although she had to admit it was possible H&B had pulled some shady deals. She remembered Uncle Joe telling her that just because someone hired you didn't mean the client was necessarily a good guy. Bad guys could hire an investigator too. She couldn't think, given Matt Halliday's pickiness and work ethic, that he'd take any shortcuts on a car restoration. Kane Blakely she wasn't so sure about, however. Big gray area there about the company's ethics and workmanship.

"So has anything happened to Mr. Halliday?" Lily's question sounded more like challenge than concern.

"Someone tried to run over him in a parking lot."

Lily shrugged. "Big deal. Andy practically got run over a couple of nights ago too, just crossing the street near our apartment. The world is full of idiot drivers."

"Whoever tried to run Mr. Halliday down was driving a light-colored pickup," Cate said.

The implication wasn't lost on Lily. She squirmed in the seat and pulled the tight tank top away from her body as if she'd been hit with a sudden heat wave.

"That doesn't prove anything! There's a zillion light-colored pickups. There's one right over there." Lily jabbed a finger in the direction of a battered tan pickup on the far side of the parking lot.

Given Lily's now hostile attitude, Cate figured this interview was over, but she dropped in a final all-purpose question. "Is there anything else you can tell me? Something I may have forgotten to ask about?"

"No." Hesitation. Lily eyed the building, as if she'd like to jump out of the car and run back to work. "Well, maybe. There was another guy at the trailer that day with Andy and Mace. Biker guy."

"A friend of Andy's?"

"He was there with Mace. Zig somebody. Right after my

brother moved his trailer into town for me, before I met Andy, I ran around with a biker guy. He and Zig were friends."

Although Cate's first thought was that Lily could possibly use some counseling on boyfriend selection, she didn't say anything. Being involved with motorcycles and motorcycle people was not a character flaw, as Mitch had pointed out to her.

"Did Zig recognize you at the trailer too?"

"I don't think so."

Cate found that hard to believe. Lily's looks weren't traffic-stopping, but her bleached-blonde hair, nightclub makeup, and curvy figure did not fade into the woodwork.

As if hearing that unspoken thought, Lily said, "I had brown hair and weighed a lot more then. Anyway, I never told Andy I'd met Zig before." She wrinkled her pert nose again. "He'd make a federal case out of it for sure."

"Do you have any idea how I could get in touch with Zig?"

"Why?"

"Because it seems likely some friend or business associate of Mace Jackson is out to get Matt Halliday. If this Zig was a good friend of Mace's—"

Lily jumped on that possibility like Octavia on a morsel of tuna. "Maybe *he* sent the threatening note!"

"I'd like to investigate that."

"Bunch of biker guys used to hang out on Saturday nights at a place called the Midnight Logger out in the sticks down near Lorane. I was there a few times." Lily sounded eager to supply information now, anything to divert suspicion away from Andy. "Somebody there would probably know if Zig was still around."

Cate wasn't familiar with the town, but Mitch probably was. "What kind of place is this where they hang out?"

"Bar. Live music. Restaurant. Little grocery store. Gas station. Lots of testosterone and ego and black leather. Fights in the parking lot."

Maybe not a five-star rating.

"Could you give me a description of Zig?"

"Short, but heavy built. Tattoos all over both arms. Bald. I don't know if that was natural or he shaved it. Usually he wore a bandana tied over it, you know, like bikers do. Heavy beard, kind of grayish. He usually wore a fancy black vest, with about a mile of fringe. And a heavy gold chain with a coiled snake engraved on the pendant." With an unexpected smile, she added, "You know, your average biker guy."

Lily went silent then, and Cate wondered if she was reconsidering the wisdom of supplying this information.

"Anything else?"

"Nope."

Cate drained the last of her 7UP and handed the empty can back to Lily. Oregon had a nickel deposit on cans. "I really appreciate your taking the time to talk to me today. I hope everything works out fine with the restraining order on your ex." She reached for her seat belt.

Lily held the two cans on her bare thighs, as if it were important the tops lined up exactly even. She made no move to get out of the car.

"Andy's been acting . . . funny lately. I've been kind of worried."

"Oh? Funny how?"

"Like he can't sit still. Jumpy. Like a little kid who can't wait for Christmas to come. Or cranky-jumpy. Like my ex when he was trying to quit smoking. But sometimes the opposite of cranky. I don't know what you call it—"

"Euphoric?"

"Yeah. Like he's high on something."

"Maybe he is," Cate suggested. The possibility seemed logical to her, but Lily slammed the cans down on her thighs as if Cate had made an outrageous accusation.

"You wouldn't understand," she snapped. "You've had an easy life. Andy hasn't. The chance to sell the bike and have a little money for a change really means something to him."

Lily had a final parting shot when she slid out of the car.

"Maybe I *will* go to Nevada or Arizona or wherever with him when he gets that money!"

"Lily, I'm sorry. I didn't mean—"

"I'll send you a postcard."

The door slam rocked the Honda like twenty big bikers hitting it all at once.

26

Cate drove by the garden center at Fred Meyer on her way home, but it was hard to focus on the comparative assets of Early Girl and Big Boy tomato plants. Or whether she wanted regular or burpless cucumbers.

Questions from her conversation with Lily kept interrupting. Were Andy Timmons and Mace Jackson good enough friends that Andy was planning vengeance for Mace's death? Perhaps had already tried it once in the parking lot? Or was Zig, or maybe some other shady buddy of Mace's, the note sender? Or did Zig even exist? Maybe quick-thinking Lily had invented him on the spot to divert Cate's attention away from Andy.

Cate didn't really make a decision about plants. She grabbed a half dozen Early Girls, another half dozen Big Boys, zucchini, and both kinds of cucumbers. On the way to the cash register she also tossed in green pepper plants.

At home, she changed clothes and impulsively picked up the phone before going out to the garden. This call didn't have anything to do with Andy Timmons, but then, this was how PI work went. You peered through various keyholes until you found something helpful.

A woman answered.

"Marilee?"

"Yes?"

"I'm sorry to bother you, but your name came up in connection with some work I'm doing, and I thought perhaps you'd want to know that Kane Blakely passed away a few days ago." The response was total silence, and lamely she added, "Or maybe you already knew?"

"No, I-I didn't know. Who is this?"

"My name is Cate Kinkaid. I'm a private investigator in Eugene." In spite of everything, Cate took satisfaction in being able to say it that way. Private investigator, without any qualifying "assistant."

"What happened to Kane?"

Cate explained about the shooting during the attempted robbery at H&B. "Mr. Blakely was in a coma after he was shot, and he never came out of it." She added the details of his burial and non-service.

"I—thanks for letting me know. This is such a shock. It's hard to believe someone would just shoot him—" She broke off and hastily added, "I mean, I do believe you, of course. It's just that we don't think of something like this ever happening to someone we know."

"When did you last talk to him?" Cate asked.

"I'm not sure . . . maybe six weeks ago."

"There's something I'd like to ask if you have a moment?"

"Yes, of course."

"As I said, the man who shot Kane was immediately shot to death by the other H&B owner, Matt Halliday. Your ex-husband, I believe?"

"Yes. I went back to my maiden name Hardee after the divorce. We don't have children and don't keep in touch."

"The thing is, Kane's shooting was first taken to be a robbery gone bad, not an intentional thing. But now there's been a threat against Mr. Halliday. So what I'm wondering is, do you know anyone who might harbor a grudge against both men, personal or professional?"

"I don't know anything about any grudges. I didn't know much about the business even when Matt and I were married, and I've never talked to him since the divorce."

"Did Kane ever mention problems, business or personal?"

"No. Kane helped me when I decided to leave Matt. He didn't *encourage* me to do it," she emphasized. "He just helped me. Emotionally and financially. Finding a lawyer too. Since then, he's called occasionally to make sure I'm okay, and we have . . . *had* dinner once in a while when he was here in Portland. But it was never anything more than friendship, if you're wondering."

"I guess maybe I was wondering," Cate admitted. "And are you 'okay'?"

"I'm doing fine. I work with an interior decorator, creating one-of-a-kind items for her clients. Kane connected me with her too. Matt thought my interest in arts and crafts was on the level of . . . oh, kids finger painting with mustard on a kitchen wall." She managed a small laugh.

"So you don't know anything about any problems in the company, unhappy clients or employees, anything like that?"

"I know Kane and Matt had troubles within the company," Marilee said. "That was the biggest reason they decided to split the business into two locations."

Cate hadn't heard that before. Her impression was that the men had simply wanted to expand the business. "What kind of troubles?"

"You name it, they disagreed about it. They were just so different. Kane was—did you know him?"

"No."

"Flamboyant. Very outgoing. He liked the limelight. Liked showing off the cars they restored. Liked—what's that word? Schmoozing with people. Everybody was his friend. Matt is much more . . ."

"Stodgy?"

"I was going to say reserved, but stodgy is probably more accurate." Marilee started to laugh but broke it off as if remembering the serious nature of this call. "Where did you say you got my name and number?"

"From Candy, Kane's ex-wife. It was in some of Kane's things." Cate didn't elaborate on how Candy got into those "things."

"I've been remiss in not being in touch with Candy. She was always friendly and nice. How is she taking Kane's death?"

"Harder than she lets on, I think. You knew they were divorced, didn't you?"

"Yes. Kane told me. Relationships are complicated, aren't they? I've been blessed with a good life since Matt and I divorced."

"Would you mind if I tell Candy that?" Cate asked.

"Not at all. I should have contacted her myself a long time ago. But, to be honest, I've wanted to put that whole era of my life with Matt behind me."

"This is kind of a personal question, but was there abuse in the marriage?"

A quick intake of breath, then big dead silence. "You mean physical abuse?"

"Physical. Mental. Emotional. Any of it can be abuse."

"What makes you ask about abuse?"

PI intuition? Lucky guess? Stab in the dark? "Sometimes it's my job to ask unpleasant questions."

Another long moment of silence, as if this might be a door Marilee would rather not open. Finally she said, "Whatever happened back then is over and done with. I've wound up feeling sorry for Matt, actually. He's not a happy man."

"Have you hidden out from him because you think he might retaliate against you in some way for leaving him?"

"I'm not hiding out," Marilee protested. "Matt could find me if he really wanted to." After a moment's thought she added, "I'm not the doormat person I was then. I could stand up to him now. But I don't see any point in making myself readily available for an unpleasant confrontation."

"That's probably wise."

"Or maybe it's a convenient rationalization," Marilee admitted. "Anyway, I have a good life now. I'm even . . . seeing someone."

"I'm glad to hear that."

"I'm just so sorry about what happened to Kane. Why would anyone try to rob H&B? I don't think they ever kept much cash there."

"I think that's true, but there happened to be a considerable amount of cash there that particular night."

"I wonder why?"

Cate hesitated, briefly wondering about the ethics of giving the ex-wife a detail that hadn't been released to the public. Cautiously she said, "I believe it was intended as a loan to Kane."

"So Kane did decide he had to ask Matt for money!"

"You knew about a loan?" Cate asked.

"Kane told me he'd had some 'business reversals' and might have to borrow some money." She paused. "No, he phrased it differently. He said get '*another* loan.' Then he laughed and said something about trading one loan shark for another.

And I can imagine, if he was borrowing from Matt, he'd pay a loan shark interest rate."

Perhaps the loan wasn't such an all-out generous gesture on Halliday's part, then?

"Did Kane ever mention a gambling problem?"

"Gambling? No. But I guess I wouldn't be surprised if he did have one. Kane was always a big risk taker." After a reflective pause, she added, "A gambler with life, you might say. I remember him driving in a demolition derby once. And skydiving."

"It seems possible that gambling debts were the reason Kane was borrowing money from Halliday."

"And someone outside the company knew the loan money would be there at H&B that night?"

"That seems to be a big possibility," Cate said.

"It seems odd either of them would have told anyone about the loan or the cash being there that night."

Exactly. "Well, thanks for talking to me. If you should happen to think of something that might be helpful in my investigation—"

"Exactly what *are* you investigating? The man who killed Kane is dead, and Matt shot him in self-defense, so . . . ?"

"There's been a threat, a written threat, on Matt Halliday's life too. It could be just a crank thing. Crackpots come out of the woodwork when sensational crimes happen. But it may be for real," Cate said. "I'm trying to find out who made the threat before the person makes good on it."

"And you suspect me?"

"It crossed my mind," Cate admitted. "My mentor in the PI business occasionally reminds me that you have to be suspicious of everyone."

"Interesting occupation."

"Anyway, if you think of anything, I'd appreciate a call." Cate added her landline number.

"I'll do that." Unexpectedly Marilee added, "You be careful too."

"Me? I don't think anyone's out to get me."

"It's Matt you're working for, isn't it? Trying to find out who's out to get him?"

"Yes."

"If someone thinks you're getting close to finding out who that person is, you could be a target too," Marilee said.

Yeah. Right. That thought had slithered around in Cate's head too, though she hadn't let it burst right out in the open. Someone might want her out of the way before she identified him. And that someone might be Andy Timmons.

"As you said, be suspicious of everyone," Marilee added.

"Thanks. I'll remember that."

◆◆◆

Cate and Mitch got the plants tucked in the ground. While they worked, she filled him in on her conversations with both Lily and Marilee. Clancy proudly produced his "buried treasure" when they were picking up their tools for the day.

"Hey, it's a shoe," Mitch said.

Clancy gave up his treasure willingly enough, and Mitch dangled it from a finger. A hint of glamour remained. Ragged leather that had once been gold colored, remnant of an ankle strap, a stiletto heel of some apparently indestructible clear plastic material with a gold cloverleaf embedded inside.

Mitch laughed. "Not yours, right? I can't imagine you ever wearing something like this."

Right. Definitely not Cate's style. Although, for a moment, it was a little depressing to think that such a fanciful shoe would never be mistaken for hers. But suddenly Cate realized who *would* have worn such a shoe. Amelia. The woman who had once owned both Octavia and this property was older, four times married, but determinedly hanging on to her long-gone youth with glamour clothes, sexy shoes, and a younger man.

A woman who was also dead. Murdered. Right here. The shoe had nothing to do with that, and yet . . .

Cate didn't believe in dark omens, but there was something about this buried treasure coming to light just now, so soon after Marilee's warning, that shot a shiver up her back. Would someone someday find one of her shoes buried somewhere, find it long after she was dead? Murdered?

Cate shook off the stab of apprehension. She got out the barbecue grill, and Mitch went to the store for steaks. They grilled T-bones and potato slices while the pleasant spring dusk gathered around them. Afterward they settled in lounge chairs on the patio and sipped iced tea.

It was a peaceful evening but rich with impressions on Cate's senses. Scent of freshly turned earth, croak of unseen frogs, lingering aromas of steak, rustles and chirps, faint wail of siren somewhere in the distance.

Cate felt a little dreamy now as she leaned back in her lounge chair. "I think I hear our seeds waking up," she said. "They know they're in the ground and are free to grow now."

"Could be." Mitch didn't sound dreamy. "I've been thinking."

Cate didn't feel like thinking, but she refrained from making some derogatory remark about his doing so.

"About this Zig guy," Mitch said. "You'd like to talk to him, right? Try to find out if he had any connection with the threat on Halliday."

Cate had a somewhat different perspective on stodgy, all-work-and-no-play Matt Halliday after talking to Marilee. Marilee hadn't openly answered Cate's question about abuse by her husband, but her wary attitude and determination to put that era of her life behind her had been answer enough. Yet that didn't change Cate's job as a PI, which was to find a potential killer before he nailed a client.

"Apparently Zig was a friend of Mace Jackson's. He could be the one who sent the threatening note to Halliday. Or know something," Cate said. "Yes, I'd like to talk to him."

"Your friend Lily said someone at this bar outside Lorane might know him. It's Saturday night. He might even be there."

Cate straightened slowly in the chair. "So you're saying . . . ?"

"I'll get the bike and we'll take a ride down there."

"To a biker bar?"

"We don't have to drink anything just because it's a bar," Mitch pointed out.

Cate had thought about driving down and trying to locate the bar on a weekday to ask questions about Zig. She hadn't thought about trying to hit it when the bikers were there doing whatever bikers did in a bar on Saturday night. But that would undoubtedly be the prime time to do it . . .

She lifted her arm to look at her watch in the faint glow of moonlight filtering through a riffle of clouds. "Mitch, it's already past 9:00."

"So? Do you turn into a PI pumpkin at midnight? Even if you do, we've still got three hours. It shouldn't be more than an hour's ride down there. C'mon, let's go!"

27

They zoomed out of Eugene on I-5 heading south. Light traffic, half-moon high in the sky, dark forests on either side of the highway. Those marvelous spots of warmer air mixed with the cool of night that passengers in a car passed through unnoticed, but on a bike hit like a tropical surprise.

Okay, even if they didn't find out anything about Zig, it was still an awesome night for a bike ride. Cate felt as if they could zoom right up into the sky, silhouetted against the moon, like those bicycles in that old E.T. movie.

The bar was easy enough to find, even in the rural area between Cottage Grove and Lorane. The oversized figure of a neon logger looming over the log building was visible from a half mile away, the blade of his axe blinking red against the sky. Closer up, another sign over the double doors spelled out The Midnight Logger in blue neon.

Nothing specifically announced that this was a biker bar, including the name, but the jungle of motorcycles in the parking area said that was what it was, at least on this Saturday night.

Mitch parked the Purple Rocket at the edge of the jungle. The bikes were in an orderly lineup close to the railed walkway along the front of the building, but farther back, the order deteriorated into an every-bike-for-itself arrangement. Some of the motorcycles were chromed up, double seated, complete with trunks and saddlebags. Others were low-slung and mud-spattered, with minimal accessories. Lots of choppers and ape-hanger-style high handlebars. A few colored streamers and flags, which Cate hoped didn't indicate biker gang connections. Although the only real requirement to fit in here seemed to be that a bike be *big*.

The Purple Rocket fulfilled that requirement.

Cate slid off and uneasily unfastened her helmet. One door of the double-doored main entrance to the bar stood open, and rowdy country and western music blasted into the parking lot. She couldn't see much through the opening, but she couldn't tell if that was because the lights were so dim or if a blue-smoke haze engulfed everything. Maybe both. Moving shadows inside suggested a dance or a brawl. Maybe both.

Off to the side, a low, metal-roofed building held the restaurant Lily had mentioned, its windows lit. An extension of that building was dark, apparently the grocery store she'd also mentioned. Gas pumps stood out front of it.

Cate clutched her helmet, reluctant to set it aside and commit herself to entering the bar. She didn't have a basic aversion to loud music, although it wasn't the noise-level setting she'd choose for gathering information.

"Are we sure this is a good idea?" she asked.

"No," Mitch admitted.

"How can we possibly find out anything in there? It's dark, noisy—" Even a little scary. "We won't even be able to find each other if we get separated."

"We go up to the bar and order a couple of 7UPs. Then we ask the bartender if he's seen Zig around tonight."

"And if he has?"

"We take our 7UPs and go find Zig. I'll hang on to you all the time."

Cate found that assurance both comforting and dismaying. Should a licensed private investigator need to be hung on to?

"And what if the bartender takes umbrage at the question, like we're being too nosy about customers? Like maybe we're undercover cops or something?"

Mitch tilted his head as if that were a possibility. "Okay, we say we heard this Zig might have a Harley for sale. It could be true." He surveyed the sea of chrome and leather overhung with scents of exhaust and dust. "Surely some of these bikes are for sale."

Cate didn't feel any burst of enthusiasm, but she nodded. "So, we find Zig. How do we start a conversation with him? If we mention Andy or Mace, we may scare him off immediately. Or all his friends will instantly gang up on us, like piranhas in a puddle."

"We can start by saying something about a good crowd here tonight. Or good music. You know, small-talk stuff."

"You sure that's what bikers talk about in bars?"

Mitch's scrunch of eyebrows confirmed what Cate already knew. He had no idea what bikers talked about in bars. But he had an answer. "We could ask him about that Harley we heard he has for sale. Or if he knows someone else who has one."

"What if the bartender says he hasn't seen Zig? Or he's never heard of him?"

"Cate, I don't have a script figured out for every alternate universe possibility." Mitch was just short of an eye roll of exasperation. "We'll just have to play it by ear."

Yeah, right. If they still had eardrums after two minutes inside the Midnight Logger.

Most helmets were hanging on handlebars or plunked casually on seats, but Mitch and Cate stashed theirs in the trunk of the Purple Rocket. She was rummaging in the trunk for her purse when an "oh no!" thought hit her.

They'd taken Clancy back to Mitch's condo when they went to get the Purple Rocket, but he'd sensed right away that he was about to be shut out of an adventure. He made such a mournful objection to being left alone in the condo that they finally took him back out to the SUV where he was content to wait, as he often waited for Mitch.

But in the confusion of doing that, Cate now realized her purse was still sitting on the counter in Mitch's condo. Everything from driver's license to PI identification card to money and lipstick was in it.

Okay, no problem. She could get along without all that. Mitch could pay for their 7UPs.

Music twanged louder with every step they took toward the bar. Three guys burst out the door and one yelled something distinctly uncomplimentary at the other two before heading across the parking lot. Cate's steak and potatoes square-danced in her stomach. She saw no way this scheme could work, and this place practically screamed "in over your head!"

She stopped short, another dismaying thought hitting her.

"Mitch, did you suggest coming here tonight on purpose to make me see that I'm no way qualified to be a private investigator, with or without a license?"

"*That's* what you think?"

"Is it?"

Mitch grabbed her shoulders and yanked her around to face him. "Cate, I have serious concerns about your *being* a PI, that's true. It doesn't strike me as the safest of occupations."

Cate couldn't argue that. She might intend to do mundane,

everyday investigative work, but killers seemed to gravitate to her. Like bikers to a biker bar.

"But I suggested coming here tonight because I wanted to help out. Now I'm beginning to think I should have settled down with Clancy in front of the TV and watched an old Garfield DVD. He likes Garfield."

"Okay. I'm sorry. I didn't mean to be unappreciative. Maybe I asked that because sometimes *I* have serious doubts about my PI abilities."

Mitch dotted a kiss on her forehead. "You'll do fine."

"It would be nice if all investigations could be conducted with nice people in cozy little tea shops or toy stores."

Mitch grinned at her. "Cate, with your luck, one of the tea drinkers would drop dead from arsenic in her tea. Or there'd be a murderous clown in the toy store."

They'd reached the two steps leading up to the main entrance. The wave of music pounded into Cate's eardrums and skin. Her teeth sizzled. She took a steadying breath before they stepped into the blue haze.

And came up against a plaid-shirted wall of muscle.

A big man, as tall as Mitch, forty pounds heavier. Marine haircut. Blue plaid shirt. Something like a miniature baseball bat hanging from his belt.

"I'll need to see some ID, please." He spoke loudly enough that Cate had no trouble hearing him in spite of the drums and guitars and voice of a singer doing a stomping version of "White Lightning."

"What difference does it make who we are?" Cate asked, half-indignant about an invasion of privacy, half-embarrassed at being here. She could see now that the shadowy movement was dancing, not brawling, but her nerves were into tornado mode anyway.

"Not *who* you are. How *old* you are."

"Oh." Cate was momentarily uncertain whether to be pleased or indignant. She wasn't in the habit of frequenting places with an age minimum, and she hadn't even thought about this. But she was certainly old enough. "I'm thirty."

"Great." He pushed them outside, where the music was a fraction below ear-shattering level. "But I need to see ID. We ID everyone who looks under forty. We got busted last year when the cops found two underage kids here. It isn't going to happen again."

"Just show him your ID," Mitch muttered. He'd already pulled out his wallet and was offering his driver's license.

"I don't have it. I left my purse on the counter in your condo."

The man used a small flashlight to check Mitch's driver's license, nodded, and handed it back to him.

"I can vouch for her," Mitch said. "She *is* thirty."

"The big three-oh," Cate said. "Some women won't even admit it when they get past twenty-nine."

"No ID, no admittance," the wall of muscle said.

"But we don't intend to drink anything." Cate could hear herself sounding a little desperate now. "We're just looking for a guy. Zig is his name. Short, heavyset, bald—"

"Look, I don't care if you came to look for your swingin' grandma or your lost dog. No ID, no admittance. Would you step aside, please. There's someone behind you."

The man let the couple behind them in without checking ID. Cate was briefly indignant. How come she and Mitch were being singled out? Then she realized that, although the couple might be wearing black leather and have helmets tucked under their arms, they were in at least their sixties. Bikers came in all shapes, sizes, and ages.

The man turned back to Cate and slightly less sternly said, "The restaurant's open. If your friend wants to come in and look for someone, you can go over there and get a cup of coffee or a burger or something."

Mitch nudged her arm. "That okay with you?"

It wasn't okay, but Cate didn't see that she had any other choice. "Okay. But I *am* thirty. I had a birthday three months ago."

"Congratulations."

"I'll walk her over to the restaurant and be right back," Mitch told the doorkeeper, or whatever he was. He grabbed Cate's elbow and turned her away as if afraid she might do something that would earn them both a whack with that weapon dangling from the doorkeeper's belt.

At the door to the restaurant, Mitch gave her another kiss on the forehead. "Calm down. I'll go play detective for you."

Cate went inside. Music from the bar was piped into here too. Not bad music, she decided grudgingly. The singer was into a good version of the old "Tennessee Waltz" classic now. A few people sat on stools at the counter, but only a couple of the booths were occupied. Cate slid into an empty one.

She had first been un-eager to go into the blue haze of the Midnight Logger, but now that she *couldn't* go in, she felt let down. Left out. What kind of a PI couldn't even get into a bar to check out shady characters?

A waitress came over with a glass of ice water. Cate asked for coffee. As the waitress was leaving, she thought of something else. She had no money to pay for coffee. Great. What now? Arrest for defrauding a place of business?

She thought about slipping out before the coffee arrived, but she wasn't eager to be out there wandering around in the jungle of motorcycles. She wasn't, in fact, even sure she could locate the Purple Rocket alone. Was there another way, a back way maybe, into the bar, so she could get in and look for Zig herself? Hey, there must be! A delivery entrance or fire exit. She could slip inside—

She booted that thought before it got any farther. If Mr. Marine or a clone caught her, he might do something more drastic than simply escort her outside. Maybe he'd call her parents. Or pastor. Or the police. The dreaded Three Ps of teenagerhood come back to haunt her from high school days.

The coffee arrived, thankfully without a demand for immediate payment, and she sipped it morosely. Not even midnight yet, and already she'd turned into a PI pumpkin.

28

The minutes dragged by. Five minutes. Cate nursed the coffee carefully. She didn't want to ask for a refill. Eight. Mitch would surely pay for the coffee when he showed up. Eleven minutes. At least the restaurant was smoke free. She didn't have her little notebook to make notes in, but she found a pen in her pocket and jotted down a rough record of the day on a couple of paper napkins. Where *was* Mitch?

Okay, she was being overly impatient. He needed time to find Zig. Make biker small talk. Work up to what Zig knew about Mace Jackson and Andy Timmons.

Sixteen minutes.

Maybe he'd decided to sit there, sip his 7UP, and enjoy the music for a while. Let her stew in her incompetence. How *could* she have walked off and left purse and ID on the counter?

Seventeen minutes.

Hey, there he was coming through the door! Cate rose in her seat and waved at him, and he turned her direction. He seemed a little unsteady on his feet as he wobbled down the aisle between booths. Did he actually *drink* something?

He slid into the booth across from her, reached for her cup

of coffee, and took a big slurp. "Caffeine," he muttered. He had a hand plastered to the side of his head. He worked his jaw back and forth.

She sniffed, catching both the smell of smoke from the bar plus another less identifiable scent. "What is that smell?"

"Beer."

"Beer?"

"I got slugged on the side of the head with a beer bottle. It wasn't empty."

She could see the dark splotch on his clothes now. She looked closer at his face. Not wobbly from drink. Wobbly from a hit on the head. The point of his jaw was already swelling.

"Oh, Mitch, I'm sorry! What happened?"

He took another sip of the coffee, then fished a chunk of ice out of her water glass and rubbed it over the swelling joint.

"I went up to the bar. They didn't have 7UP, but I got a Sprite. I asked about Zig. The guy said he'd only been working there a couple weeks and didn't know any Zig. He pointed to some guys sitting over at a table and said maybe they knew him. I took my Sprite and went over there. There were eight guys at the table. They all looked like your description of Zig," he added, sounding as morose as she'd been feeling.

"And they hit you with a beer bottle?"

"No, they were okay guys. Friendly. They dragged up another chair and made room for me to sit at the table with them."

"Did they ask why you wanted to find Zig?"

"Yeah. I said he was a friend of a friend, and they seemed okay with that. They just talked back and forth—shouted, actually. You couldn't really talk in there. Anyway, they shouted about who Zig was and was I sure it wasn't Zack instead of Zig, and someone asked, what was his ride, and I didn't know."

"So then they hit you with a beer bottle?"

"No. Then one of them said something about, hey, wasn't he that guy had the old Moto Guzzi—"

"What's a Moto Guzzi?"

"Disease? Pizza? But probably it's some brand of bike I never heard of."

"And then they hit you with a beer bottle?"

"No. Then someone suggested maybe that red-haired Rita from Springfield was Zig's old girlfriend and somebody else said wasn't that her sitting up there on a bar stool. So I went over to talk to Rita on a bar stool. I asked her if she knew someone named Zig." He paused and dipped into the glass for more ice. "And *then* I got slugged with a beer bottle."

"Rita hit you?"

"No, some guy I hadn't even seen walked up behind me and yelled something about, hey, stay away from her, and then he whacked me alongside the head." Mitch ran a finger over his teeth as if making sure they were all still attached.

"He thought you were trying to pick her up?"

"That was my general impression. He didn't want me talking to her anyway."

Cate was fairly clear on the biblical instructions about getting hit. If someone struck you on the right cheek, you should turn the other cheek to him also. Did that apply to a whack with a beer bottle in a biker bar?

"So what did you do?"

"I didn't have a chance to do anything. I was still wiping beer out of my eyes when some other guy slammed a fist in the jaw of the guy who hit me. Then Rita clobbered that guy with a big black purse the size of a suitcase. Somebody shoved her off the bar stool and she bumped into me, but I guess she thought I bumped her and she whacked me with the purse too." He felt the back of his head and then his nose. "I crashed into the floor, and somebody stepped on my hand."

Cate looked at his hand. It didn't have an actual imprint of a boot heel on it, but a couple of knuckles were scraped raw.

"Did they call the police?"

"I don't know. Chairs and bottles were flying and a table went down on top of me. I crawled out from under it and then through a whole forest of legs and feet. When I finally had a chance to stand up, it looked like half the bar was in a big brawl."

"What about Rita?"

"Last I saw, she was swinging that purse like she intended to mow 'em all down. The music was still playing. And people who weren't fighting were dancing like nothing was happening."

Was there a designated musical accompaniment for a biker brawl?

"I'm going to have to sit here for a few minutes before I get on the bike again." Mitch shook his head as if trying to dislodge the lingering cobwebs.

"I'm sorry about . . . everything." Cate had never had any big desire to learn to operate the Purple Rocket herself, but now she wished she could do it. Then she could help Mitch out to the bike and they could just disappear into the night.

"And I didn't even find out anything about Zig," Mitch added glumly. "I guess coming down here wasn't such a helpful idea after all."

"It was a great idea." But sometimes even the best of ideas didn't work out. That was PI work.

Cate dipped another napkin in the ice water and carefully

cleaned around the raw spots on Mitch's hand. The lump on his jaw was getting bigger and his nose redder. He was using his other hand to prop up his head now.

She looked up when the door of the restaurant flew open and a woman strode in. Uh-oh. A woman with red hair and eyeliner that swooped into dark wings at the outer corners of her eyes. And a big black purse with metallic studs and fringe. With the strut of a one-woman parade, she headed for a booth beyond Cate and Mitch but stopped short when she spotted Mitch. She was short and a little chubby, young enough that the guard guy would have checked her ID, but not as young as Cate had thought at first glance.

The woman leaned over to look closer at Mitch. Cate half rose in her seat, feeling protective. Mitch was in no condition to be on the receiving end of another slugger swing with the purse.

Instead, with what sounded like real concern, the woman said, "Hey, you okay? I wondered what happened to you." Only then did she seem to notice Mitch wasn't alone. Her blue eyes gave Cate a frosty inspection. Cate had the impression the woman would rather have found Mitch sans probable girlfriend.

Cate half-expected a surly grunt from Mitch. *Yeah, sure. I'm great. I always sit around holding my head in my hands as if it's a soggy squash about to fall off the vine.*

But Mitch was nicer than that. "I'm fine." Although he did glance warily toward the door as if expecting a beer-bottle-wielding biker boyfriend might be following her.

"Did I hit you? I didn't mean to. It was kind of dark in there."

Mitch waved a dismissive hand. Well, actually it was just a fingertip wave, as if his joints weren't all that well connected at the moment.

"I don't know what's wrong with that idiot Maxie. It's not as if I *belong* to him or something. None of his business who I talk to."

Mitch apparently wasn't going to ask the question, but Cate, with her own wary glance at the door, did. "Where is Maxie now?"

"I told him to get lost. Go back to whatever rock he crawled out from under. Dumb creep."

Hopefully that meant Maxie wasn't out there recruiting reinforcements with beer bottles to launch a full-scale assault in the restaurant.

"Have the police arrived?" Cate asked, also hopefully.

Rita gave her one of those what-planet-are-you-from looks that she seemed to get a lot lately. "Why would they call the police? It was just a little fight. Not like it was a riot or something."

Cate hadn't been aware of a rating system in biker bar brawling. Learn something every day.

"Oh. Well, that's, um, good, then," she said. Then, uneasily wondering about the dismissed "dumb creep" and where this left Rita, Cate asked, "Did you and Maxie come here together?"

"Yeah, we rode down from Springfield together."

Cate considered that statement with concern. They couldn't just leave Rita stranded here. But three on a bike wouldn't work. Rita wasn't as hairy as Clancy and she had fewer legs, but she was, well, bigger-bottomed.

"Do you have any way to get back to Springfield?" Maybe they could go home, get the SUV, and return for Rita.

"Sure. Not a problem. I came on my own bike—'05 Harley," she said, with obvious pride.

The woman didn't make any move to leave, and finally Cate asked, "Would you like to sit down?"

"Sure. I'm Rita."

"Cate." She pointed across the table. "He's Mitch."

"Hi, Cate and Mitch." Rita slid into the booth beside Cate and set the impressive purse on the seat between them. "You asked me about somebody, didn't you?" she said to Mitch. "Before crazy Maxie bashed you."

"We're trying to locate a guy named Zig," Cate said, since Mitch was concentrating on working his jaw back and forth again.

Rita shook her head. "I don't know any Zig."

Cate offered the description Lily had given her.

Rita shook her head again. "Sounds like at least ten guys I know. Where you guys from?"

"Eugene," Cate said.

"If you ever need a good manicure or hand massage or pedicure, I'm at Heavenly Hair and Hands." A glance at Cate's fingernails suggested Cate had better sign up for a full treatment. As soon as possible.

Rita's own nails were quite spectacular. Long and purple, with a different flower painted on each one. Except one of those flowers looked ominously close to a sprig of something illegal.

"I'll remember that," Cate said. "Heavenly Hair and Hands."

As far as Cate could tell, the conversation had now covered all possible connections between them. However, since Rita didn't seem inclined to go anywhere, she decided it wouldn't hurt to toss out a couple other names.

"How about Mace Jackson? Do you know him? Big guy, ponytail, skulls tattooed on his knuckles." *Dead*, although she didn't add that.

Skull-decorated knuckles didn't faze Rita. "I know a guy

with a skull on the back of his bald head, but no knuckle skulls."

"Andy Timmons? Have you heard of him?"

Another negative shake of head. That seemed to cover any possible mutual acquaintances they might have. Cate thought of one more.

"Kane Blakely?"

"Nope. Who are all these guys anyway? I'm here most Saturday nights and I don't know any of them."

"Oh, they're just guys. I don't know that they ever come here. Actually, the skulls-on-knuckles guy was more into bicycles than motorcycles, I think. Andy Timmons has an old Indian bike he's trying to sell."

"Yeah? Hey, I maybe met him. This friend of mine was into old bikes. Bought 'em to fix up and sell over the internet. Got some crazy prices for them. I went with him a while back to see this old Indian bike he'd heard some guy had. Skinny little guy. With an oversized mustache. And ego."

"That could be him."

"Those old Indians are worth a bundle, but this guy wanted about double what the bike was worth, Tuffy said."

"Maybe that's why he hasn't sold the bike yet. Although I heard he's about to make a deal. Does your friend Tuffy know Andy well?"

"I remember him saying even if the guy came down on his price, he wouldn't invest a nickel in it without making sure it wasn't stolen."

"Andy seems to have something of a reputation problem that way. Although I've heard that someone checked on the bike, and it wasn't stolen," she added.

"Yeah? Tuffy said later if he'd realized who the guy with the bike was, he wouldn't even of gone to look at it. Something about his name. I think the guy was using a different name now than when Tuffy knew him earlier."

Rita fished a piece of ice out of Cate's popular water glass and crunched on it. Cate considered this latest bit of information with interest. It plugged in with what Lily had said, that Mace had called Andy by a different name. Lily had thought it was a mistake made because Andy and Mace didn't know each other very well. But maybe it was no mistake. Maybe Mace had called him Artie because that was really his name.

"Do you know what name your friend knew Andy by?"

"If Tuffy mentioned it, I don't remember."

"Did he say anything more about Andy? Drugs, maybe?"

"I don't remember him saying anything about drugs." A sideways glance suggested the question of drugs was unwarranted, maybe irrelevant. Which Cate took to mean, what's a few illegal substances among friends? "I got the impression that Tuffy knew something about Andy from way back. Maybe that was why he was using a different name now."

Did Lily know all this? Cate didn't think so. Was she really thinking about taking off for Nevada or Arizona with Andy?

"Could you tell me where I could find your friend Tuffy and talk to him?"

"I thought it was this Zig you were hot to find."

"I need to talk to various people for my . . . project."

"Well, you aren't gonna find Tuffy." Rita blinked, not exactly overcome with emotion, but apparently touched by something. "He's dead."

"What happened?"

"Got hit by a hit-and-run driver right outside his bike shop over in Yoncalla a few days ago." She blinked again. "I remember him saying once that he didn't want to wind up an old biker sittin' around reminiscing about the good ol' days. And he didn't."

Tuffy got killed by a hit-and-run driver. Matt Halliday was run down by a vehicle, probably with intent to kill. Nothing said the incidents were connected, of course. But maybe hit-and-run was Andy Timmons's murder method of choice? Maybe he'd decided Tuffy knew too much about his past and gotten rid of him. Halliday was his next target, according to that threatening note. And was Cate somewhere in that condemned lineup too?

29

Some noisy friends of Rita's tromped in. She stood up and apologized again to Mitch for hitting him with her purse. Cate *oofed* when she lifted the purse off the seat and handed it to Rita. Maybe that was the time-saving system of bodybuilding: carry a purse heavy enough to act like a weight machine. With the side benefit of always having a secret weapon available. Rita moved off to another booth to sit with her friends.

Cate and Mitch huddled there for another twenty minutes until he said he felt un-groggy enough to handle the bike. He paid for her coffee, left a good tip for the length of time they'd occupied the booth, and they wound their way through the bikes to the Purple Rocket. Two bikes smoked out of the parking lot ahead of them, but three more arrived.

Maybe the biggest and best brawls were reserved for after midnight.

By then, the weather had done the Oregon thing, and the awesome night had morphed into scudding clouds. Mitch drove carefully on the freeway, a little slower than usual. A light sprinkle had started by the time they chugged up the driveway to Cate's house.

Cate stepped off the bike, opened the trunk behind her seat, and dropped her helmet inside. Mitch just sat there, balancing the bike with one foot on the ground. "You okay?" she asked.

"When I'm writing my memoirs, I may not include the Biker Bar Incident." After a slight pause, he wiggled his shoulders and added, "But yeah, I guess I'm okay."

No doubt thinking again that being a PI wasn't the safest occupation. Not exactly optimal for the PI's friends, either.

"I did find out some interesting information about Andy Timmons tonight, and I appreciate that. Thanks."

"Asking Rita about those other names was good thinking. I'm glad the evening wasn't a total waste."

Cate thought he was just going to zoom off, but he pushed up the faceplate of his helmet and leaned over to kiss her. Scents of smoke and beer still drifted around him, a fog invisible but potent, and kissing in a motorcycle helmet was rather like trying to kiss with oversized braces. But, in spite of a clunk on her jaw with the chin guard on his helmet, Mitch's determination turned it into a memorable kiss.

Perhaps catching a whiff of his own scent, he muttered, "I'm going home and taking a shower."

"You might throw those clothes in the washer too."

"I could keep them as mementos of the night. I've never been in a bar fight before."

Saying "first time for everything" didn't seem like a helpful comment, so Cate just leaned over and dropped a careful kiss on his nose. He waited at the end of the walkway until she was safely inside. She watched from a window as he made a slow descent rather than his usual zoom down the steep driveway to the street.

Inside, Octavia jumped down from the window seat with a welcoming meow and then accompanied Cate to the bathroom. Cate stripped off her clothes and kicked them into a pile to dump in the washer. They hadn't come in direct contact with either smoke or beer, but the scents seemed to be immortalized in the fibers anyway. Octavia curled up in the sink and kept Cate company while she showered. She toweled off, still thinking the same thought that had dogged her all the time she was under the hot spray of water. *Now what?* She didn't relish the answer that came to mind, but it was something that had to be done.

◆◆◆

They hadn't discussed the next day, but Mitch showed up at his usual time for church together. Cate ran out to the SUV to meet him so he wouldn't have to run through the rain to come into the house. Last night's sprinkle had expanded into a downpour, fresh-scented but not mood-lifting. She climbed into the SUV, and Clancy gave her his usual slurpy welcome. Mitch, in dark glasses in spite of the rain, handed her the purse she'd left at his condo before their visit to the biker bar.

His swollen jaw wasn't too noticeable now. But probably only because, when he pushed the dark glasses back on his head, it was overshadowed by a spectacular black eye.

Cate gave a little gasp when she saw it. "I didn't realize you'd gotten hit there too."

"Neither did I, until I got up this morning. Maybe I bumped into someone's knee when I was crawling around down there on the floor. Or maybe that's where Rita's purse got me."

No doubt any number of dangerous possibilities when you were on the floor in a bar brawl.

"Can I do anything to help?" Cate asked. Technically she wasn't responsible for his injuries, but she still *felt* responsible. She leaned across the seat and brushed a fingertip around the black eye. "It's kind of attractive, actually, in a tough-guy way. Very macho. Even mysterious."

"No photos, please," he muttered.

A new family filled Uncle Joe and Rebecca's usual spot in the third row of seats at church. Most people already knew why they were missing, and Cate explained to a few who didn't. Mitch kept the dark glasses on in church, but the bump on his jaw drew some curious looks and questions. He merely said, "Long story," and didn't offer details.

After church, Mitch offered Sunday dinner somewhere, but Cate could see that at the moment, his eagerness for dinner rivaled his enthusiasm for another jaunt to the Midnight Logger. She suggested he go on home and take it easy for the day, and he didn't argue. She had her own project in mind anyway, and she didn't want Mitch involved. She'd already caused him enough grief by getting him into a bar brawl.

Back home, she changed into jeans and heated a can of noodle soup for lunch. The rain wasn't letting up. Water slid down the concrete driveway in a silvery sheen, and small rivers burbled along the curbs down on the street. She'd just poured the soup into a bowl when her landline phone rang.

"Belmont—" She broke off and corrected that. "Kinkaid Investigations. Cate Kinkaid speaking."

"Hi, Cate, this is Seth Erickson in Salem. You remember me? The guy who didn't get to take you to dinner?"

"Yes, of course. Nice to hear from you. Did you think of something?"

"I don't know that it means anything, but I thought I'd tell you."

Cate made an encouraging murmur.

"There used to be two women working in the office, but the second one moved down to California somewhere. She'd done the bookkeeping, but Kane didn't replace her. I guess he could do it well enough himself to send on to the CPA, where it got coordinated with the Eugene books. Or something like that. I'm not much into bookkeeping, as you can probably tell."

"I see." Though she didn't really see where Seth was going with this.

"So that was a while back, and then a month or six weeks ago, some bean-counter guy showed up to look at the records. This according to Angie. I saw him myself a couple times because he must have been there a couple days. Looking for lost nickels or whatever it is those audit guys do."

"Was an audit something that was done regularly?" Cate asked.

"I have no idea."

"Was it Mr. Blakely's idea to do this?"

"No idea about that either. Although I remember Angie saying he seemed surprised when the guy showed up. He came out and worked in the shop while the guy was there, and he seemed kind of jittery. I wondered if maybe the guy was from the IRS."

"I suppose that would make anyone nervous. Did you hear anything more after it was over?"

"Angie said she was really curious and kind of hinted around to Kane what the guy was doing. She said Kane just made a joke about it. He got all mournful looking and said something like, 'Oh, it's a disaster. They're onto us. They've found out about those ten tons of hubcaps we shipped to Lower Slobbovia to be made into radiator caps for jet airplanes.' Angie said it kind of scared her for a minute, but then it finally occurred to her that we've never had ten tons of hubcaps, let alone shipped them anywhere. And jet planes don't have radiator caps."

"I've heard he was kind of a tease," Cate said. Kane had

also, she realized, effectively dodged giving Angie any real answer about what the bean counter had been doing in the office.

"So I don't know that this means anything. But I thought I'd tell you. I mean, that dude was looking for *something*."

"Thanks. I appreciate your calling me."

"It also gives me an opportunity to say that the dinner and movie offer is still open. I could be persuaded to drive down to Eugene, so you wouldn't even have to make the trip up here."

"Thanks, Seth. But I really am still involved."

Although maybe not for long.

"And thanks again for calling," she added.

Cate tossed Seth's information back and forth in her head. The bean counter could have been an IRS auditor, as Seth had suggested. But, if it was a private auditor, and Kane was surprised, Halliday must have sent him.

A routine thing, to determine whether the Salem branch should be closed? But the CPA could surely have provided those figures. Was Halliday checking up on the figures Kane was turning over to the CPA?

◆◆◆

A little after 3:00, Cate grabbed an umbrella by the garage door as she went out to her car. By the time she parked at the convenience store, she figured it was close to Lily's break time.

Inside, she spotted Lily at the cash register. She circled around to the refrigerated shelves in back and picked up a couple of cold drinks. She grabbed a bag of chips on the way to the cash register. Only one person was ahead of her.

She set her purchases on the counter. "Hi, Lily."

Grunt. With all the hospitality of a door slam in the face of a bill collector.

"I was thinking maybe we could share your break again."

"I'm really busy," Lily said.

Oh? Unlike the sunny spring day when Cate had been here before, today the convenience store could be a poster store for economic downturn. One older man glumly inspected the packaged sandwiches, and a tired-looking woman with a baby on her hip studied a tabloid photo showing some movie star proudly displaying her sleek belly only six weeks after giving birth.

"I'm in no hurry. I can wait," Cate said.

"I don't want to talk to you." Lily rang up Cate's purchases, dumped them in a plastic bag, accepted a ten-dollar bill, and gave her change. "Have a nice day," she added, managing to make it sound like a voodoo curse.

The older man selected a sandwich, and Cate stepped aside to let him pay for it. When he left, she moved up to the counter again.

"I don't have any questions to bother you with today. I just need to tell you something."

That wasn't totally accurate. Cate had wanted to ask what Lily knew about the Andy/Artie name thing. But she'd settle for warning Lily that Andy's past might mean she was in a more dangerous relationship than she realized.

"Something I think you need to know before you move off to Arizona or somewhere with Andy," Cate added.

Another brush-off wouldn't have surprised her, but Lily showed a hint of reluctant interest when she folded her arms across her chest, spread her feet in a belligerent stance, and said, "So tell me."

"Could we go out to my car again?" Was this how Lily's brother had felt when he'd tried to talk sense into her? Like he might as well talk to one of those chunks of firewood? She held up the plastic sack. "I bought snacks for both of us."

"It's raining."

Irrefutable logic there. It *was* raining, pouring down heavier than ever. Cate started to point out that she had an umbrella, but then she realized Lily wasn't even looking at her now. Cate turned and saw a figure clad in a khaki raincoat just coming through the door. No hat, and drops of rain beaded his dark hair and mustache.

Andy recognized her, Cate could tell. One thing about tomatoes-on-fire red hair, even if the rest of you was forgettable, people tended to remember the hair. Had Lily told Andy that Cate had been here snooping for information about his connection to Mace?

"Hey," he said. He didn't look ready to attack or run to avoid her, but neither was he giving off happy-reunion vibes. "Some rain, huh?"

Cate could go along with Andy's small-talk ploy, but she made a quick decision. If Lily wouldn't talk to her privately, she'd have to do it another way. Lily needed to know this.

"Hi, Artie. Yeah, some rain."

If she thought surprising him with the name would send him into a tailspin, she was mistaken.

"Ah, the busy private investigator." Andy dipped his head in mock deference. "Hard at work snooping in everyone's business."

"What's that mean?" Lily demanded. Her eyes narrowed as if she was ready to do battle with someone, but she hadn't decided on the appropriate target yet.

"She turned up the fact that I use a different name now than I used to," Andy said to Lily.

"You never told me that!"

"It's no big deal." Andy gave an oversized shrug in the oversized raincoat. Was he hiding something in there? The

279

raincoat could conceal anything from a jumbo rolling pin to an assault rifle. Cate calmed herself with the thought that Andy hadn't known she'd be here, so no reason he'd have come armed.

"When I was a kid down in Sacramento, I was Artie," Andy went on. He looked at Lily, not Cate. "My mom made me use my stepdad's last name. Now I use my middle name, Andy, and my real last name, Timmons. Arthur Andrew Timmons. My stepdad was a jerk," he added, as if that explained everything.

Apparently it did to Lily. She turned to Cate with a triumphant smile. "See?"

"Was that the name you were using when you—" Cate broke off, because she didn't know for sure what he'd done. She tossed in a generic substitute. "When you got in trouble with the law down there?"

"Who says I got in trouble with the law?" The mustache wiggled as Andy smiled. "My mom had enough of those my-son-is-student-of-the-month stickers to cover every bumper in the neighborhood."

"Was down in Sacramento where you were friends with Mace Jackson?" Cate asked.

"I knew a lot of guys down there. Surprising how many of them have moved up here. God's country, isn't that what they call it?"

"How about somebody named Tuffy who buys and sells bikes?"

"It's none of your business who Andy's friends are," Lily snapped. Andy nodded pleased agreement at this show of support.

"What was the stepfather's name that you used?" Cate asked.

280

"You don't have to answer her questions," Lily said. "She's just a private detective, not anyone important."

"I guess I won't answer then."

Even if she wasn't getting answers, Cate doggedly kept on. She tried for a conversational tone with the next question. "So, you've made a deal with Halliday on your old bike?"

"Is that what he says?"

"He says he hasn't even talked to you."

Something flickered in Andy's dark eyes, but all he did was shrug again. "I guess his memory is going bad, then. You know how it is with those old guys. Hey, babe, isn't it time for your break?"

"Yeah. I was thinking, it's too wet for anything cold. Let's get some coffee from the machine. And donuts. Those good cream-filled ones. We can sit in the back room." Lily gave Cate a glance and defiant toss of head to make sure she knew she wasn't included.

"Sounds good to me," Andy said.

Lily had a parting shot for Cate. "I'll be sure to send you that postcard, so watch for it."

Cate tightened her grip on her plastic bag. Outside, she zapped her umbrella open and headed for her car with the unpleasant feeling that she'd just been outmaneuvered. By weasely little Andy.

The wind suddenly grabbed her umbrella and whipped it inside out. An appropriate ending for the meeting she'd just had. She tossed the ruined umbrella in a trash barrel and slogged on through the rain and wind to her car.

◆◆◆

Cate tried to call Mitch later, but he didn't answer and she decided he'd probably turned everything off. Maybe he'd even gone to bed this early. She also called Candy and told her that Marilee was living in Portland, doing fine with some creative work for an interior designer, and "seeing someone." Candy asked if she was getting anywhere identifying who'd sent the threatening note.

"I'm working on some leads."

Except those leads had fizzled into dead ends, Cate decided glumly by the time the conversation with Candy ended. She was reasonably certain Andy Timmons had a significant misdeed of some kind in his past. She took time now to search the internet, but without knowing the last name he used in California, she might as well be surfing a vat of noodle soup for information.

All she had was suspicions. That Andy had a closer relationship with Mace Jackson than he was admitting. That he was the top-rated candidate for authorship of the threatening note. That he had deadly plans for Matt Halliday. And if she got in his way, maybe deadly plans for her too.

But she hadn't a shred of evidence to prove anything. Should she warn Halliday anyway? Or would it look as if she was using busywork to pad the bill for PI charges but not actually accomplishing anything?

The phone rang while she was trying to decide. Uncle Joe. Rain was hammering the coast too, but he and Rebecca weren't coming back to Eugene any sooner than planned. They were busy eating crab fresh-caught that day and playing pinochle with some new friends down from British Columbia.

Cate didn't give Uncle Joe any details of the case. It was Kinkaid Investigations now, her responsibility, not his. But she'd made up her mind by the time the call ended that she couldn't keep her suspicions to herself. Even if she didn't have concrete facts, she had to warn Halliday that Andy Timmons may have sent the note. Andy could be planning to use the old bike to maneuver Halliday into some dangerous situation, such as getting him alone somewhere, without arousing his suspicions.

Cate got back on her computer and started a report for Halliday. She used her notebook for details about her trip to Salem, although she left out more details than she put in. Nothing about staying overnight with Candy, nothing about Candy's later call with the phone number for Marilee. She tried to decipher what she'd written on a restaurant napkin at the Midnight Logger last night, but wrinkles and dampness had turned the words into some alien language. They read as if she'd been drinking something stronger than coffee. *Dsrik??* must have meant something when she scribbled it on the napkin, but she now had no idea what.

She ended the report with an admission that she had no proof Andy Timmons was dangerous, but she suspected he'd sent the threatening note. She added that at this point she had no immediate leads to follow, and, a question. Did he want her to stop the investigation now or keep digging?

◆ 30 ◆

On Monday morning, Cate called H&B to see if Halliday was in the office today. The report she had for him was likely a final wrap-up, and she wanted to deliver it to him in person and emphasize the danger Andy Timmons possibly presented. Radine said he'd gone up to the Salem branch early that morning, but he should be in sometime after lunch.

Cate used the morning to begin the process of officially setting herself up in business as Kinkaid Investigations. She applied for a business license and talked to Uncle Joe's agent about insurance and bond. She ordered new business cards. She changed the phone listing to the new business name. She called the shooting range and made an appointment with an instructor for Friday morning.

She headed for H&B about 2:00, but Halliday still hadn't returned. Radine said he was hauling a car down from Salem.

Radine eyed the envelope sticking out of Cate's purse. "If you have something for Matt, you can leave it with me."

"Maybe he'll come in before I leave. I'd like to talk to him for a minute. Is everything okay with Mr. Halliday?"

"He hasn't mentioned anyone trying to kill him lately, if that's what you're asking. Though I think the threat in that note is kind of getting to him." Radine sounded resentful, as if the note were somehow Cate's fault and Cate wasn't doing enough to protect her boss.

Hey, I'm an investigator, not a bodyguard, Cate mentally protested. But that silent protest didn't do anything to assuage the guilt she felt for not coming up with information solid enough to put someone behind bars for conspiracy in Kane's murder. And save Halliday from being targeted by that person also.

"I told him I thought he should take some time off and go on a vacation way off somewhere," Radine added. "But you know Matt. Work, work, work."

Cate nodded. "A vacation would be a good idea, considering all the strain he's been under." It would also get him out of this danger area. "Okay if I go out and talk to Shirley for a minute?"

"Sure."

Shirley looked up from her computer when Cate pushed through the door to the warehouse. "Hey, Cate! I haven't seen you for a while."

Shirley had gotten her hair cut, taking away most of the wiry curl and leaving a surprisingly flattering short pixie style. She hadn't changed the boots, however. They still looked capable of flattening old cars.

"Everything going okay?" Cate asked. "You never did get to a Fit and Fabulous session, but your hair looks great."

"I decided fit and fabulous was too much of a stretch for me. But I went to church yesterday." Shirley laughed. "Don't look so shocked. It isn't like I took a UFO ride with a herd of little green aliens."

"How did this happen?"

"Jerry asked if I'd like to go with him. He goes every Sunday.

Reads the Bible too. So I went." With a shrug of real or feigned indifference, she added, "I didn't have anything else to do yesterday morning."

"Are you going again?"

"I might."

"Okay, I'm all the way astonished," Cate admitted. "About you and Jerry both. You're, um, dating?"

"Dating? Oh no. We just kind of, you know, hang out together."

"Isn't that what kids call it these days?"

"I'm no kid. And I sure don't have any plans for getting involved with someone as young as Jerry," Shirley stated.

"I didn't plan to be a private investigator either, but here I am. God had different plans for me. Maybe he has different plans for you too." Especially considering the church-and-Bible surprise.

Shirley frowned. "Sometimes it feels as if God might be messing around in my life," she grumbled.

"Jerry sounds like a pretty good guy. And he isn't all *that* young."

"I remember eight-track tape players and shag rugs. He doesn't."

"I do too," a male voice behind them said. Jerry grinned, a smile that lit up his plain face. "I remember reading about them in a history book. They came along about the time the wheel was invented, didn't they?"

Shirley made a face at him, but then they both laughed. She might not have plans for getting "involved" with Jerry, but Cate could see that he had a different agenda. And, apparently, patience. That brought a smile to her face too. Yep, God was "messing around" here, at work in Shirley's life. Jerry's too.

Way to go, Lord.

On her way through the front reception area, Cate gave Radine the report to pass along to Halliday. She got a call from Mitch just as she was scooting into her car in the parking lot. He and Lance had to make an unexpected trip up to Portland for an evening conference with several of the top men in the company buying Computer Dudes. They'd be staying overnight for a breakfast meeting the following morning.

"What about Clancy?"

"Actually, I'm calling from your place, wondering where you were. Could he stay with you? I can leave him here in the SUV because we're taking Lance's car to Portland, and you can take him inside when you get here. If he and Octavia have territorial disagreements, you can put him out here for the night."

"Sure. That's fine."

"Thanks. Lance just got here. So we're off. I'll talk to you later."

◆◆◆

The SUV was parked in front of the garage doors when Cate got home. She let Clancy out and snapped a leash on his collar before taking him inside. He and Octavia usually settled into a wary truce if they were around each other for a while, but the first few minutes of each encounter were always tense as a Hatfield and McCoy confrontation.

Today they went through the ceremony of stiff-legged dog and porcupine-furred cat, but Octavia claimed the window seat while Clancy was still leashed, and he had to settle for a throw rug near the sofa. Octavia probably wished she had the hands to make a kid-face of thumbs in ears, fingers flapping, but she could use the anatomy she had to do queenly-smug quite effectively.

When the rain let up temporarily, Cate took Clancy for a walk around the neighborhood. Usually walking with Clancy was fun, but this time a new thought nibbled her nerves. While Mitch and Lance were in conference with the company, would he accept their offer of the job in Seattle? Or would that black eye and lumpy jaw make a difference to them? Mitch wouldn't volunteer details, of course, but if they specifically asked, she knew he wouldn't lie about the injuries. Would they rescind the offer? That gave her mixed feelings. She didn't want him to take the job and move off to Seattle. But neither did she want his trying to help her at the Midnight Logger result in the loss of the job opportunity.

◆◆◆

The rain had apparently been gathering strength for a new assault, and raindrops bounced off the concrete by the time she climbed the steep driveway up to the house with Clancy. Back at the computer, she looked for information on a new case, finding a witness to an accident for an insurance company. Not exciting work, but the kind that paid a PI's bills.

The landline phone rang about 7:00. Cate jumped to answer it—Mitch?—before remembering if it was Mitch, he'd have called her cell phone.

But, for the very first time, she didn't stumble when she briskly answered the call the new way. "Kinkaid Investigations, Cate Kinkaid speaking."

"Cate, this is Lily. I guess you, uh, remember me?"

A snarky question about "were the coffee and donuts good?" came to mind, but Cate managed a neutral tone when she said, "Yes, of course."

"I don't know if I should be calling you, but, uh, something's come up."

"Is there something I can help you with?" *Maybe we could get together and write a Dear John letter to Andy?*

"The thing is, I heard Andy talking on the phone a little while ago. I don't know for sure who he was talking to, but he asked the person if he had the cash money. So I'm thinking it was that Halliday, about buying the bike. And then, a few minutes ago, Andy left."

"Did he take the bike with him?"

"No, it's still sitting here."

In the middle of the living room floor.

Was this Andy's plan to set Halliday up so he could carry out the threat in that note? Had Halliday read her report yet about possible danger from Andy?

"Did this person call Andy or did Andy make the call?"

"I don't know. I was taking a shower, and when I came out, he was on the phone."

"Is he meeting Halliday somewhere?"

"I don't know for sure that it *was* Halliday he was talking to. I mean, maybe Andy's selling pot again, and he was checking to make sure the buyer had cash." Lily's ambivalent feelings about Andy, half-protective, half-accusing, were surfacing again. "It seems kind of strange that if this is about selling the bike, why didn't he take it with him?"

Good question. Halliday surely wasn't going to hand over a hefty amount of cash without getting the bike on the spot. She wouldn't if she were selling something to Andy.

"Then the guy must have said something about meeting him in a warehouse, because Andy said, yeah, he'd meet him in the warehouse. And then he sounded like he was kind of teasing or something because he said, 'Not eager to introduce me to your friends at a barbecue or fancy dinner, huh?' But

I have no idea what that was about or what warehouse he was talking about."

Cate didn't know what the "friends" taunt meant. But she had a good idea of the warehouse where they were meeting.

"He went in your pickup?"

"We don't have anything else to drive."

"Anything more?"

"I can't think of anything. The guy said something else and Andy said, 'Yeah, yeah, I can do that.' You can't tell much when you're only hearing half a conversation," Lily fretted.

"So what, exactly, are you worried about with this?" Cate asked bluntly.

Long pause before Lily finally said, "I'm not sure. When Andy left, he gave me a big kiss and said to start packing. We could take off for Nevada right away, because we were into some big bucks now. Or maybe we'd take a vacation in Hawaii first. Big bucks," she repeated, but she sounded apprehensive, not as if she were looking forward to packing for Nevada or vacationing in Hawaii.

"Lily, I really don't think you should go off to Hawaii or Nevada or—"

"I know what you think about Andy!" Lily flared. Cate heard her take a scratchy breath before she went on. "The thing is, I think he took a gun with him. But I don't know why he'd take a gun to sell that stupid old bike."

Cate remembered a finger jabbed in her back. "A real gun?"

"Yeah. A real gun. He keeps it in the bedroom. He doesn't know I know it's there, but I do. It's duct-taped to the underside of the bed. Except I looked and now it's gone. I-I'm scared. I'm afraid Andy is going to . . . *do* something to someone." Pause while she struggled with those mixed feelings again. "I'm afraid someone might do something to Andy."

Either was possible, Cate agreed.

"Sometimes I feel like I don't know Andy at all. I mean, he'd never even told me about the different name thing. Or that he knew that Mace Jackson."

"Maybe you should call the police."

"And tell them what?" Lily flared. "That my boyfriend left the apartment, and *maybe* he has a gun? That *maybe* he's meeting someone about selling a motorcycle, although he might be out there selling pot to someone in a warehouse somewhere? Or, for all I know, maybe selling the gun."

Okay, not a report likely to send the police scurrying to find Andy and slap handcuffs on him. Yet Matt Halliday could be in serious danger if he thought he was meeting Andy about buying the bike and Andy had a much darker purpose in mind. She'd gotten to the point where she knew enough about Matt Halliday that she didn't really *like* him. There was a dark side to both his personal and business relationships. But *her* personal and professional standards said she couldn't let him walk into an ambush.

"I'm not sure why you called me."

"I couldn't think of anyone else," Lily snapped. "But I can see now, it was a really dumb idea."

"Look, I'll see what I can do," Cate said. "If you hear from Andy, or he comes home, you call me right away, okay? So I won't be wandering around out there in the dark trying to find him." She gave Lily her cell phone number.

"Okay. And, uh, thanks, Cate."

A donut with that would be nice.

Cate first tried to call Halliday at the H&B number. It was past business hours, of course, but Halliday must be at the warehouse if he and Andy had a meeting set up there.

Except Halliday, if he was there, wasn't answering the

phone. The H&B number got her a recording of Radine giving the business hours: 9:00 to 5:30 Monday through Saturday, closed Sundays except by appointment.

She looked up a home phone number for Halliday and tried that one. No live response from Halliday, but an answering machine did invite her to leave a message. She was reluctant to announce her suspicions on an answering machine, but she was afraid Halliday might simply ignore a request to call her even if she said it was an emergency. She finally did leave a message advising him not to meet Andy alone, that it could be dangerous. She added both her business and cell phone numbers and asked that he call her back immediately.

Which did not give her a feeling of having completed her duty satisfactorily. Now what?

◆ 31 ◆

She decided on a quick run out to H&B. If Andy was already there, which meant a strong potential for danger, she'd call 911. She wouldn't earn points with police, Halliday, or Andy if the two of them were in the warehouse calmly negotiating on the bike when the cops arrived. She'd look like a paranoid redhead, the type who imagined a gun-toting outlaw behind every bush.

She'd take that risk. Making certain Halliday hadn't set himself up for a hail of bullets or a lone shot in the back was more important. She figured Andy was capable of either, and she had to warn Halliday.

She paused briefly by the gun hanging in its holster from the hook on the wall. Take it along?

And do what with it, since she didn't yet know how to put bullets in it, let alone aim and shoot?

She momentarily wished she had that voice-activated wrist-watch-style cell phone Mitch had once given her, but it had disappeared. She suspected Octavia had a secret stash of treasures somewhere, but her cat just purred when asked that question.

Cate made sure, however, that her cell phone was in quick-draw readiness in her jacket pocket.

She was halfway to H&B, windshield wipers in a losing

battle with the onslaught of windblown rain, when an un-happy realization hit her. She'd run out of the house in such a hurry that she'd neglected to put Clancy out in the SUV. Octavia and Clancy were now alone in the house. She groaned. Disaster in the making. Anything from a festival of shredded furniture to a cat-and-dog demolition derby. Try explaining *that* to an insurance company.

But she couldn't take time to turn around and go back. If Andy was already on his way to meet Halliday, she didn't have much time.

She whipped into the parking area at H&B and hit a puddle hard enough to blast a spray of water over her driver's side window. She pressed the button to run the window down to clear it and peered at a pickup and a car chained to a flatbed trailer standing under the lone yard light. The car Halliday had apparently gone to Salem to get, a big-finned '50s model that looked as if it had been in an urban riot. No other vehicles in the parking area.

Good. Even though Andy'd had a head start on her, she'd gotten here before him. Her whoosh of relief vanished when she angled the car around and two lights flashed at her from the building. Another car murderously headed straight for her! She jerked the steering wheel and screeched the brakes.

Well, no. She slid her hands across the wheel, then shakily wiped each palm on her jeans. Not another vehicle about to run her down. Her own headlights reflecting back to her from the front window of the building.

Get a grip, Ms. Licensed PI.

She shut the car lights off, and the glaring lights coming at her disappeared. Now all she could see through the rain was dim light from inside the office area. A closer peer over the steering wheel showed her the light came from the open door to the warehouse at the rear of the room. Halliday must be back there waiting for Andy.

She closed the window and opened the car door a crack. She'd just warn Halliday about the possible danger and make a quick retreat. She didn't have to wait around for Andy to arrive. Halliday could call 911 himself.

She fingered the cell phone in her pocket. Or maybe she should make that call right now. The police could be here when Andy arrived.

And do what? Andy would be righteously indignant and come up with an innocent excuse. He was here to sell his old bike. *Something wrong with that?* He'd slither away, free and clear.

Stick with the original plan. Warn Halliday.

A sudden inspiration made her click the H&B number on her cell phone again. Maybe the ringing phone would bring Halliday out of the warehouse and she wouldn't have to go inside.

She let the phone on the counter ring until Radine's voice kicked in again. No movement inside the building. Just that oblong of light marking the warehouse door.

She slid out of the car but left the door unlocked, just in case. Just in case what? Whatever.

Wind hammered the rain against her back and dribbled a cold trickle down her neck. A harder blast rattled something on the battered car on the trailer. A wind-whipped plastic bag sailed by and hit the front of the building. It clung to the window like the misshapen remnant of some tattered ghost.

Okay, knock off the imagination. Yes, she'd have preferred a windless, rainless evening, but there was no reason to be apprehensive.

Oh? So how come her palms were slippery enough to surf

on, and streams of nervous perspiration raced like whitewater rapids over her ribs?

Does the PI need her mommy?

Maybe not Mommy, but having Mitch here would be nice.

Now she was right in front of the door. A branch blown in from somewhere hit the metal siding of the warehouse with a tinny *whap*. A stronger *flap-flap* sounded as if a section of siding or roof had come loose. She had to wipe her hand before trying the knob.

Good thing there wasn't a dry palm test, or she'd never have gotten her PI license.

She turned the knob. Had she been hoping the door would be locked, and she could just say "I tried," and trot on home? It wasn't locked, of course. Halliday had no doubt left it open for Andy. Even with rain blowing in, she kept the door open a crack behind her as she called his name. "Mr. Halliday? Are you here, Mr. Halliday?"

No answer.

Rain made an indistinct rumble on the office roof, but it was hitting the metal roof out in the warehouse like a dozen watery jackhammers blasting full speed.

She took an uncertain step toward the light streaming from the open warehouse door. Another pause, and then she grabbed a breath deep enough to expand her voice to compete with the hammer of rain on metal roof. "Mr. Halliday, hey! Are you here?"

No answer.

She took another step and tried to stretch toward the door without getting too close, straining for any *different* sound from the warehouse. Rustle . . . whisper . . . murmur? Nothing. Beneath the pound of rain, silence. A very *dead* silence . . .

Had Andy already been here, made good on his threat, and gone? Her feet took root on the concrete floor. Was Halliday in there dead?

Another thought unrooted her feet, and she rushed for the door. Maybe not dead, maybe wounded, needing help—

The warehouse light blinked out just before she reached the door. She threw out a hand to grab the door frame and keep herself from skidding headlong through the dark opening. It didn't stop her. She careened into the solid body of a live person who'd risen up like a 3-D apparition. The force of her rush carried them both into the warehouse. Fear grabbed her as the figure clutched her arm and held her upright.

"Cate! I heard you calling me—"

Relief as she recognized the voice. Which didn't stop the flow of perspiration waterfalling over her ribs. She peered at him in the faint light coming through the front window from the yard light outside, but all she could see was a shadowy blob. "Mr. Halliday! I'm glad you're okay. You scared me."

"I'm sorry. I didn't mean to startle you. Is something wrong?" He was almost yelling to be heard over pound of rain on metal roof.

"What happened to the lights?" Cate yelled back.

"I heard you calling so I ran to the door. I must have accidentally hit the switch."

"Did you read the report I left with Radine?"

"No. I was late getting back from Salem, and everyone was gone by the time I got here. Was it something important?"

"Then you don't know that I think Andy Timmons is the one who sent that threatening note—"

"Who?" he yelled.

"Andy Timmons! The guy I located for you, with the old Indian bike. And if you're meeting him here—"

A dark shape barreled out of the blackness and whammed into Halliday. Something flew out of Halliday's hand and clattered to the floor. Halliday slammed into Cate as he went down, and she hit the floor too. Her shoulder crunched into the solid concrete, and her head hit the metallic shelf beyond.

She lay there disoriented as a battle raged only inches away. Rolling bodies, striking fists, grunts and oofs. She shook her head, trying to clear the shooting stars behind her eyes and the ringing bells in her ears. A kick slammed into her leg. She scrambled away on belly and elbows to get out of the combat area. One of the shelf units loomed beside her. In spite of the stars and bells, one thought burst into her mind, sharp and clear.

The phone! Call for help—

She fumbled in her pocket. Kleenex, a mint—no phone! The collision of bodies must have knocked it out of her pocket. She got to her knees and frantically ran her hands over the concrete, searching for it. The wrestling bodies crashed into her again. She fell sideways.

A gunshot boomed and echoed through the warehouse.

Another crash as a kick or shove banged the door to the front office shut. Total blackness. Cate huddled against a metal something on a bottom shelf. Sharp points prickled her back. But the points weren't moving, and they didn't have a gun, so pressing into them felt safer than moving away. Who *did* have a gun? Halliday? Andy? Because the other person must be Andy.

A simultaneous boom and a flash of flame shot into the darkness from the barrel of a gun. But this came from farther back in the warehouse. A huff of exertion near her, then a flash of gunshot. Another gunshot from yet another direction. An answering gunshot from behind her.

How many shooters *were* there? How many guns? How many flying bullets?

She took a deep, steadying breath. At least as deep as she could with her ribs aching, knees throbbing, and nerves shooting flames of their own. No, surely not more than two shooters. Just Halliday and whoever'd taken him down there at the doorway. Which had to be Andy. But they were moving around, moving fast, so neither could use the flashes of gunshot to pinpoint the other's position. Another boom and the bullet pinged into metal only inches from her head.

She didn't think they were shooting at her. They couldn't see her any better than she could see them. Which didn't mean that the next wild shot wouldn't get her in the crossfire.

She had to get to the door, get out of here—

Except she now had no idea where the door was. The blackness and booming gunshots completely disoriented her. If it weren't for gravity holding her body down, she wouldn't even know which way was up.

Up. That was where she needed to be. Up! Higher, out of the line of fire.

Find one of those ladders that moved along the shelves on rollers.

She grasped a metal upright on a shelf unit and inch by inch eased to her feet. Even in the noisy clatter of rain on roof overhead, any different sound, any creak or rustle or grunt, might bring a hail of bullets from one or both trigger-happy gunslingers.

She found the edge of a shelf and worked her way along it. She was going toward the rear of the building . . . wasn't she? Maybe. Maybe not. The loose section of roofing rattled and flapped. Overhead, the hammering rain sounded like the drumbeat of some zombie band playing music to wake the dead.

A ladder! She felt for the bottom rung, then eased around to where she could step on it. A shot and flame from a gun only a few feet away, then hurried steps as the shooter ran to get away from an answering shot which came almost immediately. It hit something off to her left . . . no, maybe her right. Sound seemed to jump and dance in this echoing blackness.

No matter. *Climb.*

She tried to picture the shelves as she'd seen them with Shirley working on them. A bottom shelf only inches off the concrete floor. Next shelf maybe two and a half or three feet higher. Two or three more shelves above that, all wide enough to hold big car parts. Her reaching hand touched something curved and metallic. A fender? Creeping giant with a bald head? Her imagination was running wild here.

She tried to be quiet, but two more shots blasted away any worry about silence. Nobody was going to hear her in the cacophony of sounds assaulting the warehouse. Hammering rain, banging section of metal roof, echoing gunshots.

Recklessly, she scuttled upward, abandoning silence for speed. Her probing hand found another shelf, but she didn't stop until the ladder ended at the top shelf.

The ladder moved as she tried to scramble from the top rung to the top shelf. She had a quick vision of herself flying across space on a not-magic ladder, careening to a deadly rendezvous with a bullet.

Two quick gunshots, not far away but, blessedly, much below her.

She slithered along the shelf, bumping into unidentifiable boxes and metallic stuff, and once something small clattered to the concrete below. She froze. Was that loud enough for the gunslingers to hear? She waited with paralyzed muscles for an answering gunshot, but none came. Thankfully, all the other noise must have drowned out the giveaway clatter.

Or maybe by now both shooters were dead.

A gunshot from the far side of the warehouse eclipsed that hope.

Hey, it wasn't a *hope*.

Well, maybe it was.

Although, beyond her own safety, she wasn't sure what she hoped for. She'd known Andy was coming here armed. Apparently Halliday had decided that even a buy-and-sell meeting with someone like Andy required firepower. Or had he figured out on his own that Andy was out to kill him, and he'd set up his own ambush?

A flame of gunshot answered, then two more shots. No limit of six shots to a gun, as in some old Western movie.

Lord, I could use a little advice here. Maybe a rescue squad?

She found a niche between a couple of cardboard boxes. She was tempted to shove one a few inches to the side to make more space to hide, but she didn't want to make some giveaway sound or knock something more off the shelf, so she just hunkered down in the narrow space available, knees tucked hard against her chest.

Another shot. Cate waited for an answering volley, but none came. A minute passed. Another. Only silence. Well, at least as much silence as was possible with what sounded like a terrorist attack on the roof.

More minutes. Five? Ten? A lifetime? It wasn't until then that she realized how cold it was in here. *Morgue* cold, the same thought she'd had the first time she was here. It seemed ominously even more suitable now. And then something touched her exposed leg. Something live.

A hand. With fingers.

32

A scream rushed up Cate's throat. She stifled it to a squeak before it escaped.

The hand jerked away. Then a scratchy noise. It sounded like a voice trying to whisper her name.

But who could tell what any sound was, with the machine-gun chatter of rain directly overhead? Halliday hadn't spent any money insulating the metal roof on the old building. All that separated her from the storm now was that single layer of thin metal.

The sound that wasn't rain pounding on metal came louder. "Cate?"

She didn't answer, and the hand grabbed her ankle and shook her leg. "Cate, that's you, isn't it?"

Andy.

"How'd you find me up here?" she whisper-screamed.

After jamming a finger in her eye and a thumb in her ear, he finally got a hand clamped over her mouth. "I wasn't try-ing to find you. I'm just trying to keep from getting killed!"

With a hand over her mouth, all that came out were unin-telligible sounds. "Umph . . . urga . . . augh!"

Maybe grunts were good. There was so much noise that

Halliday probably couldn't hear voices, but if he did hear, he'd start shooting again. Upwards this time. Which was where she was.

She whipped her head back and forth to get away from the hand and clawed at his head with her fingers. Free! She scrambled along the shelf but didn't get more than a few inches before he grabbed her ankle again.

"Why *wouldn't* he try to kill you?" The accusation came out louder than she intended. She lowered her voice to a fierce whisper. "You came here to kill him!"

"No, I didn't—"

Liar, liar, pants on fire. Which really didn't seem like sufficient response to being trapped on a shelf with a would-be killer and a lot of old car parts. "You tried to run him down in a Walmart parking lot too!"

"Shut up and move over so he won't hear us."

Reluctantly, not because she wanted to hear anything Andy had to say but because she was afraid voices might bring a fresh volley of gunshots, she twisted and squirmed until she was side by side with him, legs hanging into empty space over the edge of the shelf. After a couple of false moves, in which his head clobbered hers and his hair tangled in her eyelashes, he got his mustache up close to her head. It felt like scratchy wire against her ear.

"Someone tried to run *me* over. I think it was Halliday."

Cate remembered Lily saying something about a car almost hitting Andy near their apartment. Which didn't mean Halliday was in it. Who could believe anything Andy said anyway?

"Where's your pickup? How come you hid it?"

He yanked her head around to talk in her ear again. "Halliday told me to park around back. Which should of made me suspicious right then. I didn't come to kill him—"

303

She turned and whisper-growled in his ear. "You sent Halliday a threatening note. You brought a gun. You jumped out of the dark and attacked him!"

He edged closer. Although there was no intimacy in the closeness. It was more like the clutch of a drowning man. His breath blew hot panic in her ear. "He pulled a gun on me as soon as I got here. Hearing you distracted him. He turned off the light so you wouldn't see me. So I took a chance and jumped him!"

"So where was your gun then?"

"I had it jammed in the waistband of my jeans in the middle of my back. It got tangled up in my shirttail."

Gun jammed into the waistband of the small of the back. Right. That was where gun-toting guys in books always put them. Apparently Andy needed diagrams to get it right.

"We've gotta get out of here!" Andy said. "Before he kills both of us!"

Another squirm so she could hiss into his ear. "Halliday may be after *you*, but he's not going to kill *me*!"

"You think he's going to let you stay alive after he kills me? He probably figures you already know what I know anyway."

But I don't know anything! Not good words for a PI. "So what do you know?"

She heard something. Her muscles went rigid again. No, it wasn't what she heard. It was what she suddenly *wasn't* hearing. Andy wasn't hearing it too because he grabbed her ear.

"The rain's letting up." More mustache in her ear. "He'll hear us!"

The rain *was* letting up, the machine-gun rattle slowing now to single-shot pings.

"Why'd you stop shooting at him and climb up here?" she demanded in a whisper.

"I ran out of bullets."

What kind of killer runs out of bullets?

"I didn't have money to buy any. We had to pay rent and Lily needed some laundry soap and garlic. Where's *your* gun?"

She didn't bother with the incriminating response that she'd left it home because her shooting lessons didn't start until Friday. The rain was definitely letting up. Now it was hitting the metal roof with only an occasional plunk.

"Besides, I didn't think he'd do this! I thought he'd just pay up."

Cate turned her head and ignored the pain of her nose bumping his head. "Pay for the bike?"

"Shut up!" he whispered fiercely. "He's doing something!"

Something skittered on the concrete floor. Scuffling noises. The shelf vibrated as something banged against a lower shelf. Then Halliday's voice.

"Timmons! You hear that?" He whacked the lower shelf again. "I found your gun." A bang and flash of gunfire followed. "They'll probably give me a medal when I shoot you!"

He apparently didn't know Andy was up here because a metallic crash sounded from across the warehouse when Halliday's bullet smashed into something there. But his shot had proved one thing. *He* was still armed. And willing to shoot even if he had to be doing serious damage to his warehouse.

But if Halliday knew Andy was without a gun to shoot back now, why was he still shooting? Why wasn't he calling 911 to get the police here?

Cate opened her mouth to yell, "Don't shoot, I'm up here," but then it occurred to her that Halliday also wasn't exactly calling out any warnings to her. That all along he'd been blasting away without any concern for her whereabouts.

More noises from below, easily audible with the hammer of rain on roof diluted to that occasional ping now. Halliday was shuffling along the unit of shelves, feeling his way, not trying for stealth now. Something crashed off a shelf. New alarm shot through her. Even in the blackness, had he figured out where they were?

No, the sounds of his shuffling footsteps went on by their hidden spot overhead. Then an oblong of light flared as he opened the door to the outer room.

"What's he doing?" Cate whispered frantically.

She had her answer a moment later when the warehouse lights burst into full bloom. Halliday had found the switch he'd turned off earlier.

Why hadn't he turned it on before this so he could see to shoot Andy, if that's what he wanted to do? Because then Andy could see to shoot him, of course.

So why, now that Andy was unarmed, wasn't Halliday talking on the phone, calling the police?

Nothing was adding up here.

"Get down!" Andy's whisper was as frantic as her own.

Cate squirmed back between the protective boxes she'd been hiding behind before Andy invaded her territory.

Too late. Halliday had spotted them. Or at least he'd spotted Andy. Something blasted right between her feet. She stared in astonishment at the hole that had erupted in the shelf, ragged edges flaring.

"Hey!" she yelped. "I'm up here!"

Two more shots blasted through the metal shelf. One punched a hole behind her. Her presence obviously was no deterrent.

Andy's howl told her where the other bullet had hit. He grabbed his backside and rocked back and forth on his other

306

hip. Another shot blasted upward on the other side of him. He scrambled awkwardly toward Cate, one hand still on his backside.

For the first time, the possibility that should have been obvious all along became news-flash real to her. Halliday was on a killer rampage. Andy might not come out of this alive. She might not either. *Why?*

Two more shots. One hit the underside of the box to her right.

She and Andy slammed into the box on her left at the same time as they tried to get away. The box skidded, wavered, tilted . . . and tumbled off the shelf. A strange thudding sound as it hit something below, instantly followed by metallic crashes on the concrete floor. Then Andy lost his balance and tumbled too. She had a last vision of the bottom of his boots facing the roof. A muffled thud, then more unidentifiable noises.

Cate froze, waiting for another upward blast of bullets.

Finally, fearfully, she peered over the edge of the shelf. She wasn't sure what she was seeing. Two legs? No, *four.* Andy sprawled atop a lumpy cardboard box. Legs sticking out from under the box. Metallic shapes scatted on the floor all around them. One darker shape was a gun.

Were both Andy and Halliday dead now? Blood seeped through Andy's jeans torn by the bullet that had ripped through the shelf and into his backside. The legs below the cardboard box lay motionless.

"Andy?" It came out a croak.

A groan, a jerk of leg, a fling of hand, a shake of head.

Like a puppet slowly awakening. Would Andy spot that gun and go for it?

Cate wasn't sure what she could do with the gun if she got to it first. But she could keep Andy from getting it.

She scrambled along the shelf, unmindful now of knocking anything off. Another box fell, then one of those car parts—a fender, maybe?—stored on the upper shelf clattered to the concrete below. She scuttled down the ladder, took a few wild steps, and fell on the gun, covering it with her body.

And found herself face-to-face with that weird clown/witch she'd seen when Shirley was cataloguing the hood ornaments brought down from Salem. It was that box of hood ornaments that had fallen.

She got a hand on the gun, squirmed around to a sitting position, and pointed the gun toward the fallen figures on the concrete. The hood ornaments littered the floor around the bodies, like frivolous decorations around a grisly tableau. She wasn't sure what to do with the gun, but she put a finger on the trigger. Would it go off if she squeezed? Or was there some kind of safety thing on it?

Andy dragged himself off the squashed box and the figure trapped below it. He staggered to his feet and grabbed a shelf for support. An ability to stand meant that even if he'd been shot, apparently no essential bones had been hit. But Halliday under the box . . . Halliday wasn't moving at all.

She had to call 911 . . . *now*! Her phone must be on the floor here somewhere. She frantically tried to search the floor with her eyes while also keeping her gaze on Andy. She kept the gun in her outstretched hands.

Old oil stains on the floor. A goldish figure of a dolphin hood ornament that had bounced all the way to the door. No cell phone.

"Pull that box off Halliday," she commanded.

"I'm shot!"

"You'll be shot worse if you don't do what I say!"

Andy stumbled to the cardboard and yanked it off the

motionless figure. Cate stared at the macabre sight in paralyzed horror. One end of the silver steer horns hood ornament protruded from Halliday's forehead. The other side was buried deep *in* his head. It gave him a ghastly unicorn-man look. Or was it a horned-demon look? His eyes stared sightlessly upward.

"I . . . think he's dead." Andy's legs went weak, and he plopped limply to the floor.

Cate slid over to Halliday and frantically felt for a pulse. She also felt a sickening sense of déjà vu. She'd done this before, felt a dead person's throat for a pulse.

And found now what she'd found then. Nothing. She tried the wrist at his side. Same results.

No, no, maybe not! She was no expert. Maybe he was just unconscious, knocked out by the blow of the hood ornament.

Then she spotted something else. The handle of a gun sticking out from under Halliday's hip. He'd fallen on his gun when the silvery horns hit him. Which meant the gun she was holding was Andy's. With no bullets. Her palms went slick around the handle. She might as well be holding Octavia's toy mouse.

She tried to calm herself. Even though this felt like a fresh tidal wave of disaster, no bullets in the gun didn't change anything. She hadn't known how to shoot the gun before, when she thought it was loaded. Which also didn't change what had to be done *now*.

"I need your cell phone!" she yelled at Andy.

"I don't have it. We only have one. Lily has it."

Cate scrambled to her feet and stumbled toward the outer office to use the landline. At the door she realized she still had the gun. She turned and pointed it back at Andy. He'd be out of sight as soon as she stepped around the corner to the counter. "Don't go anywhere!" she yelled. "Don't even move!"

Don't figure out that this is your gun with no bullets.

She grabbed the H&B phone and punched in the numbers. When the operator at 911 answered, she gave what she realized even as she was speaking was a garbled version of what had happened. Gunfight. Injuries. Maybe a death. Send police and ambulance. The address. The woman wanted her to stay on the line, but Cate wasn't going to wait here by the phone where she couldn't see what Andy was doing. She slammed the phone down and ran back to the doorway.

In the movies, a guy with anything less than a fatal gunshot wound could do anything from battle werewolves to romance the heroine, but Andy wasn't doing anything impressive. He was just lying sideways on the floor with a silvery bear ornament in one hand. An ooze of blood from his wound puddled behind him on the concrete.

"Put it down," Cate commanded. She used a motion of the gun for emphasis. She wasn't giving him any chance to deceive her into thinking he was helpless and then have him pull a surprise attack with the bear.

"I'll bet you don't even know how to shoot a gun."

True. But she had lessons scheduled. That probably wouldn't be a convincing point, however, even if the gun was loaded. Which it wasn't. She bluffed it. "Try me."

He set the bear on the floor. "None of this is how it looks," he complained.

"I see a man who's probably dead. Killed by a hood ornament in a box you knocked off the shelf."

"A box *we* knocked off the shelf. You hit it too!"

Okay, if you wanted to get technical, true. She braced herself against a metal upright supporting the shelf they'd been sitting on. Her arm was getting tired holding the heavy gun. It felt like a weak branch that might droop any minute. She'd never heard anything about this being a problem for criminals.

"We'll let the police sort that out," she said. "It shouldn't take more than five minutes or so for them to get here."

"Look, I know I'm not one of the good guys in your world." Andy kept a wary eye on the gun. He might not think she knew how to use it, but he wasn't taking any chances. Apparently he did, at least, think it was Halliday's loaded gun. He hadn't seen what she'd seen.

"Right. I don't see any wardrobe of white hats." Cate kept her eyes on Andy. At least, watching him, she didn't have to look at Halliday's body. With that ghoulish horn in his head. "I heard you were in on something big down in California."

"That Tuffy jerk and his big mouth, right? So I was with some guys who robbed a gas station and killed a guy once. I didn't know that's what they were doing. I was just sitting in the car drinking a Dr Pepper." He managed to sound unfairly victimized. "I got off with some time in juvie."

Cate eased her elbow over to rest on the shelf, but she carefully didn't change Andy's view of looking down the shooting end of the gun. She hoped the hole in the barrel looked big as a cannon to him.

"Anyway, I didn't come here tonight to kill Halliday. I just wanted my money. He said he had it."

"What money? You didn't bring the bike."

Andy scrunched around on the concrete, apparently looking for a more comfortable position. Or maybe to get a few inches farther away from the horned body. "Halliday was supposed to give me some money to . . . uh . . . kind of forget something."

"Forget what?"

311

"What I knew."

That evasive statement was hardly informative, but Cate pulled a startling fact out of it. "You were blackmailing him?" The tip of the gun sagged. She yanked it up again.

"I figured fifty thousand wasn't too much for me to keep quiet when he was willing to pay thirty thousand to have his partner killed."

Startled and curious as she was at this claim, Cate shook her head. She didn't want him muddling up her head with wild stories. "Save it for the police."

"No, I need to tell *you* before the cops get here! Or you'll give them some crazy story about me and Mace Jackson in some screwball conspiracy to shoot Blakely."

"Conspiracy is beginning to sound likely."

He looked at the bizarrely horned body. "But it wasn't like that! And there wasn't anybody to send him any threatening note. He must have sent it to himself."

"Sent it *himself*? That's crazy."

"He wanted it to look like somebody who was part of a plan to kill Kane Blakely was after him too. So nobody'd start getting suspicious of *him*."

"But he hired me to find out who sent the note."

Andy considered that briefly. "He knew you couldn't find anything. It was just more of his plan to make himself look like a next victim."

"You're making all this up!"

"I wish I were." Andy sounded unexpectedly doleful. He glanced at Halliday again. "I wish it were all some big ol' bad dream."

Cate strained to hear the sound of sirens coming. Like Halliday's pulse, nothing.

"Okay, you listen to me, because this is what happened. I

came in here a while back and tried to sell my old Indian bike to Halliday, right?" Andy talked fiercely and fast, so fast the words almost ran together. Apparently, he was afraid police might arrive before he could get them out.

Cate was in no big hurry. She braced her tiring arm with her other hand. "But Halliday thought it might be stolen and didn't want it."

Andy snorted. "He knew it was probably stolen. He could see the old numbers had been filed off. But I didn't steal it. Some guy gave me the bike when he couldn't pay me some money he owed. But what Halliday wanted to pay for it was downright robbery."

"He said he checked and the bike *wasn't* stolen."

"That's the trouble with you! You believed everything Halliday said. After you found me, he told you he'd never talked to me. Right?" Andy didn't wait for an answer. "Big lie. He talked to me, all right. Because he figured on killing me. That's why he wanted you to find me! So he could kill me!"

"So I should believe a blackmailer instead of a respected business owner?"

Andy didn't argue that detail. "Halliday didn't shoot Mace in self-defense. He had killing him planned right from the start. Except it was *me* he planned to kill that night, not Mace."

"How could it have been you?"

"Do you have to keep pointing that gun at me?"

"Yes."

Andy heaved an injured sigh. "Okay, it was like this. Halliday figured I was a crook when I was first came in here. He could tell the bike was probably stolen. I'd been smoking pot, and maybe he could smell that too."

Not exactly impeccable character references.

"So he looked me up a little while later—"

"He couldn't find you. That's why he hired me."

"Shut up and listen. He found me at that trailer park. He tap-danced around what he'd come for for a while to see how I'd feel about doing something . . . not legal. I figured he had in mind stealing a car or bike or something, and I made it plain I was up for most anything if the money was right."

"Of course."

"So then he said there was thirty thousand in it for me. And to get it, I'd bust in here that particular night, shoot the guy who *wasn't* Halliday, and grab the money. Which would be my payment for—"

"Killing Blakely!"

"So I said yeah, I'd do it."

"Why would Halliday want his partner dead?"

"How should I know? You think I should have asked him to give me a notarized statement that Blakely was a danger to society or something?" Andy didn't wait for an answer to the facetious question. "I just figured it was a good way Lily and me could buy a trailer and move to Nevada or somewhere. Before her brother convinced her I'm a scumbag."

If the name fits, wear it. "Did you tell Lily?"

"No way. She'd have gone into orbit. But then, I had second thoughts. I mean, I've done some, you know, not too legal stuff, but I've never *killed* anyone. And I didn't want to."

"So you, what? Got Mace Jackson to do it with a deal that you'd split the money?"

"No! I was just telling Mace about it. He always thought I was kind of a dumb punk, and here I was, being asked to be a hit man."

"You wanted to look like a big shot to him."

"I guess." Andy shifted uncomfortably on the floor, but he

314

didn't lose sight of the gun in her hands. "But then I said I wasn't going to do it, and he started bugging me for details. Finally he offered me two hundred bucks for the information." Andy looked down. "So I took it."

"You sold Blakely's life for two hundred dollars."

Andy apparently chose to ignore that ugly fact. "But Halliday hadn't let me in on the *full* plan. After his hired gun kills his partner, he kills the killer. Wraps it all up in a neat little package. Killer is dead and no one knows anything and Halliday's a hero for offing the bad guy."

The facts of what had happened that night lined up with Andy's scenario.

"Except Halliday was all shook up after he shot the guy and it wasn't me," Andy said. "Because now he knows there's someone running around who knows the whole story. The truth. And that someone is *me*."

Cate reluctantly rearranged the facts she had. She felt squeamish about accusing a dead man of lying, when he couldn't defend himself, but if she viewed those facts from a different perspective . . .

Blakely gambled. Heavily. It was a good guess he'd asked Halliday for the loan to pay off either a gambling debt or a loan shark debt he'd taken out to pay off a gambling debt. Earlier, there was an audit of the Salem records. Had Halliday had it done because he suspected his partner of embezzling company funds to finance his gambling? And found embezzling was the reason the Salem H&B was so unprofitable?

Halliday could have made that into a criminal case and probably sent Blakely to jail. Which wouldn't bring back the embezzled money and would be very bad publicity for H&B.

So Halliday had figured out a different solution. Get rid of Blakely. His death would take care of everything neatly.

No more financial pitfalls with a partner who was gambling and embezzling. With the bonus of getting back at the man he thought had helped his ex-wife escape him, and the huge bonus of a half-million-dollar insurance payoff for the company.

Plus the neat twist that no one would ever know because he'd dispose of the killer. In self-defense. No loose ends.

A win-win situation.

Halliday had even arranged for a witness to his self-defense tactic. His first choice had been loyal Radine, but Shirley had made an acceptable last-minute substitute.

No wonder Halliday had yanked that ski mask off the killer's face! He was expecting Andy, but he could tell the dead man's big, muscular build was all wrong for the wiry little guy he'd hired to do this. So then he had to find and get rid of that guy who knew the original plan. But Andy and Lily had moved, and Halliday couldn't find them.

Enter helpful Assistant Private Investigator Cate Kinkaid.

"So, see, I just kind of got caught up in . . . all this. I'm no killer," Andy added righteously.

"Just a blackmailer."

"Not a killer," he repeated stubbornly.

"I'd also guess, even if you weren't in on the actual killing that night, there may be some legal technicalities about selling a robbery-murder scheme to a buddy."

"A good lawyer can figure out stuff like that."

"You also didn't think things through very well," Cate pointed out. "Thinking Halliday would meet you here and just meekly hand over a bundle of money. He'd already hired one man killed and killed another himself."

"A stupid guy with a bullet in his butt, that's me," Andy agreed morosely.

I couldn't have said it better myself.

This left a few loose ends. That fire at the hospital. Coincidence, or Halliday's attempt to get to Blakely, since he wasn't dead yet? Halliday's story about someone trying to run him down in the parking lot. Another lie, or creative inspiration for trying to do the same thing to Andy?

A riff of guitar music made them both jump.

Andy started to say something, and Cate yelled, "Be quiet!"

She pinpointed the location this time. It was coming from under the next shelf over. She let go of the shelf she was leaning against and moved the gun in a slow arc to keep it aimed at Andy as she unsteadily inched her way across the aisle.

She knelt beside the bottom shelf and ran her hand in an arc under it. Except something moved. She yelped and yanked her hand back. Mouse? Lizard? Snake? Spider?

But she needed that phone.

She felt in her pocket, found a tissue, and wrapped it around her hand. It didn't feel like much protection. There was probably a reason armored vests weren't made out of tissue paper. The phone was still tinkling.

She lay down on the floor and swept her hand farther under the shelf. The phone skittered out. She floundered after it and finally snatched it up. Still working! She took a moment to look at the caller identification.

"Mitch!"

"Cate? You sound funny."

She squirmed around until she was sitting instead of sprawled flat on the floor.

"Is something wrong? Are you okay? Where are you?" The questions shot out like word bullets as Mitch's sixth sense apparently kicked into gear. "What are you doing?"

"I'm, uh, waiting for the police."

"Are you okay?"

Cate took a moment to inspect her extremities. Her adrenaline was running so hot she realized she might not have felt it even if she'd been shot. But she didn't see any blood or holes anywhere.

"I-I think so."

"I'm almost afraid to ask, but *why* are you waiting for the police?"

"There's a man with a horn in his head lying on the floor a few feet away. I think he's dead. There's another guy with a gunshot wound in his . . . bottom. He's alive."

"Cate, I'm still in Portland so I can't get there fast enough to help, but I'll call—"

"You don't need to rush in and rescue me! The police are on their way. The man with the horn in his head isn't going to do anything, and I'm holding a gun on the other one."

"The gun Uncle Joe gave you?"

"No, a different one." She decided adding the information that she didn't know how to shoot it and it had no bullets anyway was information he didn't need. More importantly, it was information that Andy, who appeared to be listening intently, didn't need.

"About this horn in the dead man's head—"

"It's not a real horn. A hood ornament kind of horn. Made of heavy metal. I'm at H&B."

"I see." Small hesitation before he said, "If you don't mind my saying so, this sounds like a really . . . bizarre situation, even for you."

Kinkaid Investigations. We specialize in bizarre situations.

She pulled the phone away from her ear as she heard something. A wail of sirens, then red and blue lights flickering beyond the warehouse door.

"I have to go now—"

"Wait!"

"The police are here. I'll talk to you later."

She looked back at Andy just in time to see that he'd struggled to his feet. Coming after her or making a last-minute break to escape?

There weren't a lot of uses for a bulletless gun. Cate used the only one she could think of. She threw it at him.

33

The gun slammed into Andy's head and clattered to the concrete floor. Andy slumped to the floor too. The police burst through the door, guns drawn.

Since she was the only one of the three people present who was in talking condition, it seemed up to Cate to say something. She waved her cell phone to get their attention, then realized that was a mistake when two guns did a synchronized swim to target her. She dropped the phone in her lap and held up her hands to show they were empty.

"I called 911."

"Don't move!"

She hadn't had in mind standing to do a song-and-dance routine anyway. In fact, she felt loose all over, as if her muscles had lost connection with her bones. And brain. She stayed on the floor, not even mindful of cold seeping from concrete to her skin.

One officer checked the body with the silver horn in the forehead. The other checked Andy.

"This one's dead," the officer beside Halliday said. "How about that one?"

Andy groaned and groggily lifted his head.

"He's alive. But he isn't going to feel real comfortable sitting down for a while. Maybe he hit his head when he fell."

"I threw that gun at him." Cate pointed to the weapon that had bounced off Andy's head. "It isn't loaded. But there's another gun under the body."

Both officers peered at the gun under Halliday but didn't move it. "Can you identify these people?" one asked.

Cate did that. She also produced a business card, one of the old Belmont Investigations cards, to identify herself. The card earned her a quick glance of interest. The Belmont Investigations name was familiar to much of the local law enforcement. Regretfully she realized Kinkaid Investigations wouldn't have that same familiarity and respect. At least not for a while. Maybe not for a *long* while.

"We have questions for you. Don't leave."

Another action she hadn't been planning anyway.

EMTs rushed in. Apparently Andy's wound was bad enough that after a brief examination, they whisked him out to the ambulance.

Photographs. Bagging of the gun she'd thrown. More officers arriving. Double-take looks at the man with a horn in his head.

Questions. Cate told an officer everything she knew, which took awhile. She didn't accuse Andy of anything, but neither did she try to downplay his part in all this. Or her own, remembering that she, too, had crashed into the box of hood ornaments that had fallen and killed Halliday. She didn't have a phone number for Lily, but she gave them the address where they could contact her about Andy.

Eventually, some two hours later, they let her go with instructions to come into the station for a formal statement the following day.

Thank you, Lord. She, too, could have been leaving here in an ambulance. Or medical examiner's wagon.

She was halfway home before she remembered that some new disaster undoubtedly awaited her at the house.

She opened the garage door with the remote, parked inside, and tentatively opened the back door. Silence. For the first time, the ominous thought occurred to her that there could be more than house destruction. There could be bodily injury. Or worse.

She tiptoed in. The silence seemed to call for it.

The first thing she saw was that the clean clothes that had been folded in a basket on the dryer now decorated the laundry room. Tank tops. Faded panties. A camisole. A couple of old bras. Strange decorations, but a titillating display for a Victoria's Secret ad they were not. She really needed an upgrade in the lingerie department.

She peered in the bathroom as she went by. Towels littered the floor. Torn shower curtain draped over the stool. Tufts of hair in the sink and tub. Both cat and dog hair.

The art of teepee-ing had apparently not gone out of style in the animal world. Her apprehension increased as she followed a trail of ragged toilet tissue down the hallway and into the living room. There, sofa pillows straggled across the floor, one with rips in the cover that sprouted foam-like jungle growths. Torn magazines from the coffee table scattered on the carpet. Then she spotted the combatants.

They were on the window seat. Clancy sprawled in the center of the seat, paws hanging over the edge. Octavia curled up between his legs.

Dead?

Clancy lifted his head and flapped his skinny tail. Octavia gave Cate a complacent stare.

Cate put a hand on each of them. Clancy turned his head to lick her hand. Octavia purred.

No one dead. No one injured.

"What happened here?"

Cate could see into the kitchen now. The paper towel holder lay on the floor, and at least a mile of paper towels blanketed the kitchen.

Innocent silence from the occupants of the window seat.

"Okay, I'm not going to ask any questions," Cate said. As if it would do any good if she did ask. What had happened here and why it resolved the way it did would undoubtedly forever remain a mystery. "Anyone want a snack?"

Everyone wanted a snack. Jerky strips for Clancy. Tuna Treats for Octavia. Cate had an Oreo.

Five minutes later, the doorbell rang. She opened the door, and Mitch wrapped his arms around her. Seeing him was so unexpected, and so was the feeling of relief that flooded her.

"I'm so glad you're here," she whispered. For the first time since she'd stepped into H&B, she felt *safe*.

Finally he asked, "Are you okay?"

It was a question he seemed to have to ask often in her line of work. He was probably thinking the same thing.

"I thought you had to stay for a meeting tomorrow morning."

"Lance can handle it. I wanted to be here with you." He didn't let go of her, but he took a half step back to look her over. He didn't ask for details, just repeated the question. "*Are* you okay?"

"Yeah." Although a vision of a man with a horn in his forehead would be with her for a long time to come.

He eyed the tangled toilet tissue, paper towels, and scattered pillows. "What happened here?"

"Octavia and Clancy made up. They seem to be good friends now."

He wrapped his arms tighter around her. "Maybe we should do more than that."

◆◆◆

Almost four weeks now, since the storm both outside and inside the walls of H&B that night. Cate was in her office working on a report about a surveillance she'd just completed for an insurance company. Mitch would be here in a few minutes. He said he'd bring something to put on the barbecue for dinner. Cate had hot dog buns from the freezer thawing on the counter.

Mitch had two more weeks helping with the transition as the new company took over Computer Dudes. He still hadn't indicated what would happen when that time was up. Lance and Robyn had already loaded up a U-Haul van and left for Dallas.

Cate had told Mitch all about the shootout at H&B, who had killed whom and why. "But I didn't exactly solve everything with brilliant detective work," she'd added gloomily.

"But your sense of responsibility put you where you were needed, or the outcome would have been much different."

Yeah, one more dead body. Could Halliday have worked the self-defense thing again with a dead Andy?

"I figure that sense of responsibility is as important as brilliance," he said.

It was a generous assessment, and she appreciated it. But he'd never expanded on that statement he'd made the night it all happened, about being more than the friends Octavia and Clancy had become.

Andy, unable to come up with bail money, was in jail with

various charges against him. It turned out that he'd had a packet of meth in his pocket when they got him to the hospital. Lily had moved out to live in the travel trailer parked on her brother's place, but she went to see Andy occasionally. She had nothing good to say about Andy, but she'd tried to take some of his favorite garlic-heavy spaghetti to him in jail. So far unsuccessfully, but she was persistent.

Senate hopeful Mark Gillerman's engagement to campaign worker Candice Blakely wasn't national news, but it had made the inside pages of newspapers around the state.

Cate had never heard, with both partners dead, what would become of the $500,000 insurance money. Halliday's lawyer was handling the estate. He'd hired Jerry to run H&B temporarily. After the legal complications with both partners being dead were straightened out, Jerry would purchase the company. Shirley had finally admitted to Cate—and to herself, Cate guessed—that she and Jerry were really and truly *dating*. She was going to church with him too.

Cate had been taking weekly shooting lessons. She wasn't any deadeye, but she wasn't missing the entire target anymore. She couldn't imagine herself ever actually shooting anyone. She never *wanted* to shoot anyone. It still bothered her just aiming at the target of a human-shaped silhouette. But if shooting meant saving someone's life sometime . . .

She'd traded Uncle Joe's big Glock .40 in on a smaller Smith & Wesson Airweight .38 that fit her hand better. It would also fit in her purse. She was scheduled for another class that would enable her to get a permit to carry a concealed weapon.

Octavia and Clancy's truce was apparently permanent. Unlike humans, who had to ratify every agreement with "whereas" and "wherefore" phrases composed by a lawyer, written on crinkly legal paper and properly notarized, Clancy and Octavia had it all settled with tail wags and purrs. They shared the window seat or playroom whenever Clancy visited now.

Mitch had a box for Clancy built to fit on the Purple Rocket. Riding in his own purple box, with goggles on, Clancy was one very cool dog.

The doorbell rang and Cate yelled, "C'mon in," as she left her office and headed for the front door. Mitch and Clancy trooped in, Mitch's arms filled with grocery bags. Clancy sported a new purple-plaid kerchief tied on his collar. Mitch headed for the door to the patio.

Cate followed. "What's all this?" she asked when he dumped everything on the outdoor patio table. She peered in the sacks.

Rib-eye steaks. French bread. Garlic-butter spread. Macaroni salad. Packaged plate of carrot sticks, celery, broccoli bites, and olives. Sparkling apple juice. Two chocolate-drizzled cannoli.

"I thought we were just going to do hot dogs." She peered into a smaller, separate sack. "Candles?" she said, astonished. "We've never had candles when we barbecue."

"We do tonight." Mitch busied himself getting the gas barbecue grill started, but he seemed uncharacteristically jittery.

He pushed a wrong button, and it took him three tries to get the grill going. He dropped a steak and had to take it inside to wash it off. He accidentally bumped into the sparkling juice Cate had just opened, and only her quick grab saved it from a crash to the concrete patio.

Cate went inside for plates and silverware and paper napkins. Octavia didn't often want to go outside, but tonight she followed Cate out to the patio. There, she found Clancy under the table and snuggled up beside him.

But a feeling like a lump of moldy garlic bread clumped

inside Cate as she watched Mitch put the steaks on the grill. She'd figured out why he was so jittery. He'd set up this candle-light and steak dinner as a break-it-to-her-easy backdrop for the news he was about to drop on her. He was leaving Eugene as soon as the transition period was over.

It's been great knowing you, Cate. Let's keep in touch.

But he was nervous about dumping that on her. What did he think, that she'd break into hysterical tears or have a hissy fit, complete with steak-knife attack and a cannoli jammed up his nose?

No way. She might cry later, but for now she'd be the epitome of grace and poise. Although she'd really have to work at it, she realized when she found herself jamming a carrot stick instead of a spoon into the macaroni salad.

Okay, she wasn't going to let him do it this sneaky way. He was arranging and lighting the candles now. She determinedly made her tone conversational rather than confrontational, but she finally asked the question directly.

"Have you decided yet which job you're going to take after the transition period ends?"

"Well, uh—"

Clancy's back thumped against the underside of the table when he suddenly jumped to his feet. Octavia yowled indignantly and raced for the back door. Clancy streaked across the yard, barking as if he were after a band of outlaws.

The table jiggled when Clancy hit it. The candle Mitch had just lit fell over. It landed in the paper napkins. Flame flared. It caught the sleeve of Mitch's shirt. He yelped and clamped a hand over the flame. It flared around his fingers.

Cate grabbed the closest available form of fire extinguisher. She dumped sparkling apple juice on his shirt and hand and candles.

"There," she said. "No harm done—"

Clancy's bark suddenly went silent. Then a small yelp. Then . . .

The Smell.

Oh, the SMELL.

"Skunk," Cate gasped.

Mitch raced across the yard to the back fence. The skunk was still holding its ground. White stripe down its back. Tail arched. Clancy rolling on the ground and making whimpery noises.

Mitch grabbed him and pulled him back over to the patio area. The skunk faded into the night, but the smell came with Clancy.

"I'll get the hose and we can wash him off," Cate said.

"We need shampoo too."

Cate got a bottle of her gardenia-scented shampoo, and together they washed Clancy, sudsing him from floppy ears to skinny tail. Sudsing themselves too. Finally she turned off the hose. Clancy wagged his tail. If any scent of gardenia clung to him, it was overpowered by the stronger smell of *skunk*.

"I've heard tomato juice will work," Mitch said.

Cate went to the kitchen. She returned with a bottle. "I didn't have any tomato juice," she apologized. "But here's a bottle of ketchup."

So they doused Clancy with ketchup and washed him again.

By that time, another scent had joined the wet dog and skunk/ketchup blend. Burned steak.

Mitch let go of Clancy and ran to the grill. Too late. Blackened leather was all that remained.

Mitch turned off the burner, and they both surveyed the scene. Burned steak. Empty bottle of sparkling juice. Dead candles. Wet, smelly dog. Wet, smelly people.

Mitch plopped onto a bench at the picnic table. "This isn't what I had in mind," he muttered.

"You never did answer my question."

"What question?"

She picked up an olive and tried to make her tone casual. "About what you're going to do when the transition period ends."

"I'm coming out of this with a rather respectable chunk of money. I was waiting until I knew how much there'd be after taxes."

"You should have plenty for making a new start, then."

He looked at her as if puzzled by her suddenly tart tone. "So I've been thinking. How would you feel about my buying into Kinkaid Investigations?"

The question was so not what Cate expected that she choked on the olive. He jumped up and patted her on the back.

"And *you'd* become a private investigator?" she asked when she could finally speak.

"That's what I had in mind."

"But you hate my being a PI! Why would you even consider being one?"

"I don't *hate* it," he protested. "I've had my doubts, sure. But it seems to be a part of you."

"Like a big ugly wart on my nose?"

"That's a rather crude way to put it."

"But it's there. Being a PI *is* a part of me."

"I realize that. I figured it was time to go along with that old saying, if you can't beat 'em, join 'em. I think my computer skills could be useful in the PI business. And I've had a little PI experience helping you."

Oh yes, Mitch had computer skills. And she had to admit he'd been helpful.

"And I see PI work as a worthwhile way to use those computer skills," he added.

"You're serious about this?"

"Quite serious."

Cautiously, she gave the possibility further thought. A two-person company could accomplish much more than a one-person one. It would make surveillance work easier. They could back each other up in tense situations. A big influx of money would make it possible to open a professional office downtown. And there was Mitch's expertise with a computer.

But.

"You'd be like I was with Uncle Joe and Belmont Investigations. You'd have to be my assistant."

Mitch nodded. "I can live with that until I get my own license. Then we'd be partners."

Partners. She saw another problem.

"I suppose you'd want a name change. Kinkaid and Berenski Investigations?"

"That wasn't exactly what I had in mind."

"Surely you aren't thinking Berenski and Kinkaid!"

"Actually, I thought Berenski and Berenski would be nice."

"Berenski and Berenski?" she repeated blankly.

He groaned. "I tried to do this romantic setting. Great food. Candlelight. Sparkling drinks."

"For a business proposition?"

"For a proposal! A *marriage* proposal. Mr. and Mrs. Berenski. Instead . . . this."

His wave of hand took in ruined steaks, dead candles, empty sparkling juice, wet dog, wet Cate, wet self. He reached over and wiped something off her ear.

Cate looked at the blob on his fingertip. Ketchup.

"I'm sorry I've made such a mess of it," he said. "I've never done a proposal before. And I sure never intended washing a dog in ketchup as a centerpiece of the evening."

Cate swallowed. "The candles were a really nice touch."

He looked at his burned sleeve. "Thank you."

"The sparkling juice and steaks too." She took a deep breath. "Except I've never heard any actual marriage proposal."

He looked surprised. "I love you, Cate Kinkaid," he said almost fiercely. He dropped to a knee in front of her. "Will you marry me? As soon as possible."

"The knee is a *great* touch."

"Thank you."

"Mr. and Mrs. Berenski? I like it. I like Berenski and Berenski Investigations too. Let's do it!"

Clancy came out from under the table and shook water all over both of them before he plopped down at their feet. Octavia padded over and started washing him industriously.

"Now you'll be around when the garden starts producing," Cate said. "Hey, maybe you're marrying me for my carrots."

"Whatever."

He pulled her to her feet and kissed her. Two wet people. One wet dog. One dog-washing cat.

One great kiss.

Hey, Lord, you did it, didn't you! Whatever plans we make, you have better ones.

With a proposal like this, Cate could hardly wait for the wedding.

Lorena McCourtney is a *New York Times* bestselling and award-winning author of dozens of novels, including *Invisible* (which won the Daphne du Maurier Award from Romance Writers of America), *In Plain Sight*, *On the Run*, *Stranded*, and *Dying to Read*. She resides in Grants Pass, Oregon.

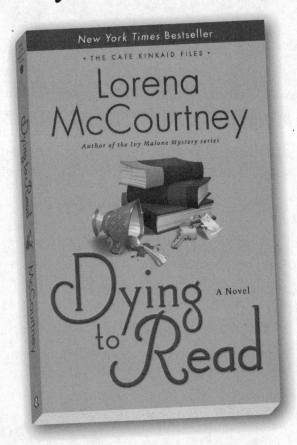

"With a clever plot that moves rapidly, this is a definite one-day read that suspense and mystery fans will **absolutely love.**"
—*Suspense Magazine*

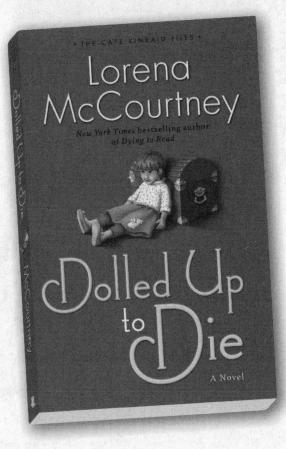

Don't Miss the
Ivy Malone Series
in Ebook

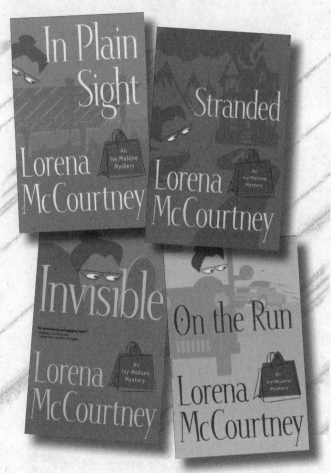

JUL -- 2014